Advance Praise:

"So gritty about every least detail, so frank about its people's needs, *Dream of Another America* might at first seem the furthest thing from a dream. Yet Tyler McMahon has worked this desperate material into a headlong tumble of jeopardy and escape, sweeping up a remarkable array of souls—mostly Central American—in a spell so vivid it seems straight out of the deepest recesses of the unconscious. As his protagonist Jacinto makes his way north to Los United, McMahon puts the reader too up against the worst monsters of that odyssey, now baking in the desert, now clinging to a train. The novel's likewise unsparing about the burdens on the family back in El Salvador, most impressively Jacinto's wounded but resourceful wife. Even if the man can survive the trip, and by some miracle get his family North as well, his story will long disturb the sleep of our all-too-comfortable slumber."
　　—John Domini, judge and author of *Movieola!*

"*Dream of Another America* is a tautly-spun, dark and stirring migration parable, an ode to the impoverished, powerless, and double-crossed south of the proverbial border, and a sensuous, fast-moving train hop of a read that is every migrant's nightmare, every inhabitant of Eden's duty."
　　—J. Reuben Appelman, author of *The Kill Jar: Obsession, Descent, and a Hunt for Detroit's Most Notorious Serial Killer*

The "dream" in *Dream of Another America* is both a noun and an imperative verb of hope: Tyler McMahon has written a *Grapes of Wrath* for contemporary America. Like Steinbeck's classic, *Dream of Another America* urges readers to confront the costs and sacrifices of the American Dream. Beautifully written, emotionally gripping, narratively propulsive, and morally important, this book should be necessary reading for every American.
　　—Shawna Yang Ryan, author of *Green Island* and *Water Ghosts*

Also by Tyler McMahon

How the Mistakes Were Made

Kilometer 99

Dream of Another America

by Tyler McMahon

Winner of the Gival Press Novel Award

Arlington, Virginia

Published by Gival Press, an imprint of Gival Press, LLC.
For information please write:
Gival Press, LLC
P. O. Box 3812
Arlington, VA 22203
www.givalpress.com

First edition
ISBN: 978-1-940724-14-0
eISBN: 978-1-940724-15-7
Library of Congress Control Number: 2017955120

Cover art: American/Mexican border © Nytumbleweeds | Dreamstime.com
Design by Ken Schellenberg.

For Marie McMahon.

I

1

THE STANDING OAXACAN DID THE TALKING; THE KNEELING
Oaxacan's mouth was already too full of piss. "Suit yourself, Guanaco. We
won't offer again." The pair had run out of water early this morning, and the
reluctant urine stream was dark as beer. The kneeler grimaced and for a second appeared to gag. But his thirst won out over his squeamish reservations.

"No thank you," Jacinto repeated. "I'd prefer to die." He held his second
and final plastic gallon-jug up to his eyes. The water level was lower than the
width of a finger.

Jacinto looked past the Oaxacans. With blurry vision, he followed their
tracks backwards through the sand, but saw no sign of the three others—
the slowest walkers in their party. Perhaps they'd given up hope and followed
their own footsteps back to Mexico sometime during the night. That was the
best fate Jacinto could imagine for them.

He turned away from the piss drinkers and took a few more steps. Over
his shoulder, he heard the men switch places. So far, Jacinto was unimpressed
by these United States of America. What sort of work might there be in a country like this, with its million different shades of brown? What would grow, in
the scorching daylight and freezing night? What could be built, without rivers
or trees? Two days of walking, and so far, only hills of rock and scrub, cactus,
and this course mix of sand and gravel all over everything.

Also, there was the sun, so large and hot Jacinto feared it might scorch his
eyelashes. He saw an airplane cross the sky—or was it a vulture? —then disappear against the brightness. Jacinto stared on until a blinding blur burned
in his retinas. He cast his vision downward, pulled his baseball cap lower over
his face.

Ahead of him, their pink-haired guide gained ground.

"*Niño!*" Jacinto did his best to speed up. "That mountain there." He pointed to his left; a cross made from sticks stood in one cleft of the hill. "We passed it already. We've walked in a circle. You're lost, aren't you?" Even with little faith in his own memory, Jacinto was sure he'd seen the cross before.

The *pollero* turned around. "You want to guide us, old man?" When their walk began yesterday morning, his pink mohawk had stood up straight atop his head like the comb on a rooster. Now it hung limp and crooked, matted locks at odd angles. "I make this trip twice a month. I could walk it blind-folded." He whipped the pink fringe out of his face.

"We paid a lot of money for this trip, boy." Jacinto guessed their guide's age at around nineteen.

"You're from El Salvador, right?" Pink Hair laughed darkly. "You don't know shit about money. But I'll tell you one thing: if I were to get lost in this desert." He pointed his thumb at his own chest. "Money would be the least of your worries. Understand?"

The *pollero* turned and kept walking. Jacinto followed close behind. He played back the words that he'd said when the two tired Oaxacans offered their piss. Did he prefer death?

Heat addled his brain. Translucent worms floated across his field of vi-sion. Forming thoughts required an effort like untying a stiff knot. There was a good chance that not everybody would make it out of this alive. If the oth-ers—the Honduran woman, the father and son from Chiapas—hadn't re-treated to Mexico or been caught by the authorities, then their lives were in danger. If these remaining four didn't come across a road or a town—even a stream, a puddle, a shelter of some kind—they would not survive another day. Jacinto was a stranger to this desert, to deserts like this. There was nothing he could do to save anybody else. What he would do, he decided, was make sure that this rooster-haired smuggler who'd put them all at risk would not outlive him. Jacinto wouldn't faint, wouldn't succumb to dehydration, and would not stop walking, until Pink Hair did.

To seal the pledge, Jacinto took the final swallow of water from his plastic bottle. It felt like hair and dust upon his parched throat. He dropped the gallon jug to the ground and kept on walking in the smuggler's shadow.

*

At last, his father's final crop of corn had sprouted. Wilmer walked the rows—planted on their hillside patch atop the ravine. With the machete his father had left behind, the boy turned up any weeds that grew near the yellow-green shoots. He was familiar with these chores from other seasons, but this was his first chance to perform them alone and unsupervised. Before leaving, his father sat him down and explained that the corn and beans would be his responsibility now, and that he was capable of it. Wilmer was, in his father's words, "the man of the house."

Once the weeding was done, Wilmer walked to the palm-frond shelter at the highest point of the parcel. He drank from the water jug he'd left under the shade. The family dog, Renegado, waited there for him, standing like a sentinel over the corn. From this high point, one could see the Pacific Ocean, the smoke from the burning cane fields along the coast, the *maquiladoras* where young adults from their village and elsewhere went off to earn little more than the bus fare there and back, the Litoral highway full of tractor trailers, and off in the distance, the tower of the Comalapa airport.

All of El Salvador was green and moist this time of year. All the men were busy and hopeful with some sort of work. At his feet, Wilmer watched a chain of ants carry off scraps from the lunch he'd eaten hours ago. Crumbs of tortilla and flecks of egg moved atop the backs of the tiny workers.

As the sun approached the horizon and the sky grew darker, little sets of light became visible upon the airport runway. Wilmer watched as one trio of yellow moved along the ground and took off into the air. It did a broad turn over the ocean then straightened out. Like most planes that left Comalapa, this one headed north.

Wilmer had heard stories about the insides of those airplanes from a school teacher with relatives in Miami. The rich from San Salvador loaded their bags full of cheese and fried chicken for their families. On the way back, they'd return with those same bags full of electronic gadgets and cartons of cigarettes.

Meanwhile, on land, his father was somewhere in between—with an extra shirt, a baseball cap, and the phone number of an uncle stitched into the waistband of his underwear. When Wilmer had asked why not simply fly to

California on an airplane, the answer was: "poor people must do things differently than rich people." Wilmer understood that explanation; it didn't upset him. In fact, as he stared out at the trucks and the factories that the gringos had brought here to his country, the ocean over which all the clothes and sugar would return to the gringos, and the airplanes in which the rich of both countries could travel back and forth with ease, the entire situation seemed laugh-out-loud funny.

A gust of dusty wind rose from the ravine, and Wilmer felt the cavities constrict inside his chest. He remembered that he was the principal reason for his father's long and costly journey, and that thought robbed him of even the absurd humor. The ocean and the sky grew a darker shade of orange, and Renegado paced in circles upon the path. In the day's last light, Wilmer picked up the machete and headed for home.

*

In the frigid desert night, it was easier to walk, but harder to keep an eye on Pink Hair. The two Oaxacans fumbled along behind, complaining bitterly but keeping a kind of dumb faith that their *pollero* knew where he was going. No moon shone above. The tattered stripe atop the teenager's head looked white under the stars.

The rest of them—Jacinto reminded himself that they'd started as seven—never caught up. If the three others were still in this desert somewhere, there was little chance they were alive.

"You following me, Guanaco?" Pink Hair didn't turn around.

"You're the guide," Jacinto said. "Isn't that the idea?"

"Not so close. You a faggot? You like to look at my ass?"

"There's not much about this that I like," Jacinto admitted. "Don Noe promised professional guides, not some punk kid who can't tell north from south, who leaves those people back there to die."

"They're not dead."

"Where do you think they are?" Jacinto asked. "Phoenix, Arizona? Houston, Texas? Los Angeles?" He'd heard those strange names spoken before as though they were paradises. Now they sounded like cruel jokes.

"Migra got them," Pink Hair said. "It's bottled water and air-conditioning now. Shit, they're probably eating better than they ever did in their homes. Those gringo jails are like hotels."

Jacinto now understood how Pink Hair saw things: failure on this walk didn't mean death to him; it only meant losing some cat-and-mouse game against the authorities.

"Those people were your responsibility," Jacinto said. "You let them down."

"They were shitty walkers!" The pale mohawk jiggled with emotion. "Fuck them!"

"You've never been in combat, have you?" Jacinto felt himself grow oddly calm.

"I been shot at before." Pink Hair said. "By gringo ranchers, by the Migra, by fucking bandits. I shot back a few times, too."

"Any asshole can run from bullets." Jacinto didn't know what he expected this boy to learn. "Combat means other people trusting you with their lives. You would make a shitty soldier. You are a shitty smuggler."

"You get what you pay for, old man."

"Holy God! Holy Mother!" One of the Oaxacans called out from behind. Pink Hair and Jacinto both stopped in their tracks. They'd listened to those two moan and curse for hours. But it sounded different this time.

"They're dead!" he cried out. "They're all dead!"

At the foot of the stony hillside, the men screamed. One of them carried a plastic cigarette lighter. Jacinto and Pink Hair scurried toward the flame.

Jacinto was no stranger to corpses, but this desert made it a much more gruesome sight. The skin blackened and blistering like an overdone tortilla, lips and gums stripped back along the teeth, the bellies swollen with gas, clothes torn to shreds—it looked as if death were the least of the afflictions these poor bodies suffered from.

He recognized the Honduran woman. The man from Chiapas appeared to shelter his child from the sun—but in another way looked to be smothering him. As the Oaxacan moved the lighter toward their hands, Jacinto saw that the two adults had pricked their fingers trying to rip open a nearby cactus—in search of water.

But there was one detail more telling than the sorry state of their bodies: one or more of them had torn up some American bills. A small pile of green paper bits lay between them, the crumbs of what little money they'd brought. Was this a message of some kind? A warning to whichever walkers would pass them? A curse on the smugglers or crooked authorities that might find their bodies? More likely, Jacinto thought, it was an act meant to liberate them from the force that led them to this desert. In death, at least, they'd be free of that dirty, bloody imperative that so many of their kin and countrymen mistook for salvation: earning dollars.

The two Oaxacans continued to curse and scream. Pink Hair finally sobbed like the child that he was. Jacinto couldn't understand why they were all so surprised.

"We're going to die here." Pink Hair put his hands over his face, too dehydrated to shed actual tears.

Jacinto spoke up: "Might I suggest a change in our priorities."

The three others looked at him. The butane flame cast ghostly shadows upon their faces. If it were up to them, Jacinto thought, they'd stand around weeping until they were dead as well.

"We have no water," Jacinto went on. "We have no idea where a town or highway is. I'm not sure any or all of us could endure another day of this. It seems to me our only chance for survival is to be found by the gringos. We won't make it across this time, but we'll be alive to try again another day."

The Oaxacans needed no convincing.

Jacinto turned to Pink Hair. "What's the best way to get ourselves caught?"

The boy removed his hands from his face and tucked the front fringe of his limp pink mohawk behind one ear. "The drag we saw back there. They drive their trucks along those at least once every twenty-four hours." With his thumb, he pointed west.

Jacinto nodded and called up a vague recollection of the sandy path the boy spoke of. He looked down at the bodies in the dirt. For a second, he wondered if they might carry them. Perhaps the gringos could offer a proper burial, send the remains to their families even. But they couldn't risk the added burden. Besides, from the looks of things, the corpses might fall apart in their hands.

The four men started off in the direction that Pink Hair had pointed. Jacinto took the lead now, the Oaxacans fumbling along behind. It was hard not to be reminded of the Conflict—enduring thirst, enduring hunger, walking for days straight only to keep death at arms' length. Jacinto swore he'd never get caught up in a madness like that ever again, and yet here he was: leading a line of scared young men. It wasn't meant to be this way.

Jacinto recalled the visits Don Noe made to his house. He was the most respected—and expensive—*coyote* that worked in Carasucia. His successful clients were the only thing keeping the village afloat. As if clairvoyant, Don Noe showed up shortly after Wilmer's third visit to the local clinic. He'd promised that things would be professional: commissioned vehicles, bribes at the border, false documents. The only thing Jacinto had to lose, back then, was the down payment.

*

It began as a tickle in the back of his throat, then a tightness in the upper chest. Wilmer reached for his water on the table. The wheezing came on so sudden and strong that his hand knocked the cup over before he could grasp it. At his feet, Renegado let out a howling bark. Clutching the end of the table, Wilmer felt as though he were held face-down in a river. He stood up taller—a vain attempt to rise above the imaginary surface.

His mother rushed in once she heard the wheezing. Wilmer closed his eyes—hoping to concentrate more fully on those constricting channels of air. Mother's hands were cool with the coarse grit of corn *masa*. She laid him out across the table, its oily cloth slick against Wilmer's back. She sang a simple hymn: "*Forgive your people, Lord/ forgive your people, Lord.*" Wilmer couldn't help but wonder why he needed forgiveness. Was this disease his fault? Had he done something to deserve it?

Mother put a wet cloth to his forehead, but he did not open his eyes. His vision floated up above his body a little bit. He pictured the inside of his chest like an anthill—a series of tight and intricate tubes subject to collapse every so often. In his mind's eye, Wilmer saw himself as an ant—covered in armor and strong for his size. Cruel children collapsed his home with sticks, but he burrowed away, clearing debris, making space for new fresh air. Don't panic, he told himself. Don't fear the darkness or the tightness. Relax.

As his breathing slowed and the wheezing subsided, his mother shoved a handful of pills at his face, all of them different colors and shapes. "Take these," she said. "Tell me if they work." She picked up his fallen water cup and refilled it from the plastic jug they kept by the cistern.

Wilmer forced a swallow. He knew that these were leftover medications, the crumbs that fell from the Health Promoter's table.

"Once your father is in the north and settled, you'll get the good medicine all the time." She stroked his forehead. "You'll get the stuff that works."

Wilmer knew the medicine she spoke of. He once had an attack in Rosario de Mora, the nearest town. At the health center, Don Toño used a plastic device to spray some down his throat. The mist was like a legion of helpful ants released all at once. He felt them grow and multiply, the tunnels forming faster than he could breathe through them. It seemed impossible that someday that spray might be in his home and always at his disposal. But it seemed equally impossible—perhaps ridiculous was a better word—that the way to make this happen was for his father to make a journey of thousands of miles. After all, that medicine was here in this country, was it not?

He thought of the planes and the sweatshops that he'd seen earlier in the day, and recalled his father's words about how poor people did things differently than rich people.

*

Watching the Oaxacans die was the worst part of the disaster thus far. They stumbled over their own feet as the rosy-fingered dawn became the yellow-fisted morning. Their tongues swelled until they could barely speak, but still they begged non-existent water from Jacinto and Pink Hair. Eyes sunk further back inside their heads. Their lips flaked and blackened. The four walkers took a break and sat for a moment in the dirt. The Oaxacans made another clumsy effort to drink each other's urine, but all they could squeeze out were a few beads as thick and dark as strong coffee.

"They're not going to make it, are they?" Pink Hair asked Jacinto, as the two of them sat watching.

"Not unless the gringos pass by soon."

"Are we going to survive?" Pink Hair was finally, appropriately, scared for his life.

"If you're right about this drag, then we will." Jacinto realized just how much faith he'd put in a track through the sand, and the words that this scared little boy spoke about it.

The sun was now high and bright in the sky. They could see their destination not so far away. For a healthy man—one well-fed and watered—it wouldn't be much of a walk at all.

"It's my fault." Pink Hair again sobbed without tears. "I'm responsible for all these deaths. Their blood is on my hands."

Jacinto had hoped the boy would recognize the stakes of this journey since they'd left the safe house. But now that Pink Hair's eyes were open, there was no joy in it for Jacinto.

"You're not responsible," Jacinto said at last. "Not fully, at least. You and me, we're pawns in this thing. The *coyotes*, the kingpins, the bosses—they're the ones that make the shit; we're the flies left to live and die in it."

"I'm going to hell for this," Pink Hair said.

It was all Jacinto could do not to laugh out loud. He stopped himself short of asking how Pink Hair would tell the difference. But for the boy's sake, Jacinto mustered up a measure of sincerity: "If you help me get these men over to that drag, then you'll have my forgiveness."

A sudden explosion, like a gunshot, rang out. Jacinto acted on an old instinct and laid flat to the ground. He heard one of the Oaxacans groan with pain, shaking his hand in the air. His body still half-crouched, he rushed over, along with Pink Hair. Was someone shooting at them?

"The lighter." The man held his own hand by the wrist. "It blew up."

Jacinto found the piece of plastic in the sand, its bottom panel blown out. The sun had heated it to the point of combustion. He'd hoped to use it to keep warm tonight. Thus far they'd avoided fires and endured the cold so as not to draw attention. He chucked the useless bit of plastic over his shoulder. "Let's go."

With an arm around each neck, he and Pink Hair helped the Oaxacans walk. Jacinto wondered if it wouldn't be easier to carry them. The dehydrated body trembled in his arms. The skin felt like that of an onion; Jacinto worried that a piece of it might come off in his hand.

They were the walking dead: a couple of four-legged and two-headed monsters stumbling their way through a landscape in which only bugs and reptiles could prosper. The Oaxacan that clung to Jacinto reached out his free arm and grabbed at the air like a frightened crab. The other one appeared to sleep in Pink Hair's arms, his legs going through the motions of walking. The day passed this way: helping the two hopeless Oaxacans walk because they couldn't stomach leaving them for dead.

"Where is my sister?" the man at Jacinto's side asked.

"She's safe," Jacinto said. "She's at home."

"This is my home." The man's words worked their way out around his dry rag of a tongue.

"This isn't your home, my friend. This is the desert."

"No, *cabrón*." The Oaxacan was incredulous. "This is my house. I'm inside my house right now."

Jacinto saw no point in correcting him.

The orange sky grew dim as they reached the drag. Jacinto and Pink Hair laid the two Oaxacans off to the side of it.

"What is this thing?" Jacinto asked. Their salvation looked to be little more than a wide line of smooth dirt.

"Drag is the way the Migra catches wetbacks. They haul a bunch of old tires laid flat and chained together behind their trucks, to make this line. Then they come back and look for footprints. Depending on how fresh the prints are—how many bug-trails go through them—they can tell how far the wetbacks have gone."

They'd risked their lives over one random line in the sand, Jacinto thought, and now they hoped to be saved by another. Not far away, he spotted some dead weeds and scrub. He set to hauling it over to the middle of the path, an improvised roadblock in case the Migra drove by fast in the night. Pink

Hair understood and helped. The two Oaxacans lay quiet in the dirt, but still breathing.

It was full dark by the time they finished the brush pile. The two of them sat down and stared as though it were a dark and silent campfire that they were too tired to light.

"When we get caught," Pink Hair said. "Don't tell them that I'm the *pollero*."

"Don't tell them that I'm Salvadoran," Jacinto replied.

"You come a long-ass way to get caught now, huh?"

"It wasn't so bad, until this part." In truth, much of Jacinto's trip had been comfortable. "We were in tractor trailers most of the way. It was crammed, but bearable."

"You went the easy way," Pink Hair said. "With a good *coyote*. Some of these fools do it on their own, hopping trains and shit. They show up at the border half dead, in no shape for the hardest part."

"Who's really the fool?" Jacinto asked. "If we all end up in the same cell in the end? At least they didn't pay the *coyote* anything up front."

Pink Hair shrugged. "It's hard to put a price on what happens down south, on the tops of those trains. The cops and the soldiers there do what they want: rob, rape, torture. They make the gangsters look like nice guys."

"Do you know Don Noe, the *coyote* that I paid for this?"

"Heard the name from other *pollitos*. He brings most of the Guanacos. But I don't meet guys like that. Nowadays, this business is a monopoly: lots of people working for one big company."

Jacinto was surprised that their mouths maintained the moisture to talk so much. His throat tasted like the clumps pulled from the bottom of a broom.

"What do you do for work, back there in El Salvador?"

"Farming," Jacinto said. "A little carpentry or masonry if it comes up. Picking coffee for extra money during the season."

"Your own land?"

"Since the Peace Accords." Jacinto nodded. "They gave us little parcels as part of the land reform. It's in a ravine, rocky and hilly. You can't do much with it other than corn and beans."

"Doesn't sound so bad," Pink hair muttered, as though momentarily wishing he were a farmer and not a smuggler.

"It isn't bad. I spent too many years looking over my shoulder every second—sleeping two minutes at a time—and I swore I'd never do that again. Being a poor farmer was fine by me. But things happen. My son is sick. There's medicine that helps, but it's expensive. Corn and beans can fill your belly, but they don't do much when you need cash."

"Someday," Pink Hair said. "Those gringos will learn to be grateful to live in a country that other people want to sneak into."

"What will happen, once they catch us?"

"The gringos are soft. We'll go to a hospital for a while, fill up with fluids, eat meat and bread, watch TV. Then we'll go see a judge and get dumped back across the border. It's the Mexicans you got to worry about."

"Will they let us make phone calls?" Jacinto reached a hand to the waistband of his underwear. There he touched the phone number embroidered in thread. That had been Mina's innovation, and already it had proven itself useful: he'd have sweated the numerals into a blur had they been written in ink. The number was that of his brother-in-law in California, a man he barely knew but who offered to receive him. It was too dark to see the digits now, but he rubbed his finger across them to be sure they'd not come unraveled.

"Shit, they'll have a phone by your bed. You can order pizza if you want." The boy's confidence didn't convince Jacinto.

"What you said before, about looking over your shoulder." Pink Hair spoke hesitantly. "Were you talking about a war?"

"Most people call it 'the Conflict' or 'the Problem' now. But war is what it truly was."

"What was that like?"

"Madness. Pure madness. It makes this—pacing in circles around the desert—seem a perfectly reasonable way to die."

As if on cue, one of the Oaxacans let out a wheezing gasp. Jacinto and Pink Hair walked over and looked down at them. Jacinto couldn't help but think of his son Wilmer—the short shallow breaths he would take once one of his attacks came on. It reminded him of the greater purpose behind this particular tragedy.

Only starlight shown above them. They'd chosen to make their voyage when there was no moon. It was difficult to see the two men on the ground. Pink Hair kept calmer than when they'd come upon the first dead from their party. Once the man finished wheezing, Jacinto checked the breath on the other one and found that he'd expired earlier and much more quietly than his companion.

"Rest in peace," Jacinto said.

Pink Hair acted as though the words were meant for him, and went off to lie on the now-cold earth. Jacinto looked up at the dense and claustrophobic canopy of stars. He tried to understand how anybody found beauty in this desert, which for the life of him still seemed a cruel and ugly place—this land that even the two vast and greedy countries on either side showed so little interest in claiming.

2

HE SAT UP WHEN HE HEARD THE MOTOR APPROACH, SO AS NOT
to be mistaken for another dead body. Two men in green uniforms emerged
from the truck, carrying a gallon jug of water. The first was Latino, and wore
a single diamond earring. Jacinto worried for a second that they'd somehow
circled back to the Mexican side of the border. It was a relief to see a pale
gringo next, older than his partner and with thinning blonde hair. From the
car stereo, loud rock-and-roll poured out in English.

Pink Hair stirred but didn't quite sit up. The officers put the gallon jug in
Jacinto's hands. He took a sip, held the liquid there in his mouth, then passed
it off to Pink Hair. It hurt to take that first swallow, the water like needles all
along his throat. It burned in the cracks that had opened on his lips and gums.
Pink Hair drank so greedily that he puked much of it back up.

The Border Patrol officers immediately went over to the bodies of the two
Oaxacans, and stood above them muttering what Jacinto guessed were curse
words. He took more swallows of water and watched. The Latino with the earring reached for the radio strapped to his chest, but Blondie grabbed his hand
and stopped him. Jacinto took this as a bad sign. The officers didn't seem to
know what to do. They paced around and argued. Pink Hair was too busy
drinking and puking to pay them any mind.

Finally, Blondie came over and asked, in poorly pronounced Spanish:
"Which one of you is the smuggler?"

"He's dead." Jacinto pointed back into the desert, the direction from which
they'd come. A terrible liar, he was glad his face was too sunburned to blush.

"There are more bodies back there?" Behind his reflecting sunglasses, the
gringo's eyeballs darted back and forth.

Jacinto nodded. "We were eight, to start." He was careful to add one fictional *pollero* to their numbers. The falsehood tasted bitter upon his tongue.

Blondie's mouth widened and he put his hands on the sides of his head. The two officers turned their backs and spoke in hushed and bothered voices for what seemed a long string of minutes.

"*Vamos*," Earring said at last. He put handcuffs on both Jacinto and Pink Hair, but in the front so that they might continue to drink water. They were placed in a backseat cage that separated them from the officers. Jacinto was sure that the inside of this truck was colder than the refrigerator Don Valentín used to for beer and cheese back in Carasucia. It was colder than nighttime in this desert. Jacinto worried that the water in the jug might freeze before he could finish drinking from it.

"Where you from, *amigo?*" Earring looked at Jacinto through the rearview mirror.

"Mexico." Jacinto detected a nervous flutter in his own voice.

"Where in Mexico?" Earring asked.

"San Luis Potosí." Pink Hair spoke before Jacinto had a chance. "We came together. He's my *padrino*." It was the first time the boy had talked all day.

"You're not going to die on us, either of you?" Earring asked. "We have a long drive ahead."

"We need water and food." Jacinto didn't like the way this conversation was going. Didn't they have a protocol for these situations? "But I don't think we'll die."

"You'll get your food and water," Earring said.

"What about the other bodies?" Jacinto asked.

"Let us worry about those bodies!" Blondie turned and spoke in a voice studded with anger and a bad accent. "We take care of the living first."

Something wasn't right. Jacinto was sure of it. Several moments of silence passed. The truck bounced down the dirt road. The desert continued uninterrupted.

*

There was little to be done in the parcel but watch the corn. It hadn't rained in several days, and even the weeds seemed reluctant to grow. If the rainy season somehow ended prematurely, it would be a disaster for this crop. The green shoots had gained a modest inch or so, and there wasn't yet reason to panic. Still, Wilmer wondered how much they had stored in their granaries, and how long it might hold out. He'd never had to worry about such things before.

To justify the trip, Wilmer collected an armful of firewood at the low end of the parcel and headed up the path. Along the way, he passed Don Chus, an older patriarch from Carasucia, known for enjoying casual conversation a bit too much.

"*Niño!*" Don Chus had a bony cow in tow. "Always working, no?" The man wore a straw hat and a wide-collared white shirt. No shoes covered his bare and leathery feet.

"Always," Wilmer said.

"It doesn't want to rain, does it?"

"Doesn't want to rain." Wilmer shifted the logs in his arms, hoping to make it look heavier than it was.

"How old are you now?"

"Thirteen," Wilmer said.

"Thirteen, and taking care of the corn on your own."

"Trying to," Wilmer said.

"News from your father?"

"Nothing."

"*Ojalá* you hear something soon."

"*Ojalá,*" Wilmer said.

"I have two sons there now." Don Chus held up a pair of fingers, like a peace sign. "One of them was incarcerated for a while, but he made it." The cow pulled hard on its rope, the black rubber of its lips sucking up weeds and stubble along the margins of the path. "One of my boys, he works hard, calls every Sunday, and talks about the day he'll come back to Carasucia." He gave the rope an authoritative tug and righted the cow's head.

"And the other one?" Wilmer asked.

"That one's drunk all the time and hardly works. No thoughts of return. Wants to find a *gringita* to marry and become legal." Don Chus laughed hard and slapped his knee. His grin revealed a mouthful of black and brown teeth. The cow saw an opening and made another go at the weeds.

Wilmer let out a small and insincere laugh, wondering what his father would think of that country if and when he got there.

*

"Hungry yet?" Blondie asked.

Between the two of them, Jacinto and Pink Hair had finished the gallon jug of water. The thirst had subsided enough so that Jacinto now noticed the cavernous hollow in his stomach.

"Yes," he said tentatively, still suspicious of the uniformed gringo. "We're starving."

The truck pulled over and parked on the shoulder of the dirt and gravel road. The officer opened his door and stepped out. For the first time, the desert's midday heat felt welcome, after the truck's relentless air-conditioning.

Blondie opened the door to their backseat cage and tossed in two brown-paper sacks. He placed another gallon of water at their feet. Hands cuffed together in front of them, Jacinto and Pink Hair ripped open the bags and found food: sandwiches made from soft, square bread, fried corn and potato chips, a bar of chocolate. Obviously, these were the lunches the two officers had brought for themselves. It hurt Jacinto's teeth at first, biting through the red disc of meat and the orange triangle of cheese.

"Don't eat so fast," he said to Pink Hair. "You don't want to vomit again."

The boy tried to slow down his chewing on the mayonnaise-soaked bread in his mouth, but hunger got the better of good sense.

The two officers left the car running and the air conditioning on. They closed the doors and walked off several yards. The older gringo made a call on what looked to be a separate mobile phone—not the radio strapped to his chest. Jacinto continued to study them while Pink Hair traded the second halves of their two sandwiches. Though he could hear nothing over the hum of the motor and the din from the blowers, Jacinto could tell that the officers were raising their voices. This was some sort of argument.

The bigger Latino shrugged and held his open palms at his sides, circling to keep his partner's gaze. He was the voice of reason, hoping to bring about a peace between them. The older blonde man was more emotional. Even the reflecting sunglasses failed to conceal his bother and anxiety. He shook his head and looked away, waving his pointed index finger at his partner, the truck, the desert. Whatever his position in this argument, Jacinto decided, it was more extreme than Earring's. Also, he was more determined to get his way.

"Don't you think this is strange?" Jacinto asked Pink Hair. "They've given us their own lunches."

"Gringos are soft." Pink Hair spoke through a mouthful of food. "Believe me: the Mexicans would let us starve."

"Have they mentioned anything on their radios about us? About us or the dead bodies?" Jacinto wished he could understand even a little bit of English.

"No." Pink Hair slowed down the starving-dog pace on his sandwich. "They haven't said anything."

In the distance, Earring put his open hands up at chest level and took a few steps backwards. Whatever his position was, he had just conceded. Blondie again reached into his pocket and pulled out that private mobile phone. He kept his eyes on his partner, and made a call.

"Something about this isn't right," Jacinto said out loud.

They drove for hours and arrived nowhere. Certainly, they weren't heading north. Based on the gigantic sun, Jacinto guessed that southwest was their general direction. He understood that this was a big desert, but shouldn't they have at least come to a real road by now, a town perhaps? He wondered if the Migra wasn't going to take them out to the middle of nowhere and shoot them in the head. Or worse, simply abandon them far from their drags even—to save the bullet. But what about the food? If they were to be killed or left for dead, why waste a perfectly good sandwich?

Nobody spoke as they drove through the desert in the ice-cold truck. Hard rock played on the stereo, while the police radios chirped out incomprehensible words. With the eating and drinking, Jacinto felt his strength return. He took off his baseball cap and scratched his head. A layer of caked salt covered the

hat all the way up past the logo of whatever American sports team it repre-
sented.

Jacinto managed to get a look at himself in the truck's rear-view mirror.
The sight shocked him. Deep new lines were carved into his forehead and chin.
Layers of his nose had blistered away. Worst of all, his eyes had that collapsed,
sunken-into-their-sockets look that he'd seen on the Oaxacans and the other
corpses. It looked like he was wearing a mask of wood and leather. In three
days, Jacinto had aged a decade.

Pink Hair fell asleep. As the truck bumped its way along the dirt road, his
head settled eventually onto Jacinto's shoulder. Some outlaw, Jacinto thought.

Jacinto wished that he could get some sleep as well, but he was too anxious about what the gringos were doing. At this stage, the hospitalization that
they'd hoped for looked unlikely. Should they have feigned being even closer
to death? Perhaps they should've puked up all the food and water—so that
intravenous feeding was their only option.

The truck crested a hill and slowed a bit. Blondie extended his finger and
spoke one syllable of English.

Jacinto looked to where the gringo pointed and saw, in a dirt lot to the
far side of their dirt road, another police truck not so unlike their own. This
one, however, was painted black and white, and was older, smaller, a different
make. Two officers stood outside of it, in all black uniforms. These men were
not Chicanos. They were Mexican.

Their truck pulled over and the two officers climbed out, leaving the motor
and the air conditioning on. One of the black-uniformed officers did the talking, while the other hung behind him, watching. He shook hands with both
their Migra agents, and looked over at Jacinto and Pink Hair in their cage.
Facing Blondie, he nodded his head as if in affirmation. Jacinto swallowed
hard and watched as their gringo officer took out his wallet and presented the
black-uniformed man with a handful of green bills.

"*Hijo.*" Jacinto jostled his shoulder to wake Pink Hair up. "We've got a
problem."

Pink Hair shook himself awake and looked out the window. "*Federales?*"
He was confused more than anything else, wondering where his hospital bed
was, with his steak and cable TV. "What the fuck are they doing here?"

"I think we're going with them," Jacinto said. "Is that bad?"

*

Wilmer walked homeward from the ravine, machete in hand, the dog sniffing at the dirt in front of him. Upon seeing the house, he remembered the fat man in the big pickup who'd first come to offer his services. The truck parked out front, its polished chrome shining. On the airbrushed rear gate the word *EXODUS* was written in a flowing script, like the coca-cola logo, before a background of pastel-colored volcanoes, lakes, and moons. A young helper waited in the cab while the fat driver came into the house.

Inside, Wilmer's mother had brought the man coffee and tamales. Father had shaken his hand and offered him a seat. The stranger wore an enormous belt buckle with a real scorpion encased in some sort of plastic or glass at its center. As he sat down, a thick roll of fat hung over his pants, and Wilmer wondered if that frozen scorpion might be able to sting him below the navel.

"In one day." The fat man spoke between delicate sips from his coffee cup. "You'll make more money than you can make here in a month."

Wilmer's mother had ordered him to clean corn in the kitchen, while she joined the men at the table. Her back was turned to him, but Wilmer distinctly heard her say "the medicine" in a tone like a tired lullaby.

The fat man mentioned several numbers—one for now, others for later. He spoke of trucks, and houses, and all of the people that he had—people here, people there. This fat man had a guy in Guatemala, another in Arizona. His friends in Tijuana came up several times. Did this stranger do nothing else, Wilmer wondered, then go all over the known world making friends and collecting people?

Once the corn was clean, his mother gave Wilmer a coin for the mill. By the time he returned with the ground *masa*, the fat man was shaking hands with both parents. His belly bulged a bit bigger with the tamales, the scorpion at his waist wiggling about more boldly.

"I'll come back next week and we can talk again." He put on his hat and went out to the truck. The loud engine turned over with a strain. The oom-pah sounds of the Mexican *norteño* bands started up mid-song. The pickup pulled away from their little house—the *EXODUS* on the tailgate barely vis-ible through the cloud of dust that blew up around him.

*

"What's our independence day?" The *federale* had a pock-marked face and a thin black mustache. He spat a little as he asked Jacinto the questions.

"September sixteenth." Jacinto mumbled his answer in a monotone, trying not to affect any sort of accent. Don Noe did make him memorize a few facts and dates, but he remained unpracticed in the subtleties of Mexican speech.

"Sing the national anthem." A small particle of saliva flew onto the table.

"*Mexicans, at the cry of war/ make ready the steel and the steed*," Jacinto sang off-key, hoping he'd be asked to stop after the chorus. His biggest fear was for any kind of question about where, in Mexico, he was from. Surely, Pink Hair was being interrogated in another room nearby. Would he stick with his story about the two of them traveling together, as *hijado* and *padrino*? Where was it that they were meant to be from? San Luis what?

"Fine then," Pock Mark said at last.

"*And may the earth tremble…*" Jacinto hit the last word hard. Isn't this what good liars did: showed enthusiasm for their fibs?

"If you're so Mexican." Pock Mark stood now, staring out of the small window in the door as he spoke. "Perhaps you're the *pollero* as well."

"The *pollero* died in the desert," Jacinto said in his controlled monotone. "That was the only bit of justice to come out of that journey. Asshole didn't know left from right. Led those poor people in circles until they died of thirst." It wasn't hard for Jacinto to summon a convincing amount of anger when he told this half-truth.

Pock Mark stood away from the window. "More people died out there?"

"Many more," Jacinto told him. Was it possible that the Americans didn't mention this?

Pock Mark stepped away from the window and sat down at the table opposite Jacinto. "Tell me what happened, in the desert."

Though he didn't fully trust this man, Jacinto felt that he had nothing to lose by telling him. The other walkers had families—people waiting back home who deserved to know their fate. "We were eight," Jacinto began, careful once again to add a made-up dead smuggler to their numbers. "The walk was only meant to take a day and a half. We carried two gallons of water each, no more. The *pollero*—the one who died—he made a wrong turn somewhere and got lost. After that, we went in circles. Once it was only four of us, I suggested that we try and get ourselves caught. That it might be our only chance for survival. Two more men died before the Migra found us. The young man and I are the only ones who survived." Jacinto was interrupted by a knock at the door.

Pock Mark rose from his seat and spoke in hushed tones to another *federale* through the thin slit of open door. A clipboard and documents were handed to him. Once he returned to the table, he checked a few boxes and made an elaborate signature at the bottom.

"I want to give you some advice." Pock Mark seemed genuine. "There are dangerous people involved in the human-trafficking business, people that wouldn't like for this story to get around. If I were you, I would use discretion. Things have changed considerably along this border. It's not as it used to be, even a short time ago. The *coyotes* don't mention this when they're recruiting clients. Once you're back in El Salvador, you might consider staying there this time."

"El Salvador?" Jacinto didn't need to fake his shock. "I am Mexican."

"You're Salvadoran." Without emotion, Pock Mark turned to the next document on his clipboard and filled that one out as well. "We can spot it from a mile away. Besides, the kid with the faggot haircut told us."

Jacinto felt anger burn bright as the desert sun. The words: *he's the smuggler* rose in the back of his throat like bile. Would it matter? Would they even believe him?

"You know," Pock Mark said. "On the border between two nations, two cultures, two ways of life—loyalty is not much of an asset."

Two officers came from outside and led Jacinto off to a ragged cell lit by a lone light bulb hung from the ceiling by wires. One overflowing toilet stood cockeyed in the corner. All the inmates looked to be other unsuccessful migrants. Most of them sat on the floor, the light bulb drawing long shadows on their tired faces, no evidence of them having been fed or watered. Jacinto stood by the bars and looked out, hoping Pink Hair might pass by on his way to a cell.

A fellow prisoner approached Jacinto there at the bars. He had a smooth face and fine, straight hair.

"El Salvador?" the stranger asked with a sing-songy lilt to his voice.

"Is it that obvious?" Jacinto wondered if his nationality were tattooed on his forehead somehow.

"I'm very perceptive."

"You're Salvadoran as well?" Jacinto asked.

"No." The man shook his head. "I'm from Quetzaltenango, in Guatemala."

Jacinto recognized the *chapín* style of speaking that he'd heard jokes about. "Jacinto." He offered his hand.

"Israel." The Guatemalan lightly squeezed Jacinto's fingers in his palm. "You're lucky, Don Jacinto."

"Lucky?" Jacinto rolled his eyes.

"Oh yes. They've almost got a full load of us already. The bus will leave tomorrow or the next day."

"The bus?"

"The Bus of Tears. Is this your first time doing this?"

"Where will it take us?"

"To my country. Usually a border town called El Carmen. You can cross the river there, but I recommend a better spot further down—Tecún Umán. The river is less bold, easier to wade."

"I'm not crossing again." Jacinto decided this as he spoke. "I barely survived this first try, with an expensive *coyote* and everything. Back home, I can at least feed my family. What good am I to them dead?"

"But in El Norte, you can do a lot more than feed them." Israel beamed. "Don't worry about one failed attempt. I've made this journey many times, no *coyote* at all, and I still get through most of the time."

Jacinto thought about what the *chapín* said. If he made the trip unassisted, he wouldn't owe Don Noe on the rest of his debt. He might not get his down payment back, but at least he'd get into the US for a fraction of the going rate. There was something a little strange about this Guatemalan, but he did seem to know what he was talking about.

The guards walked another prisoner past them and Jacinto remembered why he was standing by the bars.

"Do they bring the Mexican prisoners in here as well?" he asked Israel.

"Mexican prisoners?" Israel laughed. "What do you mean? Mexico has no law against crossing the border."

"It's all Central Americans in here?"

"They might lock up a *pollero* every once in a while, for the bribes. Other than that, it's just us, waiting for the Bus of Tears."

3

THE BUS WAS A RATTLING METAL BOX. THE SEATS HAD ALL BEEN ripped out to make room for more migrants. A chain-link wall separated the driver from the rest of it. Apart from the wheels and the windows, it wasn't so different from the cell they'd all been in the day before.

While no less comfortable, something about the bus was more hopeless, Jacinto decided. Watching Mexico go by in the wrong direction, he couldn't help but feel like a colossal failure.

A sheet-metal grid was bolted over the open windows. Still deep in the Sonora desert, it was a barely breathable brand of hot highway air that came in at fifty miles per hour. Prisoners crowded the windows in the hopes of fresher breath.

"Everyone hugs those windows now, but wait until we get into the Sierra Madre." Israel had again found his way to Jacinto's side. "Then they'll be huddling together in the front of the bus, trying to keep warm."

"Don Israel, don't take this the wrong way, but why have you taken such an interest in me?" Jacinto spoke tentatively. "Not that I don't enjoy your company. And I can see the advantage of having allies in our current situation. But I'm a liability. I've never made this trip before. And I'm giving up after this attempt. Why not befriend one of the other men? One who can offer more help than I can?"

Israel smiled broadly; he had perfect teeth—gleaming white with no metal among them. "I told you before, Don Jacinto, that I'm very perceptive. I can see things that nobody else can see. Recently, for example, you have suffered bad fright and sore trouble, have you not?"

Jacinto looked down at his hands. They rested upon his thighs like two corpses. He thought of the sun-dried bodies in the desert, how close he'd come to becoming another one of them.

"Also, I can see that you are not a base man, lacking spirit. These others..." Israel used his lips to point at the fellow passengers. "They plan to pursue vice in El Norte—women and alcohol. Or if not vice as such, then material things—cars and televisions. They are in no way wise or upright men. I can see that you're different. It's a gift of mine."

"You're some kind of *brujo*, is that what you're telling me?"

"Some people call me that. Others call me worse. More accurately, I'm called a healer. To be honest, I don't see the need for so many labels. I have certain talents, and I lack others—like everybody else."

"I don't believe in those things—*brujeria*, herbalism, bone-setting." Jacinto stopped himself just short of adding heaven and hell to the list.

"I'm not asking you to," Israel said.

Outside, a small town materialized out of the desert. For fractions of a second, the scenery was broken by a couple of concrete buildings, a bodega and a pool hall, a few old cars, and a dirt lot full of bizarre stone statues—angels and dragons and mermaids with ample breasts. The town disappeared just as quickly. Once again, desert was the only thing to see.

"Why do you make the trip?" Jacinto asked. "What are your reasons?"

Israel smiled again. "I have no land. I can't even feed my children in my own country. Not so long ago, I went to California only for the grape-picking season. I'd bring the money back and pick coffee. Now, the border has become difficult. I stay in the north until I can't bear it, then come back."

"Don't you like it up there?" Jacinto asked.

Israel shrugged. "The money's good. And I like the gringo cigarettes." He smiled. "But it's not the same as one's own home. I'll never understand those that go for good, who lose any wish to come back or even send news. I think everyday of returning to Chela."

Jacinto stared out the window, trying hard to be thankful that he still had a small bit of land to raise corn on, that he didn't have to make this trip over and over.

"What about you, Don Jacinto?" Israel asked. "Why have you come on this trip, if you love your *patria* so much?"

"My son." Jacinto had a simple answer to that question. "He has a disease of the lungs. Asthma."

"Have you tried a cleansing?" Israel took a professional curiosity—if black magic could be called a profession. "Shark's fin oil is meant to be help with such a thing."

"We've tried everything." This was true. In desperation, Mina took Wilmer to a *yerbero* not far from their village. He made a tea of sage and *chipilin*, and cracked an egg on the boy's chest, but the asthma refused to go. "There's a good medicine, but it's quite expensive."

Israel nodded, the smile gone from his face.

"How much longer will we be on this bus?" Jacinto asked.

"Days, my friend. But it will feel like months. All the seasons of the year pass by on the Bus of Tears."

*

When he saw that shining air-brushed pickup in front of his house, Wilmer prepared for the worst. Renegado sprinted along at his heels, wondering why his master didn't walk faster in this final stretch homeward. In all likelihood, if they heard first from the smuggler and not the smuggled, the news would be bad.

Their house consisted of two enclosed rooms that backed up against the main road. The living space was open on three sides—one was the normal entrance, one was by the freestanding kitchen, and the other opened to the yard with the cistern and latrine. Wilmer was about to enter through the near side. He heard his mother preparing a cup of coffee for the *coyote* and stopped himself short: maybe both of them would speak more freely if they didn't know that a child was present. He grabbed Renegado by the skin of his neck and pulled him around the house the long way.

The unmistakable *EXODUS* mural on Don Noe's tailgate still looked brand-new. As before, a bored young man sat in the driver's seat—a chauffer, a bodyguard, or perhaps both in one. He leaned out the window with a lit cigarette, dark glasses over his eyes. Wilmer smiled as he passed, but the man in the truck didn't appear to notice.

He heard his mother take the coffee to the other room. The cup and saucer clanged down upon their dining table. Wilmer gathered Renegado in his arms and sat behind the adobe kitchen, where he could see into the main room. The pinging of the just-boiled pot helped cover his noise.

"I have some good news and some bad news for you Niña Mina." The fat man spoke in a tedious, folksy drawl, as though he enjoyed too much the sound of his own voice.

"Please." Wilmer's mother had no patience for this song and dance. "Is my Jacinto alive?"

The fat man rotated his cup upon his saucer. "He certainly is alive. That's the good news."

Wilmer watched as his mother crossed herself and closed her eyes. Renegado fidgeted in his hands, and Wilmer squeezed tighter, as though this were his own silent, thankful benediction. The dander from the dog's fur tingled in his sinuses. Wilmer heard his mother's next question: "And the bad news?"

The cup clanged against the saucer.

"He's not in Los United," the fat man said. "He's in prison on the Mexican side. If they discover his country of origin, he'll be sent back to the border with Guatemala. If he manages to pass himself off as a Mexican national, then he's already free."

This was a confusing turn to Wilmer. As far as he knew, *coyotes* guaranteed their services. They were obliged to keep trying until their clients made it successfully to the other side. Wouldn't they know for certain where his father was?

His mother was equally confused: "So then, you will take him again, no? Either from Mexico or all the way from Guatemala. It's part of our deal."

The fat man let out a long breath. "That's where this situation gets complicated. It seems your husband did something very damaging, something he was given explicit instructions not to do. He turned himself in to the authorities—surrendered, so to speak."

Wilmer didn't breathe at all for a moment. He felt Renegado's lungs inflate and deflate while his own were frozen.

"Not my Jacinto," she said.

The fat man ignored her. "This cowardly act of his, it jeopardized the fate of several other travelers."

"Jacinto would never do such a thing!"

The dog squirmed in Wilmer's hands, associating that tone of voice with an imminent beating.

"I've spoken by telephone to the *pollero* who was there, as well as to my associates in Mexico. I'm sure I don't have to tell you that these are powerful and dangerous men, men who do not enjoy having their business disrupted by a *pinche* Salvadoran who gets thirsty and tired of walking."

His mother left his field of vision, but Wilmer could hear her sobbing. His father? Tired and thirsty? He was known for working harder than any man in Carasucia. The other farmers made jokes about it.

"Now," Don Noe continued. "I have argued the case with my superiors, and explained that you are of scarce resources. No harm will come to you, Niña Mina, but the debt must be paid as soon as possible."

"The debt?" Wilmer's mother lost what was left of her composure. "Can I pay you in tortillas and chicken feathers? Because that's all I have!"

"Calm yourself!" The fat man raised his voice. It hurt Wilmer's ears to hear his mother referred to in the second-person familiar, as though she were a dog. Even his father always spoke to her with the formal address. "Be thankful that nobody is considering more drastic measures. My associates don't suffer this kind of irregularity with good humor."

The fat man stood up from the table and pointed one stubby finger at Wilmer's mother. The scorpion on his belt buckle shimmered in the late afternoon sun.

Two villages to the north, in La Bolsa, a house caught fire last year. Further back, in Ahuachipilín, a household of girls were beaten and raped by strangers in the night. Both acts were blamed on a delinquent family debt to an organization of *coyotes*.

"Now." Don Noe regained his composure and sat back down. "I'm not accusing you of anything. But please understand the importance of appearances. Debts cannot be forgiven because a husband loses contact with his family, or because a wife hasn't heard from him. I know it may sound heartless, but that sort of thing could set a dangerous precedent."

Wilmer's mother pulled herself together.

"So then," the fat man continued. "If your husband contacts you, please let me know immediately."

"We have no phone. How will he contact us?"

"Who was meant to receive him in El Norte?"

"My brother."

Don Noe nodded a few times, processing the fact that they did have kin in the north, therefore the means to pay northern-style debt. "Perhaps you should give him a call, ask if he's heard anything, if he can offer any help. We'll speak to our own people. Someone might be able to tell if your husband was deported or released." He slurped the last of his coffee, tipped his hat towards the woman whose life he'd just ruined, and left the house from the side opposite Wilmer's hiding place. The oom-pah of *norteño* music—sounds of mischief and glee—started strong and then faded as the truck pulled away. Wilmer heard crying coming from his mother in the other room. He let go of Renegado, who shook a few times and spun in circles, thinking all of this a part of some new game.

In the main room, Wilmer's mother had her head down upon the table. She sobbed into the oilcloth. With light steps, Wilmer entered and put a hand on her shoulder. She wasn't surprised by his presence. In spite of the tears and worry, his mother was still beautiful. Wilmer saw the way men and boys from the village looked at her when she left the house. Her hair still had its tight curls and shiny black sheen. Though Wilmer was meant to be the man of the house, she was taller and stronger than him.

"I'm sorry," he said. He was sorry for his worthless lungs and for his powerlessness to help her with this problem that he had caused. He wanted to apologize for all of these things, for the family's entire predicament, but was sure she'd shush him. "I'm sorry," he said simply, over and over, pretending—for her sake—that he didn't even know what for.

*

Israel's description of the bus ride turned out to be painfully accurate. In the days that followed, they sweated through the desert then shivered through the highlands. They crossed a tall suspension bridge over a nearly dry river. Jacinto's lifelong fear of heights forced him to back away from the windows, and crouch against the bus floor. He was nearly in a fetal position by the time they were back on solid ground.

Somewhere outside of the capital, they spent one night in a detention facility and were consolidated with other deported Central Americans—from other parts of the border. They were fed a nighttime and then a morning meal of beans, tortillas, and salt, and reloaded early the following day. The driver changed, but the bus stayed the same.

Watching out the window as they wormed their way up one of the valleys, Jacinto was shocked at the immensity of this vast, overgrown city. Mexico's capital made San Salvador seem small and intimate by comparison. Staring down at the DF from a hill, all of human civilization looked like some sort of plague attacking the earth—a slow-spreading cancer of smoke and concrete, not unlike a fungus overtaking an ear of corn.

The roads grew worse as they made their way south. Jacinto's ass was bruised from so many hours on the bare metal floor. They bounced high in the air whenever the bus crossed the "speed bumps"—which were inexplicably placed in the middle of major freeways in this part of the country, and for which the driver did not slow down.

Jacinto studied the faces of his fellow prisoners. How many of them, he wondered, will turn right around at the Guatemalan border and try this again? How many of them had fought in a brutal civil war? All that killing and dying and starving in the woods—for countries where a hard-working man couldn't even get a job.

A train whistle sounded faintly over the rumbling of the bus. Israel opened his eyes at the sound. "Not much longer now," he said to Jacinto. "That's the train, the one that takes us north."

"Where are we?" Jacinto asked. It was night. Outside was a dense forest only visible in the truck's headlights.

"Chiapas." Israel pronounced the name ominously. "The Beast."

Jacinto remembered what Pink Hair had said about the southern jungles—the atrocities that occurred to solo travelers on the tops of the trains.

"At this rate, we'll get to the border after it closes, spend the night on board, then they'll take us across in the morning."

"Do you know where we can find some food, in Guatemala?" The desperation in his own voice was hard for Jacinto to hear.

"We'll see what we can do," Israel said.

"How do I get back to El Salvador?" Jacinto asked.

"It's not so far." The pings of raindrops against the roof blended with the sound of the motor. "You could hitch-hike in a couple of days. Cane trucks should still be running."

The thought of home was bittersweet for Jacinto. He hated being treated like a criminal. And before being caught, he hated thinking like a criminal—looking nobody in the eye and keeping a convincing lie always on the tip of his tongue. He never wanted to get caught up in something that caused death again. If the war had taught Jacinto anything, it was that killing breeds more killing. The only way out was to avoid such a course in the first place.

But how could he face his son? What explanation would satisfy Wilmer? The boy can't breathe because his father couldn't complete a journey that women and children from his country made successfully every single day, which Israel had made dozens of times?

As the double-edged nature of his dilemma grew unbearable, the bus hit what felt at first like another speed bump. Jacinto was launched so high into the air that he bounced off the ceiling. A hot coal of pain burned into his forehead, just above his brow. On the way down, he couldn't tell which side was the floor of their metal box. A storm of knees and elbows pelted the length of his body. Migrants shouted. The bus tumbled downward and around. The crack of breaking branches and the wash of wet brush drowned out the engine. Then, at once, the noise, along with the motion of the bus, stopped short.

For a moment, all that could be heard was the drumming of rain against the steel of the bus, and the running of what sounded like a small river not so far away. Seconds later, the men began to scurry like chased animals. Old shoes slipped about in search of traction. "This way, *cabrón*," somebody shouted.

Jacinto touched his forehead and felt the wet warmth of blood there. A stiff hand materialized under his armpit and helped him up. He had to straddle a v-shaped floor underneath him—one foot on either angled wall—and walked the length of the bus. With his hands, he felt the opening that the others had found. The chain link at the front of the bus was undone from one side. It made enough of a gap to slip a body through. From there, the side door—now facing up and hanging slack—could be crawled out of like a hatch.

"*Vamos*, Don Jacinto." At his back came the steady soothing voice which he knew to be Israel's.

Outdoors for the first time in days, Jacinto felt a surge of energy and life not unlike what he'd gotten from that first bottle of water in the desert. In the moonlight, he saw the other men scatter. Most ran back towards the road, hoping to find the train tracks, perhaps.

"This way, Don Jacinto." Israel grabbed his upper arm and gestured upriver.

They took off in a clumsy running stumble over the stones and mud of the bank, uphill and in the opposite direction from their fellows.

"Do you know where you're going?" Jacinto asked several minutes into the walk.

"So much of this jungle looks the same," Israel said. "But I think this is the place. Oh, yes. Here we are."

Their pace eased once it was clear that nobody was in pursuit.

"Do you think anyone was killed back there?" Jacinto asked.

"If the driver lived," Israel answered without pause. He'd obviously considered the same question. "Then he wasn't foolish or cruel enough to try and stop the rest of us. Most likely, our cage is what kept us safe."

Though it was too dark to see, Israel surely grinned at that bit of irony.

"This way." Israel turned abruptly at a tight but well-worn path that left the river and led straight uphill.

"Water," Israel said once they'd gone several yards up. At the side of the path was a small spring, a crack between two rocks really, where a thin trickle fell toward the river below. Israel used his hands to pass himself a few mouthfuls, then gave Jacinto a chance.

The water tasted more sweet and pure than any he'd had since the gringos saved his life in the desert. As Jacinto drank, Israel picked the leaves of some plants growing at the foot of the spring—his vision somehow unencumbered by the dark night or the canopy of trees. He stuffed the leaves into his pockets, said, "*vamos*," and continued to lead Jacinto.

Soon, the path turned much steeper. They grabbed onto the weeds and branches at its sides. This far from the road and the river, the jungle now howled with birds, monkeys, and God knows what else. As it grew more vertical, their path resolved itself into a set of rough-hewn stone steps. They were going straight up a nearly sheer mountain.

Once at the top, Jacinto thought he must be hallucinating—sleepwalking, perhaps. Clear of the jungle canopy, the light from the waxing young moon was like a sunrise to his straining eyes. A four-sided limestone structure stood before them—a room of sorts—with a roof comb like the photos Jacinto had seen of Tikal, like a more authentic version of the concrete-covered one in Tazumal. The steep hill that they'd been climbing for the last several minutes had turned out to be an enormous stone building—only the top of which remained exposed from foliage and soil.

"What is this place?" Jacinto asked.

"One of our cities," Israel said. "One of many holy places that the gringo scientists have neglected to find."

"Is this a pyramid? A Mayan pyramid?" Jacinto was incredulous.

"It's a temple, a sacred place. And the people who built it—our ancestors—they didn't know they were Maya at the time." Israel took one bunch of leaves from his pocket and sprinkled them, with an exhausted sense of ceremony, over the large slab of limestone that lay flat inside the little room.

"We'll stay here tonight and keep dry." Israel gestured to the limestone room behind them. "Please, if you have to piss or shit, go all the way to the bottom."

Jacinto nodded. The two of them bedded down on the cool stone of the temple floor, where a thousand years ago a high priest might've cut out a peasant's heart and offered it up for a bountiful harvest.

4

DESPITE HIS EXHAUSTION, JACINTO WAS TORTURED BY DREAMS. He shook himself awake midway through the night. The sound of Israel's snores nearby offered some comfort. Jacinto recalled what his companion said about pissing on the temple, and rose to make his way down.

It was a treacherous descent upon the stairs and then the steep earth that covered the rest of the stairs. The jungle howled all around him. One violent and piercing cry sounded above the others—a monkey or nocturnal bird that was long since extinct in El Salvador. At one time, Jacinto's home country was covered in a jungle as lush as this one, full of trees and water and more than enough resources.

Once on flat ground, he unloaded his bladder, an act which stung after all the dehydration and piss-holding he'd been through in the past several days. The jungle was doubly dark underneath the canopy. Jacinto stared into the blackness as he finished.

At first, he feared his vision played tricks on him. He blinked and squinted, but it refused to disappear: two red dots glowed in the darkness, as close together as a pair of eyes.

Jacinto's thoughts leapt to pythons, caimans, and jaguars. He tried not to move, and fastened up his pants without looking away from the eyes—burning like the ends of twin cigarettes in the shadows. Jacinto wished he had a machete with him. Back home, he'd never be without one under such circumstances.

Whatever this creature was, it moved closer. A smell like wet fur and sulfur filled his nostrils. Its low grumbling sound didn't betray the animal's identity. Jacinto had heard that you must protect your throat if attacked by a big cat—a jaguar or ocelot—but beyond that he had no idea what to do. He couldn't count on outrunning such a beast, and knew that fleeing might trigger a predatory instinct. He maintained eye contact and took a cautious step backwards.

The animal did not fear him. It advanced to match Jacinto's retreat. Soon, he could see its whole outline. This was no cat. In fact, it looked canine—but with shaggy, tangled hair. He thought of the televised nature documentaries he'd seen on the public channel back home. Was there some breed of dire wolf that survived in the jungles of southern Mexico?

Jacinto did his best to avoid sudden motions, and prepared to be pounced upon. He'd cover his face and throat with his arms. Perhaps he should lie still and hope to be mistaken for dead—the possum's strategy. The low gurgling growl grew louder.

With a backwards step, Jacinto went down to one knee. He put his hands over his face so that his fingertips reached his hairline and his forearms covered his windpipe. Gentle but trembling, he laid down onto one side upon the ground, the moist itch of the brush all along his waist and bare arm. He pulled his knees toward his belly, tighter into a fetal posture, in hopes of protecting the vital organs. His eyes now covered, Jacinto couldn't see the creature, but its raspy rumble and rank odor grew more intimate.

This is it, he thought to himself, this is how it ends. He didn't long for heaven then, only for a peaceful, dreamless sleep. Was it wrong to feel some relief? Was it wrong—after days of aimless walking through the desert and years of dodging bullets in the mountains—for Jacinto to take comfort in finally being killed by the claws and teeth of another species? Unlike immigration policy or communist uprising, he could at least wrap his mind around becoming a meal for something higher up the food chain. This was a timeless, respectable way to die. If only he knew the name and nature of the beast about to take his life.

He sensed its presence behind his ear, and tried to press himself harder against the ground. Jacinto hoped it would go first for the fleshy part of his thigh or shoulder. Even a bad bleed or gut wound would mean death out here. His heartbeat quickened and his teeth knocked together. As he steeled himself for that first strike, Jacinto wondered how long Mina and Wilmer might wait to hear from him before assuming the worst.

But what he felt next wasn't painful or piercing or even pressure. It was the flutter of a wet tongue upon his ear. The soft lick was followed by warm breath and then a ruf-ruf like a barking dog. Jacinto thought of Renegado back home.

Sure enough, as he released his arms from around his head and sat up, Jacinto found himself face to face with an everyday dog. It had a short, clean coat of hair—so white it seemed a source of illumination there in the otherwise dark jungle. The black creature with the red eyes was gone.

Still at eye level, the little white dog stared at Jacinto. It gave his face a friendly lick, and its breath had a smell like squash cooking. Suddenly calm, Jacinto stood up. The dog took several bouncing strides in the opposite direction, upon what looked to be a path. It turned back toward Jacinto and let out a couple of sharp barks, as if wanting him to follow.

Jacinto took a tentative step. The white dog continued. It was hard to believe such a well-worn trail existed in a jungle this dense, but the dog knew exactly where it was going. It sped up, stopping to look back a few more times, but still gaining ground. Before Jacinto knew it, he was running behind the dog at full sprint, struggling to keep up. The dog went so fast that after a minute or two Jacinto was winded. He lost sight of his leader and couldn't tell where the trail had been. Turning back now, the first signs of sunlight came up to the east.

At their makeshift camp atop the temple, Jacinto lay down beside Israel again and was instantly able to sleep, even on the cold limestone floor.

*

The next time the *coyote* showed up, Wilmer was shitting in the latrine behind the house. It was night. As the motor passed then stopped outside, Wilmer knew it to be Don Noe's by the *norteño* music blasting out.

The latrine's walls were *bajareque* and only the first couple feet were filled in with mud. Through the bamboo slats, Wilmer could see his mother in the main room, sweeping the dirt floor. He stood and did up his pants.

The smuggler's bleating cow of a voice: "With permission."

"Pass," Wilmer's mother said without enthusiasm.

"Thank you, Niña Mina."

"Have you heard anything about my Jacinto?" She continued to sweep the floor.

Wilmer was glad that she didn't fall all over herself to fetch him coffee and the like.

"Your husband is dead," Don Noe said.

The sweeping sounds stopped short. Wilmer felt the ground undulate below his feet. He feared, for a moment, that the cement slab was giving way, and that he was about to fall into a two-meter deep pit of his family's own excrement. With a hand against one of the corner beams, he regained his balance. Breath came quick and shallow through his upper chest, but he did his best to control it.

"What happened?" his mother asked.

"In the Mexican jail, he took his own life."

There was a silence. Renegado let out a tired yawn from the floor of the latrine. Wilmer visualized the little passageways through his chest expanding, ants digging them out. The next sound he heard was laughter.

Wilmer looked up and saw his mother cackling out a fierce laugh and tossing her head back. With that broom in her hand, she resembled a witch. Don Noe stood there looking puzzled.

"Get out of my house, you fucking liar." For some inexplicable reason, hearing his mother say this immediately put Wilmer's breathing at ease.

"If you'd have told me that he'd died in the desert, that he'd been shot by some gringo rancher, stabbed by a gangster or drowned in the Río Bravo I'd have believed you. But I know my Jacinto. I marched beside him in Guazapa. He didn't hang himself in some *pinche* Mexican prison." She laughed again at the audacity of the lie.

"This husband of yours." The fat man recovered from his initial shock—having better prepared for incredulity than for laughter. "His actions have proven much more cowardly than you make him out to be."

Mina went back to her sweeping and Wilmer looked about for where he might find a weapon of some kind. His machete hung inside the bedroom, on the other side of the house. Would that teenager be waiting out in the truck as usual? Wilmer left the latrine. By the cistern, a rusty hoe and shovel leaned in the dirt.

"You realize, of course, that this does not excuse you from your debt, Niña Mina."

She kept on sweeping, knowing now that there was no advantage in staying on the *coyote*'s good side.

"I've thought about what you said the last time," Don Noe went on, "regarding your lack of money."

Wilmer stepped lightly around the house. He knew his mother kept an old cut-off machete near the kitchen for opening coconuts and halving sugar cane.

"It's occurred to me." Don Noe's tone dropped into that menacing register that he'd used last time to describe his mysterious and murderous associates. "That perhaps there is another way you could settle your debt to me." He put his hand—it looked like a plucked hen—on her hip.

Wilmer hurried around the house. On the far side of the kitchen, he could no longer hear the voices. He found the old machete stuck in a stump by his mother's grinding stone, a groove well-worn into its underside from so many coconuts and chicken necks.

"Listen to me," Don Noe hissed through clenched teeth. "I'm offering you a solution here. Forget your pride for a second and take it seriously."

When Wilmer rounded the corner of the side door, he saw the fat man shaking his mother by the shoulders as he spoke. She squinted and turned her head away, as though his words were harsh light.

"Mamá!" Wilmer spoke from the threshold, the machete at the end of his arm. Renegado barked from his heels. "What's happening here?" He did his best to stare the fat man in the eye.

Don Noe turned to Wilmer and took his hands off the woman. "Nothing happens, *hijo*." A wicked smile formed on his face. The thick mustache bristled at the sides like the tail of an animal about to strike. Now it was his turn for cruel laughter.

"Be careful with that *corvito*, son." With his lips, Don Noe pointed toward Wilmer's machete. "You could hurt yourself." The fat man took a small black revolver from the back of his waistband and tucked it into the front, by the scorpion belt buckle. He had to suck in his stomach to get it settled there.

Wilmer swallowed and gripped the machete tighter. He felt his lungs constrict.

Don Noe's vigorous laughter exposed the gold frames around his front teeth. He stuck two fat fingers into his mouth and made a loud whistle. The engine—along with the oom-pah music—kicked to a start outside. Wilmer's windpipe was reduced to a pinhole now, but he would rather simply die than let the fat man see him wheeze.

"Think about my offer," Don Noe said to Mina. "It won't get more generous than that."

"And you." He turned to Wilmer. "Be careful with your little toys." The fat man laughed again, then turned and left the house.

As the truck drove off, Wilmer collapsed onto the floor. The effort to breathe was like trying to suck a grape through a drinking straw. His mother spread him out and sang her "Forgive your people" hymn. She fetched a wet rag from the cistern and put it against his forehead. From the kitchen, she carried out a cup of lukewarm coffee—one of the only home remedies that they'd found effective. Wilmer choked down a few swallows. Renegado howled like a wolf.

"Forgive your people, Lord," sang Wilmer's mother. The caffeine took effect and Wilmer felt his airways expand a little.

"Don't you believe what that man says." His mother set Wilmer's head on her lap and stroked his damp hair. "Your father isn't dead. Something has happened to him, but he's not dead."

Wilmer knew that she wanted to protect him, spare him more trauma. He was used to translating what adults told him into the always-more-miserable truth. But for some reason, in this case, he felt that his mother was sincere.

"However," she continued to stroke his hair, to tuck it back behind his ears. "In the meantime, you and I must find a way to earn some money."

*

In the morning, Jacinto woke alone upon the limestone floor, the sun now shining and the animals quiet. Outside, Israel sat on the top step of the temple with an enormous bunch of small, fat bananas to one side of him, a pile of peels to the other.

"Good morning," Jacinto said.

"Same to you. Have some breakfast. They're a little green, but not bad otherwise."

Jacinto helped himself, happy to eat anything at all. The end of the stalk looked to be severed by teeth and fingernails. During the conflict, finding a ripe banana tree was a great luxury. Here he was all over again.

"In the jungle, last night." Jacinto spoke with his mouth full. "I saw a dog."

Israel stopped chewing and spit yellow mush from his mouth. "What color was it?"

Jacinto hadn't expected such a reaction. Nothing ever surprised Israel. "White."

"You saw a white dog? Here? Last night?"

"That's right," Jacinto said.

"Which way did it go?"

"That way." Only as Jacinto extended his finger did he realize that it was pointing north. "I chased it for a few minutes, but couldn't catch up."

Israel's hairless face erupted into a wide grin. "This is very good news."

"What are you talking about?" Jacinto asked. "More witchcraft?"

"My friend, you've seen the white *cadejo*." Israel was ecstatic.

"I don't believe in such things." Now that the word was mentioned, Jacinto recalled the legendary ghost dog that was meant to appear in the night like a boogeyman.

"For a moment, I feared that you'd seen the black one, which is much more common and always brings misery."

Jacinto thought of those eyes in the darkness, the foul smell and the rattling growl. He didn't mention it to Israel, not wanting to fan the flame of his superstition.

"But the white *cadejo*." Israel stood up now and broke off a few of the biggest bananas. "He is a helpful spirit, a guide." Inside the temple chamber, Israel bowed his head and placed the fruit upon the limestone slab. "In my opinion, Don Jacinto, you should reconsider going home. Come with me, to the north."

Jacinto looked down at the empty banana peel in his hands. He didn't buy the black magic. But the memory of running with that dog felt right and whole-some, correct somehow. Sitting atop this temple—from a time when a whole separate series of lines cut up this continent—the troubles with the Migra and the *coyotes* felt small, fleeting. Also, Jacinto still couldn't swallow the thought of returning to Carasucia in failure, to watch Wilmer gasp for air because his father couldn't find his way through some damn desert. Unlike the nebulous revolution that those starving guerillas muttered about during the conflict, his son was at least worth dying for.

"Fuck it." Jacinto turned to face Israel. "Let's go north."

II

5

BRINGING ALONG THEIR HALF-EATEN BUNCH OF BANANAS, JA-
cinto and Israel returned to the river and bathed there. They soaked their
clothes and beat the filth out upon the rocks. Jacinto handled his underpants
carefully, so that the stitched-in phone number would not fray.

Naked but for their sneakers, the two of them carried their clothes to a
sunny spot downriver where they draped them over a small tree to dry. They
each had the same four items: t-shirt, trousers, underwear, and baseball cap.
Jacinto had brought a long-sleeve shirt with him as well, but it had been lost
somewhere between the desert and the jail cell.

"Nothing is more brutal than an angry belly." Israel took his underwear
off the branch. "I'd rather start off with something besides bananas in mine."
With his teeth, he ripped a hole in his own underwear, and from there proceeded to tear the entire waistband off.

"Agreed," Jacinto said.

"How are you at making fire?" Israel tested the elasticity of the cloth band.

"Out of practice," Jacinto admitted. He'd not used friction to force a spark
since the peace accords were signed. "But I remember how it's done."

Israel found a forked branch and snapped away at each end until it had a
Y shape a little bigger than his hand. He wrapped the waistband around the
two ends several times, until the tension satisfied him.

"You need not be fast. Have it lit before nightfall." Israel knelt by the river
and gathered round rocks. "I'll see about a little meat."

With an improvised slingshot and a few stones under his armpit, Israel
went off into the jungle. If not for the Nike sneakers on his feet, one wouldn't
know that Europeans had ever arrived on this continent.

The hard part was finding dry tinder. Jacinto scoured the spots where the sun broke through the jungle canopy until he had a handful of crisp leaves and sticks. He carried this tinder back to their place by the river. Next, he threw a few round stones against the larger boulders of the river bed until they broke. He picked through the chards and chose one rock-half with a useful rough edge.

Near the bush where their clothes were hung, he found a patch of river cane and harvested one dry, dead shoot. With his half stone, he made a point, like a pencil, on one end of it, then twisted it between his palms: it drilled straight and true. He had a harder time finding a softwood hearth. But as the sun grew higher, more dry spots revealed themselves. A young *zapote*, choked to death by the *matapalo* vine, lay collapsed in a clearing. Fragments of dry dead wood, in various shapes and sizes, lay littered about. Jacinto filled his arms.

Back by the river, he notched a split section of the *zapote* with his broken rock. With the tinder, he made a small nest. He took the sharpened stick between his hands and began to drill.

The process was tedious. Jacinto spent an hour at it, blistered one of his hands, and hadn't even drawn smoke. Though dead, the *zapote* was still moist. He looked around and broke off a green branch with a wide curve. With one of his own shoelaces, he strung it like a bow. He used his cutting rock to make a palm-size piece of the sinewy banana stalk. The drilling cane twisted into the bowstring, he could now create more friction simply by sawing back and forth. With the chunk of banana stalk in his blistered hand, he applied downward pressure into the hearth piece.

The new method proved far superior. Jacinto soon had a tiny ember. He dumped it into the nest of dry tinder then lifted the whole bundle and blew onto the coal. Smoke puffed out—once, twice, a third time. On his fourth blow, a few orange flames leapt up. He placed the bundle back on the ground and dressed it with the best splinters of *zapote* and *matapalo*. He kept blowing until the kindling took to fire. Next he dragged over two large logs, and placed them close enough to dry out.

The initial burst died down but the fire kept many respectable coals. Jacinto sat hypnotized, as though it were some great work of art that he'd created, his masterpiece. The bigger logs finally took to burning. He surrounded them with a ring of stones. On sticks, he skewered a few of the greenest bananas from their bunch and placed them over the fire. The day drew toward its end. He couldn't see the sun from so deep under the canopy, but he watched the pink sky in patches through the trees.

"A good fire, Don Jacinto." Israel appeared without a sound. Still naked but for his sneakers, he dropped two fat iguanas on Jacinto's lap. "Those bananas smell nice." Israel grinned. "We eat well tonight, no?"

They took the bananas from off the skewers and replaced them with iguana. The thick skin bubbled and crackled amidst the flames. The two men ate the bananas while the meat roasted. It had been a long time since Jacinto had tasted iguana. There were so few of them left in El Salvador, and those were small and skinny. He wondered if Wilmer and the other boys his age would learn to hunt and make fire. For that generation, survival skills would mean learning the English language and the geography of Mexico.

They let their dinner char until it was black and blistered. Mina always favored boiled iguana, skinned before serving. Tonight, however, Jacinto knew that he'd eat every bit of the rubbery hide.

Israel declared the meat done and handed Jacinto one of the skewers. The two of them ate like starved dogs. Starting with the fleshier bits along the belly and haunches, Jacinto tried his best to balance bites of the flaky meat with chewy skin. If a piece fell, he picked it up off the dirt and put it straight into his mouth. Israel used his thumb to pry cheek flesh from a cavity below the eye. Jacinto took care not to cut himself on the sharp, splintery bones. They ate the skin right down to the claws, and along the tail until it was nothing but the leathery nail of the spine. Jacinto felt his stomach swell with the extremes of hunger and binging.

Once they'd eaten the eyeballs and the tongues, and sat sucking at other holes in the skulls, Israel finally spoke: "Missing a little salt, no?"

"Salt would be nice." Jacinto smiled at the thought of it.

"But you know what they say: the best spice of all is hunger, and because the poor never lack that, they always eat heartily."

"Who says that? I've never heard it before." Jacinto enjoyed the saying immensely.

"Maybe it was in a movie." Israel leaned on one arm and picked his teeth with a sharp iguana bone.

"Will we go back to the temple tonight?" Jacinto asked.

"Might as well stay here." Israel shrugged. "Fire will keep the bugs away, and we can keep watch on our clothes."

"We start our journey tomorrow?"

"That's right." Israel gave a somber nod. "My hope is that authorities have their hands full with the rest of our busload—that we will travel in their wake, so to speak."

"It's nice to be off that bus, to be out of that cell. In truth, even if it is more dangerous..." Jacinto moved one log closer to the heart of the fire and it popped with sparks. "It feels nice to be travelling without a smuggler."

"You wait. This is the easy part. Tomorrow, things get difficult." Israel laid himself all the way down now, and inched closer to the fire.

Jacinto adjusted the logs again, and did his best to enjoy this moment: a full belly, a warm place to sleep—without much thought for the journey they'd have to start tomorrow.

In dreams, Jacinto returned to his early childhood, a time he scarcely remembered, a stage that hardly seemed part of his life at all—like the womb. In Chalatenango, before his family lost the farm, he was Wilmer's age. His father would give him a good horse and a big hat, and send him to check fences or look for lost animals. Other families came to their house to purchase cheese. His older brothers were always out working the cattle. His sisters lived with their hands in a bucket of curds and whey. At every meal his mother served meat and milk. His father had a job for any man willing to work.

*

Wilmer and his mother made their way to Rosario de Mora. It was late morning, so the bus was relatively empty, save for a chicken farmer carrying several basketsful of live white hens. The driver's son—younger than Wilmer—acted as *cobrador* and came through collecting fares. Mina, seated by the window, took the change purse out from her bra and retrieved two coins. She reached across Wilmer's torso and handed them to the boy.

Wilmer kept a keen eye out for how the local cornfields were doing. He was glad to see that his crop was higher than several others, but it was obvious that all of them could do with a bit more rain.

At the south end of town, the bus came to a stop. No passengers had risen or approached the door, and Wilmer craned his neck to see what they'd stopped for.

Two young men climbed aboard. One wore a loose black t-shirt, the other a sleeveless white undershirt. Both had sloppy monochrome tattoos on their arms and faces. The one in the undershirt spoke to the driver. He was the taller of the two and had the letters "MS" written on his forehead in a gothic script. Wilmer's mother crossed herself with her hands.

Wilmer knew that the Mara Salvatrucha had increased its presence in Rosario. The rumor around the village was that they'd taken over the local high school—an outstanding location, for recruitment in particular—kicked out the teachers, and used the classrooms as their headquarters. The Ministry of Education complained to the authorities. But when the police were finally sent in, they found themselves outnumbered and outgunned by the gangsters. Now, it looked as though the Mara was collecting a cut for transportation through town as well.

The bus driver held his palms up in the air and shrugged. The gangster in the tank-top grew annoyed with him. The other, in the black t-shirt, wore wrap-around sunglasses and a shaved head. He stood silently behind.

At last, the bus driver handed over a wad of bills. The gangster slapped him on the cheek, then turned towards the passengers.

"*Vaya señores*," he said. "Sorry to interrupt your trip. Myself, along with my associates, have been placed in charge of security on all buses travelling this route. In exchange for this valuable service, we are asking for a small collaboration on your part."

With his hands extended, they went up the aisle, collecting change from the passengers. Wilmer's mother reached into her bra and pulled out two tarnished fifty-*centavo* coins. She reached across Wilmer's torso and dropped them into the gangster's hand. He stopped and stared down at the coins.

"*Señorita*," the gangster said. "I don't trifle over *centavos*."

"Please," Wilmer's mother said. "I have only enough money for one phone call to the states. That's our sole reason for coming to town. I'm trying to contact the boy's father."

The gangster turned to Wilmer once he was mentioned. Their eyes met. In addition to the "MS" tattooed on his forehead, there was a bluish teardrop drawn onto the side of one eye. He moved on up the aisle.

The two *mareros* negotiated for a while with the chicken farmer—apparently, chickens required special protection—until both parties agreed on a sum. Wilmer watched the driver's son, the *cobrador*. He sat in the first seat behind his father's and silently sobbed into one of his arms, pressed against the green vinyl seat-back. Poor boy, Wilmer thought: all the money he'd made so far had gone to the gangsters, and he'd had to see his father turn helpless in their presence. Still and all, Wilmer thought as the two tattooed men left the bus, the Mara had shown his family more mercy than their *coyote* had.

*

"*Vamos*, Don Jacinto," Israel said. "Best we go early, before the bandits wake up."

It was still dark out, but the frantic sounds from the birds and monkeys betrayed the coming dawn. They put on their now-dry clothes, filled their pockets with the last from their bunch of bananas, and went to the spring.

On what may well have been the path that the white dog led Jacinto down the other night, the two men walked with hurry. The first light trickled down through the canopy, and Jacinto struggled to keep up.

Finally, at the crest of a small hill, Israel stopped and crouched down. "There," he whispered. Below them, following a bend in the river, was a single train track.

The two of them stared at it from their crouched position. Jacinto didn't see the need for whispering; there was nobody around. It was bittersweet to see those tracks cut the jungle into two halves, the first sign of modern civilization they'd come upon since fleeing the bus two days ago. Jacinto beheld the path out of the jungle with a heavy heart.

"The train slows for the curve. This is a good place to jump on. If you have anything valuable, put it in your shoe or up your ass now. Somebody will try to take it from you soon enough."

"I have nothing," Jacinto whispered back.

*

At the north end of Rosario, they disembarked the bus at the ANTEL station. It being a Saturday, there was a line. Wilmer watched as wives and children spoke into the receivers along the walls—spouting the local gossip, complaining about teenage misbehavior. Younger children stood on chairs and spoke into the phones, mostly saying yes, yes, yes to their father's questions: Have you been good? Did you get the clothes, toys, or school supplies that I sent? Do you miss me? Do you remember how I look? The mothers would go back on, and always there was a ritual exchange of suffering—how difficult it is here all alone. Then some stone-faced specifics—what could be done with a bit more money.

"Yes, Niña Mina?" The ANTEL operator was a kind man with dark skin and coarse hair, several teeth framed in gold.

She took out the well-worn piece of graph paper with the phone number of her brother in California written on it.

The ANTEL operator dialed the number and listened through a headset. "Number two," he said, pointing to one of the phones along the wall. Wilmer followed his mother over to it, then listened as she spoke.

"Chano, is that you? It's Mina."

In the pause, Wilmer studied his mother's expression. Surely, Uncle Chano would waste no time telling her if her husband was there with him. Mina's mouth flattened out.

"Chano." She fought her way into the conversation. "Any news from Jacinto?" She stood nodding her head, staring across the room but seeing nothing.

"No, we've only heard from the *coyote*," she said. "He lies to us. He says that Jacinto is dead."

Wilmer watched as a few heads turned toward his mother. He saw, for the first time, just how far-fetched their story must sound to others.

"The son of a bitch still wants the money, you see. That's the problem."

All of the ladies waiting in line, as well as several of those who had their kids on the phone, turned an ear towards their station now. Wilmer glared at the most shameless of the eavesdroppers—a tall, lopsided woman with teeth like a horse's. He offered his best stink-eye until she turned her head.

"No, no." His mother struggled to explain the mess to Chano. "The coyotes claim that Jacinto went to the authorities, that he turned in his whole party. Then, in prison, they say that he hung himself. Can you imagine? It's all lies. He's somewhere out there in between, and now we have this debt. The only contact information he has is your phone number, Chano."

Tears stained his mother's cheek. The other women rolled their eyes. For the first time since the fat man's last visit, doubts crept into Wilmer's mind like bugs into sweetbread. Perhaps his father had died. Perhaps he'd taken his own life even. Was it possible that he'd endangered his fellow travelers by seeking out the Migra? Wilmer had seen the way other boys put their fathers up on pedestals. Even the laziest drunks in Carasucia were great heroes in the eyes of their sons. Did he now suffer the same bias? Were hope and denial obscuring the truth in the minds of both Wilmer and his mother?

This train of thought was broken by her screaming voice: "With what money, Chano? With what money am I to pay this debt and forget Jacinto?" Only once she'd slammed down the phone did Mina notice all of the other women staring. She composed herself at once and went to the operator's desk.

"Five," the man said, holding up as many fingers.

She handed him the only bill left in her purse, then turned to Wilmer and said: "We'll have to walk home."

But Wilmer had already figured that part out. "Some clouds have moved in anyway. It won't be so hot."

*

After hours of waiting in silence at their spot on the hill, Jacinto laid back into the grass and pulled his baseball cap over his eyes.

"Psst." Israel shook him. "Make yourself ready, Don Jacinto. Train coming."

Jacinto sat up. After several long seconds he heard a mechanical sound.

"Hope you're a fast runner," Israel said. "Go for one of the ladders. Boxcars are good because they have the flat tops. Be ready to jump at any time."

A reluctant whistle—a sound like a wounded animal—came from the far side of the bend. They kept still. Soon the grind of the engine was audible from where they sat.

When the train finally came into sight, it looked as impossible as that Mayan temple had two nights before. The locomotive had a flaking paint job of blue and yellow, amidst the jungle's endless greens. It was like a cartoon machine passing through a scene from real life. Israel held an open palm against Jacinto's chest, his eyes darting all over. Finally, when the locomotive rounded the bend, he let go his hand and shouted, "Now!"

The two men scrambled down the hill. Their feet slid though the loose soil. Once at the bottom, Jacinto found his bearings and struggled to keep up as Israel took to a sprint alongside the train. This was more difficult than Jacinto anticipated: to run at full speed upon uneven ground without looking at his feet or where he was going, whilst scanning the train for some sort of perch— a handhold which was within reach but also high enough to clear his feet of the wheels. And if he tripped over one of the roots, holes, or railroad ties littered before him, he'd either miss this train or be ground to burger beneath it.

Ahead, Jacinto saw Israel take hold of a grab-iron on the boxcar passing them by. Once his feet were planted on the train, he reached out a hand. Jacinto made a lunge for it, but only managed to graze Israel's fingertips. Off balance, he stumbled and kicked one heel with the other toe. The train sped up as it left the bend. Jacinto resumed running, but the boxcar gained ground on him. Desperate not to lose track of Israel, he mustered the speed for one final grab. One last feature looked like it could hold him: a rusted latch sealed with a padlock upon the boxcar's cargo door.

He made an all-or-nothing lunge, lifting his feet high into the air so as not to let a pant-leg or shoelace get caught in the wheels. All of his weight hung by the ends of his fingers, hooked on the thin metal of the latch. He set to pulling himself up. The train's weight shifted, and his blistered palm was pressed into the rusted metal. Jacinto groaned with the pain. He swung his feet up so that they pressed against the sides of the boxcar, did his best to mentally separate his hand from the rest of his nervous system, and climbed.

The crease between the cargo door and the car allowed him some perch. Unfortunately, with the motion of the train, it pinched around his fingers and toes. After a few painful tries, he found that if he pried it as wide as possible with his shoe, he could keep the door from slamming upon his fingers. Once he worked his way up far enough, so that his feet stood atop the latch where his hands had started, he looked up and hoped the roof was within reach.

Above him, he saw Israel, leaning far down the car and extending an arm. Jacinto reached out. The blister on his palm gave a fierce burn as they clenched hands. At last, Jacinto was able to rest a forearm upon the train's roof, and from there it was a simple matter of hoisting up his lower body the rest of the way.

The instant the ascent was over, Jacinto held his injured palm in his good hand and—teeth and eyes clenched tight—let out a painful, bellowing growl. Out of breath, he stopped wailing and opened his eyes.

To his shock, dozens of people sat staring at him. Still huddled under blankets and old coats, a mass of human beings—men, women, and children— already rode atop the train. They wore tired expressions of defeat and hunger.

"That's good, Don Jacinto," Israel whispered in his ear. "Make them think you're a bit crazy."

He turned to his friend and was surprised to see his perpetual grin replaced by a stone-faced scowl. Was there something to be feared in these fellow travelers?

*

Indeed, the weather was more pleasant on the way home—some cloud cover and a nice breeze. At the south end of town, they passed the Mara Salvatrucha's tax-collecting outpost, and Wilmer could feel his mother's hatred harden for the gangsters.

Without meaning to, Wilmer let his eyes meet with the teardrop man's. He didn't feel the same hate that his mother did. He had more animosity for those nosy women back at the ANTEL office. That gangster had shown more understanding—and less intrusion—for their plight.

Teardrop gave Wilmer a little nod as they passed, and Wilmer returned it. Without any good reason, he believed that nod to be an acknowledgement of their mutual fatherlessness.

As they left the town limits and headed downhill into the country, the clouds turned dark and dense. Soon, a rainstorm was underway. Within seconds, they were both soaked.

"What luck," his mother said sarcastically.

"This is good for the corn." Wilmer was sincere. The two of them walked on through the rain.

*

Most of the morning went by uneventfully. The men sat silent side-by-side atop the train, hugging their knees to their chests and avoiding eye contact. The day warmed up with the rising sun. So far, Jacinto thought, this wasn't such an unpleasant way to travel.

Jacinto did his best to look right through his fellow passengers. But he couldn't stop staring at one young boy, who looked to be about Wilmer's age. His clothes were ragged and his face covered in railroad soot. Every so often, he opened his coat and took a few deep breaths from a small glass jar. It took Jacinto a minute to recognize the glossy bloodshot sheen in his eyes.

"That child." Jacinto leaned into Israel's ear. "He's sniffing glue. Is he by himself?"

"Correct," Israel said. "Each time more children ride like this, looking for the mothers and fathers that left them behind. They discover vice along the way."

"Who would abandon a child that young?"

"Happens more often than you think, Don Jacinto. Many folks, they go north with the intention of loyalty, but their intentions change over time."

"I abandoned my family once," Jacinto said. "I don't ever intend to do it again."

"Just wait, my friend. You'll see more tragic things along this trip than a child sniffing glue."

The land flattened out before them and Jacinto assumed the train's route was heading closer to the coast. The dense jungle relented a bit and gave way to forests speckled with agriculture—a cornfield here and there, peanuts, some sugarcane. They passed a large ranch and the cows looked up at the migrants, indifferently chewing away at piles of dry grass. Jacinto wondered what would happen if they had to jump and run from the train here, with no jungle to hide in.

After a long straight stretch, the tracks grew serpentine again, and the forest choked out the fields and homes.

In the night, Jacinto and Israel took turns sleeping atop the boxcar. Before closing his eyes, Israel told Jacinto to wake him the moment anything unusual happened: if the train slowed, if anyone suspicious approached. The air was cold and the moon filled up. Many of the migrants sought out other spots to sleep.

After only an hour or so, Israel sat up. "Try and get a bit of rest, Don Jacinto," he said. "We may not be able to stay aboard all night."

"Okay."

Jacinto found it easy to sleep atop the train. Somehow, the act of sitting still and watching all day long had exhausted him. In dreams, he returned to his childhood. This time, he remembered when the FMLN first showed at the family ranch. By then, the conflict had swept much of the countryside. The young men were the first to abandon the surrounding villages, then the old folks and girls. Jacinto's parents pulled him out of school just before the army came to recruit the little boys. His father stubbornly clung onto the farm and the semblance of their old life.

Jacinto would realize years later that his family was, in many ways, an anomaly in that chapter of El Salvador's history: a medium-sized landowner, not one of the fourteen families who owned all the big haciendas and controlled the government and military, but not penniless sharecroppers either. They didn't fit neatly in on either side of the rich/poor divide. Still, the time would come when everybody had to pick a side.

It might be nice to say that it was populism or ideals that drove his family to take up with the Frente. But in truth, they were simply the first to show up.

The thin guerillas came to the door and Jacinto's father didn't refuse them. Within hours, they'd slaughtered every animal on the ranch. Fires were built right there in the fields, and those men and women—starving and armed—cooked their beef until it was black as coal. His mother and sisters slapped out tortillas for hours, draining the family granaries.

Jacinto remembers standing in the doorway at his father's side, watching the guerillas scrape at rib bones with their teeth, their bellies swollen from so much food so fast.

"Are these the good guys or the bad guys?" Jacinto asked.

His father let go of a long sigh and said, "They're the ones we'll have to go and fight with."

One of his sisters came past with another basket of tortillas.

"We're going to fight?" Jacinto asked.

His father nodded. "We've put it off long enough. Help your brothers pack up some cheese and salt."

Jacinto did as he was told. They filled old rice sacks with food and provisions, and assembled personal bags with extra clothes and matches. His brothers put on their sturdiest boots.

The sound of the gunshot didn't surprise anyone. Jacinto figured, at first, that the guerillas had found another cow or pig somewhere. Seconds later they heard a woman scream.

Jacinto and his brothers followed the sound out toward the kitchen. There, they saw their mother crying over their father's body. His mouth and hands were wrapped around opposite ends of the bird rifle. The back of his head had exploded in a mess of blood and blood-soaked matter—colors and hues that young Jacinto was used to seeing only during the slaughter. He was confused, more than anything. As his mother continued to sob, Jacinto's oldest brother explained that their father decided to die here on his own land, rather than in the mountains to some stranger's bullet.

The confusion that followed his father's death haunted Jacinto like a specter ever since. There were days when he thought his father a coward for checking out on the family in such a needy hour. Other times, he saw it as an act of fearless self-determination. It was a riddle, which tangled together manhood and responsibility in a confused knot, and would likely puzzle Jacinto until his own death.

"Wake up, Don Jacinto." Israel shook him out of his memory dream. "We need to go."

Jacinto rose. All around him, the migrants mobilized. One jumped off the front end of their boxcar.

"What's happening?" Jacinto asked.

"Checkpoint." Israel helped him to his feet. "This is the part where we run."

Jacinto's eyes were unaccustomed to the dark and he could see no solid ground at the base of the train, only blackness. He heard more bodies go thud against the earth. The train was slowed. The boxcar shook beneath him with the motion of the jumpers.

"Ready?" Israel asked.

"Ready," Jacinto said.

The fall was further than he'd anticipated, and he collapsed upon his knees and hands. The ground was a rough grade of pointed gravel. Brakes squealed as the train approached a full stop. Flashlight beams jiggled from the front end.

"*Vamos.*" Israel grabbed Jacinto's upper arm and pulled in the opposite direction. The gravel gave way to firm-packed dirt. Bodies of other migrants bounced off them in the dark, and soon Jacinto found himself pushing back with his arms. The police flashlights gained on them from behind.

"Here," Israel said at last, and cut to the left, towards a stand of trees.

"Careful, Don Jacinto. This way." Israel held down a strand of barbed wire, so that Jacinto might climb over it. Jacinto straddled the wire and then, once on the other side, held it down for Israel.

They were inside of a cornfield now, the ears only slightly shorter than Jacinto's head at full stance. Between rows, they took off running. The crisp leaves scratched at their faces and opened little cuts on their hands. Jacinto's eyes had begun to adjust, but still he followed only Israel's t-shirt, keeping as close to it as he could.

Their crouched sprint relaxed to a brisk walk. Finally, the two men stood still and turned around. As their breathing slowed, Jacinto heard a sound come from back by the train. If he had to guess, he'd say it was somebody opening watermelons with a club.

"What is that?" Jacinto asked in a whisper.

"The police," Israel answered. "They're beating the migrants."

"Why?" The question sounded naïve to Jacinto, even as it left his lips.

"What else would they do? They don't have enough handcuffs or jail cells for all of them."

"Are there a lot of checkpoints like this one along the way?"

"Chiapas is the worst," Israel said. "They figure it's easier to catch us here, in the skinny part of Mexico."

For a moment, the two men shared only the sounds of their own breath and the hard beatings they'd barely escaped.

"Let's stay here for a while," Israel said. "It's safer than moving around."

They crouched low among the darkened ears of corn, and awaited sacred dawn.

6

MORNING IN THE CORN FELT A BIT LIKE HOME TO JACINTO. Cocks crowed as the sun rose. Bakers on bicycles rang their bells, delivering the daily bread. Jacinto and Israel checked to see that nobody watched, then left their field for a dirt path shaded by tall trees.

Both men kept their baseball caps pulled low over their eyes. A few early-risen farmers passed by them, machetes in hand. By the looks of things, the corn here would be ready to fold soon, within a day or two in some cases. In others, it was time to plant beans or squash at the base of the stalks. Jacinto contemplated, for a moment, the state of his own field back in El Salvador. Would Wilmer know when the ears were ripe enough to begin drying? How many might he harvest fresh so that Mina could make tamales and *atole*?

One farmer passed them—an old man with a face wrinkled from years working in the sun. Jacinto knew he wasn't to make eye contact, but he couldn't help staring at that deep-furrowed face a bit too long. The old man returned with a scowl.

"Don't stare," Israel whispered.

"Sorry," Jacinto said. "Should we try and get some work here? Their corn is ready to harvest."

"No." Israel was resolute. "Here the *campesinos* turn migrants over to the authorities for money. They're not to be trusted."

"These people? But they're farmers, poor people. Why would they do that?"

"I just told you why: for money."

"But this village..." Jacinto was confused. "They must receive *remesas* from El Norte."

"Hah!" Israel whispered a mock-laugh. "This area sends more workers to Los United than anywhere in Mexico."

"So why don't they sympathize with us?"

"Because we're foreigners." Israel shrugged. "They think migration is a right exclusive to Mexicans. The joke is that these people barely knew they were part of Mexico before we started crossing through their land. Most don't speak Spanish." Israel looked from side to side. "I find that people tend to be patriotic only when there's profit in it for them. A starving man would eat his own flag, were it made of cheese."

"I suppose." Jacinto felt disappointed that his sole idea so far had turned out to be such a bad one.

"Forget about working here, Don Jacinto. Wait until we get further north. Chances are any wages we'd earn would only be stolen before we made it through the Beast."

*

"Bring me *elotes*," Wilmer's mother told him. "As many as you can carry."

Wilmer walked to their parcel with an empty grain sack, leaving his father's machete at home. Renegado followed at his feet.

The corn was tall and ripe, ready for harvest or drying. He snapped off the fresh ears and cleaned them of their outer leaves to reduce the weight. It was hot, itchy work. His mother planned to sell the fresh corn as tamales, *riguas*, or even *atole*. But Wilmer worried they'd end up with an empty granary if they neglected to dry enough for the rest of the year's tortillas. In seasons past, this had never been an issue. The family had eaten all the *elotes* that the three of them could hold, then dried the rest.

Once his sack was half full, Wilmer set it down and carried the corn back to it. Renegado tired of following him, and lay in the shade of the *palapa* at the top of the parcel.

The sun was high and hot by the time Wilmer filled the sack. He twisted up the top and tied it shut with a length of twine. The full load doubled over as he hoisted it upon his shoulder, like a limp body. Once it was up, he shifted the weight until comfortable and started for home.

Renegado sniffed and pissed along the sides of the path. It was a Sunday and few men were at work in their fields. In fact, the only other worker Wilmer passed was Don Chus, dragging that reluctant cow of his like a form of piety.

"Aha!" he said. "Young Wilmer already has his *elotes*. It's the hour of the *atolada*, no?"

"My mother's going to sell at the party." Wilmer kept walking, not wanting to get sucked into a conversation with a load on his back.

"Save one for me," Don Chus shouted over his shoulder, then pulled hard on the cow's rope.

*

Israel and Jacinto stole some ears from the last cornfield they passed, then sat by the bank of a small river and chewed the under-ripe kernels. Israel still had his makeshift slingshot. He took it from his trousers and tested a few smooth stones.

"Going after iguanas?" Jacinto asked.

"No time for that." Israel smiled. "Mangoes."

Somehow it had escaped Jacinto that a large mango tree was a little ways upstream. Israel had good aim. He knocked down the lowest-hanging fruit with the first few shots.

"So tell me, Don Jacinto. There was a civil war in your country as well; was there not?" Israel fished out the green mangoes from where they'd fallen in the water.

Jacinto nodded. "In yours too, no?"

Israel raised his eyebrows. "They called it a war. It didn't look much like the wars I've seen in the movies. Only men with evil hearts carrying guns, killing women and children. New bodies left out in the road every morning. Poor people made food from flowers and much less. That was how I first came to Mexico: a refugee camp not far from our bus-wreck. Before that..." He handed the fruit to Jacinto, but failed to make eye contact. "I did many things I'm not proud of."

An awkward span of seconds passed in which Israel only stared down at the river, as if looking for more stones. Jacinto felt compelled to say something: "I know the feeling."

"Were you in the army?" Israel reached down and rolled a wet stone between his fingers.

"No," Jacinto said. "I was with the other side."

"I see." That seemed to be the right answer. "The side without gringo rifles or canned food."

"That's right."

"Your side wanted revolution." Israel let go the elastic and the rock slapped against the leaves.

"That's what they said, anyways." Jacinto saw no falling mangoes. "Damn near won, too. We were part of the General Offensive. The Frente captured the Guazapa volcano. It's full of nooks and crannies where we could hide, and only fifteen miles from downtown San Salvador. Nahuatl warriors once used the same tact against the Spanish conquistadors."

"What happened?" Israel asked.

"The gringos took the Frente seriously then, and sent help to the army. Things turned hard for us. The gringo officers called that volcano 'asshole hill,' because they planned to wipe the whole thing clean. They sent in troops at first, then planes and helicopters." Jacinto remembered those days: trying to get a couple of shots off before running like mad. Mina carried the first-aid kit along with her rifle. Once the bombs began to fall, it became a game of chance and speed, the stakes of which were death and dismemberment. "They say that volcano is the most-bombed piece of land in this hemisphere," he said. "After that, the Frente spent ten years slowly losing the war."

"Tell me something." Israel turned to him at last, while the stone rolled between his fingers. "Did anything good come out of that revolution?"

Jacinto shrugged. "Some people got land, I suppose. I did as well, but it's much less than what my family owned before the conflict." His mind went through the political and military reforms. None of them seemed worth one life, much less tens of thousands of lives. "I met my wife," Jacinto heard himself say at last. "That's the best thing that came out of it for me."

Israel grinned, apparently satisfied. He shot his other rock and a cluster of mangoes fell from the tree.

*

Back at the house, Mina had everything set: a big borrowed pot, salt and sugar. She stood sharpening her knife with a *guacal* of water and a stone.

"Well done," she said as Wilmer set the sack of fresh corn at her feet. "Go and cut me some banana leaves."

Wilmer did as he was told. There was a grove in the back of the house, and he used the machete to cut from among the youngest leaves, still curled into tubes and perfect for wrapping food.

Tamales de elote, the fresh corn dumplings that were her specialty, came wrapped in the corn husks themselves. Perhaps she planned to also make *riguas*—the grilled corn cakes which were less common, and always cooked on a banana leaf.

Inside, his mother had opened the sack and stood shucking the corn.

"What is this party all about?" Wilmer put down the machete and the leaves and set about helping her.

She shrugged. "The ADESCO called it. They say a gringo is coming."

"A gringo?" Wilmer pulled back a thick layer of outer leaves. "Coming to Carasucia?"

"That's what I heard." She freed a fat *elote* from its stubborn husk. "Something to do with the water problems."

"A gringo is coming to bring us water?" Wilmer snapped the shriveled end off a cob. "Is he an engineer? Or some kind of magician, perhaps?"

His mother laughed. "Some say he's going to live here in the village."

They both laughed out loud.

"A gringo living here in Carasucia." Wilmer could hardly keep a straight face at the thought of it. "All of us trying to go up there, and one gringo wants to come here and live with us."

The grins left their faces at the mention of going north. Wilmer understood that he'd taken their joke a half-step too far. They worked through the rest of the sack in silence.

*

The men walked downriver, peeling skin off the mangoes with their teeth, and then gnawing the tart green flesh down to the seed. After a while, they came to a small wooden bridge where train tracks crossed the water.

"No bend here, Don Jacinto." Israel led the way to a ditch on one side of the tracks. "We'll have to catch it at speed."

Jacinto nodded, determined to do a better job of train hopping this time around.

They didn't wait long for a freighter. Jacinto took the lead this time, anticipating the train's velocity and making a solid grab for the first boxcar that passed. Israel caught a ladder and the two of them reached the top at once.

Jacinto was shocked to see several familiar faces from the day before. The boy with the glue jar was there once again, though he hadn't escaped as cleanly from that last checkpoint. A bad welt swelled around one eye, its purple hue showing through the black railroad soot that covered all of him.

As the Chiapas countryside rolled by in the afternoon sun, Jacinto allowed his confidence to grow. After all, this was meant to be the worst part. Why had he paid that fat man any money in the first place? Israel was equally competent, his help as free as friendship.

Once again, Jacinto found himself staring at that young glue-sniffer, sympathizing—in spite of himself—with the boy's self-imposed plight. He still reached into his coat every so often to huff. His jar, it seemed, had survived the police raid more intact than his head.

*

The ADESCO was a kind of village counsel formed years ago. A group of men from the prominent Carasucia families, they reveled in calling each other by their titles—president, treasurer, vice president, and so on. Wilmer wasn't aware of them ever having completed any useful project in the community.

They'd certainly gone all out for this party. Set up on the one paved street in the village—a two-block span that ran alongside the football field then wrapped around to the school—they'd brought in a small stage, many chairs, and some big speakers. Old *ranchera* music blasted out as set-up went on.

Mina made the pot of tamales at the house. As they were in their final stages of steaming, she sent Wilmer ahead to build a fire in the portable grill she'd dusted off. The contraption was nothing more than the iron rim of a car wheel welded to three thin legs of rebar. Wilmer brought the best pieces of their firewood, along with matches and some plastic bags. The teenager on the microphone chanted strings of nonsense words and twisted a few knobs on the old stereo it ran through. Wilmer's fire grew big and smoky, then settled into some fine coals—their redness nearly invisible under the bright sun. He fanned it a few times with his hands. Small clouds of ash puffed off.

Once Wilmer saw his mother rounding the corner—a *guacal* of *masa* on her head, the clay *comal* under her arm—he rushed over to help.

"Gracias, *hijo*." She was happy to unload some of the weight. "Run and get me the pot of tamales. Be careful, it's still hot."

Wilmer headed back to the house.

Though his mother had already done it once, Wilmer re-drained the pot. The oily, starchy broth spilled out onto the dirt. Chickens ran over to pick at it, hoping for a few wet clumps of grain.

He put a thick rag upon his shoulder, another in each hand, and hoisted the pot. As he left the house, a caravan of new cars pulled up across the street—all of them white passenger SUVs from the last few years, a series of logos painted on their doors. Sure enough, not one but several gringos stepped out, along with a group of Salvadorans obviously from the capital. They carried black bags over their shoulders, with logos matching those of their cars.

Two men from the ADESCO were there to meet them, shaking hands and speaking to the gringos with slow, methodical Spanish. They walked over to the party; Wilmer followed in their wake.

*

"Look alive, Don Jacinto," Israel whispered into his ear.

Jacinto turned to face him. With his lips, Israel pointed to the far end of the train.

A young man hopped onto their car, with long hair and a black stocking cap, bare-chested with black jeans, a large gothic "MS" tattooed across his belly. In his hands, he carried a baseball bat. He turned back and helped another young man land on their car. Taller than the first, he wore a shaved head and a baggy white t-shirt. This one carried a machete.

Once they were both aboard, the two young men sized up the group of migrants. Jacinto followed Israel's lead and kept his head bowed. Making their way down the car, the one with the bat shook a handful of change in the faces of the travelers, as if this was a bus ride and he was the *cobrador.*

Their first customer, a young woman who'd obviously gone out of her way to make herself dirty and unattractive, gave them a couple of coins without protest. Baseball Bat stared down at the money and stepped away, but Machete wasn't finished. He placed the point of his blade in the middle of her chest, between the buttons on the over-sized American-football-logo jacket that she wore.

She refused to look up at him, but did undo the jacket. Underneath she wore a tank top. Above it, on her chest, the words "I have AIDS" were carved into her skin, an alphabet of straight scars done with a sharp blade.

Jacinto heard himself gasp. Though the self-diagnosis might have been a lie, the gangster was disgusted enough and moved on. Another old man obliged them with coins before they came to Jacinto and Israel.

Baseball Bat leaned over and shook his handful of coins in Jacinto's face.

"We've got nothing." Israel did the talking. "Police took everything at the checkpoint yesterday."

As the gangster stared him in the face, Jacinto found it hard to avoid eye contact. It wasn't true, what Israel said about the police, but perhaps the *mareros* had heard of that raid and were inclined to believe it.

"Maybe you're lying," Machete said from behind.

"We're not in the habit," Israel said, still cheerful. "But we have no proof other than empty pockets."

Baseball Bat pushed his head closer to Jacinto's. The gangster's face muscles tightened up as though he were taking a shit.

Jacinto was filled with hatred for these two bandits, who preyed on the weakest and most vulnerable of their countrymen. He could handle running from foreign authorities—it was their job to harass him—but not these shiftless punks.

"Stay here," Machete said. Baseball Bat's breath was warm and rank against Jacinto's face. Machete went to the little gas-huffing boy and kicked him in the side. The boy startled and shifted around, trying to protect the bruises already raised by the police. The gangster muttered threats and demands for money. With his free hand he grabbed the collar of the boy's coat and attempted to pick him up by it, like a kitten. The glue jar jostled free and rolled atop the boxcar. Machete picked it up, his blade pointed down at the boy. He took the lidless glass jar—a blackened rag stuffed halfway inside—and gave it one long inhale. Israel remained quiet. Jacinto couldn't help but scowl.

"Here." Machete staggered a bit as he handed the jar off to Baseball Bat. He stood up taller above Jacinto—who still sat upon the boxcar roof—and took the jar in the same hand as his loose change. Through Baseball Bat's legs, Jacinto watched as Machete resumed tormenting the little boy. He slapped him with the blunt sides of his blade, demanding money. Jacinto looked straight up. Baseball Bat's eyes were bloodshot and blinking rapidly. His head swayed a bit as he breathed out the fumes.

It was opportunism more than bravery. Jacinto saw a single window for action, and knew there'd not be another like it. With all the force he could muster from that sitting position, Jacinto thrust the arc of his hand straight into Baseball Bat's crotch.

The gangster groaned in pain. His bloodshot eyes bulged in their sockets. Jacinto drove his hand further upward, planting one foot to get more leverage. Between his thumb and fingers, he clamped testicles. The glue jar bounced off Jacinto's chest as the gangster dropped it. His handful of coins jangled against the roof of the boxcar.

Jacinto remembered the bat only a second before the gangster did, found the wrist with his free hand and pulled it straight down. Between the huff of glue and the nauseous pain, it wasn't hard to break Baseball Bat's balance, even from below. The train swayed upon an uneven bit of track. As soon as Jacinto saw the gangster's knees lock, the weight shifting to the toes of one foot, he knew he had won. He let go the wrist, grabbed a handful of the ratty hair spilled out from under the stocking cap, planted his other foot underneath him, and increased his death grip on the man's balls. Jacinto stood all the way up as he pulled on the lock of hair.

Once he realized that he was going off the train, the gangster rolled with it, hoping for more clearance, perhaps. Jacinto didn't wait to watch him land. He immediately cursed himself for not seizing the bat somehow. Machete charged him straight away, muttering "*hijo de puta.*" The other migrants screamed and scrambled to the sides.

Jacinto had some experience dodging machete strikes. The good news was that the gangster threw haymakers, losing balance with every missed swing. The bad news: they were running out of boxcar fast, and once they reached the end, Jacinto would be able to dodge nothing.

After the next swing, Jacinto went for it. He took one long stride and got a hold of the machete-wielding wrist. But his opponent was quicker than he thought. The gangster stepped back and twisted free of his grip.

Now Jacinto was fucked. He was off his fighting stance, had the wrong foot forward, and left his back exposed and within striking distance. He looked down off the side of the fast-moving train. Another set of tracks ran parallel. His choice was to jump off onto a bed of steel rails, wooden corners, and gravel—or to risk a cut in the abdomen from a rusted machete. Or, if he hesitated a fraction of a second longer: both.

Jacinto was sick of fleeing and hiding, of being forced off the train. He lifted his knee as he stepped across, hoping to take the blow in the leg rather than the torso. The gangster had already drawn the machete back, and had wisely moved to the right in order to pin Jacinto against the side of the train.

A breaking sound rang out over the noise from the tracks. Jacinto looked up and saw the gangster's face covered in blood. Behind him stood Israel, the broken rim of the glass glue-jar in one hand.

The gangster reached for the badly bleeding cut above his brow, filled with bits of broken glass. Jacinto punched him below the ribcage and he doubled over even more. In a quick blur, Israel applied some kind of wrist lock to the gangster; his arm straightened all the way to his shoulder and he leaned his head down to his knees. Israel held him by only the thumb and wrist, like something out of kung-fu movies. Jacinto watched dumbfounded as his friend casually stripped the machete from out the gangster's hand, then threw him off the train. In his head, he replayed their earlier conversation, about Israel doing-things-he-wasn't-proud-of during his war.

Jacinto noticed himself hyperventilating. His limbs twitched from all the adrenaline, and it was hard to tell which shaking was caused by his body and which by the train. He looked up and down his arms and legs and could scarcely believe that he found no wounds. Israel handed him the machete and squinted to work a shard of glass from his hand. Jacinto tested the machete's metal edge against his thumb. The thing was so dull, he realized, it probably wouldn't have broken the skin.

The huddled migrants looked up at him with terror, not gratitude. Perhaps they knew what to expect from the Mara Salvatrucha. They were more fearful now that this weapon was in the hands of a devil that they didn't know.

The woman with "I have AIDS" carved into her chest went after the coins spilled during the fight. When her eyes met Jacinto's, she backed off, and re-dropped them.

"Go on," Jacinto shouted. "Take back whatever was taken from you."

The cut-chest woman and the old man went for their coins. The little glue-sniffer stared off into the woods on one side of the train, more upset over his lost drug than anything else.

Jacinto sat down on his now-empty end of the boxcar. He hugged his knees to his chest, the dull and rusted machete hanging from one hand. This was not what he wanted: more violence. Why not wait until the gangsters had collected their coins and gone?

Israel, as usual, seemed to read his thoughts. "Don't feel bad, Don Jacinto. Those men and their kind are responsible for horrible things." Israel continued to nurse the bloody palm he'd cut open on the glass, sucking at the wound so as to dislodge more glass.

"Do you think they survived their falls?" Jacinto asked.

"So long as they didn't hit their heads," Israel said. "I've been thrown from the train at a comparable speed. Broke my ankle and lost a bit of skin, but lived."

Jacinto stared down and watched the ground whiz by below.

"We'll be out of the Beast soon," Israel assured him. "Oaxaca is very beautiful, and there they treat strangers as brothers."

*

Mina's clay *comal* heated upon the wheel-rim grill, every available inch of its top surface covered in *riguas*—blackened banana leafs lining each of their sides. Once she saw Wilmer round the corner, she shouted: "*los tamales, las riguas!*" in the drawn-out inflection that signaled food-for-sale.

Wilmer set down the pot and helped her. Both items were two *colones* a piece, so most customers paid with single coins and didn't need change. His mother was fast and efficient on the grill. Their clientele were mostly gawkers, staring on as the gringos continued to glad hand with the local authority figures. Music still played over the speakers, but they'd shown mercy on the visitors' ears and turned it way down.

As the crowd increased, Wilmer's job grew simple. He took coins from hands and put *tamales* in their place. Every so often, someone would offer a fiver or a ten, and he'd make a little change.

"*Vaya señores.*" A voice boomed through the tinny microphone. Wilmer dropped one last tamale into a hand and took back his two coins. The crowd hushed and focused their attention onto the stage. Wilmer turned to his mother and saw that she was quite happy with the sales.

"Well, done, *hijo*," she said in his ear, then set about slapping together another set of *riguas*. The pot of *tamales* was nearly empty.

Wilmer tried to listen to the boring speeches that the men from the village gave: offering thanks to God and to these gringos, blessing the future generations of Carasucia, talking about the day that water would come. In between the blessings and hyperbole, Wilmer pieced together that there were indeed plans to build an aqueduct here in the village.

His mother's new batch of *riguas* hit the hot clay of the *comal* with a sizzle.

"It's true," Wilmer whispered to her. "They want to bring water to the village."

"*Ojalá*," she muttered.

Wilmer turned back to the stage and heard another rumor confirmed: there would indeed be a gringo coming to live with them.

He was the final speaker of the event. Taller, younger, and more causally dressed than the rest of the men on the stage, he looked foolish. His Spanish was tedious, and he seemed terrified to speak in public. How would he handle living among these people, if he's frightened even to talk to them?

His collared shirt and trousers looked like they were borrowed from a bigger man. The spectacles he wore were the smallest Wilmer had ever seen, and they almost disappeared at certain angles. The blonde hair was soaked with perspiration, and the pink skin of his face was either embarrassed or sunburned or both. Wilmer was thankful that this gringo wasn't long-winded. Certainly, he didn't enjoy the sound of his own voice the way the other speakers had.

Once the speeches were done and the event descended into a drone of applause, Wilmer's mother called out the distinctive "*los tamales, las riguas!*" that let everyone know she was in business.

"So it's true," Wilmer whispered as he took the lid off the tamale pot. "That gringo is coming to live here."

"I wonder if he needs his clothes cleaned."

A smaller fury of sales followed as the event wound down. Once again, Wilmer found himself in the hunched trance of exchanging coins for tamales. He reached into the pot and pulled out the last one. Waiting for him was a hand with a ten-*colon* bill, higher than most of the other hands he'd been servicing. Wilmer looked up and saw that it was the same blonde gringo.

"One tamale please," he said in passable Spanish.

Wilmer reached into his back pocket for change.

"*Licenciado.*" Don Felix took the gringo by the elbow. "Put your money away. Surely, this fine member of the community will give that to you as a gift." He glared at Wilmer.

Wilmer turned to his mother.

"Maybe you're capable of giving money away," she snapped at Don Felix. "I'm not running a charity here."

Looking outraged, Don Felix pulled out his index finger and started: "*Oye!*"

It took the gringo a second to understand. "No, no, no!" he said—the most assertive tone Wilmer had heard him take thus far. "I want to pay."

That hushed both sides.

"If I'm going to live here," he went on. "I can't have everyone giving me things for free."

Wilmer quietly made the change while Don Felix glared on.

"*Gracias*," Wilmer said as he handed the coins to the gringo. "If you need your clothes cleaned, my mother is very good at that as well."

Don Felix breathed out through his nostrils.

The gringo nodded and smiled, his mouth already full of tamale.

*

That night, Jacinto and Israel slept in a graveyard along with many other migrants. They'd quit the train once it slowed toward what appeared to be a routine stop. At least nobody chased them this time.

Any other night, Jacinto might have found it eerie to lie among graves. But he was too tired for superstition. The dead didn't scare him as much as the living did lately.

Without discussion, Jacinto assumed that the two of them would take turns sleeping and keeping watch tonight. They bedded down alongside a flat, concrete tomb. Jacinto found a corner where the paint had worn thin, and set about sharpening the stolen machete on it. The surface had the right level of grit, but he needed a bit of water to do a proper sharpening job.

"Not now, Don Jacinto," Israel said. "There will be time for that tomorrow." With one hand Israel scooped at the loose dirt. For a second, Jacinto wondered if he meant to unearth a body, or perhaps dig himself a shallow grave. But Israel made only two small niches in the ground, one for his shoulders and one for his hips, then lay down on his side—something Jacinto hadn't seen done in a long while.

"Where did the *coyote* take you?" Israel's eyes were now closed. "On your first attempt?"

"Some fucking desert," Jacinto said. "I didn't know exactly where, to be honest."

"Likely you headed toward Ajo," Israel said, "in Arizona."

"That sounds familiar."

"It's crazy, the ways we go now. When I began picking grapes, it was easier to cross the border than to cross a busy street. We gathered at the checkpoint in Tijuana, and a pack of us would all run at once." Israel grinned, his eyes still closed. "The officers would come after us, but it was like the lions hunting gazelles in Africa: they might get one or two, but most of us would make it. And if you did get caught, you could simply try again the following night."

Jacinto smiled at the notion, wondering how much harder the crossing would become as the years went on.

"There were few *coyotes* back then. No need for them."

"What happened?" Jacinto asked.

"Everything changed after the NAFTA. First, it was only that bit near Tijuana that tightened up. They built their walls and whatnot. Now, everybody's been forced eastward, into the mountains and the desert. Now the smugglers are more powerful, and more expensive."

Jacinto remembered the fires and the rapes in the villages near Carasucia, undertaken upon the orders of powerful smugglers. He wondered if Don Noe ever used such tactics on his own delinquent clients.

"And the funny part is," Israel continued. "We don't stop coming. If anything, those without documents stay longer because it's so much harder to cross. Only a few of us are foolish enough to still come back and forth."

Israel stopped speaking. The loud sounds of the insects overtook everything. Jacinto was reminded of the night not long ago when he saw those two creatures—one black and one white. He tightened his grip around the machete, as his friend snored softly from the ground.

7

JACINTO WOKE TO CHIRPS FROM THE DAY'S FIRST BIRDS. THE rosy-fingered dawn had blossomed all around him.

"Morning." Israel sat on the ledge of the tomb, something inside of his mouth.

As Jacinto rose to his feet, he felt sore in his joints and limbs, as if he were the one beaten up yesterday in that fight atop the train. The shoulder and hip holes they'd dug were too short for his long torso.

Israel stared stone-faced across the graveyard. He shifted the machete around so the blade leaned against his knee, then spit out whatever it was he'd had in his mouth.

His back still tight and crooked, Jacinto turned to see what Israel stared at. Across the cemetery, a pack of tattooed gangsters leaned against a mausoleum smoking what appeared to be a joint.

"Son of a bitch," Jacinto muttered. "They're not the same ones as yesterday?"

"No." Israel kept his gaze fixed. "They're teenagers, getting high and giggling."

Jacinto ran his fingers through his hair and rubbed the crusts from his eyes. What he would do for a cup of coffee right now. All around, other migrants emerged from the grass and the graves—waking up, taking stock of the day. Jacinto looked forward to leaving this, the skinny part of Mexico.

"Here." Israel handed him a cluster of strange green pods. "Don't eat the seeds or the skins. There's a little flesh in between that you can suck off, then spit out the rest." He popped one in his mouth, as if to demonstrate.

Jacinto followed suit. The thin film of fruit was bitter and tart—like an under-ripe berry. "Tastes like shit," he said through a full mouth.

Israel spit his out and grinned. "Did I not mention that?" He popped another in his mouth. "Come. Let's go before these *locos* start acting stupid." He handed Jacinto the machete. The two of them rose to cross the graveyard.

They walked with a deliberate calm, like one would to pass a wild animal, not wanting to draw attention from the *mareros*. As they went, several of the other migrants stirred. A few followed them.

The machete seemed to weigh a hundred pounds as it hung from Jacinto's hands. The gangsters at the far side sized them up. The two or three migrants that gathered in their wake hoped to pass themselves off as members of the same party, all under the protectorate of this dull length of steel.

Jacinto did he best to avoid eye-contact, but before they left the gate he stole a glance at the pack of teenagers. The tattered tube of smoldering paper and weed passed down the line of them. Jacinto gasped a little when he saw the small hand that took it and the small face that drew a lungful of its smoke: it was the bruised boy he'd seen so often on the boxcars, the one who'd been nearly beaten by members of this same gang. Their eyes met for a moment, then Jacinto followed Israel out the gate of the graveyard.

Now outside, the two men took long, determined strides. They walked a hundred yards up a dirt path—too narrow for cars. One older man and two women from the graveyard followed close behind, not taking the hint. Finally, Israel turned around and confronted them.

"Look," he said. "We're not able to help you."

Jacinto was shocked. Israel had been such an undeserved guardian angel to him—it was strange to see this side. Still, he didn't disagree: they couldn't take care of anybody else, certainly not anyone more helpless than themselves. But that fact failed to comfort him as he stared into the eyes of their three followers—a man who looked much too old to be making this trip on his own, and two women who might've been sisters. Jacinto silently hoped that they weren't leaving any children behind.

"Believe me," Israel went on. "We're all better off in smaller groups, lest we draw too much attention."

The old man looked down at the ground, his pride hurt.

"The train is that way." Israel pointed. "It's good to get on it early. You'll be in Oaxaca soon, where the people have a grain of understanding." He turned and continued on.

Jacinto followed, more thankful than ever to have cemented the friendship when he did. He recalled the words of the mustachioed *federale* at the border, about loyalty not often being an asset.

"We'll see about some food and water before we catch the train," Israel said. "It's quite flat here, no? Might be hard to find a river."

But it felt good to walk for a while with the machete in his hand. Jacinto could almost fool himself into believing he was on his way to harvest *elotes* from his very own field. Their path merged onto a wider dirt road, one where motor traffic might pass. They found a small stream at last, but both were hesitant to drink from it. The water had a shiny film of oils from fuel and laundry soaps. They sat by it for a while and washed their hands and faces. Jacinto found a stone up the bank, wet the machete, and set to sharpening. Israel wandered off.

Perhaps an hour passed before Israel returned, a shit-eating grin across his face. "How's the machete?" he asked.

Jacinto gave it a rinse and felt the edge with his thumb. "Sharp enough to shave a Spaniard," he said.

"You're going to like what I've found." Israel smiled.

They broke off from the road and walked through weeds until they reached a wooded hillside. There, poking out above the trees was a tall palm with a cluster of coconuts attached. The two men grinned and giggled, their faces cast upward. Climbing palm trees was never a skill that Jacinto could claim—a deficiency he blamed on his paralyzing fear of heights. As soon as they reached the base of the trunk, Israel removed his sneakers and his t-shirt. Through a combination of tying and tucking, he made the shirt into a strap attached to each of his feet. He put the blade of the machete between his teeth, and set to scaling the tree.

Jacinto headed further up the hillside, clear of any falling debris. Israel climbed freakishly fast, his arms hugged around the trunk and his two feet working together to push him upward. His speed increased as the tree grew thinner near the top. Clouds of dust puffed off the palm fronds with his first strokes of the machete. Jacinto watched in suspense as his friend swayed about so many stories up in the air. The cluster drooped low beneath the fronds as Israel severed its woody tethers. Finally, there was a silence as the bunch fell through the air, then a sound like a broken marimba once all the coconuts hit the ground.

Israel descended faster than he'd gone up, and handed the machete to Jacinto. He worked through the husk in just a few strokes, clipped off a flake of the hard inner shell, then drilled a hole through the tender white membrane with the machete point. He handed it to Israel as though he were a roadside vendor.

"Only the straw is missing." Israel laughed and took the first slurp. "They're mature!"

"And they are many." Jacinto went to work on the next one.

They drank all the coconut water they could hold, then sliced them open and ate the almost-crunchy meat. Both their bellies swelled visibly with the feast. The two of them lay in the shade digesting, neither willing to leave any coconuts uneaten.

"You know what," Israel said. "The elite gringo soldiers—the ones with the floppy green hats—they know how to use coconut water intravenously, for blood loss and the like."

"Is that so?" Jacinto half-expected a punch line to follow that random bit of trivia, but none came.

"It's good that we eat and drink now," Israel changed the subject. "We've an unpleasant part to go through next."

Jacinto sighed, then rose and opened a couple more of the coconuts.

After a short nap, they walked a long way. Israel took great care with how they next approached the tracks. This hot, dusty country was a far cry from the jungle where they'd begun hopping trains.

"We'll have company, Don Jacinto." Israel barely turned over his shoulder to speak. "It's important that we keep a low profile, especially with that machete."

"I understand," Jacinto said.

But in truth, he didn't understand. And he was not prepared for the sight once they finally found the railroad tracks. A full-blown shantytown had been erected, a village of migrants on their way north, all of them undoubtedly Central Americans. Makeshift tents and lean-tos fashioned from scraps of tin and cardboard lined the sides of the main drag. On a spit, one man roasted what looked to be three small mice over a fire of burning plastic bags. Several others gathered to watch and beg.

The residents offered suspicious glares to Israel and Jacinto, taking note of the newly sharpened machete that Jacinto carried. The place reminded him of the refugee camp in Mesa Grande where he finally reunited with Mina.

"Are all of these people going to ride the same train?" Jacinto whispered his question into Israel's ear.

"Not all at once," Israel said. "This is like the waiting room. The train moves too fast through this stretch for anybody to jump on."

"Why don't the police raid it?"

"Sometimes they do. But the migrants are many and they can hear them coming from a long way off. They'd simply scatter in all directions. It's easier for the cops to wait and stop the train. Mexican police don't like to run very much."

"Incoming!" a voice shouted.

The entire camp came to life. A few young men who'd been lying on the rails climbed off. Several people crossed from one side to the other. In the distance, Jacinto heard the grind of an engine. The air horn sounded as the locomotive broke the horizon—a casual act of mercy on the part of the conductor.

Israel and Jacinto took a few steps back and watched as it came. Its speed was shocking, far too fast for train hopping. But the bigger surprise, for Jacinto, was the crowd of people already aboard. He could hardly see the metal of the cars for all of the bodies piled upon it, clinging to every side of it. And it wasn't only the boxcars. Human beings were stuck to the sides of the rounded tankers as well, hanging by whatever they could get their fingertips around, defying gravity like tics stuck to a dog's neck.

Jacinto stared in awe, the train-made wind washing all over him. Where would he climb on even if this thing were at a full stop?

"Come on," Israel said. "Let's keep walking. We'll try the next bend."

The spot they found was at a tight curve in the tracks. Other migrants waited there as well, in the shade of a big *cedro*. All took note of the machete. Jacinto wondered how he would board the train with the thing.

Israel managed to talk one of the strangers out of a cigarette. He came back and sat beside Jacinto, drawing a deep breath from the filter then turning the thing around to examine the ember at its end. After two puffs, he extended it towards Jacinto.

"I don't smoke," Jacinto said.

Israel shrugged. "In our situation, it's bad luck to decline charity."

"Fine." Jacinto took a puff of smoke into his mouth, held it there for a second, then coughed it out, nearly dropping Israel's precious cigarette.

Israel took it back from him. "Like this," he said. "First I draw it into my mouth, then down into my lungs." He demonstrated and passed the half-spent cigarette back to Jacinto. This time, he got it, and immediately felt a tingling head-rush, along with a foul taste all through his throat.

"Here it comes!" somebody shouted.

Israel took the cigarette back and gave it a long pull. They stood. The metallic squeal of the brakes hissed in Jacinto's ear. He continued to cough. The men who carried bags or backpacks slung them over their shoulders. Israel threw down the cigarette, then took the machete from Jacinto's hands and put it between his teeth again, as he had when climbing the coconut tree.

"Look alive, Don Jacinto," he managed to say through a mouthful of metal and clenched teeth.

The squealing sound of brakes overtook everything, and the train slowed almost to a complete stop. Two men grabbed a ladder on the first boxcar that passed. Every other inch of it was too covered with people.

This time, the train hopping was less about running, more about finding a space. Jacinto followed Israel in a frantic dance alongside the tracks, sizing up each car for some sort of perch. He felt like he was playing fullback on the soccer field back home, on guard against a wily offensive player who wouldn't commit to either direction.

Finally, near the end of the train, Israel went for a tanker car that had only a few others on it. There was no ladder, simply a bar to grab onto and a kind of step welded to the sides. Even once they hoisted themselves all the way up, it was quite uncomfortable: all four of their feet sharing a steel square meant for one, a length of rebar rubbing at their hips. The rounded sides of the tank offered nothing to hold onto. This train made their previous rides look like first class.

*

The gringo moved into a cinderblock house which had sat empty for several years. The owner lived on a big spread to the south. He'd put the little house on this bit of land in town when an NGO was giving away building materials. Wilmer approached with an empty rice sack.

The place was a mess. A set of gutters scattered across the lawn. The cistern was in disrepair, and needed cleaning. Through the open door, Wilmer could see half-full boxes and gadgets scattered about.

The gringo had been dubbed "Don Jefe" by the village elders. He sat on a plastic chair with a guitar across his knee, studying a piece of paper on the floor.

"Do you know how to play that thing?" Wilmer asked.

Don Jefe startled. He put the guitar against the wall behind him, as though he were embarrassed. "Hello," he said. "Come in."

The house was poorly designed. The ceiling was too low, and all the windows and doors were along one wall. Beads of perspiration tingled on Wilmer's forehead the second he stepped inside.

"Do you have any dirty clothes?" Wilmer asked. "My mother will wash them. Five *colones* now, while it still rains. But the price goes up, once the dry season starts."

"How does she wash clothes at all, during the dry season?" the gringo asked.

"Same way all the other women do. They load the clothes onto the bus and take them down to Santa Cruz." Wilmer pointed south. "They wash in the river there, then bus the wet laundry back here to the village to dry."

Don Jefe nodded, confused. And he'd come here in order to solve the village's water problems? The very thought was enough to make Wilmer laugh out loud: this young man, who couldn't even properly connect his gutters or clean out his cistern, he was going to bring running water to each household?

"Here." Wilmer handed the gringo the empty rice sack. "Fill this up and I'll take it over to my mother."

"Right." The gringo nodded. "Have a seat." He motioned to the plastic chair that he'd sat in a second ago.

Wilmer sat down while Don Jefe rummaged though his things in search of dirty clothes. An old wooden door was propped up on cinderblocks, to make a kind of desk. The surface of it was scattered with books and papers. Wilmer found a photograph among the mess and picked it up. It was a group of gringos, indoors, holding cans of beer. Their faces were contorted from laughter or bright light—nobody looking at the camera. Wilmer wondered why anybody would bother to take a photograph of such a thing. He dropped it back onto the desk.

"Done!" The gringo plopped the now-full sack in front of Wilmer, wearing a self-satisfied smile as though finding his laundry were an achievement.

Wilmer stood up. The two of them stared at each other for a second.

"The money?" Wilmer said.

"Oh yes!" Don Jefe went to his overcrowded desk and dug up a leather wallet. He took out a five-*colon* bill and handed it over.

"Thanks." Wilmer started to get a handhold on the sack to heft it to his shoulder, but paused for a second. "Can I ask you about something?"

Don Jefe raised his eyebrows.

"My father, he's trying to get into your country. He's going...well, 'wet' is the term that we use."

The gringo nodded, for once understanding perfectly.

"Is there any way you could help him? Ask for permission or some papers of some kind?"

The gringo looked down. He shook his head and brought his gaze back to Wilmer. "I'm sorry," he said. "I'm just a private citizen. There's nothing I can do."

Wilmer nodded. He trusted Don Jefe on this count. It wasn't difficult to believe in his incompetence.

"I'll bring this back once it dries," Wilmer said.

Don Jefe helped him heft the bag up onto his shoulder.

*

Hours went by clinging to that little piece of steel as the train swayed and jolted. Israel and Jacinto took turns holding the machete. Israel developed a method of stretching his legs by holding the rail with both hands and doing a deep knee bend. The train picked up more migrants each time it slowed through a turn. They gained elevation, leaving the lowlands of the coast behind and heading to the mountains.

When Jacinto stood up, he could see all the migrants crammed atop the other cars. Some had erected little shades of plastic or cardboard to protect themselves from the sun. The air felt cooler and cleaner, but it was hard to get a full breath between all the exhaust from the locomotive.

Israel didn't like the ride any more than Jacinto did. He nudged Jacinto to take over the machete. Once they'd made the hand-off, Israel went into one of those knee bends that seemed to offer him some relief.

With all their feet crammed together on that tiny step, one hand on the metal railing and the other around the machete's plastic handle, Jacinto leaned back against the smooth side of the tank and let his tired eyes close for a second. He tried hard to remember why it was he rode this train. There was some sort of higher purpose, wasn't there, which would redeem all of this discomfort?

He felt the train's rhythm change abruptly. A gust of cool wind washed over him. Upon opening his eyes, he nearly dropped the machete. The entire train was somehow flying through the air, hundreds of yards above a rushing river. Once he summoned the courage to look down, he saw the spindly wooden skeleton of the bridge that held them up. The blood drained from his face.

Israel bounced up and down in his squat position, nonplussed. Along with all the other riders, he didn't seem to mind. Sweat lined the insides of both Jacinto's palms. The soles of his feet itched and tingled. The river below was blue, but white flecks showed the violence of the water against the rocks. It had cut out a ravine with sheer walls on either side, green tufts of forest at their tops.

Though it was among his deepest and longest-held fears, as Jacinto stared down into that emptiness below him, he also felt the desire to jump off and get it over with.

"You okay?"

He barely heard the words. Vertigo made the river turn a little, as though it wanted to become the sky.

"Don Jacinto?"

The hand on his shoulder made him tremble and hold on tighter. Suddenly, there was another abrupt change in the cadence and timbre of the train's music, and Jacinto saw solid ground alongside them once again.

"What's the matter with you?" Israel's usual telepathy for such things seemed to be off.

"It's nothing." Jacinto took his first deep breath in several seconds. "I don't like high places."

Israel chuckled. At first, Jacinto's feelings were hurt. But after a second or two, he laughed along with his friend.

"It's funny, no?" Israel said. "The difference between the things we fear and the things which truly endanger us."

"It doesn't seem funny at the time."

"My mother, she had the gift that I have, that's where I get it from. She used to say that our fears and our hopes are one and the same."

Jacinto thought about that suppressed desire to jump from the train, but said nothing.

*

Wilmer's stomach felt a sinking sensation as he saw the pickup parked alongside their house again. He pressed on, the sack of dirty clothes over his shoulder, telling himself that this is how it would be for a while. Until they paid off the debt, they'd have to endure visits from the *coyote*. At least this time, they had some money to put toward what they owed.

Inside the truck, the same sun-glassed teenager sat waiting. Wilmer walked past him. The radio was on and played *norteño* music. Wilmer wouldn't hide this time. When he crossed the threshold into the house, his breathing grew shallow and forced. The first thing he saw was that same small black revolver shoved into the back of the fat man's jeans.

Wilmer dropped the sack onto the dirt floor with a thud. "Can I help you?"

Don Noe turned around, a smug grin under his bristly mustache. "Look who's here," he said. "Come inside, son. I was just discussing some important matters with your mother."

"Here, you without-shame." Mina came in from the kitchen with the instant-coffee jar she'd used to store the tamale money. "You put this against my debt. Then you get out of here and go harass somebody else."

Wilmer focused all his energy on his breathing. He wouldn't let it go beyond his control. His chest rose and fell. The fat man thumbed through the bills.

"This is your first installment against your debt?" His smile transformed into a tight scowl. "This is chump change." His finger pointed right in Mina's face.

In and out, Wilmer whispered to his lungs and throat. Inside and out, don't panic.

"This will pay the interest on what you owe me." The sly smile returned to the fat man's face. "It's been several weeks, after all. But the principal remains the same." He put all the bills into his back pocket.

Wilmer's fury ran thick as mucus, lining the insides of his lungs and windpipe. It was enough anger to drown in. His mother was a crying statue, staring at the ground while the tears rolled down her cheeks.

"There is an easy way to solve this." The *coyote* lowered his voice and put a fat hand up to her cheek. "You could be free of your debt tomorrow, Niña Mina. You're lucky that I'm such a gentleman. Others in my position would simply take what's owed them." He went to put his other hand on her hip, but Mina slapped it away.

"Don't touch me," she snapped.

At that moment, Wilmer didn't care about money, didn't care about medicine, didn't care about where his father was. All Wilmer wanted from life was the chance to push his machete into that man's fat belly, all the way up to the handle, and watch the blood and air drain out.

After Mina's outburst, Renegado rose and barked. The *coyote* rolled his eyes and shook his head, still bewildered by the woman's stubbornness. "What is the purpose of loyalty to a dead husband? It makes no sense."

"My Jacinto's not dead, you lying sack of shit."

This statement didn't ring true to Wilmer anymore. It sounded desperate. And even if it was true, what use was a live father if he wasn't here to help with this problem?

"And a good day to you too, Señorita." The fat man tipped his hat and turned to leave. He bumped Wilmer in the shoulder on his way out, knocking the boy off balance.

The second the *norteño* music started outside, Wilmer dropped his guard, doubled over and wheezed. His mother rubbed his forehead for a second then went to fetch the now-cold coffee she'd gotten into the habit of saving throughout the day.

*

Hours later, signs of civilization revealed themselves. The hillside wilderness resolved into squares of tilled or cleared land. Cattle stood in paddocks— chewing their cud and sniffing each other's asses, looking smug with all their space and leisure.

Clusters of houses and buildings sprouted along the sides of the tracks. Jacinto felt a pit in his stomach, anticipating the next stop. He disliked being so close to the far end of the train. What if the police came at them from this side? His legs were so cramped and numb, he wasn't sure they were capable of running.

"Give me that." Israel took back the machete.

Jacinto was glad for that. If they did get caught up in another raid, he feared what he might do with it.

As a town blossomed all around their train, crowds of people gathered alongside the tracks. Jacinto squinted his eyes. It looked as though the mob was throwing things at the migrants. Stones? Bottles?

He swallowed hard. They'd be easy targets here against the side of the tanker. And among the last cars as well, the locals will have perfected their aim by then. Where do people get so much hate from? Jacinto wondered. Does it not exhaust them the way that enduring hate exhausted him? Is it so easy for them to make a living that they have that much energy left over for hatred?

"Look alive, Don Jacinto," Israel whispered in his ear.

He knew by that familiar phrase that this was no time to contemplate the why's and how's of his fate. This was the time to dodge fate's blows.

The first one hit right in the chest. It was so slow and soft that he caught it in his arms. He'd expected stones or broken glass, but instead the mob was throwing...bread? The object in his hands was a soft bun wrapped in a plastic bag.

He looked at the faces alongside the tracks. They were all well worn from work in the sun, with the long straight hair of indigenous blood. They weren't full of vitriol, as Jacinto had feared. They were shouting blessings to the migrants: good luck, Godspeed. And they were throwing them food.

Another plastic-wrapped bundle flew up and Israel caught it, machete tucked under his armpit. Jacinto grabbed an oily tamale wrapped in a banana leaf. Near the end of the crowd, an old woman in a red woven shawl handed up a one-liter plastic soda-bottle filled with water. In a rush, Israel handed the bread and machete to Jacinto and reached way out—one hand on the railing, and took the water from her, shouting his thanks. The train rolled on past the crowd now, the kind men and women offering thumbs' up or folded hands in prayer.

"What was that?" Jacinto asked, still in awe of what just happened, off-balance from the unwieldy objects in his hands.

"The kindness of strangers." Israel held out a pinch of his t-shirt in the front, so that it made a kind of pouch where they could set the food. The jug of water was wedged between his knees.

They ate like machines, partly from hunger and partly to be rid of the food so they could better cling to the train. The small pieces of soft bread were stuffed with a smear of beans and strings of creamy cheese. It tasted incredible to Jacinto, the perfect food for a starving man. It could've been eaten without teeth. The tamale was different than those he was accustomed to—a courser grind of *masa*, many more vegetables and odd seasonings.

"Why don't they hate us the way they do in the other villages?" Jacinto tossed the banana leaf to the ground.

"We're in Oaxaca now." Israel spoke through a full mouth. "Never have I reached this state and waited long for aid from strangers."

Once the food was finished, they passed the water back and forth and took long drams. This was more difficult, now that the train had regained speed. Though it might've been useful later, they threw away the plastic bottle once they were done with it.

"Get down!" came from one of the cars ahead. Then there was a sound like something tearing, and human gasps. One body flew by only a few feet from the train, turning somersaults before it hit the ground. Then another airborne human hit Jacinto right across the chest, startling him so bad that he bumped the back of his head against the iron of the tanker. The body bounced off as quick as it had come, but a smell like a burning chemical lingered in Jacinto's nostrils.

"Power lines," Israel said, before being asked. "One must stay low when riding on top, to avoid the power lines."

Jacinto's heart beat hard inside his chest. He pushed his whole torso flush against the tanker car, terrified of whatever passing thing might kill him if he leaned too far away. Through the thin layer of metal, he heard liquid sloshing inside the tank.

Israel turned back toward him, and showed surprise at the pale terror upon Jacinto's face. "Relax, Don Jacinto." He spoke as one might to a child. "I'll keep you safe from such things. Those are only small dangers. I'm an expert on them."

Even when Israel extended a hand to Jacinto's shoulder—a gesture meant to comfort—Jacinto flinched at the touch. The awful odor stayed with him for a while, foreign but now intimate. Jacinto wasn't sure if it came from burning clothes, hair, or flesh, but to his own nose it had become the scent of death itself.

The sky grew dark around them and he wondered how much longer they'd spend on this train.

They rode on through the cold night and other towns until the train stopped at a switching yard in the early morning. Jacinto and Israel, along with many other migrants, climbed off and walked away without hurry and without anybody chasing them.

Jacinto's legs felt like foreign objects. They dragged underneath him, brushing at the ground like two stiff brooms.

"No police here?" he asked.

"We're out of the skinny part now," Israel said.

The cool dawn threatened to become a sweltering day. They walked along the tracks for a while, past a couple of hobo camps where other men rested. They broke off the tracks and found a shade tree not yet taken. The two of them collapsed underneath it and slept for a couple of hours, until the heat of day became too much.

"Hard to hunt for our food around here." Israel picked at the dirt with the point of their machete.

"Any work to be had?" To encourage blood flow, Jacinto banged his fists into his thighs.

"Coffee," Israel said.

"I can pick coffee," Jacinto said.

They rose and continued uphill, away from the tracks, until the paved road turned to dirt.

8

IT WAS JACINTO'S EXPERIENCE THAT THE OWNERS OF COFFEE fields everywhere were exploitive bastards. As it turned out, this was the one thing he did know about Mexico.

Within minutes of meeting the bosses at the hacienda, Jacinto and Israel were already in debt to them for at least one day's work—to pay off their overpriced sacks and a morning meal in the dining room.

Still, Jacinto was glad to find employment. It was a job he knew well. Most of the bushes grew in the shade, which made the work more pleasant. The food in the dining room was tasty, the coffee fresh and strong. Nobody asked about his country of origin.

They picked the first crop of the season. Jacinto's nimble fingers went after the cherries from a kind of muscle memory. The other pickers were few. Most likely, local *campesinos* were still busy with their own crops. Jacinto filled his sack before anybody else, and brought it to the scales. If they stayed here for a week, he figured, they might be able to take a bus to the border.

They worked on through the rest of the day, picking each bush clean of its red berries, hauling the sacks of already-fermenting fruit over to the weigh station, where the suspicious foreman eyed their loads for rocks or under-ripe berries.

Jacinto's hands were cut by the leaves. The thin limbs of the coffee trees whipped at his forearms like switches. But once the sun went down and it was too dark to pick, the foreman peeled off a few Mexican bills, and pointed out the tin pavilion full of old hammocks where they were welcome to sleep.

They ate their supper sitting on wooden benches in the dining room, another simple but hearty meal of beans and eggs. Stacks of thin Mexican tortillas sat on the tables. Jacinto folded them over into threes so that they approximated the thickness of what he considered a 'real' tortilla.

"You're a good worker," Israel said between mouthfuls. "You'll make good coin once we get to the north."

"There's no coffee in the north, is there?"

"Work's work." Israel shrugged. "It's easier up there."

Israel had paid off his sack and meals, but had yet to make any cash.

"It feels good," Jacinto admitted, "to work outdoors, and to be compensated at the end of the day, none of this running and stealing business."

Israel's smile looked a bit forced. He wasn't enjoying this as much. "You'll do fine in Los United, Don Jacinto."

After dinner, they found a place to hide their machete and slingshot in the rafters of the sleeping pavilion. Jacinto slept well in his dusty hammock, and rose before anybody else to begin the picking.

*

In Rosario, they waited for hours amongst coughing children and crying babies, all eager for their medicine. Flies circled at eye level, in hopes of someone vomiting in the waiting room. To Wilmer, this health center seemed the biggest source of infection in the municipality.

The door opened and a boy covered in red sores—little white bumps at their centers—exited with his mother.

"Paredes!" the nurse yelled.

Inside his office, Don Toño finished paperwork from the previous patient and ushered Wilmer and Mina in. They sat down in a pair of plastic chairs. Wilmer wondered which had been occupied by the boy with the sores.

"His condition," Mina started. "I fear it's gotten worse. He's had several attacks in the last month."

Don Toño looked up. Sweat stained the underarms of his heavy khaki uniform. "He has asthma. It doesn't tend to get better, at least not at his age."

Don Toño rose and went to the medicine cabinet. With his back to them, he sorted through the most popular pills.

"The tablets you gave us last time, they don't help much," Mina said. "The one that comes in the spray form, that was quite effective."

"I understand." The rattle of medicine bottles punctuated his speech. "But there's no more of that. They resupply us at the beginning of the year. Until then, I have what I have." He placed a couple of pill jars on the desk in front of them.

"It's just that the attacks." Mina's voice wavered. "They come so often. And all I can do is stand there helpless."

"These pills aren't meant to be used in the moment of the attack. He must take them hours before any exposure to dust, smoke, or mold."

Wilmer wasn't offended that Don Toño only spoke of him in the third person. It was, after all, his mother who needed to be convinced.

"Before exposure to smoke or dust?" She threw her hands up. "When, around here, is one not exposed to smoke or dust?"

"Mamá," Wilmer muttered, embarrassed.

"Niña Mina." Don Toño leaned against the front desk and let out a sigh that seemed to contain a day's, a week's, possibly even a career's worth of frustration. "This office isn't meant to treat long-term illness. Your son needs medication; we agree on that. I can't tell you how to get it."

The three of them shared a few seconds of silence before Don Toño opened the door once again.

*

Israel and Jacinto spent the next week this way. They woke early and worked hard, ate simple meals, earned cash, and slept soundly in their hammocks.

It was cool in the mornings, clumps of cottony fog strung about the hillsides. Jacinto knew to pick as much as possible before dawn, while dew still clung to the berries and the extra moisture increased each sack's weight. By the time the breakfast bell rang, he'd already picked a full load. He left the sack by the weigh station and went in to eat.

During the morning meal on their fifth day of work, several more pickers arrived. They were a ragtag mix of people—some dressed in Mayan-style woven shawls and hats, others in second-hand American t-shirts and fake designer jeans.

"Where are they from?" Jacinto asked Israel across the table.

"All over Mexico, I suspect." Israel spoke softly. "Mexicans have a long history of travelling far in order to find work."

The foreman was quick to sort everybody out with a sack and a debt. Several of the newcomers abstained from breakfast and went straight to work.

The job grew more difficult with more people, but there was still plenty of coffee to be picked. The newcomers spoke several languages—indigenous dialects as well as crude urban slang. Their skill with this type of work was equally wide ranging.

It pained Jacinto to see a slow mover claim a loaded bush, or to watch one pick green cherry from a tree yet to ripen, but he did his best to keep a low profile. The first pick of the morning had been lucrative, and he was grateful for that.

In the afternoon heat, everyone's pace lagged a little, even Jacinto's. He worked his way through a dense stand of trees—a spot that had been overlooked because of the time it took to haul a sack in and out. He stumbled across an overgrown but well-loaded bush and went to work on it. A stocky, curly-haired man sidestepped into the same tree and said, "mine."

Jacinto looked up from the berries.

Curly scowled at him. "What?" he said, all but begging for confrontation.

Jacinto breathed out of his nose and said, "nothing." He then lifted his sack and walked away.

Israel stood uphill. He nodded at Jacinto then popped a ripe coffee cherry into his mouth.

*

During a dry spell, Wilmer decided it was time to fold the corn. He hadn't much enjoyed the *elotes* this year—their taste tainted by anxiety over storing enough dry corn for the coming year's tortillas, and made bitter by the memory of the fat man stealing all the money Mina had made from her tamale sales.

The field was dusty and hot. Wilmer wore long sleeves to keep from cutting his arms on the course leaves of the corn stalks. While Renegado waited under the *palapa* at the top of their parcel, Wilmer made his way through the crop. One by one, he pressed the dull edge of the machete into the stalks, and broke each so that the cob would hang there to dry. Many times, Wilmer had watched his father perform this task. This was the first time he'd done it by himself. It wasn't so difficult. Care had to be taken not to sever the entire stalk or to dislodge it from the ground. A soft touch was called for, but Wilmer was in no hurry.

Once the corn was all folded, Wilmer and Renegado headed home empty handed. Don Felix and one of his sons—a year younger than Wilmer and called Moises—approached on the path, carrying a bag of dry beans and *guizotes* for planting.

"Good morning, *hijo!*" Don Felix smiled wide and greeted Wilmer, perhaps to make amends for their harsh exchange over the gringo and his tamales.

"Morning," Wilmer answered.

"News from your father?"

"Nothing yet," Wilmer said. "Still in route."

Don Felix placed an unwelcome hand on Wilmer's shoulder. "Do you know who can ensure that your father arrives safely at his destination?"

"God?" Wilmer kept his sarcasm as subtle as possible.

"Correct!" Don Felix didn't catch it, but his son seemed to, and sent a stink-eye back Wilmer's way.

"One of these nights, you and your mother should come to our church. We'll pray for your father's safe passage. We prayed for this water project, and God will soon grant us that."

"I'll tell her." Wilmer resumed walking.

"You do that." Don Felix raised his eyebrows and turned to continue on his way. "And Wilmer: tell your mother to come to the ADESCO's meetings about the aqueduct. They're quite important."

"I'll tell her," Wilmer said again.

Before he returned to the house, Wilmer saw the Gigante Express motor-cycle come down the road. He felt his pulse quicken and a tingle in his fingers and toes. Could it be coming to their house? This would mean that his father was alive and well, had arrived in the north, and was earning dollars already. Without meaning to, Wilmer's lazy walk became a half-jog up the street. Renegado sprinted ahead, excited.

But before they made it even halfway, the motorcycle passed by their house, and turned into the home of Don Felix's oldest daughter, whose husband was in the states.

*

Once the dinner bell was rung, a line formed at the weigh station. The mean, curly-haired man was a couple spots ahead of Jacinto and Israel, but paid them no mind.

With Curly's bag on the scale, the foreman undid the sack and checked the berries with his hand. "Too green," he said. "Already I told you: only ripe berries. I'm not paying you for this green shit anymore." The foreman gestured to the next man in the line.

"Son of a whore," Curly snapped. "It's only a few that are green. Here." He found a worn-out plastic bucket and pulled it over to his sack—now at the side of the line he'd been squeezed out of. By hand, Curly frantically sifted out the under-ripe cherry from his bag and threw them into the bucket. The foreman ignored him and weighed the next pickers in the line.

Jacinto hefted his sack onto the scales. The foreman glanced at it, nodded his head, and took out his billfold. He was the first get paid. Everybody else was still working off their sacks and meals. Curly erupted once he saw what was happening.

"What is this?" he shouted, hoping to elicit some kind of outrage from the other pickers as well. "You're giving money to this *pinche* Centro-American? This immigrant? And you're not paying us?"

Jacinto wondered what he'd done to betray his nationality this time. What slip in speech or mannerism had given him away? He kept his head down, tucked the bills into his pocket, and found himself unconsciously reciting the Mexican national anthem inside his own mind.

"You know what I ought to do." Curly leveled an index finger at the foreman now. "I ought to go to the police and tell them that you're hiring illegals."

A gunshot rang out from the other side, and the entire line flinched. Jacinto ducked. Walking toward them was an older, well-dressed man with glowing white hair and cowboy boots. He held a smoking pistol in one hand, lowering it as he walked.

"I'll tell you what you ought to do." The old man's gun was a tarnished silver six-shooter. It looked like an antique. "You ought to get off my property this instant. And if you go to the police, give my brother-in-law my greetings."

Curly's face grew so tense it looked as if a blood vessel might pop through his forehead. He turned his furious gaze towards Jacinto. By way of exit, Curly kicked his sack over so that the coffee spilled across the ground, then walked off to the road.

The *finca* owner put his pistol into a leather holster straight out of an old western movie and walked off towards the dining room. Israel hoisted his own sack upon the scales. Jacinto looked around at the other faces in the line, trying to gauge their sympathies.

During dinner, nobody sat near Jacinto and Israel. They were served beans with scoops of brownish avocado and fried plantains. Without thinking, Jacinto folded one thin tortilla over into thirds.

In a whisper, he asked Israel: "How did that man know I wasn't Mexican? Is it because I fold up my tortillas?"

Israel shrugged. "Everyone's heard about how hard Salvadorans work. Maybe that's what did it."

Anticipating a crowd in the sleeping pavilion, they ate fast and dropped their plates off first. Both of them pissed upon a stand of coffee trees on the way, then settled into hammocks. Jacinto took the wad of bills from his pocket and shoved it down the front of his underwear. With his thumb, he checked to make sure that the phone number was still stitched inside his waistband. Despite the chilly night air, Jacinto had no trouble going to sleep, and was thankful for another night in a decent hammock.

*

After dinner, Wilmer sat at the table and started on the day's homework. Outside, his mother banged the gringo's clothes against the concrete washboard. This year, Wilmer started English classes. The teacher gave them pages of fill-in-the-blank sentences to complete. Verbs he didn't understand had to be conjugated to agree with their subjects. All the students knew that their teacher didn't truly speak the language, and never bothered to read through their homework.

Outside, past the kitchen, Wilmer watched the evangelicals on their way to the nightly service. The men wore long, collared shirts and the women covered their heads with white scarves.

"Brother...Brother," sounded their nightly greetings. "God bless you... God bless *you.*"

Mother's cloth snapped hard against the *lavandero.* She ground her bar of soap into a stiff pair of gringo trousers. At Wilmer's feet, Renegado lifted his head and perked his ears a little, keeping watch on the church-goers as they passed. Don Felix and the other men from the ADESCO went by. The new religion was perfect for them; they all so loved to speak in lingo and judge others.

Wilmer turned back to his homework. Little pictures beside the English sentences were meant to explain the meaning. Cartoon gringos performed actions that Wilmer didn't recognize. They walked with backpacks and boots on.

John _____ through the woods. (to hike)

A gringo in glasses leaned his way into a bizarre sideways posture—a thin pole in each of his hands and two odd boards strapped to his feet.

Rick _____ on the snow. (to ski)

Outside, Wilmer heard his mother sigh and reach deep into the cistern for another *guacal* of rinse water. It was almost empty. They needed more rain.

Singing began from the evangelical church. It was hard to pick out any lyrics other than the odd "Jesus" or "spirit" here and there. The voices blurred together into a cacophony of praise.

Wilmer turned back to the page. A bearded man sat at a compact table with a cup and saucer. There was a window beside him, and beyond that a landscape of trees with little lines suggesting motion. This one, Wilmer understood.

Billy rides the train. (to ride)

*

In dreams, Jacinto slept atop a train again—jostling with the bumps and creaks of the track. Slowly, he came to realize that he wasn't dreaming, and certainly not on a train. The shaking that he felt was from somebody rooting through his pockets, moving the hammock in the process.

Jacinto tensed his body and blinked the sleep from his eyes. His hands went straight for the wad of bills at his crotch. "What the fuck?" he muttered, half-awake.

The figure shifted instantly and Jacinto felt pressure on his throat. He was able to make out Curly's face above his own, even in the scarce moonlight. But his vision soon grew blurry as the pressure increased around his throat. He thought he heard Curly say "money," but Jacinto couldn't say a word back. He tried to fight the big man off. He sent his fists bouncing off Curly's ribcage several times. He pushed back against the forearms that choked him, but Curly had the advantage of size and gravity. A stream of foamy spittle dripped out Jacinto's mouth and down the side of his cheek.

He'd never felt anything like this before. In spite of the years he spent at war, this type of fight was still foreign to him. Jacinto couldn't help but think of Wilmer's condition, and the irony of it all: the father making the journey so that his son could breathe, and here he was, choking to death while still in route.

A ringing grew in Jacinto's ears and his vision turned to a grainy glistening like colored sand. He could feel Curly's anger communicated through the hands around his neck. What was meant to be a robbery was now a full-blown act of rage. And such an intimate act it was, this murder. Jacinto could sympathize with his killer. He felt an equal anger for his circumstances. For a second, Jacinto felt as though the two of them were becoming one person, that his life-force was being absorbed by the man who snuffed it out.

When the pressure ceased upon his windpipe, Jacinto thought he'd died. The first breath felt so foreign to his lungs, he doubted it was breath at all, but surrender—like when a drowning man finally lets the water in.

He then felt a flow of hot liquid down his side and wondered if he'd pissed his pants. But this was all the way up by his chest. The body pressing down upon him then tumbled over onto the floor.

Israel stood at the edge of the hammock, puffing air and drenched in sweat. The liquid all over Jacinto's chest was blood, looking black in the moonlight. The machete they'd hidden in the rafters—which Jacinto had forgotten all about—was stuck halfway out of Curly's ribcage.

"Shoes," Israel said. "Now."

Jacinto did as he was told. Still seated in the bloody hammock, he laced his sneakers tight. All around the pavilion, faces stared out from their hammocks, wisely wishing not to get involved. An old Indian woman crossed herself.

For a half-second, Jacinto's self-preservation instinct yielded and he turned to Curly, wondering if he might be saved. The steel blade was shoved so far into his torso that the puddle of his blood grew like a rising tide across the rough surface of the concrete floor. His chest still rose and fell with breath. Jacinto again remembered Israel's cagey words about things-he-wasn't-proud-of during his country's war. Jacinto was about to turn the body onto its back, utter something encouraging, take the blade out perhaps.

"*Vamos*," Israel said.

Jacinto followed him into the night, thinking that now they were actual outlaws rather than technical ones.

They ran down the dirt road from the *finca*. Jacinto struggled to keep up. A set of headlights appeared in the distance, coming toward them. Israel broke off to the side of the road. They lay flat amongst the coffee while the police jeeps bounced up the road. Jacinto remembered what the *finca* owner said about his brother-in-law.

Jacinto pulled a couple of berries off the nearest tree, popped them into his mouth, and hoped for a small burst of energy from their caffeine and sugar. While the dust settled on the road and the jeeps continued on their way, Jacinto felt a well of sadness open up within him. He wouldn't wake up early to pick tomorrow. There would be no hot breakfast. A man might be dead.

"*Vamos,*" Israel said again once the police were past them. Their pace increased now, and they jogged all the way to the railroad switching yard where they'd been a few short days ago.

They were the first travelers atop their boxcar this time. As the rosy-fingered dawn blossomed all around them, the two waited for the train to move. Finally, the engine turned over and the locomotive ground its way down the track. A small burst of migrants ran out from the shadows and jumped aboard.

"Throw away the shirt," Israel shouted into Jacinto's ear.

Jacinto felt silly for not thinking of this before. He took off the shirt with its wine-dark bloodstains and tossed it over the side. From the far end of the car, a couple of youngsters stared. His pants were also stained, but that could've been mistaken for the marks from coffee cherry or the like.

Now that Jacinto finally had something worth stealing—and nothing with which to defend himself—he was more suspicious than ever. But they were lucky with this particular ride. This train was long and it traveled fast, without stopping or slowing down. The small load of stowaways on board had plenty of space to stretch out.

In the middle of the day, Jacinto felt hard sun on his back, and he wished he had some piece of cloth, bloodstained or otherwise, with which to cover him from the elements.

Between the engine and the rush of air, the noises atop the train had a way of blending together and cancelling everything else out, until it became something similar to silence. Jacinto had a long time to think about what happened back there in that sleeping pavilion. Though they hadn't bothered to speak for several hours, he leaned over into Israel's ear and shouted "thank you" over the noise.

Israel nodded, then put his mouth to Jacinto's ear. "He would've killed you. I had no choice."

"Will he survive?" Jacinto asked back.

Israel shrugged. "Depends on blood: how much he loses, how fast they can get him some more."

9

THEY RODE ON THROUGH THE DAY. THE LANDSCAPE GREW LESS green, more grey and industrial. Jacinto knew without asking that they were approaching that overgrown monstrosity known as the Distrito Federal. His skin was dry and soiled from a combination of sunburn, wind, diesel exhaust, and the relentless dust. They'd have a hard time finding rivers or springs to bathe in around here.

The train slowed in a rambling wasteland of factories, garages, grain silos, and fuel tanks. It crept along at a snail's pace for a while, but nobody bothered to jump off. By the time they reached a full stop, it was late in the afternoon.

Jacinto and Israel walked for a while in what they assumed to be the direction of more residential environs. The town—if you could call it that—had the feel of desertion. Even when they finally came upon a street with what looked to be homes, nobody was inside them.

They walked further. Jacinto hoped to find someplace he could buy a shirt. If they looked respectable enough, there was no reason not to take a bus for the next leg of their journey.

They turned a corner and understood where everybody was. An entire city block burst into Technicolor with flowers, ribbons, colors, and people. Skulls, whole skeletons, guitars, hats, donkeys—all made from paper or sugar, all adorned with bright yellow bouquets. Upon closer look, they saw that this block was the cemetery, cleaned and decorated, each tomb adorned with marigolds and sweet bread.

"What is this?" Jacinto asked.

"I think it's the Day of the Dead." Israel, for once, was just as surprised.

The two of them walked past the graveyard. The smells of tamales and eggy buns cut a cavern into Jacinto's stomach. As the sky grew dark, they came at last to a small storefront where a vendor exchanged goods for money through an iron cage. The front of the shop was full of skeleton dolls and candles, but there was also a single replica jersey of the Mexican national football team.

Jacinto waited nearby while Israel dealt with the shopkeeper. He looked into the windows and doors of the houses along the street, everyone preparing for a feast. Parents lit candles and hung skulls in their windows. Children carried cups of *atole* and tequila out their doorsteps—offerings for the dead, Jacinto assumed. Back in El Salvador, they tidied up the tombs and left flowers for their departed relatives on this day, but nothing compared to this level of pageantry.

Israel shoved the jersey into Jacinto's chest. "The vendor says there're no long distance buses leaving the local station until tomorrow," he said. "We'll have to improvise where we sleep tonight."

Jacinto pulled the jersey on over his head. "Let's walk for a while."

They moved on. It grew cold as the dark descended. Relatives and visitors came in and out of doorways until a late hour. Eventually, the two men found themselves in what looked to be a wealthier neighborhood. The houses stood tall and proud, set further back from the road.

"Could we call Los United, now that we have a little money?" Jacinto worried about what Mina and Wilmer were left to think.

Israel rolled his eyes. "The thing is: it's best to buy a card with lots of time. For only one call, it's not wise. And we'll need all the money we made if we are to buy bus tickets."

Jacinto sensed hostility towards the phone call, maybe even towards the bus ride. But what good was all the cash they'd earned, if it were lost to bandits atop trains?

The lights were turned out in the neighborhood now. The cold had settled in. Jacinto put his hands deep into the pockets of his trousers and shivered, worried about how he'd ever get any sleep tonight.

Israel bent down at an offering left upon one darkened doorstep. He picked up a piece of sweetbread and tore it in half, offering the bigger piece to Jacinto.

"Are we supposed to do this?" Jacinto took a sheepish hand from his pocket. "Is it not...for the dead?" How had he suddenly turned into the more superstitious of the two?

"They're not as hungry as we are." Israel grinned. "The spirits take the essence of these foods. But afterwards, humans eat the real thing. It's part of the celebration. In this house." he pointed with his lips. "They didn't bother to bring them in. If we don't eat, it will go to the dogs."

That was all the encouragement Jacinto needed. The bread tasted incredible. The dough was rich and moist and the outside wore a dusting of sugar crystals that dissolved in his mouth and stuck to his fingers. They drank from a cup of *atole* that was set out as well. It had gone cold and separated, but still it was tasty—having been well-seasoned with hunger.

"For the cold." Israel held aloft a dainty cup of clear liquid, then sipped down half of it and grimaced.

Jacinto was no drinker, but did not decline. He hoped it would indeed help with the chill.

Israel identified it as, "*mezcal.*" Jacinto slurped it down, felt the warmth along his throat and chest. Certainly, it was more palatable than the *chaparro* or *aguardiente* he'd sampled back in El Salvador.

They walked on through the damp foggy night and found another abandoned offering—tamales this time. They dug in without reservations. The Mexican tamales were different than the ones Jacinto knew. Wrapped in corn husks and full of pork, they were small and firm, easier to eat with one's hands. Afterwards, Jacinto felt the burn of chili peppers in his mouth, something he wasn't used to but which he hoped would further stave off the cold.

His belly was full after the second offering, and Jacinto could now focus all of his worry on where they'd sleep. It might be better to walk all night long, rather than spend hours shivering on the cold ground. There was little talk between them as they made their way. When he saw it, Jacinto first thought it was a hallucination—the equivalent of thirsty walkers seeing lakes in the desert. But Israel saw it too. He ran over and bent down. There on the doorstep of a large and darkened house was a stack of wool blankets and two pillows.

"Is this what I think it is?" Jacinto asked.

"They leave them for the dead, so they might rest after their long journey," Israel answered.

"These Mexicans take better care of their dead than of the living."

They laid down right there in the doorway to the large house, where they could get a bit of shelter from the wind. The wool of the blankets scratched against his skin, and the bedding smelled of mildew. Still, Jacinto could scarcely remember the last time his head lay upon a pillow. He fell asleep at once.

*

Raindrops pinged atop the corrugated metal roof. Mina sat on her bed, which doubled as a couch for watching television. "Tell me about the field."

"With this rain, I can plant beans tomorrow." Wilmer stood by the TV set and turned the knob through the few channels they received.

"When can we dry the corn?" Mina asked.

"Soon. Once there's more sun." He paused at the public station. On the screen, an alligator broke the surface of a brown river. Wilmer's father loved these nature documentaries. Not otherwise interested in TV, he often lost hours to such programs.

Wilmer turned to ask if she wanted to watch this. But when he saw the sadness in his mother's eyes, he changed it back to a dubbed American movie. A child had been kidnapped. In his baritone voice, the heroic father character decided to take matters into his own hands.

"I'm going to the ANTEL tomorrow." Mina sounded as if she'd just then made up her mind. "Would you like to come?"

"No." Wilmer sat down beside her and kept his eyes on the screen. He thought of how all those people stared at them in judgment the last time. "I've got the beans."

*

In the morning, Jacinto awoke to a steel-toed boot in his side. Above him stood a man in a black uniform, a shotgun strapped across his chest.

"*Amigo*," the man said. "Time to go."

The guard was young and nervous. Perhaps he feared that Jacinto and Israel were, in fact, dead relatives resting after a voyage through the afterlife. The black cap he wore was not of any official police force. As in the wealthy *colonias* of San Salvador, he was a private security guard, his salary paid by the neighborhood residents.

Jacinto nodded, blinked the sleep from his eyes, and went to stand. Israel followed suit.

"A bus station?" Jacinto asked in a raspy, dry-throated voice.

The young guard pointed in the same direction they'd been walking last night. The two men had traveled several miles since leaving the train yesterday, and were now in a much different sector of this sprawling metropolis.

They passed by more pageantry for the Day of the Dead. In the daytime, they could see altars inside all the homes and businesses. Yet another cemetery overflowed with crosses, marigolds, and sugar skulls. A small procession passed them by, its parishioners carrying their offerings and skeleton dolls. A few small children tagged along, dressed as animals and superheroes.

They passed by some small cafeterias, where the smells of brewing coffee and fresh baked bread made Jacinto finger the bills along his crotch. But he knew he couldn't indulge in such things, not if he hoped to buy a bus ticket, and possibly have a little left over to make an international call.

Soon, they came to a dusty corner office alongside a gravel lot full of buses. From the doorway, Jacinto stared at the information board: a series of cities he'd never heard of, with numbers in a currency he was still unfamiliar with. They backed away a few steps to talk things over.

"Why don't I handle this," Israel offered. "Let's see the money."

They scooted over along the cinderblock wall that enclosed the parking lot. With discretion, Jacinto took the wad from out his pocket. Israel pooled their grimy bills together and counted them against Jacinto's chest, trying not to draw onlookers.

"Well." He sighed. "It's not enough for Tecate or Nogales. We could maybe get to Juarez, but that wouldn't leave us much for food."

Jacinto simply nodded, not able to offer any helpful input on the matter. Israel entered the office. Across the street, there stood a small bodega. In addition to the seasonal flowers and candies, they had a sign which advertised pre-paid calling cards. Apparently, this country didn't have a public phone service like ANTEL in El Salvador. He reached down to the waistband of his underwear, and pulled it up above the front of his pants. A spattering of stains, like freckles, ran all along it—either from the juice of the coffee berries, or blood from that awful incident in the sleeping pavilion, or perhaps a mix of both. Jacinto read the phone number to himself, wrapping his mouth around the sounds of each digit. Though it was a couple of steps removed, this was his only lifeline back to his home and family in El Salvador. He wanted them to know that he was alright, that he'd be traveling on a bus for one long leg of the journey, no more dangerous trains.

He stared into those stitched numbers, the work done by Mina's hands, as though it were a fire or the ocean, something hypnotizing to watch. Then, down in one corner, he saw a bit of unraveled thread. He could still make out the number of course, but one corner had begun to fray.

"Alright then." Israel appeared at his side. "I had to give our friend the dispatcher a little something to avoid questions about our identification."

Jacinto let the elastic snap back against his waist.

"We're going to Chihuahua. It's not on the border, but it's close to Juarez. There's work there, as well as short-range smugglers."

"Alright."

"This is all we have left." Israel held up a few dull-colored bills. "It's best we buy food here rather than along the way. We'll be on the bus until tomorrow."

Jacinto nodded, understanding that a call was out of the question.

They walked across the street to that same bodega. Jacinto stayed silent as Israel bought their rations for the trip: a bit of cheese, some fresh tortillas kept wrapped in cloth behind the counter, a large bottle of water.

The bus stopped and started its way through the city. The seats were more comfortable than the old school-buses Jacinto knew from El Salvador. He sat by the window, his long legs crammed into the seat in front. Israel sat in the aisle, the plastic bag with their food wedged between his feet. There was no talking. Jacinto had sensed a divide growing between them since the struggle at the coffee farm. As they moved further into this unfamiliar Mexico, Jacinto felt helpless, dependent on Israel for everything.

Once the bus broke free from the city's traffic and sooty air, it gained speed along a smooth and empty toll highway. Jacinto enjoyed the landscape, the velocity breaking the heat a bit.

"Can I ask you something?" Jacinto said. "How did you learn to use a machete like that?"

Israel pulled his baseball cap down over his eyes, crossed his arms before his chest. "In our war," he said. "That was how things were done. The gringos, they sent men to instruct us."

A long moment of silence passed; even the bus's engine noise seemed to diminish.

"Did you mention something about abandoning your son? That you did it once and wouldn't ever again?" Israel asked the question matter-of-factly. He was now owed an equally awful truth, to balance the scales of their personal histories.

"That's right," Jacinto said, "in my war." That night wasn't something he enjoyed talking about. "We had our little bunker up in the mountains. It must have been an old stable or something. Mina was pregnant but fought the entire time. She had no choice. We'd listen to Radio Venceremos; they gave us codes and whatnot. We were told that the army was on its way to raid our camp. They knew our location and were coming on foot. We were all packed and ready to evacuate when Mina went into labor. She couldn't run with us, there was no way. I wanted to stay with her, but she wouldn't have it. 'There's no reason for you to die here along with me!' she said. 'Don't be stupid!'"

Jacinto turned to Israel, as if hoping to be judged, but all he got was a downward tipped baseball cap.

"I was young, you know. I always did what I was told. The rest of the guerillas agreed with her. They took her weapons and gear—the idea being that an unarmed woman in labor might be spared. If I was there, there'd be shooting."

Jacinto recalled the crackles on the radio, the worn-out wood of the table, the threadbare sheet that he spread over it. Mina's logic: don't be stupid. Don't be stupid. At the time, it didn't seem an act of abandonment. It didn't seem much of an act at all.

All through that war, nothing felt like survival. It was all a matter of how long to suffer and how soon to die. He never expected a return to anything like a normal life again. To believe that he would not catch a bullet in the back eventually, or step on a mine—this was unthinkable in those days. Even on the eve of Wilmer's birth, if Jacinto had been told that he'd one day be father to a thirteen-year-old son, he'd have laughed out loud. He'd just as soon have believed that he'd one day be president of that so-called republic.

"How did you find her again?" The question came out from under Israel's downward cap.

"What?" Jacinto jumped off that train of thought.

"Your wife, how did you find her again?"

"At the refugee camp, in Mesa Grande, Honduras. The baby came early; the army came late. She carried the newborn through the mountains, then across the Rio Lempa. He was a year old before I met up with them again."

"You're lucky," Israel said. "You all got another chance to be a family."

"That's right," Jacinto said. "We did." He felt his eyes grow heavy. Though it hadn't been long since they were awoken by that security guard, he had more lost sleep to make up for.

*

Finally, the night of rain had filled the cistern and softened the ground. Wilmer's mother left early for the ANTEL, to try her brother on the phone again. She walked this time, to save the transport tax to the Mara Salvatrucha. Wilmer felt bad for not accompanying her, but he'd soured on the experience of all the walking and waiting just to watch his mother receive more bad news. Besides, he had work in the field.

Years ago, his father had fashioned a portable seed-bin from half a plastic bottle and a bit of twine. It hung from one shoulder or the neck, like an apron. With the *guizote* in one hand, a person could reach into the open piece of plastic and draw out a seed, without fumbling through the folds of a plastic bag. Wilmer filled the device with dry seed beans.

It was still cool when he and Renegado left for the field, the *guizote* over his shoulder and the seeds in his other hand. The houses in Carasucia had hardly stirred. Most likely, the men waited to see if the rain had truly stopped.

Planting beans was a task that Wilmer had done before, though never very well. A long stick with a bit of iron at its tip, the *guizote* went easily into the moist earth. His father could drop a seed right into the hole without bending over, but Wilmer often missed. He leaned down a little, and many times had to go back, pick up his seed, and tuck it into hole he'd made.

Thankful for this rain, Wilmer also worried that if they didn't get another full day of sun, his corn might not fully dry and would risk rot or fungus. A sky of high grey clouds wouldn't betray its intentions.

Wilmer spent hours this way, depositing beans at the base of the corn. With any luck, their vines would soon climb the stalks before the corn finished drying. He wondered where his mother was now. Still at the ANTEL perhaps. He hoped she'd keep it together. The thought of her losing composure again— in front of all those gossipy women from town—filled Wilmer with dread. The idea that she might be successful, that his father might be there in California at Uncle Chano's house—that possibility had already faded from Wilmer's imagination.

*

Jacinto blinked the sleep from his eyes. In the morning light, he saw an iron structure at the side of the road. Painted red, it consisted of an enormous upside-down fishhook-shaped bar, and then a smaller triangle below.

"What is that?" He pointed at the window.

Israel turned his head. "It's art, a sculpture. They call it 'the Gate to Chihuahua.'"

Jacinto kept on staring, watching as the sunlight crept over the horizon and illuminated that hunk of iron which looked so much like a machine.

"Here," Israel said. "We should finish our food before we get off. It won't be long now."

They wrapped bits of cheese inside the cold tortillas, and washed them down with sips from their gallon of water. Soon, the bus was in another cement wasteland of highways, exits, and overpasses all tied up into knots. They entered a layer of smog and dust not unlike the one they'd left behind in the

D.F. In fact, when the tires crunched onto the gravel lot and finally came to a full stop, the office was nearly indistinguishable from the one they'd left. Jacinto wondered if they hadn't simply made a big circle all night long, and come back to where they'd started.

The doors opened and passengers piled out of the bus. Jacinto's legs trembled underneath him, remembering how to walk. He wondered what they would do now. Look for work? For the train tracks?

Israel came to a stop in front of a woman with a cart full of tall metal pots. The aroma of coffee drifted off. From his back pocket, Israel withdrew a few small coins. He spoke to the woman about prices—Jacinto still didn't understand the Mexican currency—then came back with one mug of coffee and a cigarette.

Though he'd not been impressed by his first try, Jacinto took the smoky drags when they were offered to him, and the two of them stood sharing their stimulants of choice, as though their chemicals might combine for a state of wakeful alert greater than the sum of their two parts.

Across the street, a truck pulled up at a small hardware store. A teenage attendant opened the gate and helped the older driver load bags of cement. Jacinto watched, the lightheadedness from the tobacco settling some. Within a few minutes, the teenager excused himself and went back to service a customer in the store.

"Look." He nudged Israel with an elbow. "They might need some help."

Israel nodded, drained the dregs of the coffee mug and handed it back to the woman with the cart. Jacinto led them across the street and hiked up his pants.

"A little help?" he said to the grey-haired driver.

The man responded only with a suspicious glare, but Jacinto picked up a bag of cement anyway. He threw it over his shoulder and carried it to the truck. Israel hopped into the bed and took it from him, starting a more orderly stack at the far end.

In his youth, Jacinto could carry two bags of cement at a time, but he thought better of that, what with a stiff back from all that bus riding. He understood that the driver may or may not pay them for this, but he decided to work hard and hope for the best.

By the time the truck was loaded, Jacinto's shoulder was covered in a grey film of sweat mixed with cement dust. His back ached as he bent to pick up the bags that sat straight on the floor. The suspicion had left the truck driver's face.

"You boys busy today?" He looked at Jacinto as he spoke. "You want to help me unload as well?"

Jacinto and Israel rode in the back upon the stack of cement bags. The smoggy air hit their faces at fifty miles an hour. Jacinto wondered where in this wide-wayed city more cement might be needed. It was as though they were trying to turn the whole thing into a continuous mass of concrete.

At the margins of town, they came to a chain-link fence and a guard with a shotgun. He exchanged a few words with the driver and in they went. The truck backed up to an excavated rectangular hole where a large gang of masons laid blocks.

A cellular phone pressed against the truck driver's ear as he climbed out the cab, talking business. He pointed to the spot where he wanted it all unloaded.

This time, with the heat of the day that much hotter, and all the dust from a construction site in the middle of the desert, the bags felt far heavier. The two of them worked from the ground until they'd moved all the cement within reach. Israel mercifully told Jacinto to climb up and work from the truck. It was his turn after all.

"*Amigos?*" The driver held his clunky cellular phone against his chest. "Are you two available all day?"

"*Oralé.*" Jacinto spoke before Israel had a chance, and used the tiny bit of Mexican slang that he'd learned.

Israel looked up at Jacinto with a tight grin. Most likely, he'd have preferred to talk price. But Jacinto had found them this job by heavy-lifting first, asking questions later. Israel appeared to appreciate that.

Gradually, Jacinto understood that their new boss was arranging for new business. How had that old man ever handled deliveries on his own? Once the cement was done, they took off down the dirt road back to town.

"What are they building out here anyway?" Jacinto asked.

"More *maquílas*," Israel shouted over the truck's diesel engine. "The gringos don't mind us doing all their work if they don't have to look at us."

Soon, they hit the highway and it was much too loud for talking.

*

On the way home, two boys approached Wilmer on the path. Both were Don Felix's sons: Moises, the one from the other day, along with an even younger one, called Jeremias. They carried empty sacks and one machete with them. When their father wasn't around, those two were notorious mischief makers. Even from a distance, Wilmer could see them punching each other in the upper arms and thighs.

Wilmer nodded as they passed, but didn't offer any spoken greeting.

Moises put his brother in a headlock—the machete dangling dangerously from one wrist—and kept walking. The moment they'd passed, Wilmer heard the older boy speak in a loud mock-whisper: "Did you hear about his father?"

Wilmer stopped walking.

"He couldn't endure the desert, and surrendered to the Migra."

The hiss of the boy's insincere hush pierced Wilmer's ear like a piece of old wire. He gripped tighter the shaft of the *guizote*. The two other boys giggled and went on.

Wilmer opted not to turn around. They were two, after all. Though Moises was a year younger, he was bigger than Wilmer.

He passed several more workers on the way to their fields as he went. Wilmer scowled at every one.

*

Their next load was all long pieces of rebar. It made the cement look easy. The truck parked at the far end of a fenced-in lot full of building materials. The driver and a clerk walked the yard with a detailed list, telling Jacinto and Israel how many pieces to take of each shape and caliber. Some of the largest pieces required the two of them to lift. Others had to be carried the entire length of the yard. With work gloves and a bit of canvas or denim over the shoulder, this work would've been grueling. With bare hands and a shoulder only protected by the football jersey, it was unbearable.

Israel's face grew bitter and distant. The driver had the foresight to start with the biggest pieces and work his way down to the smallest. But with the exhaustion, each bar felt heavier than the last.

Even the ride was miserable, balanced atop a load of jangling metal bars, pinching at their toes and ankles and allowing no comfortable perch. The construction site where they arrived was slowly growing into a factory of equal size to the last, but in a younger stage of development. The carpenters banged out molds inside the geometric holes of excavated earth. The iron busters were impatient for their materials. All the rebar had to be unloaded into the same separate piles as it had been in the yard. Jacinto had to use even his tired brain as he unloaded, every rusted piece sawing away at his shoulder.

By the time they were done, his fingers were curled up and swollen. Israel didn't speak. But the boss was happy with their work. He peeled them off a side of bills before they started the trip back to the city proper. Jacinto studied Israel's face and was glad to see no obvious sign of dissatisfaction.

The driver took them to the same street corner where they'd met up that morning—where Israel and Jacinto had enjoyed their coffee and cigarette.

"Be here first thing tomorrow," the driver said, "if you want more work."

"*Oralé,*" Israel answered, the bit of sarcasm in his voice meant only for Jacinto.

Each man in his own silent state of ache, they ordered food from the same woman who'd served their coffee. She took big flour tortillas, filled them with beans, rice, and a bit of what looked to be finely chopped beef—then wrapped it all up. Though the rust and the cement dust on his fingers lent a bitter note to the supper, Jacinto was happy to have something that could be eaten fast and without utensils. They finished the food in less than a minute. Israel paid and purchased a sole cigarette. As they walked away, he passed it off to Jacinto every so often. This time, Jacinto was thankful for the mild way it suppressed his still-lingering hunger.

"Where will we sleep?" he asked.

"Wherever there's *maquiladoras.*" Israel let out a breath of smoke. "There's migrant camps."

The sun had already quit the horizon. The sky was now a dark mix of oranges and blues in the very last light of the day. Israel led them off the street by a large apartment building. He found the dumpster at the far end of the car park, and wasted no time jumping into it. Jacinto stayed outside, listening to the crumpling of plastic bags and the low gongs from the metal floor, looking to see if any residents were watching them.

"Here we are," Israel said at last. Over the rim of the dumpster flew a hooded cotton sweatshirt with a blue stain all down the front of it. It was huge. Jacinto cast the wretched garment about his shoulders and the sleeves dangled below his hands. Israel emerged wearing a false leather coat obviously made for a woman. They continued on their way, now a bit more ready for the cold desert night.

Just as Israel had predicted, an enormous hobo camp stood on a hillside across from the first of the industrial zones. Entire families were set up there. In makeshift shacks of cardboard and corrugated metal, they cooked suppers and put children to bed. Adults prepared for another hard day of sewing together clothes for gringos to wear once or twice and then discard.

Initially, Jacinto had misgivings about bedding down in one of these camps. But now, in the glow of the cookfires and with the sound of the brooms scraping across the few tiny squares of earth where this city would tolerate them, he saw that they were all humble hardworking people like him.

At a careful distance, Israel and Jacinto followed a little girl in a pink Sunday dress carrying a five-gallon bucket. Sure enough, she led them to what appeared to be the shantytown's water source: a dug-up and exposed piece of PVC pipe with a plastic valve spliced onto it. The girl filled her bucket as a matter of habit. Once it was full, Jacinto approached and helped her hoist it up upon her head.

The spigot to themselves now, the two of them drank and washed their hands, careful not to wet their clothes before the cold desert night. Most of the families had gone to bed by the time they returned to the camp. Without speaking, they bedded down beside a cookfire that looked to be abandoned for a shack further up the hill. Every joint in his body aching and tired, Jacinto slept like a dead man.

10

THEY PASSED SEVERAL DAYS THIS WAY: WORKING LIKE MULES while the truck driver watched from the shade and arranged more work over a cell phone. Their dumpster jackets helped protect their shoulders and backs while they carried the most unwieldy cargo. They cut costs and saved their wages. Israel handled all the money. Jacinto hardly saw a phone during this time, and forgot all about the call he'd wanted to make.

One of the families in the migrant camp agreed to feed them supper for a small fee—and to let them sleep on an old mattress left outside of their shack. They were a kind couple, with two children. But everyone was so exhausted by the end of the day, there was little talk or visiting.

Israel and Jacinto awoke each morning before sunrise. They were first to the water spigot, and by now had scrounged up a couple of empty plastic bottles with which to carry the day's drinking water. They walked into town, bought coffee and a cigarette from the same woman at her stand, and waited for the driver, who often had a pickup arranged at the hardware store across the street. Jacinto's hands grew callused in a whole new set of places, after more than a week of working iron and concrete blocks. He preferred the bags of cement. They were the right size, fit on his shoulder, and didn't tear at his hands.

After a long day of loading rebar and bricks—a day that stretched well into the night—their employer informed the men that he'd not be able to pay them until the following morning.

Israel's face tightened up like a fist. "What are we to do for food tonight?" he hissed. "What will my children eat?"

It always shocked Jacinto to see dishonesty come so easily to Israel in a pinch. Their whole friendship was based on an inexplicable confidence.

"I'm sorry." The silver-haired driver did look apologetic—even if he knew better than to believe the bit about the children. This man had been good about paying them so far. Why not give him the benefit of the doubt? After all, he held the cards.

"Show up with our money tomorrow morning." Jacinto did his best to sound stern. "Or we don't work."

"*Oralé.*" The truck driver nodded and drove off.

Jacinto put a hand on his friend's shoulder. He could feel Israel trembling with adrenaline.

"It's alright," Jacinto said. "We've got plenty saved up. It's only one night. He'll pay us in the morning."

Israel sighed. He took some coins from his pocket and laid them on the wooden cart of the vendor—the one person who seemed to work longer hours than they did in this town. She knew he wanted a lone cigarette.

"Don Jacinto." Israel leaned in for her to light it. "We'll never see that man again."

They walked back to the camp in dark silence, Israel keeping the cigarette for himself.

In the morning, Jacinto let him sleep in a bit later than usual, and filled up water bottles for the both of them.

"Let's go." He shook his friend's shoulder. "Time to get paid."

At their street corner, the morning grew late. Jacinto sipped coffee while Israel counted and recounted their savings against the cement wall. Across the street, the hardware store opened and filled orders. Gradually, he understood that Israel had been right: their employer had abandoned them over one day's lousy wages.

"Well." Israel put his hand on Jacinto's shoulder. "I think we have enough to cross, provided we spend nothing between here and the border. Do you prefer a river or a tunnel?"

"I can't swim," Jacinto said.

*

Once the harvest was in full swing, Wilmer went to the field each morning. He broke off the driest ears of corn, and carried a sack-load home on his back. At the house, his mother strung up a ratty, worn-out hammock above a blue tarp in their courtyard. They put all the cobs in the hammock and tied it closed with a bit of twine. Wilmer and his mother then beat the bundle with two long sticks. The kernels fell through and pitter-pattered against the tarp. The dry leaves and naked cobs were caught inside by the hammock strings.

The dust forced them to turn their heads and squint their eyes. Each bundle required several minutes of full-blown whacking from the two of them. Once the cobs would yield no more kernels, they picked up the tarp by each corner, and dumped its contents into their tin granary. If Wilmer were lucky, he might get two sacks done before he had to bathe, eat lunch, and dress for his afternoon school session.

*

They walked along the non-toll highway heading north outside of town. Israel's anger about the lost money subsided, now that there was nothing to be done about it.

They backpedaled on the road's shoulder with their thumbs out. Semi trucks blasted by and nearly knocked them over with their gusts of wind.

"Only eighteen wheelers on this road?" Jacinto asked.

"It's all commercial traffic. The rich folks and the expensive buses take the toll roads."

A big green tractor with two trailers flew past, honking his horn as though in warning.

"Why would anybody stop to pick us up?" Jacinto meant the question for himself as much as for Israel.

"You never know," Israel said. "Many of the truckers have ties to the *coyotes*. It's a similar business, when you think about it."

"So, we're looking for a *coyote* now?"

Israel stretched his thumb out wide, but the approaching semi switched to the other lane. Air brakes hissed as it passed.

"Not like the one who took you all the way through Mexico. We're after a *pollero* of sorts—somebody who's connected enough to pay off the right people and lead us through without hassle. It shouldn't cost much."

"How will we find this person?" Jacinto fought off unpleasant memories of Pink Hair.

Israel laughed. "After we get a bit further north, everything changes. Crossing the border becomes like growing corn where you're from: everyone's in the business or connected to it somehow."

An unmarked semi with a bad muffler slowed down as it approached them. After a second or two of dust and noise, it ground to a stop on the shoulder a hundred yards ahead of them.

"*Vamos.*" Israel took off running and Jacinto followed.

The door on the passenger side swung open.

"To Nogales?" Israel asked, then climbed aboard.

Loud *norteño* music blasted inside the cab. Jacinto climbed onto the sleeping bunk in the back, while Israel rode shotgun. The truck driver shared his Marlboros, and Israel couldn't hide his satisfaction.

Once again, Jacinto experienced that city-desert-city landscape transition that he'd come to associate with this part of Mexico. Once they were well into the rambling industrial outskirts, the truck driver turned down the volume on the cassette player.

"So then," he said. "Where is it that you two are going?"

Israel picked up another of the man's cigarettes, this time without an offer. "To Nogales, of course."

"No." The truck driver shifted the tone of his speech. "Where are you *going*? What's your final destination?"

Israel let out a mouthful of smoke. "Why do you ask? Do you know anyone who can help us?"

"It's possible." The driver kept his eyes on the road.

"We're on a tight budget," Israel explained. "We only need the most basic. It's not our first time doing this. No bells and whistles, if you know what I mean."

Jacinto had no idea what was meant by any of these innuendos. And though it wasn't his first crack at this border, he seemed to understand it less and less with each passing hour.

"Perfect," the truck driver said. "My cousin has a safe-house full already. The *polleros* are all lined up. You'll pay a bit to cross with them. They'll take you to the bus stop on the other side."

"That sounds reasonable."

"Factor in a little something for my finder's fee, and I'll take you straight to him."

"Of course," Israel said.

*

Wilmer's day was off to a late start. He and his mother were in the middle of beating on their first batch of corn cobs when Don Felix approached with a couple other members of the ADESCO. Don Jefe, the gringo, followed behind them, wearing a funny-looking pair of rubber sandals.

"Niña Mina." Don Felix removed his straw hat. "With permission."

"Enter." Wilmer's mother wiped her brow with a forearm.

Don Felix used his big hat to wave the dust out of his face and entered their courtyard. He smiled and nodded at Wilmer. "Niña Mina, we've come to talk with you about the water system."

"Is that right?" She pressed the point of her stick to the ground and rested her weight against it.

"It's about to become a reality, this project. By next summer, there will be water running to all the houses in Carasucia."

"How nice." Wilmer's mother showed little patience. She would believe these men's promises once she saw them come true.

"The materials will come from a pair of NGOs. The community will provide the labor. That's the agreement. You've not attended our recent meetings, have you?"

"Unfortunately not," she said. "We've been busy, with the harvest."

Wilmer watched the gringo's expression. He appeared to follow the pseudo pleasantries of the Spanish conversation, his face braced for bad news.

"The arrangement we've come up with works like this: To secure the rights to their water connection, each household must give two days of work per week. We hope to break ground soon, and to complete the aqueduct in several months."

"That sounds fair." For the first time, Wilmer's mother showed some interest in what these men were saying. "My son can work on Saturdays, and I will fulfill the other day."

Wilmer was about to say that he could skip school. Don Jefe's lips cinched together in a tight line.

"That's actually why we're here, Niña Mina. In the meetings, the community set some regulations about who could and could not do the work. It was all very democratic and correct. We can't have young children or very old folks, you understand."

"I see," she said.

Wilmer felt a hollowness in his stomach.

"What exactly are the requirements?" Mina asked.

Don Felix looked down, swallowed, then looked her in the eye again. "Males. Healthy men ages sixteen to fifty."

"My son works very hard, and..."

"I'm sure that he does," Don Felix interrupted her. "But the community voted on this. I can't go making exceptions. Also..." He turned to Wilmer. "Is it not true that you have a condition of some kind?"

Wilmer dropped his gaze downward, as if to stare in judgment at his worthless pair of lungs.

"Many of the families who lack an able-bodied male will pay a day laborer to work in their place," Don Felix went on. "Perhaps you could do the same? I'm sure they wouldn't charge more than they do for work in the fields. Don Jacinto is in the north now, is he not?"

"He hasn't arrived yet." Mina picked up her stick and held it outward like a sword. "There's been some trouble with his *coyote*. But we should hear from him soon, before you break ground perhaps. If not, I suppose I'll keep hauling my laundry to Santa Cruz, won't I?" She cocked her stick back and prepared to strike. "Now, if you'll excuse me, we have more work to do."

"Of course." Don Felix replaced his hat, and turned to leave.

Wilmer's eyes met the gringo's. He offered a sort of shrug on his way out.

Once the men had left, Wilmer and his mother resumed beating their bundle with more fury than before, and didn't stop for even after the kernels had ceased to drop upon the plastic tarp.

*

That same evening, Jacinto found himself following yet another herd of frightened migrants. Between the truck driver and the teenager who now led them, Israel had handed over all their money.

More than a dozen and all of them men, they walked through a slum quite similar to the one Israel and Jacinto had slept in back in Chihuahua. In the distance, Jacinto spotted the tall sheet metal fence on a hillside. Razor wire—put there by the gringos—lined the top. Graffiti—put there by the Mexicans— lined this side.

The great concrete rectangles of the *maquiladoras* loomed on the hills, lit up by floodlights and surrounded by tall lengths of chain-link, as though somebody might want to break in and fill ink cartridges for a few extra hours.

The whole group took a wide turn and made their way up a drainage channel. The only source of illumination came from a flashlight in the hands of their tall teenage *pollero*. Soon their progress slowed. Jacinto stared ahead and saw that they were about to enter some sort of underground chamber. He touched what he thought was Israel's upper arm.

"This is the tunnel?" he whispered.

Israel grunted in the affirmative.

Inside, the round caverns were moist and dark. A thin ribbon of filthy water ran past at their feet, shining whenever the *pollero's* flashlight came their way.

The smell was a foul mix of death and feces, and Jacinto for once wished that he was in that desert again, where at least he could see his own shadow and tell north from south.

As they followed the group, Jacinto held onto a pinch of Israel's shirt. Despite the frightened line-up's best efforts to be discreet, each step and whimper echoed throughout the concrete caverns.

"Who the fuck?" came a sudden shout from behind.

At the end of the line, Jacinto turned around and was blinded by another flashlight. As his pupils constricted and his vision adjusted, he saw what appeared to be a sharpened screwdriver pressed to his sternum. He put his open palms up at his sides. Working backward, he followed the point of the weapon up to its plastic grip, then to a tiny hand that held it. He recognized the soft fingers of a child. Then, at a spot between the thumb and forefinger, he saw the three blue-black dots meant to stand for "*Mi Vida Loca*"—the crude gang tattoo.

Jacinto then stared into the face of the child that threatened him—a face that only came up to his own chest. For a second, Jacinto felt he was looking into the eyes of his own son.

"Who the fuck are you?" The voice wasn't this little boy's, but that of a girl, another child, coming from behind. She held the flashlight and shook it in Jacinto's eyes.

"*Tranquilo,*" came another voice, this time from the opposite side. The *pollero* stepped and splashed his way to Jacinto's end of the line. "Didn't Manuel tell you? We're taking a group tonight. We paid him this afternoon."

Now with several flashlights in the mix, Jacinto could see more. It was a whole crowd of kids before him—a gang in every sense of the word. Their skin was pale and moist, their eyes big and bloodshot. Did they ever leave these tunnels?, he wondered. Were they some sort of amphibian race that no longer needed light or fresh air to survive, but lived only off filth and moisture, like fungus? He stared into the feral eyes of the silent boy that still held the screwdriver up. Jacinto wanted to ask where his parents were. He wondered how his own son might answer that question lately, so many weeks into this journey.

After a minute or two it seemed that the *pollero* had sorted things out to the satisfaction of the kids. The little boy withdrew the screwdriver. Jacinto let his hands fall slack at his sides and released a full breath.

Just then, the boy lunged at him with the screwdriver, letting out a high-pitched whoop. Jacinto jumped backwards and tripped over Israel's shoe, landing in the dribble of water at their feet. The kids laughed and high-fived at the prank, then wandered off into the darkness of their tunnels.

The *pollero* returned to the head of the line, and Israel helped Jacinto up.

"Who are they?" Jacinto asked.

"Just some kids who live down here. They're sort of the landlords of these tunnels. The smugglers—of both drugs and humans—have to pay them off in order to pass."

They carried on through the tunnel, moving faster now, with greater purpose. Jacinto couldn't wait to get this part over with. His back and trousers were soaked in the filthy water. He cared less about which country he ended up in, more about getting out of this tunnel as soon as possible. The line grew longer and thinner, sloshing through the puddle at their feet.

Jacinto heard the group flee before anything else. Their feet splashed about and they sprinted in all directions at once. Again, he held onto a pinch of Israel's t-shirt and followed him even as he ran through the dark. It wasn't until a second later than he heard the "*alto, alto,*" shouted in a bad gringo accent and then a tin whistle chirping like a football referee's.

The group moved over and on top of each other. The scattered like a herd of wildebeests, leaving their slowest or dumbest to be eaten by the predator.

A light shone in Jacinto's eyes from the other direction, a light much stronger than any he'd seen from the smuggler or the gangsters.

"This way," somebody—hopefully Israel—whispered into his ear.

They ducked low and crawled their way into a sort of side cavern, a small artery off the main branch. They put their backs to the wall and listened to the shouts and movements coming from around the corner.

"What the fuck is this?" Jacinto whispered.

"Gringo Migra," Israel answered. "Very strange. I think the Mexican cops are down here as well."

They stayed frozen in their place for several minutes. Israel was right; as the authorities walked about only a few yards away, Jacinto heard Mexican voices as well as gringos. They had at least a couple of the migrants in custody, but most of them seemed to have run and eluded capture.

"I don't understand," Jacinto whispered once the police voices faded to a different direction. "Why wouldn't the gringos simply seal this tunnel off if they know it's being used for smuggling?" He'd assumed it was a secret.

"Can't," Israel said. "This thing is for drainage. Their Nogales would flood as well if they cemented it shut. That's how it is with neighbors." Israel lowered his tone. "You're always connected to them, whether you like it or not."

From above, they could hear a woman cry and shout. From the sounds of it, the gringos had caught her but were handing her over to the Mexicans. She cursed and screamed in the voice of a young girl. She must be one of the gangsters, Jacinto thought, not a fellow migrant. Perhaps they were the real target of the police.

*

"Here." Wilmer dropped the sack of laundry on the gringo's floor.

Don Jefe startled at the sound. He stood tending a pot of the coffee on the stove and nearly spilled hot water down his arm. "Oh, Wilmer." He put a hand up to his own chest. "Thanks."

The sun had just risen. Long beams of light came in between the bars on the east-facing window.

"Give me a minute," Don Jefe said. "I'll get your money."

Wilmer nodded.

"Can I ask you something?" The gringo killed the flame on the stove and found his wallet on the wood-door desk. "Do Don Felix and the other ADESCO men have something against your mother?"

"My parents fought with the guerilla during the war," Wilmer explained. "Almost everyone else in Carasucia fought with the army. We've always been outcasts. More so now that they have the evangelical church."

Don Jefe nodded. "Here you go." He handed over a bill. "I'm sorry about the water situation. I thought your mother would be able to send a laborer. I never expected your family to be left out."

Wilmer shrugged and stuffed the bill into his pocket.

"It was the community's decision," Don Jefe said apologetically. "We made those rules and we must follow them. Everything has to be fair."

"Oh yes." Wilmer didn't hide the sarcasm in his voice. "Can you imagine: if life wasn't fair? That would be unthinkable." He turned and left the gringo's house.

*

Jacinto was fully soaked in the tunnel water, a solution of piss and industrial chemicals. They didn't hear a peep from the police for a long while, and decided that perhaps now was their chance to move.

Israel went first. Jacinto followed. Soon, they were able to stand up straight. Jacinto's eyes finally adjusted to the darkness, but he wouldn't have known which way to go without Israel there.

"Look." Israel pointed.

There at the far end of the tunnel was a sort of iron gate—its two doors open and revealing a vertical stripe of rosy-fingered dawn that nearly blinded Jacinto's dilated eyes.

"Let's be careful," Israel said. "Cops could've posted somebody there to watch it."

Once they reached the opening, they paused before crossing. Outside was a drainage ditch like the one where they'd entered.

"There it is," Israel said. "*La Usa.*"

Jacinto blinked madly as his eyes adjusted to the light. He stared into it as though hypnotized. The next sound he heard was similar to the wheeze that he knew well from his son's asthma attacks, a sound he associated with sorrow and helplessness. As Jacinto turned his head, he wondered why Israel might make such a noise.

His friend dropped to his knees and let out the gurgling hiss of a horse choking on its bit.

"Fucking cops," came a small voice from behind.

Yonder stood the little boy who'd threatened Jacinto at the beginning of this underground journey. There, in Israel's back, was the sharpened screwdriver that had been held to Jacinto's sternum not so many hours ago.

"We're not the cops," Jacinto said stupidly.

The boy shrugged, looking bored by this exchange. He took off running back into the darkened complex of tunnels. Outside, the American sun rose higher and shined a column of daylight onto the two men.

A caterpillar of frothy spittle formed in one side of Israel's mouth. He fell onto one hand and in a raspy reptile speech uttered: "take it out."

Jacinto wrapped his hand around the bloody screwdriver and pulled. He paused to stare at the long and sturdy needle which had been meant for him. "I'm sorry," he heard himself whimpering. "I'm so sorry."

Israel lay down in the puddle. Blood-tinged bubbles sputtered and spurted through the contaminated water. One of his lungs seemed to be pierced. There was a time when Jacinto knew a protocol for this sort of wound. But now, he could only bear witness to his friend's suffering and mutter his stupid apologies.

A bright light shone at the end of the tunnel. Voices barked syllables in a foreign tongue. The gringo police, Jacinto thought, as though they were on television as usual and not alive, a couple hundred yards away.

"It's okay. The Migra is over there. They'll get you to a doctor. I'll see to it." Jacinto turned his head up. "Over here!" he screamed. "Help!"

"Don Jacinto," Israel coughed out, his face stretching and contorting around the words.

"Yes," Jacinto said. "What can I do?" He was eager to fulfill any near-death requests his friend might have.

"Run," Israel said.

"What?" Jacinto asked as if he didn't know the meaning of the word.

"I won't survive this," Israel hissed. "I've had my fill of wounds before and I can tell that this one is different. Death has come for me now."

"That's not true. Hold on for a few minutes…" But Jacinto heard the doubt in his own words. His conscience had traded heavily on ambiguity—a grey area between injury and death—with those gangsters atop the train and again with Curly in the coffee fields. He would no longer hide behind uncertainty.

"Run, you fucking idiot!" The act of screaming seemed to cause Israel great pain.

Jacinto dropped the weapon, nodded to his friend, and did exactly as he was told.

III

11

IN THE MORNING LIGHT OUTSIDE THE TUNNEL, JACINTO FELT
as though he were learning to see, a kitten with eyes newly opened after the
first few dark days of life. The drainage ditch was banked in by high walls. It
wasn't hard to know which way to run. Once he finally came to a road, he was
shocked to find what looked to be a familiar face. The young *pollero* who'd led
them into the tunnels stood beside a minivan with blackened windows. He
pulled people into it, saying "Let's go! Let's go!"

Jacinto ran to the van and was the last person shoved inside. All of the
seats and furnishings were stripped out, so that it was little more than a metal
box with a sheet of plywood along the bottom. Many of the other members of
their party were inside, as well as a few strangers.

The human odors of fear and sweat filled the van and made it hard to
breathe. The *pollero* rode shotgun and exchanged curses with the driver. Both
men were upset about the police raid and terrified of punishment from their
superiors. Soon into the journey, Jacinto realized that their destination lie far to
the west. He was sure this was more travel than he'd paid for. Their deal was
for nothing more than passage into Nogales, Arizona. Perhaps the smugglers
thought better than to leave anyone behind for the Migra to find.

Jacinto sat on the plywood and leaned back against the sliding door of
the van. He did his best to enjoy the speed and the distance, the illusion of a
destination and a purpose. The sickening grief over Israel fermented inside his
gut—turning more potent and acid as it aged.

It was late in the morning once the van finally turned off the highway.
It bounced down a dusty gravel road, the suspension clearly not meant for
this cargo of people. Jacinto looked around and saw that they were in a citrus
grove. They parked amongst trees and a few low wooden buildings. He nearly

fell backward as the *pollero* slid open the door. Men jumped out and pissed wherever they stood. Jacinto stretched his legs, still waiting to wake up from the nightmare that was the last twelve hours.

He found himself strolling along the side of a man-made irrigation pond. In the brown earth that surrounded it, he found a couple of small stones—bits of gravel really. The morning in the desert was still and windless, the pond's surface an unblemished sheet of glass. It reflected the gigantic sky above this, the country that Jacinto had been travelling so long to reach. He threw one of his rocks in and watched the ripples travel from its center all the way to each of its man-made shores.

"*Vamos, Vamos,*" he heard from the buildings. It seemed that the smugglers and the farmers had reached an agreement of some kind. Jacinto went to join the commotion, motivated by curiosity as much as anything else. He tossed the other stone in before walking off, and let his mind's eye linger on the waves it now sent across the water's surface.

A foreman from the farm explained the rules and protocols. The whole experience still felt surreal, but Jacinto found that he understood this Latino foreman—a middle-aged man with a deep voice, a straw hat, and a salt-and-pepper mustache—better than anybody else. His Spanish sounded more familiar to Jacinto than anything he'd heard in months. Was it possible that this foreman was Salvadoran?

Curious and distracted, Jacinto didn't truly hear what he would be paid per pound or when. At the end of the brief talk, all of the men took up a ladder and a basket. Jacinto was the last to follow. When he approached the grey-mustachioed foreman, they stared each other in the eye. Not finding any words, Jacinto took his supplies and fell in behind the rest of the workers.

It wasn't until he began picking fruit that Jacinto could see the good fortune he'd stumbled into. He'd expected, once the van stopped, to be held hostage until he could contact somebody to send more money, or to take on a debt against the first of his American wages. But it seemed that these smugglers were in cahoots with this particular farm, and that this group of men paid for everything in full, including their job placement. In all likelihood, they lacked family or friends in this country.

The work itself was foreign to Jacinto. His fear of heights didn't help with the ladder climbing. But the trees weren't so tall, and picking was picking, up to a point. Jacinto got badly scratched from the course leaves of the trees, and the oils from the fruit often stung in the cuts, but it was easier on the back than many of the doubled-over tasks he was used to back home. Most fortunately, the trees were many and the men were few.

Though he'd been up all night and his eyes strained with unrest, Jacinto was able to lose himself in the work. As he'd always done in times of trouble, he focused on the labors at hand— the ripe fruit, the weight of the basket, the distance between here and the next loaded tree. During the war, he'd often been thankful for long, uphill marches and heavy loads. Such tasks exhausted his body so that his mind might rest.

Cold came quick to the high desert, once the heat of the day subsided and the sun retreated behind mountains. Much to Jacinto's surprise, the men were paid out—in the first American dollars he'd ever earned—at the last weigh-in of the day.

A converted truck arrived selling food: Mexican combination plates, hot dogs and hamburgers. The workers all studied it, until one man stepped forward and ordered from the female attendant. When his turn came, Jacinto pointed to a picture on a plastic-covered menu and in short order was handed a Styrofoam plate with beans, rice, and some sort of sliced meat in a dense reddish brown sauce. She took one of his bills, and gave him back others. Jacinto had no idea whether or not it was a bargain. After dinner, many of the men stripped and bathed in the pond, whooping and giggling at the cold shock of it. Jacinto was too tired to join. Between the sleepless night before and the long day of labor, he hoped to make it through until morning without nightmares. He lay down on one of the creaking bunk beds provided them, still covered in dust and dried filth, a bit of Israel's blood soaked into his trousers.

He was haunted by guilt and second-guesses over leaving his friend in the tunnel. Everything about it rhymed and resonated with the awful memory of his pregnant wife in that stable during the war. Jacinto didn't fancy himself a hero. But he'd come to believe there might've been virtue in simply being there both times, even if only to witness a suffering he couldn't fully share. He closed his eyes and reminded himself of the underlying truth to both cases: in the big picture, his presence or absence would not have made one damn bit of difference.

*

After several mornings of beating out hammock-loads of corn, their tin granary was finally full. It was a Saturday when Wilmer harvested the last of the dry ears from the field.

Once all was said and done, they had two full sacks left over.

"We could take some out of storage," Wilmer suggested. "It's only us eating now."

His mother shook her head no. "Rain could come late next year and we'd be stuck. Besides, we don't even know the market price."

Wilmer nodded. She was right. If they needed to sell more, they might as well wait a few months. Between the two of them, they could carry this load. Any more and they'd need to hire a porter in the city. Wilmer hauled both heavy bags to the street while his mother dressed for the trip.

When the bus came, the *cobrador* was kind enough to help heft both sacks in through the rear door. Wilmer and his mother took up the entire last row of the bus: the two of them on either side of the aisle, a sack of corn in each of the window seats beside them.

Once they came to Rosario, the gangster with the teardrop tattoo boarded the bus. He didn't bother with speeches this time. Instead, he simply walked the length of the aisle, gathering change like a second *cobrador.*

Wilmer swallowed hard, and felt a familiar tightness in his chest. He wondered if Teardrop remembered them, or if he would again be as merciful as the first time. But once the gangster made it to their spot in the back, Wilmer's mother was ready with some coins. She dropped them into his fist and he turned around. At the front of the bus, Teardrop patted the driver on the shoulder and disembarked. The whole thing was over without any words exchanged.

The rest of the bus ride was less eventful. It had been months since Wilmer had travelled to the capitol, but little had changed. They went up the hill to the highlands of Los Planes de Renderos, where rich San Salvadorans had their houses. Mormon missionaries knocked on gates. Kids from the private schools walked to the park for their recess. Gringo tourists asked directions to the Puerto del Diablo—that rocky outcropping that some of them were crazy enough to climb.

As soon as they started downhill, the houses shrunk. Vendors sprang up on the sides of the road. *Bolos* lifted bottles of rubbing alcohol to their mouths. Soon they passed the zoo, with its foul smell, emaciated elephant, and always-sleeping lion.

By that time, they were in the city itself. The low cloud of diesel fumes hung in the air and made Wilmer's lungs tingle. The bus stopped at the cathedral. Wilmer and Mina rose to exit. Again, the *cobrador* was kind enough to help them with the corn. He set a bulging sack on each of their shoulders.

Wilmer followed his mother through the central market, stepping around the legless beggars and the passed-out drunks, past the vendors with their shelters of black plastic, their tables of saints, chains, and baseball caps. *Pupusas* sizzled upon oily griddles, beside the color-coded buckets of beans, *masa*, cheese, and *chicharrón*.

Wilmer's shoulder ached by the time they reached the grain trader, but he refused to complain in front of his mother. She set her bag down upon the scale, and then summoned the clerk from behind his counter. Wilmer threw down his sack beside hers.

The clerk was a thin, clean man with wire-rimmed glasses. He moved the weights on the scale and scribbled a number down on his yellow pad. On one of the sacks, he undid the twine at the top and ran his hand through the inside. He withdrew a few of the kernels, shook them there in his palm, and appeared satisfied. Another man came in and set to hauling the sacks away. Behind the counter, the clerk counted out their money.

"Is this it?" Wilmer's mother asked, when presented with the handful of bills and coins.

"Sorry." The clerk shrugged as he spoke for the first time. "It's been a good harvest. Prices are low."

It wasn't hard to believe him, with that efficient and businesslike air. The man had a personality as cold and fast as the market itself.

Mina nodded, thanked the clerk, and started for the door. "*Vamos* Wilmer," she said. "Let's buy food with this money before it too gets stolen from us."

*

The days of the week passed like this in a relative blur of work and sleep, the smells of sweat and citrus so constant in Jacinto's nostrils that he hardly noticed anymore. His acceptance of Israel's death came to him in waves, like the rising and breaking of a fever. Some days, he understood it as a casualty of the voyage, a calculated risk that Israel took over and over again, knowing the stakes better than anyone. Other times it felt like the ultimate injustice, a final sign that this journey was ill-conceived from the start. Jacinto remembered the two creatures he'd seen in the jungle that night. Had that event been misinterpreted? Was it, in fact, a sign that they should go no further? Or was it simply the nature of things that good luck and bad luck always follow one another, like two dogs chasing tails?

Jacinto made little effort to socialize with his fellow workers. Though he'd missed it in the welcome speech, he gathered that they would have Sunday off, and that the Mexicans were excited by this. Many of them quit early on Saturday afternoon. They bathed in the pond while the sun still shined.

There was no line when Jacinto brought his sundown load to the weigh station.

The foreman helped lift the basket onto the scales. "Don't work too hard," he said. "There's more time than there is life."

Immediately Jacinto recognized the Salvadoran phrase. "*Puchica*," he said in response. "I haven't heard that in a while."

"*Puchica*." The foreman laughed as he repeated the nonsense word.

"You're a *guanaco* as well?" Jacinto asked.

"That's right," the foreman said, "Beto." He extended his hand.

"Have you been here long?" Jacinto asked him, in awe that one of his countrymen could rise to a managerial role in this nation.

Beto nodded. "Since the conflict, really."

Jacinto stopped himself short of asking which side this man fought on; he didn't much care, and nothing good would come from the question. "It's very impressive, that you've become foreman," he said instead.

"We work harder that anybody else. That's why the Mexicans resent us so much. If a gringo gives a *guanaco* half a chance, we always climb their ladder. You'll see."

On the dirt road that led into their camp, an old car—one of those wide American sedans so rare in El Salvador—approached. A plume of brown dust followed behind. The chassis nearly bottomed out against the wheel wells, from a bad suspension and a heavy load. Loud *norteño* music pounded out the windows. The car rounded the curve by the weigh station and headed on to the workers' barracks. As it passed, Jacinto saw several heads inside.

"What is that?" he asked.

"That's the party." Beto smiled. "Take my advice, Don Jacinto. You go have a beer with those men. Spend a little of your money. If you seem too disciplined, too hardworking, it can draw attention, and create problems."

Jacinto recalled the incident in the coffee field, and needed no further explanation.

As it turned out, he couldn't have avoided the party even if he'd tried. The bunkhouse was overtaken by it.

The oom-pah of the *norteño* music came not from the car stereo, but from a big silver boom box which now sat on top of the car and resonated with its fiberglass roof.

The man in charge of the party car was a big Chicano with a shaved head. He popped open the trunk to reveal an ice chest full of tall silver cans, sweating with the cold. In another box, he had several open packs of cigarettes, and sold them to the workers one-by-one. A teenager—perhaps the man's son or nephew—helped with the transactions. Jacinto's colleagues rushed to thrust their money upon them in exchange for the ice-cold cans of American beer.

Soon, Baldy revealed a cardboard box with two different bottles of tequila and a stack of small plastic cups, like the ones the health promoter gave out with his medicine. The Mexicans bought each other shots, then grimaced and grunted after downing them.

Once everyone seemed to have his initial thirst for alcohol quenched, Baldy took out a duffel bag full of new clothing. The workers wasted no time rooting through the selection. They found the old-fashioned cowboy shirts that the older generation preferred, as well as the baggy blue jeans and bright baseball caps that were suited to the youngest amongst them.

More than anything, Jacinto was impressed by the resourcefulness of the bald entrepreneur. Perhaps it was a bit exploitive, but he certainly had identified the needs of his market.

"Hey, El Salvador," one of the men shouted "Have a drink with us!"

Jacinto saw that this colleague was already red-eyed with the liquor. He'd anticipated something like this, and approached the cooler with his money. The Mexican drinker also took out his cash, but Jacinto waved it away. He didn't wish to get into a tit-for-tat drink-buying situation.

"One beer please," Jacinto said.

Baldy handed over a can and made change for one of Jacinto's bills.

"Also," Jacinto said. "Do you have cards for making phone calls?"

"Where do you need to call?" Baldy asked.

"California."

Baldy motioned for Jacinto to follow him around to the driver's side of the car. From above the sun visor he took out a stack of multicolored cards. "You sure you don't want an international one? To call...your country?" He fanned them all out in his hands, as though they were playing cards.

"My family has no phone," Jacinto said. "I'll leave word with my brother-in-law in California, and they'll call him from the public phone. It's our only option until I have a place to receive calls."

"That's cheap then." Baldy picked out one card from his deck. "This will give you half an hour. That's the smallest denomination they make."

Jacinto shuffled out his wad of American dollars, in the same manner that he'd just been shown the phone cards. Baldy smiled at his ignorance, then plucked one of the bills from the fan.

"Where are all the other people that rode in with you?" Jacinto saw that the back seat was now empty, but was sure there'd been others when the car first arrived.

Baldy's grin turned sly. "The ladies are just dolling up a little." He slapped Jacinto on the shoulder then motioned with his head to the far side of the bunkhouse. "But don't you worry; they'll be back soon. You know how women are." He raised his eyebrows conspiratorially.

Jacinto put the phone card in his back pocket and finally opened his can of beer. The first sip was surprisingly mild and watery—less bitter than the rare beers he took in El Salvador. He studied the label for a second and tried to guess how it might be pronounced.

"Hey Guanaco!" That same drunk Mexican shouted over the music. "I meant a *drink*, not a beer!" He gave a bill to the teenaged helper, who poured a plastic cup full of amber tequila.

Jacinto reluctantly walked back to the party proper and took the cup from the man, doing his best to smile and nod as if he were actually thankful.

The drink-buyer ordered a shot for himself as well, and led Jacinto through a ridiculous rhyming toast—up and down, to the middle, now to the inside—and the two of them slurped the tequila. Jacinto felt the burn work its way through the back of his throat down to his chest.

The other man breathed hard out his mouth. Jacinto took a long gulp from his beer to wash the tequila down. He felt his shoulders tighten up and so rolled them in their sockets a couple of times. As he went for another pull from his can of beer, the other men broke into a chorus of hoots and whistles.

From around the corner of the building pranced three women, all in tight-fitting tops and high heels. The prettiest of the three was young, probably a teenager. Small, with straight dark hair and smooth skin, she wore blue jeans cut off high at her hip. She seemed the most self-conscious, the only person other than Jacinto looking awkward at this party. The other two were older, and heavily made up. They wore clunky jewelry, short skirts, and wasted no time shaking their hips with the music.

"*Bueno muchachos*." Baldy used one hand to turn down the volume on the boom box, the other to cup around his mouth. "This is Rosita." He pointed at the youngest one—uncertain atop her high heels like a fawn with spindly legs. "Christina." The tallest one blew a kiss as she was introduced. "And Maria." Maria was quite fat. She put her hands on her hips and batted her eyelashes at the men. "They are more than happy to dance with you," Baldy continued. "Anything more than that, you must talk to me first." He turned the music back up.

The party took on a sour note for Jacinto. This bald man's business became less impressive once its prostitution wing was revealed. He had another sip of beer and watched as the drunk who'd bought him the tequila handed a wad of bills to Baldy. While the two older women did their best to dance with several partners at once, this man dragged little Rosita by her hand, off into the darkened orange grove, while she stumbled behind atop her heels. Jacinto finished his beer and decided to have another.

The party kicked into high gear. The men took turns dancing with Christina and Maria. The cool fizz of a fresh beer filled Jacinto's mouth—he thought of how far he'd come since nearly dying of thirst in the desert. He deserved a little celebration, did he not? Isn't that what people did?

All the men broke out into a giddy cheer once a new song came over the boom box. It was *"Tres Veces Mojado"*—the ballad of a Salvadoran crossing three international borders in order to come and work in the United States. All of the men rushed to put a hand on Jacinto's back and sing along. Inexplicably, Jacinto found that he knew the lyrics as well: "When I came from my land of El Salvador/ with the objective of arriving in the United States/ I knew I would need more than courage/ I knew I might end up in the road..."

He slammed his beer against those of the other men, these brothers in the struggle to make a little money and provide a life for their families, feeling a kinship he'd not felt since travelling with Israel.

From the corner of one eye, he saw that same drunken coworker return, along with the little girl in the cutoff jeans. The two of them joined the group dance, and sang along to Jacinto's song: "How can they call me a foreigner/ in Central America, given its situation both political and economic/ for many now there is no other solution..."

Jacinto held no grudge against anyone. All of them—the prostitutes and their pimps included—were doing the best that they could, here in the desert night with the accordion playing loud. Somebody passed him another shot of tequila and he gladly downed it, thinking it not so harsh this time, certainly more palatable than the *guaro* the local drunks in Carasucia made such a fuss over—the *guaro* that he'd so rarely sampled.

Somehow, Jacinto found himself dancing with little Rosita. He felt this was a good deed of sorts, as if he was protecting her from these other rough men. Did she appreciate it? Another of the new men then took the little girl by the hand and dragged her off. Jacinto slurped his tall beer. The song changed, but the men were still desperate to keep the party going.

Jacinto felt a bit of melancholy creep in through the side door of his psyche and wondered if more tequila might shut it out. He paid for his own shot for the first time all night. Before Baldy had a chance to make change, Jacinto drained the plastic cup. He went to return his wad of bills to their home in his back pocket, but first he measured them between his thumb and forefinger. By their width, he judged himself a rich man, who need not worry over spending a little on beer and spirits tonight.

With a renewed sense of purpose, Jacinto returned to the dance floor. He found himself dancing with Maria now. For the first time all night, a slow song came on the boom box. Maria pulled him tight against her. She took one of his hands and placed it on the curve of her hip. The soft warmth of a woman's flesh was something he'd not felt in ages. He smelled the chemical perfumes of her shampoo. Inside his pants, an erection formed and Jacinto did nothing to hide it. He felt Maria lead him by the hand over to Baldy at the cooler. Jacinto pulled that wad of bills from his back pocket again—an act he'd been conditioned to do each time he stood before this man. Baldy took nearly the whole wad, and Jacinto stood there wondering what for.

The irresistible tug on his arm returned, and Jacinto found himself in the darkened orange grove, beneath a nearly full moon. No words or anything else were exchanged. In the night, following along in silence, he feared that he was about to be smuggled yet another time. Maria pushed him to the ground at the base of an orange tree, then straddled him. The entire weight of her body lay heavy on his lap now. She proceeded to grind against him, hard, grunting and groaning. Jacinto heard himself grunting as well, but his sounds were from the real discomfort that this woman was causing him.

She mercifully shifted a bit of her weight onto her knees and Jacinto caught his breath. Aided by the full moon, his eyes adjusted to the night. Maria reached her hands up behind her head and undid the band that held her hair back. She then squirmed her way out of the tight blouse and bra. With her arms on either side, she displayed her giant breasts before Jacinto. This sight made Jacinto forget the circumstances for a second. The pendulous weight of them, the areolas as big around as tortillas—he froze as though spotting some rare nocturnal bird here in the grove.

Next she undid a fastener on her skirt and pulled it upwards. Jacinto had rarely seen a naked woman apart from his wife. That was the trigger that sent his rapidly sobering brain all the way back to his own country, where Mina waited faithfully for him, while he wasted money on vice—beer and prostitutes.

He found himself hyperventilating: shallow, rapid breathes working their way up from his lungs. Where Wilmer might suffer from a lack of oxygen, Jacinto now suffered from abundance.

Maria had her hands on his pants now. Jacinto looked down and saw what had to be his erection inside her pork-shoulder of a fist. In truth, there was a split second of pleasure there, but it was followed by so much self-loathing it barely registered. When Maria did go to mount him again, this time without those thin layers of cotton and polyester between their bodies, he managed to utter the word, "no."

"No?" Maria was incredulous.

"No," he whispered it now, his palms held toward her, his fingers spread, his hands shaking like leaves the ends of his wrists.

She shrugged, and withdrew the big thigh about to lie across him. She did not, however, let go of his stubborn erection, and Jacinto realized that she'd misunderstood the refusal. Kneeling by his side now, her round hand furiously moved up and down.

Jacinto was taken aback. His mouth opened wide but no sounds came out. As suddenly as the act had started, the whole thing was over. Notes of pain accompanied the orgasm. His whole body squirmed there in her grip. Maria let go as soon as she saw him climax, and left him to spill his seed all over his own belly.

"*Esso*," she whispered over and over, drawing out the last syllable, as though the quantity of his ejaculate were somehow testament to her prowess as a lover.

Jacinto laid his head back, horrified by the experience. His desperate mind searched for justification. He reminded himself that the other men in the bunkhouse had wives back home as well. But that was little help. He'd once prided himself on being unlike all those other husbands—living with secrets and half-truths in a constant state of jealousy and mistrust.

Maria wiggled her way back into her clothes, then walked off toward the party.

Jacinto blinked his eyes several times, hoping he might have dreamed this night. Soon he understood that he'd have to spend some time revising his own opinion of himself, that this was not something he could chalk up to the trouble built into the voyage. Unlike the tragedies he'd witnessed in the desert, on the coffee farm, and in the tunnel, for this sin Jacinto had nobody but himself to blame.

12

HE WOKE IN THE MORNING AT THE SAME SPOT IN THE ORANGE grove. A terrible headache shone in one side of his skull like a second sun. Jacinto sat up and rose to his feet, thinking for a moment that he must get to work. But on his way back to the buildings, he remembered that nobody picked on Sunday.

A loud engine turned over. The laborers all stumbled out of the bunkhouse and piled into the old flatbed truck parked beside the weigh station.

"*Vamos*, Guanaco," one of the men shouted. Jacinto ran over and climbed aboard. All of the workers ducked down close to the bottom of the truck, behind the wooden walls at its side. Once Jacinto was aboard another migrant closed the gate behind him.

"Stay low," the man spoke right into Jacinto's ear, over the diesel engine. "It's not legal to do this here."

Jacinto crouched as he was told, but didn't understand why. Was it illegal to ride in the back of a truck? What sense did that make? Why would lawmakers care about such a thing? And why would anyone buy a truck, if not to carry others?

As they started down the driveway, Jacinto studied the faces of the men, fearful a taunting might come his way. How much would they know about his escapades with the woman last night? He touched his navel and was repulsed by a crust of dry semen there.

But what he found, as they bumped their way along the dirt road out of the camp—the dust rising up to meet them—was that each of his colleagues suffered from a similar state of shame. They were all burdened by guilt over wasted money and stupid behavior, and each of them had to shoulder those personal weights on their own.

Jacinto had no idea where they were going. He wondered if it might be church. Instead, the truck stopped at a little clutch of stores lined up around a parking lot. Don Beto let down the gate and motioned for them to all get out. The landscape was similar to the one he'd walked through for days, save the road and some power lines. Jacinto was puzzled by this place. Why would anybody build their shops in the middle of nowhere? Where were the houses? How do the customers without cars buy anything?

The other men wasted no time heading into the store. A line immediately formed at the sole payphone outside. Jacinto remembered the phone card—the one wise thing he'd done last night—and reached into his back pocket. He closed his eyes and had the odd urge to say a little prayer of thanks when his fingers felt it there.

He took his spot in line behind the payphone, and studied the complicated instructions written on the card in a tiny script.

"Excuse me." Jacinto touched to arm of the man before him in line. "How do I use this?" he showed his phone card.

"Easy." It was the same red-eyed Mexican who'd bought him that first shot. "Just dial this number." The man pointed to the one on the card. "The voice will ask you for a code. Then you dial this." He pointed to a second, shorter string of digits. "Then dial the number that you want."

Jacinto rehearsed a conversation with Chano, Mina's brother. Tell my wife that I'm in Arizona, he would say. Tell her that I have a good job which pays and that soon I'll send money to the house. I had a hard trip through Mexico, and was incarcerated for a while, but the good news is that I did the voyage without the help of a *coyote*. So we need not pay off any debt now. Don't fret over the down payment, Jacinto would advise her. It's true that Don Noe should refund it, but we're better off with him out of our lives.

The plan took shape as he practiced relating it to his brother-in-law. He wondered if Chano might offer advice or even money for Jacinto's travel to California. From now on, he resolved, he would be a good and faithful husband and father. He'd lost less than a week's wages, after all. No point worrying over that now.

Jacinto grew nervous as the line inched forward. Most of the men called Mexico, and told their families they were safe. The story of their chaotic tunnel crossing was related so many times in the course of that afternoon at the payphone, Jacinto imagined that soon all of Mexico would know about it.

He heard the same words muttered over and over: I miss you; it's difficult here; the work is hard; we're all suffering; yes, the money is good; yes, I'll be sending more soon.

Finally, Jacinto's turn arrived. He was pleased to hear the mechanized voice speak slowly and in Spanish. The receiver was warm against his ear. The man from the line had been right: it wasn't difficult to follow the instructions. He reached for the waistband of his underwear to enter the final set of numbers.

What he saw then was the cleverest of cruel jokes that fate had yet played on him. The last two digits of Chano's phone number had come unraveled from the rest. A wad of thread lay tangled into Jacinto's pubic hair. He remembered the loose stitch he'd noticed in Chihuahua, how he'd neglected to do anything about it. He thought of all he'd been through since then: all the cinderblocks and lengths of rebar he'd lifted and carried along his waist, all the crawling through tunnels, the picking of oranges, rubbing upon branches and the rungs of ladders. With a nauseous sinking feeling, he thought of the woman grinding against him last night.

The men in line looked on with suspicion. Through the earpiece, the robot apologized for not understanding the number. He could figure this out, Jacinto decided. He had eight out of the ten digits. How hard could it be to guess the last two? He put in the first several numbers then made up the rest. Many times, he'd rubbed his fingers along that embroidery, but he'd rarely stopped to read or memorize the digits. Was there a two there? Perhaps a five?

Somebody answered on the other line: "Hello."

"Chano!" Jacinto blurted out. "It's me, your brother-in-law!"

A gringo voice responded in English, and Jacinto knew he had the wrong number. He apologized, as if the voice on the other line could understand, and then started over.

His finger trembled with nerves and the hangover, but slowly he was able to get that robotic voice again, and make it to the point of dialing the number from his underwear. He needed a method. There were only ninety-nine possible combinations, after all. Rather than random numbers, he started with a pair of ones. As he listened to the rings, he realized that zero-zero should be the real starting point, but no matter. He'd come back to that, if he needed to.

Again, a gringo voice on the line. Jacinto said nothing this time. He hung up and started over. The men behind him grumbled. They were likely to grumble more.

"If you have nobody to call, give someone else a chance," one of them muttered.

Jacinto pushed their voices out of his head. He'd waited through the long sappy conversations; they could wait through this. On his seventh or eighth try, a voice finally answered in Spanish.

"Chano!" Jacinto yelled. "Is that you?"

"No," the voice replied. "There is no Chano here."

"Do you know a man named Chano? A Salvadoran, in his late..."

"I don't mix up with *pinche* Salvadorans!" The call ended with a slam and a dial tone.

On the twelfth attempt, the line behind him was relentless. There was a slight sense of relief when the robotic operator told Jacinto that he lacked enough money for another call. He walked away in defeat and dropped his wasted phone card onto the pavement of the parking lot.

Inside the convenience store, Jacinto felt the cool blast of the air-conditioning, a sensation he knew only from his time in the Migra truck months ago. There was a Gigante Express counter inside. Jacinto recognized the logo from the motorbikes that cruised around the village on weekends dropping off envelopes full of *remesas* for the families left behind.

The clerk recovered from the flurry of business that their party had caused him. Their due diligence done to the wives and children back home, the workers now spent their money at the store—chips and soda, cigarettes, tall cans of cold beer.

"Excuse me," Jacinto said to the Gigante clerk. "Could I send some money to El Salvador?"

"Name and address?" He placed a document full of empty squares down on the counter between them.

"Guillermina Paredes," Jacinto said. "Cantón Carasucia, Rosario de Mora, San Salvador, El Salvador." He hoped that was all the information he would need.

"And the amount?" The clerk kept his face down, rapidly filling out the form.

Jacinto reached into his pocket and pulled out his remaining bills, all of them twisted and oily from the many hands they'd passed through, most of them change from the bald merchant.

With an irritated sigh, the clerk straightened out the money and counted it. "Look," he said. "I can send this for you, but frankly it's not even worth the fees we charge."

In defeat, Jacinto stared down at the pathetic little stack of bills.

"You're better off buying yourself a beer and a hot dog. Come back when you have at least fifty dollars or so."

Jacinto nodded, refusing to unload his own guilt upon this man. As instructed, he walked over to the cooler where the beer was kept. He opened up the glass door and felt the frosty air wash over him, soothing his dry eyeballs. He touched one of the silver cans, the shape and color of which he remembered well from last night. Would one of these rid him of his hangover, as all the village *bolos* used to swear? Would it give him back that invincible feeling he'd enjoyed so briefly?

His fingers wrapped around it and were ready to pluck it out, but at the last second he fought off the urge. In the next cabinet over he found a coca-cola. He paid at the counter and went outside.

The carbonation and the sugar felt incredible against his dry mouth and tongue. He would be good from here on out, he decided. He would save up his money and send it back to his family. He would keep trying to contact Chano, even if he had to dial all ninety-nine possible numbers. Back at camp, he would beg a pen and paper and write down the rest of the numbers before they came unraveled as well.

Once he finished the soda, Jacinto—suddenly starving—went back inside and bought two hot-dogs, nearly spending the last of his American money.

*

"You'll have to harvest the beans on your own, *m'ijo*." Wilmer's mother checked the mirror and tugged at the formal clothes that Wilmer associated with trips to church. "I know of no other way."

"But the *maquílas*? They pay next to nothing!" It was common knowledge that even in a long day of work at those sweatshops, a woman could barely earn her bus fare there and back.

"Perhaps." Mina shrugged and took the last sip from her coffee. "But I'm making nothing at all here. Maybe there's a chance I could…become a supervisor or something."

"Be careful," Wilmer said. "And return before dark." It was equally well known that bad things befell women outside those factories.

"That's why I'm leaving so early." She walked to the curb to wait on the bus.

Wilmer followed. The pink dawn spread from one corner of the sky, like a spilled cup of liquid. Already, the group of some twenty men—Don Felix and his pet gringo at their lead—walked uphill, picks and shovels over their shoulders, on their way to the aqueduct.

"It's true," Mina said as they both stared out at them. "They're going to bring water to the village."

"And we'll be the only house without it," Wilmer added.

His mother sighed. A cock crowed from not far away.

"They say the *mosos* are making forty *colones* per day," Wilmer said.

"Is that right?" Mina stared up the road. Her bus broke the horizon and rattled its way toward them. "If your father were still here, he could work the two days for us, and still earn almost two hundred a month."

Wilmer refused to think about where his father might be right now.

Mina signaled for the bus to stop, then turned to say goodbye. "Take care of yourself, my son."

"You do the same, Mama."

She boarded the bus, and found a seat by the window. It went off down the hill, without another stop in Carasucia. Wilmer kept watching until it was nothing more than a thin cloud of dust and diesel exhaust.

*

Fueled by shame over the way he'd wasted his first week's worth of American wages, Jacinto worked like a mule during the second week. He woke before sunrise, and picked the most loaded tress before the others were up. He timed his trips to the weigh station when there was no line—so as not to lose any time picking. He counted and recounted the money he'd made, until he was familiar with this American currency—how much he could earn in a day, in a week, in an hour. At dusk, he'd bathe in the pond after the others were done. Most evenings, the Mexicans played cards under a lone light bulb and listened to a Spanish radio station. Jacinto came in from his bath and fell asleep instantly, in spite of the noise.

Each morning, he'd wake in the dark with back and arms still aching from all the work, sit on the edge of his top bunk, and contemplate a later start, an hour or two of extra sleep. He asked himself, as the dawn cracked at the far end of the horizon, what he would tell his wife and child if he were to speak to them right now. If they asked what he had accomplished, what could he say? What had he done and what had he earned since leaving them behind? What were the ends that justified all these awful means? The wad of bills growing inside of his back pocket was his only imagined answer. And as it grew in size, a better answer it seemed to be. If it was big enough, he imagined, perhaps it would redeem everything else that had occurred.

Late Saturday evening, Jacinto had his final load on the scales when Baldy's party car rumbled down the driveway, blasting music and riding low with its cargo of booze and sex. Jacinto could only watch it from the corner of his eye.

"You better hurry." Beto the foreman counted out bills. "You'll miss the party."

"Not tonight," Jacinto said. "They'll have to get by with the Mexicans' wasted money. They won't get any from me."

"Suit yourself." Don Beto handed him more folded bills.

Jacinto went to the pond and spent a long time bathing. He held himself so low in the water that only his face was exposed, looking up at the bright stars against the desert sky and listening to the whoops and giggles coming from his fellow workers. The night air was much colder than the sun-baked water; it was hard to pry himself out.

Inside the bunkhouse, the men danced and drank. Fat Maria noticed Jacinto walk in. She grinned, raised her eyebrows, cupped her fingers round a shaft of air, and mimed the act of jerking him off—as if inviting him for another round. Jacinto turned away.

He walked straight to Baldy and asked for a phone card. This time, Jacinto understood how much it cost, and didn't show any more cash than he needed to. He considered buying a new shirt, as his football jersey was soiled, but didn't feel like looking through the box with all this noise and commotion.

"Guanaco! One drink!" That same red-eyed Mexican held a lone index finger up in Jacinto's face.

"Not tonight," Jacinto answered. "I've got some debt to pay down tomorrow." He pushed his way past the man, went to the back of the bunkhouse and lay down. With a pillow pressed against one ear and the other buried in the mattress, he fell asleep with no trouble.

13

OUT OF HABIT, JACINTO WOKE UP WITH THE SUNRISE ON SUN-
day morning. He dragged himself up to the side of the bed but saw by the
empty beer cans and cigarette butts everywhere that this was, in fact, a day of
rest. For the first time, he lay back down and slept for another glorious hour,
until the desert heat forced him up again.

While the rest of the men continued to sleep, Jacinto walked around the
farm and enjoyed the quiet. Later than normal, Beto's wife put out the coffee
urn and sweetbread. He helped himself to both. Don Beto soon came out of his
own house and poured a cup.

"Morning," Jacinto said.

"You're up early, for a Sunday."

"Never was any good at sleeping in," Jacinto said.

Beto looked out at the trees. "Almost finished," he said. "You have any
idea where you're headed to next?"

Jacinto had given little thought to when the harvest might end. "California," he managed.

"That's good." Beto nodded. "They'll still be picking grapes for a while.
Maybe apples as well."

"How much longer will there be work here?" Jacinto asked.

"Another week should do it, don't you think?" Beto looked out across the
trees that were his charge.

"That sounds right," Jacinto admitted. "Where will all these men go afterwards?"

"Most of them came only for the harvest. Once we get into December,
there's not much work around here. They'll go back to Oaxaca, Chiapas,

Sinaloa, wherever they're from. A few might stay on and try to break into construction or something."

The first few workers wandered out from the bunkhouse—now baking with the morning sun on its tin roof. Jacinto gathered that they'd partied less hard than last week, now thinking seriously about the money they needed to bring home with them. They took their coffee and sweetbread, and soon enough Beto climbed into the flatbed and fired up the engine.

*

Wilmer's mother was off in the factory. The corn had all been sold and put up; the beans still grew. It was Sunday: no school. Alone with the dog in an empty house, Wilmer felt helpless. The thought of the men and boys from the village—those only a couple years older than him and with healthy lungs— out earning money day in and day out. He thought of his mother off sewing gringo clothes. There had to be some way for him to help out, financially.

Lacking any serviceable ideas, Wilmer went into the bedroom and reached for the dial on the television. He stopped himself short of turning it on. Renegado stared from the doorway and cocked his head. Wilmer made the same pensive gesture back to the dog.

He turned down to his mother's unmade bed. It was a wood frame with a network of twine strung both ways across it, topped by a thin foam mattress. Wilmer couldn't remember when or how, but he knew his father had built it. What he did remember was sitting here in the evenings—after dark but before dinner—with his father.

Mostly, they watched the wildlife documentaries. His father preferred those to the local news, the dubbed American movies, the soccer matches, the professional wrestling. His face would show an uncharacteristic sort of wonder for the big cats of the African Savannah, the marine mammals of the north and south poles, even the insects and reptiles of the Amazon jungle. Often, Wilmer had seen the episodes so many times he knew the narrator's lines before they were spoken. But his father had a way of forgetting it was on television at all.

Perhaps he enjoyed seeing what the world might be like without people, to escape inside a story without even a hero to demand one's attachment.

Wilmer pulled the plug out from the wall and lifted the television off its table.

*

At the little store, Jacinto went straight for the payphone. The line was smaller this time, many of the men having made contact and seeing no need for a weekly report. Nobody bothered him as he went though his phone-number count-off. He had the first eight digits written out on a piece of paper, and so didn't need to go back to his underwear with each attempt. This time, he was discreet as he asked the poor folks on the other line if they spoke Spanish, and if so, if they knew a Chano Barrera. Between the two cards, Jacinto had checked off twenty-some of the possible ninety-nine combinations.

As the robotic operator informed him that he lacked sufficient funds for another connection, an old American car—similar to Baldy's party-mobile—pulled into the lot and parked beside the flatbed, its engine still running. There were four Mexicans in work clothes inside.

"Two more!" The driver opened his door and shouted at the men from Jacinto's group. "Two more for California!"

Jacinto's first instinct was to ignore them and go straight to the Gigante Express counter. But the mention of California caught his attention.

One of the youngest Mexicans in his party went up and spoke to the driver. They engaged in a furious exchange of words, then of dollar bills. Jacinto went to investigate.

"You're going to California?" he asked the driver.

"Right now," the man said. "To pick grapes near Santa Barbara. Fifty dollars. Are you in? It's our last spot."

Jacinto was taken aback. He'd meant to send all the money to his wife, but this was too good an opportunity to pass up. His current job would expire in a week, and he'd be left without work or the foggiest idea how to find Chano.

"I'm in," Jacinto heard himself say, thinking it a brave moment of opportunism. He paid his fare and climbed into the back seat of the still-running car,
wishing he'd at least had a chance to buy some food first. By way of goodbye,
he managed a brief wave to Beto, who sat in the driver's seat of the flatbed. The
car turned and left the lot.

As they pulled onto the broad desert highway, Jacinto felt as if he were
in an American movie. Some hours passed, and the romance quickly drained
from the experience. The car had a bad shake in the front end, which only got
worse as their driver insisted on seventy miles per hour or more. All the windows were down, but the only air that came in was hot, dusty, and laced with
exhaust fumes. They pulled off at a convenience store. Jacinto went straight to
the restroom and drank metallic-tasting water from the tap. The driver filled
the car up with gas while the other men bought beer and cigarettes.

Jacinto had eaten nothing but this morning's sweetbread. Not wishing to
experiment, he went with the nearly pronounceable hot dogs. This time, the
clerk was a gringa. She made change and pointed at several bottles of condiments in one corner of the store.

Jacinto smiled, said, "okay," in his best fake English, then went over and
doused his meal in ketchup and mustard.

Back at the car, the men took up a collection for gas. Jacinto realized that
his week's wages weren't going to take him much further than their destination. On the road again, the other men drank beer from those tall American
cans. The desert gave way to a rambling urbanscape, full of intertwined highways and enormous parking lots, stores as big as the factories he'd seen in
Chihuahua and Juarez. The traffic grew thick and slow, which helped stop
the car's frantic high-speed shaking, but didn't help the heat. Then, as if out of
mercy for the six of them in that sweltering car, a thick layer of clouds came
in and let go fat drops of rain that popped against the fiberglass roof like a
military drum.

"Los Angeles." The driver extended one of the fingers from around his
beer can and pointed toward the tall buildings in the distance. Jacinto stared at
it for a second, wondering if that was where Chano was, someplace down there
in that sprawling metropolis which back home they referred to as "the second
biggest Salvadoran city." Over the course of this drive, he'd begun to recognize that California was much bigger than he'd anticipated, and that finding

his brother-in-law might be more complicated than going there and looking around.

Through the rain and the near darkness, the driver weaved his way up and around a complicated series of ramps, bridges, underpasses, and overpasses. Jacinto wondered how he could possibly know where they were going. How could all these roads coexist? They seemed to be tied up into concrete knots. He was torn between considering this wide-wayed city a marvel of gringo engineering or simply a maze of pavement gone berserk.

"You been here before, Guanaco?" The driver spoke over his shoulder.

"No, never." Jacinto wondered how this man could possibly have guessed his nationality.

"It's big." He took a sip from his beer. "Big and crazy."

"I'm trying to find my brother-in-law," Jacinto said. "He lives in California."

"Where in California?"

"I don't know," Jacinto admitted. "I have his phone number, but the last two numbers are missing."

"Let me see the number," the driver said.

Happy to stumble into a bit of help, Jacinto passed him the scrap of paper.

"*Hijole!*" The driver shook his head. "This a San Francisco number. That's way up north." He turned and passed it back to Jacinto. "You got a long way to go, brother."

Jacinto stared down at the paper. He felt a little disheartened, but at least he was headed in the right direction.

Once free of the Los Angeles labyrinth, they found themselves on a smaller road. Soon, they had a view of the ocean. This came as a source of tremendous comfort to Jacinto. He'd not seen the Pacific for many months. He thought of Wilmer back in the village, how he might have a view of this same sea from their little parcel. This time of year, the rains would be ending in Carasucia. Perhaps Wilmer was harvesting the last of the beans. The sight of this shoreline, where the dark sea collided with the American landmass, it made Jacinto feel—for the first time in this foreign land—that he had some notion of where he was.

The rain let up as they drove on. Jacinto continued to enjoy the seascape. Wind chopped up the ocean's surface. It took on a flat and reflective sheen under the dull light of the overcast sky. The sun made an appearance through a thin belt of clarity in between the water and the cloud layer at the horizon. As it set, the whole sky turned an eerie mix of reds and blues. The road left the ocean behind and headed inland through the dark. The men all seemed anxious to reach their destination, wherever that was.

*

The old TV was heavy and unwieldy. Wilmer could barely keep it aloft while waiting for the bus to town.

The *cobrador* opened the back for him, and helped to lift the set into a seat near the rear. Wilmer sat down beside it. There was a man in Rosario who dealt in such appliances. Wilmer hoped to get at least fifty *colones*.

At the entrance to the town, only one gangster boarded the bus. It was the same tall one—with the teardrop under his eye—from the last time. Everyone aboard seemed to know the drill by now. Teardrop walked the aisle and collected coins from each of the passengers. Wilmer sat beside the oversized television, several rows behind any other passenger.

Teardrop looked him in the eye and shook a handful of coins in Wilmer's face.

"I have nothing," Wilmer said. "The bus fare was the last cash in our house. I'm taking this TV to Don Rodrigo's, so that we can afford oil and salt. Take it, if you have to." Wilmer realized that what he'd said was true, and that truly, he didn't much care what the gangster did to him.

To Wilmer's surprise, Teardrop's stern face burst into a smile. He winked at Wilmer and punched him playfully on the shoulder. "You worry too much," the gangster said, then turned and left the bus.

*

It was quite late when the car finally turned off the paved road and onto a dirt and gravel driveway. The young Mexican boy from the previous farm had fallen asleep and now his head tumbled on and off of Jacinto's shoulder, the way that Pink Hair's had done months ago.

Finally, they pulled to a stop amongst a couple of other old cars on a strip of dirt surrounded by trees. The driver left the motor running.

"Is this it?" one of the men asked, disappointed.

"This is it." The driver cut off the engine.

From out of the brush and woods, two men emerged, each carrying a flashlight. The driver climbed out and spoke with them. They seemed to know one other. Slowly, the rest of the men left the car. Jacinto tapped the sleeping boy on the shoulder and motioned for him to come with.

The driver and one of the flashlight men were in a hushed but heated conversation. Finally, the two of them turned to the rest of the party and said: "This way, let's go."

The men followed him along a dirt path through the woods, the sounds of insects loud in their ears. It was colder here than Jacinto expected, and he wished he still had the jacket he'd scrounged from that dumpster in Chihuahua.

In spite of the cold, he was happy that they'd ended up in a place like this, far from those crowded and sprawling cities that they'd passed through. He had no experience picking grapes, but was sure he'd learn. This forest forced him to recall the time he'd spent in the jungle with Israel, and how that was, in many ways, the easiest part of this whole trip.

Soon, their narrow path opened up to a broader clearing, full of makeshift shelters. Tarps strung across trees, lean-tos fashioned from scraps of plywood and corrugated metal. It was a full-blown squatter camp, presumably for the laborers of this vineyard. Taking a rough inventory—the cook-fires now smoldering, cots and hammocks strung up haphazardly, bottles of water perched in the trees—Jacinto realized how good he'd had it back at the citrus farm.

They were led to what looked to be an abandoned shelter. There wasn't much of a roof left to it, but there were a few mattresses and hammocks. One of the men with the flashlights showed up carrying a stack of wool blankets.

"Here it is," the driver said to them. "This is where we sleep."

Jacinto took one of the blankets and curled up in a hammock. He didn't know what to make of this situation. The driver obviously had some clout with the men who'd showed them in. Still, he didn't feel welcome. Were these hosts—who'd given them the blankets and a place to stay—working for the farm or simply fellow migrants acting out of kindness?

Despite the cold and the awkward cant of the hammock, Jacinto had little trouble falling asleep.

14

HE WOKE BEFORE THE SUNRISE, BACK ACHING FROM THE NIGHT spent in a short hammock and the previous day spent in a car. Jacinto rose and walked into the woods far enough to take a piss. His fellow travelers still lie strewn in hammocks or on old mattresses atop the dirt. Jacinto decided not to try for more sleep, and instead walked up to the main part of the camp.

An old woman with long braids—in the Indian style Jacinto had seen in Chiapas and Oaxaca—tended a cook fire and a makeshift gas stove. She had a wooden table set up with a couple of mismatched plastic chairs.

"Breakfast, *señor?*" she asked once she saw Jacinto.

"Yes." He sat down.

She brought him a child's plastic cup with sweet coffee. Jacinto heard the familiar sound of eggs hitting hot oil. By the time he was through with the coffee, she served him a plate with two well-fried eggs—their edges brown and crisp—along with four thin tortillas—re-toasted on the stove, a thin black blister in each of their centers. She placed a dish of salt on the table as well.

"Thank you," Jacinto said.

She refilled his coffee.

Jacinto finished the meal in seconds. The sun emerged beyond the hills and trees. Birds squawked to welcome it.

"How much?" Jacinto asked.

"One dollar." The woman held up a single finger.

"Do you have any water?" Jacinto fished money from his pocket.

She fetched him a jar and poured it full from a cleaned-out coke bottle. He placed a bill on the table, then went back to his pocket and weighed it down with one of the odd-shaped coins he'd struggled to learn the value of. Several other men approached, already dressed for work. Jacinto relinquished his seat.

She gathered the money, said "gracias," and cleared away his dishes.

Jacinto milled about while the other workers came out of their shelters. He did his best to stretch his back, reaching his arms up above his head, twisting at the waist. Soon, the other members of his travelling party arrived in the clearing. They all seemed to be waiting for instructions from their driver, who was silent but alert. As a group, all of the workers started off, the night chill not fully gone.

They left their canopy of trees for the vineyard proper. It was quite beautiful, Jacinto thought, these grapevines in the morning: the manicured rows of green, punctuated by red-purple fruit, the golden hills in the background and beyond them a clear sky growing bluer with the rising sun. This was good growing land. Little wonder so many of his countrymen ended up here.

The men gathered by a barn, where a couple of gringo bosses awaited them. A huddle took place between one of the gringos, Jacinto's driver, and the man who'd shown them where to sleep last night. Jacinto recalled his car ride with the Migra—reading the gestures and hand signals, while more powerful men spoke in English about his fate.

The gringo boss looked impatient. The two Mexicans pleaded. Finally, the gringo pointed to one group of waiting workers. He said something in English and signaled them to start work. From the sheltered side of the barn, they each took one from a stack of plastic crates. The rest of them formed a crude line. A few at a time, the gringo ushered them on—like the captain of a schoolyard team picking his players—then slowed down when only Jacinto's party was left. The driver, along with one of the men who'd ridden in the front seat of the car, were given work and told to go on. The other four of them were denied— offered only the gringo's horizontal palm and the apologetic shaking of his head.

"All these grapes," muttered the Mexican boy who'd slept on Jacinto's shoulder last evening.

Though disappointed, Jacinto was glad to have an answer either way.

"Come on." The other man from the front seat of the car was stoic. "We'll go into town, wait for work on the corner. I've done it before. It's best to get there early."

They walked back out the road upon which they'd come. Nobody spoke.

Not long into their walk, an old pickup rumbled its way down the road. At the wheel was a gringo farmer. The man from the front seat, who seemed to know his way around, stuck out his thumb and the driver stopped. The rest of them climbed into the back while their new leader rode shotgun.

It wasn't long before they found themselves on the outskirts of a town. The truck dropped them at a street corner in front of what appeared to be the largest hardware store ever built. Several Latinos stood manning the corner already, and Jacinto didn't need to be told that they were about to join them, in hopes of day labor.

They waited in a rough line, the work served out on a first-come, first-serve basis.

"It's late already," one of the men said as they walked up.

A white van driven by a Chicano contractor came by shortly and took many of the men away, leaving only Jacinto and his cohorts waiting as the day wound down. From the parking lot of the hardware store, a brand-new pickup appeared with a load of lumber in the back. The well-dressed gringo at the wheel held up three fingers.

The four men remaining on the corner—all of them having travelled here from Arizona—looked at each other in confusion. How would they decide who got left behind? Was it possible to negotiate with this gringo, ask him to consider a fourth?

Jacinto looked into the eyes of the young boy he'd ridden beside in the car. "Go ahead. I'll stay here."

Nobody wasted any breath talking him out of it. The three climbed into the gringo's pickup, perched atop the lumber, and offered Jacinto nothing more than a wave as they went off. He sat down on the curb and admitted to himself that the workday was well underway by now, and he'd need to find a place to sleep tonight. At least he'd gotten that good, cheap breakfast when he did.

Shortly into his despair, a vehicle pulled up at the corner, and Jacinto rose to meet it. It was one of those rounded Volkswagen vans, the ones used for public transport in Mexico City. The stereo blasted out a fuzzy brand of rock and roll.

"*Trabajo?*" A young gringo with long blonde hair leaned out the passenger window and shouted.

"Yes." Jacinto wondered how many other Spanish words this man might know.

"Only you?" The gringo spoke with a slow and heavy accent.

"I'm the only one left."

He turned to the driver—who had a bushy brown beard, the rest of his hair pulled back behind his head like a girl's. They exchanged a few words of English. The driver shrugged.

"Do you want to help us?" The passenger asked.

"Yes." Jacinto nodded.

The gringo reached around behind his seat and opened the sliding side door of the van. "*Vamos*," he said.

Jacinto climbed in. The van was a scattered mess of clothes, blankets, and what appeared to be electrical equipment. His two employers were what Jacinto would label hippies—long hair, casual clothes, loud music. They were meant to be lazy; Jacinto wondered what they needed his help for.

"Excuse me," Jacinto asked. "What sort of work will we be doing?"

The blonde turned down a knob on the stereo. "We need to move something big. It's a…" he seemed to struggle for the Spanish word. "Like a piano."

Jacinto nodded. It sounded easy enough, and probably meant riding in the van most of the day.

"I'm called Tomás," the passenger said, then pointed at the driver. "This is Josue." Obviously, he was translating the names for Jacinto's benefit.

"Jacinto." He offered a little wave and smile of greeting to each of them.

"Where are you from, Jacinto?" Tomás seemed to relish the opportunity to practice his Spanish.

"El Salvador." Jacinto thought he might pass for Mexican with these two, but for once there was no need.

"El Salvador!" Tomás turned around in his seat, excited. "La Libertad?" he asked.

"My home is close to La Libertad." Jacinto nodded. "Only forty-five minutes by bus. Much faster in a private car. My wife goes there to buy fish sometimes. In the dry season, the women from my village wash their clothes in a river nearby."

"Very good waves there." Tomás held up both his fists with upward-pointing thumbs. "We are surfers. We go to Mexico at least once a year for waves. Someday, we want to go to El Salvador."

Without meaning to, Jacinto burst into laughter, slapping his knee at the absurdity. "I'm sorry." He regained his composure. "It's funny to me: the idea that a gringo would want to go to my country, considering how many of us come here. I don't mean to laugh."

But Tomás and Josue weren't offended. In fact, they both smiled along with him.

"We love to travel, especially for waves." A song came on the radio that called for Tomás's attention, and he turned it up. Both gringos sang along.

Jacinto leaned into the soft upholstery of his seat, finding this country more bizarre with each passing hour.

Before long, they arrived at a great complex of low buildings used for storage. The van trawled its way down one row of orange doors until Josue spied the one he was after. He killed the motor and unlocked the storage unit. The door slid open with a rumble. Inside, it was packed full of gear. Jacinto didn't see a piano per say, but there were plenty of speakers, cables, and stands.

"*Bueno.*" Tomás walked over to one strange-looking piece, an old case with odd latches and handles, atop of a set of rickety wheels. "This is the heavy one."

They rolled it around to the side door of the van, near where Jacinto had ridden. All the thing's handles were rendered useless by the height of the van off the ground. Their only option was to lift the top-heavy piece by the very bottom, just behind the wheels. On the first attempt, the far end didn't clear the edge of the van, but they juggled themselves around until it worked. Once that was over, it was a simple matter of packing the smaller items in around it.

When they looked to be done, the gringos took two shiny stream-lined boards—like flattened canoes—from the back of the storage unit. "For surfing," Tomás said. There was that word again: this odd art they wished to practice in El Salvador. They strapped the boards to the roof of the van, then locked the door to their unit.

As Josue started up the car, Tomás took out his wallet and offered Jacinto two twenty-dollar bills. Jacinto was shocked. They'd been working for less than one hour. His guess was that they'd be loading and unloading like this all day.

"*Vamos.*" Tomás smiled.

Jacinto nodded and put the bills into his back pocket. They'd been careful to leave a thin column of space along the rear bench seat for Jacinto to sit on. Once again they were off, bouncing around in their van and blasting rock and roll.

"Lunch?" Tomás shouted over the back of his seat.

"Okay," Jacinto said. It was midday, after all, and his appetite had returned.

They stopped at a Mexican restaurant with an outdoor patio. The waitress brought them three menus, glasses of water with ice, a basket of fried tortilla triangles, and a cup of red Mexican sauce. Though the coldness hurt his teeth, Jacinto gulped down his water.

"*Tres Margaritas*," Tomás said to the waitress, without consulting anybody.

Jacinto looked up at him alarmed. He'd hoped to get out of this lunch without spending all the money he'd just made.

"I invite you." Tomás winked, as if reading Jacinto's mind.

On the menu, Jacinto recognized a few of the words from his time in Mexico, and luckily there were pictures of many of the dishes. He settled on one that looked simple and separated, unlike those Mexican specialties where all ingredients come wrapped or cooked together as one, loaded with the spicy sauces so beloved in that country.

Their food order was taken and they received their drinks. Jacinto expected to endure the margarita the way he did with other spirits. Instead, he found it delicious. Sweet and tart, it killed the taste of the alcohol.

"*Salud*," Tomás said, and the three of them clanged their glasses together.

"So." Tomás checked his watch and turned a bit serious. "Do you want us to drop you off at that same corner? I guess you probably won't get more work today. We can take you someplace else if you prefer."

"It doesn't matter." Jacinto now asked the question of himself. "I suppose I'll go back to that corner tomorrow to look for work. But what I really need is someplace to sleep tonight, someplace where I won't be bothered by the police or anybody."

"Wait," Tomás said. "You don't have a home?"

"Not in this country." Jacinto smiled. "I rode along to the vineyards last night in search of work, but there was none. They sent me to the corner."

"Where do you want to go?" Tomás asked.

"I have a brother-in-law somewhere in the northern part of California," Jacinto couldn't remember where the driver had said he was. "I'm trying to find him, but I only have part of his phone number. Jacinto took the piece of paper from his pocket, and placed it on the table between them.

Tomás picked up the scrap and read the eight digits. "This is a four-one-five number. It's in San Francisco. We're playing Santa Cruz tonight." He opened up his hands and raised his shoulders as though this were the simplest thing in the world. "Come with us, and you'll be in the same city as your brother-in-law by tomorrow afternoon."

Just then, the waitress brought out their food. "Careful, hot," she said to Jacinto.

What he'd ordered turned out to be a big production. Onto the table, she plopped down a still-sizzling iron platter, an assortment of meats and vegetables bubbling and trembling upon it. Next, she set down a normal plate with beans and rice and all of those Mexican condiments. Finally, he was given a basket of thin tortillas. Had Jacinto accidentally ordered more than one lunch?

He looked up in embarrassment, expecting to see his gringo friends laugh at him or worse: feel that he'd taken advantage of their invitation. Instead, they were busy eating their own meals.

"But Jacinto." Tomás covered his mouth with a fist. "How did you get here in the first place? Did you come with one of those smugglers?"

Jacinto took another sip of the yellow-green drink. Was it alright to tell them the truth? His first instinct was to be discreet about his ordeal. But he couldn't bring himself to mistrust these two. He was in their hands, at any rate—at their mercy. In exchange for all their generosity, the least he could do was be sincere.

He started from the beginning. He told them how he'd hired Don Noe, only to be lead in circles in the desert until almost all of their party died. He told them about the Bus of Tears, the wreck that resulted in his friendship with Israel. All the hardships and near misses along the way: the gangsters, the coffee farm, stealing food from the dead in Mexico City, sleeping in the squatter camps in Chihuahua, and finally that awful dawn at the mouth of the tunnel, watching Israel die at the very doorway to this nation.

His gringo friends cringed at times, gasped at others, but couldn't look away. Every so often, Josue tapped Tomás and asked for an explanation. Tomás would translate a phrase or two under his breath. Sometimes, Tomás asked Jacinto for clarification, but he followed it all quite well. Their food went cold during the storytelling.

Once they were caught up to the present day, all three turned back to their plates and ate. Jacinto devoured his meal—or meals, really. The drink had given him a tingling light-headed sensation for which food felt like the only cure. He made small tacos with the meat and vegetables, the beans and the cream. The waitress refilled his water regularly. Soon, nothing remained on any of the plates spread out before them. Jacinto hadn't felt this full since the coconut binge he'd had with Israel, one incident which he'd neglected to share with his two new friends.

"That's amazing, your story," Tomás said. "I'm sorry for all you went through."

"It's not your fault." Jacinto smiled.

The waitress brought over their check. Tomás picked it up, while Jacinto went into his pocket for money.

"No *hombre*," Tomás said. "We invite you."

"Thank you," Jacinto said. "I'm lucky to have met you two."

"It's nothing, so long as you don't mind carrying our instruments a few more times tonight."

It turned out that they had a long distance left to drive. The first bit followed the sea, then the road turned inland through a stretch that bisected those same brown and green fields he'd seen earlier, near the vineyards. With the big meal, the drink, and the afternoon sun warming him through the windows, Jacinto fell asleep despite the loud rock music.

*

The transition from morning classes to afternoon classes was a chaotic af-
fair. The overworked teachers said goodbye to the youngest students—some
of whose parents waited outside—while older children made their way reluctantly in to the same desks and chairs. A bottleneck of small bodies formed at
the gate. Wilmer pushed his way through it along with students from his and
other grades, all of them in matching blue pants and white-collared shirts.
From behind, he heard the familiar false whisper of Don Felix's young son,
Moises.

"There goes the orphan," Moises hissed to one of his friends, for Wilmer's
benefit. "His father was such a coward, he turned himself in to the Migra."

The friend from the lower grade giggled, not so much at the statement,
but at the audacity of saying it within earshot of Wilmer. Anger beat inside
Wilmer's chest like a second heart. His limbs trembled.

"Now he's in some jail," Moises could barely keep up the conceit of the
hushed tone, "sucking the dicks of Mexican prisoners."

That was the breaking point. Wilmer's backpack disappeared. He flew
onto Moises. Wilmer didn't waste time striking, but went straight for the
throat. The two of them were about the same height, though Moises was more
solid and thicker limbed.

All around them, children screamed and cleared a space. In an instant,
Wilmer was on the ground atop Moises. Both his thumbs tucked into the folds
of the boy's fleshy neck. Moises's fat hands were on each of Wilmer's forearms,
but their grip slowly grew weaker. Raspy coughs crept their way out from the
Moises's mouth, along with foamy tendrils of saliva. For once, it was Wilmer
who controlled how much air entered into another's lungs.

Several sets of arms suddenly hugged him from behind. Wilmer lost his
sense of up or down. His eyes were covered. His arms were wrapped up and
his body was being carried through the air.

*

When he awoke they again drove along the coast, and for the second time in this country, Jacinto watched the sun set over the ocean. They'd been on the road for over five hours, and must've travelled hundreds of miles. One could cross the whole country of El Salvador in that time. But in California, it seemed an unremarkable thing to do with an afternoon. How long would it have taken Jacinto to travel this far on his own? Meeting these two gringos was a great stroke of luck. He hoped they were right about the city in which Chano lived.

In the dusky light, they drove into a small town and finally came to a low building with a gravel lot. Another carload of hippies waited there for them, and there was an exchange of greetings in the parking lot. Tomás introduced Jacinto to the three others in turn, one of whom spoke Spanish.

Jacinto shivered with the new night's chill. Josue noticed this and immediately dug through the van.

"*Toma*," he said a moment later, the first words of Spanish Jacinto had heard him speak, and offered a warm jacket.

"Gracias," Jacinto replied.

They spent the next hour or so ferrying equipment from the vehicles to a small stage inside the building—which turned out to be a bar of sorts. Jacinto had long since gathered that they were musicians, but all the plugging in chords and taping down wires made him wonder if they weren't some breed of electricians as well.

After an hour or so of setting up, noise finally emerged from the speakers. The sheer volume shocked Jacinto. It was as though they were aiming to entertain people in a bar next door to this one. He'd heard *conjuntos* and *bandas* perform before, mostly at the fiestas in Rosario, but he'd never been this close or heard anything quite this loud.

It began as a cacophony of each different instrument. Josue played that massive item Jacinto had been hired to help them lift, an instrument with keys that sounded something like the accordions from *norteño* bands. Tomás was one of several electric guitar players, and that other Spanish speaker sat in the back at a set of drums. After a few minutes of noise-making, all of them came together to play an actual song. They stopped after a few bars and spoke instructions into the microphone, to a man near the back at a massive control center of switches and knobs. This routine went on for a bit: playing together, then pausing for one member of the band to speak into the microphone, until everyone seemed satisfied and they climbed offstage. It was already dark out and still there were no people inside this bar, other than the musicians, a couple of employees, and Jacinto.

Somebody walked in with several long, flat boxes and spread them out across the wooden counter of the bar. Finally, this was an American food that he recognized: pizza. He'd never eaten it himself but had seen it in movies and television, and knew that it was available in the capital of his own country.

All the musicians dug into it straight away, without plates or utensils. Jacinto watched them eat with an almost anthropological fascination—like one of those nature documentaries he'd seen back home. Only here it wasn't lions or elephants, but gringos—feeding in their natural habitat.

"Jacinto!" A shout came from over his shoulder. "Eat!" It was Tomás, and he was quite insistent.

Jacinto shrugged his shoulders and did as he was told.

More than anything, this food reminded him of pupusas: a bit of dough, cheese, meat, and tomato sauce that could be eaten with one hand. Perhaps such a thing existed in all cultures. It was a treat, nonetheless. Jacinto fancied himself a real international traveler for a second or two, spending time with his gringo friends, eating exotic foods and hearing the foreign music. Once the pizza was done, Tomás placed a big glass of beer in Jacinto's hand.

Soon, people came inside. They paid money at the door and ordered drinks from the bar. All of the musicians disappeared for a while. Jacinto did his best to keep a low profile in one corner, wondering if he was expected to pay for this music as well. The house lights dimmed and the crowd gathered before the stage. They were young people, men and women, some as dirty and unkempt as the band members but some well dressed.

Soon, it was difficult to walk through the bar, as every inch of the floor was covered with people. A spotlight shown on the stage and the crowd let out a rowdy chorus of whoops and hollers. Tomás was the first to walk out from the back. He waved to the crowd and picked up his instrument. The rest of the band followed behind him. Tomás spoke a few words of English into a microphone on a stand, then played a prickly, angular line on his guitar. Soon, the group reached their peak of volume, but somehow it didn't seem as loud with all the bodies filling up the space and making noises of their own.

Jacinto had expected the area in front of the stage to become a kind of dance floor where couples might step and twirl. Instead, the whole crowd undulated back and forth as one, like they were all involved in some bizarre collective dance step. Though chaotic, it did feel less likely to result in fights.

This rock and roll music was not something that Jacinto had ever taken seriously before, but he had to admit that his new friends were good at what they did. He couldn't see any reason why their music shouldn't be on the radio station they'd listened to all day. After a couple of the loud fast numbers, they played a softer song, like a *corrido* or *bolero*, with Josue singing from behind his giant keyboard. It was quite lovely, the slower number. The crowd swayed from side to side. Jacinto wished that he understood the English lyrics—now shouted aloud by several members of the audience as well.

*

Wilmer's teacher took him home. Perhaps they cancelled class for the rest of the day. She treated him as though he were sick, insisting he lay down in the hammock.

"Where's your mother?" she asked.

"Working," Wilmer answered, "at the *maquilas*."

Miriam pulled a plastic chair away from the table and sat down facing Wilmer's hammock. "Now tell me what came over you this afternoon."

Wilmer wished the school would simply punish him for his actions and not waste time fretting over his motives. He didn't want their mercy and didn't care to discuss it. Miriam and the other teachers had always been kind to Wilmer. But now he recognized their affection as something more akin to sympathy. His condition meant he was worthless at sports and physical mischief. This ineptitude was erroneously equated with studiousness.

Wilmer had no desire to be a good pupil anymore. It had gotten him nowhere.

"He talked about my father," Wilmer said. "He's been spreading lies about him for a while now. There was no other way to shut him up." He put on his best stone face.

*

After a false stop followed by relentless cheers and stomps from the crowd, and then another song, the band finally quit playing. Jacinto's eyes stung with the late hour and the cloud of cigarette smoke that hung about the bar. Only after things quieted did he notice the ringing in his ears.

The musicians did a lot of handshaking and conversing with their fans, but wasted little time getting to the business of breaking down their equipment. All of them fetched more beer, and Tomás again shoved one tall glass into Jacinto's hand.

It was just as tedious to get their things packed and reloaded into the van, and the men were all tired and soaked with perspiration. To Jacinto, these might as well have been the most famous musicians in the world. It was humbling to see them all do the grunt work of packing their things up again.

Once all their gear was stowed, it was well after midnight. Jacinto wondered where they planned to sleep. An intense back-and-forth went on in English between the two drivers. Soon, they were caravanning down an empty road.

They stopped at last at a dirt lot on a bluff above a beach, the white of the breaking waves lit up under the moonlight. The group of them stood together and looked down at the sand and the water. There was a moment of agreement in English and then they all went back to their vehicles.

The gringos undertook a whole other kind of unpacking. They used flashlights and carried out blankets and sacks. The other car had a case of beer and a cardboard box filled with firewood. A cold breeze came from off the sea and Jacinto was again thankful that Josue had offered him the jacket. These men must've been as well versed in setting up camp as they were in setting up their instruments. A pair of tents was erected in an instant.

Jacinto made himself useful by manning the fire pit. One of the gringos offered him a pack of matches, and he struggled to light a handful of cardboard scraps in the wind. Eventually, he got it going and the dry hardwood caught easily. The gringos congratulated him on the bonfire, and all of them gathered around it on the sand, nursing cans of beer. One of them had an old acoustic guitar, and strummed out a couple of songs.

One by one, people grew sleepy and went off to bed, some in tents, some in sleeping bags upon the sand. Jacinto was slower in finishing his beer than the others.

"This spot is for you." Tomás, who sat beside him, patted a sleeping bag and bedroll.

"Thank you," Jacinto said.

"Tomorrow, we'll take you to San Francisco."

Jacinto nodded. "Did you all earn money tonight?" he asked.

Tomás shrugged. "Enough to pay for the gas."

"Your music was good," Jacinto said. "The crowd enjoyed it."

"Thanks." Tomás took a long slurp from his beer. "It's what we love to do."

"It's nice," Jacinto said, "the way you do what you want to, with no worry over the profit and the loss involved." Jacinto thought of how few things in his life, how few of his decisions, could be described this way.

"We're lucky," Tomás said.

Jacinto crawled inside the sleeping bag that had been laid out for him, and curled a bit closer to the fire.

15

JACINTO WAS THE LAST TO WAKE IN THE MORNING. THE SMELL of coffee brewing beckoned him out of the sleeping bag. One of the bearded gringos from the band tended to an overflowing pot on a small gas stove. Two of the others stood and pointed towards the ocean. Jacinto rubbed his eyes then followed the line of their fingers. There, out among the waves, were two figures—presumably Tomás and Josue—dressed in black and laying upon those odd watercrafts they'd kept strapped atop the van the whole day before. Jacinto watched them struggle for a minute or two, the waves having their way with them. The other gringos laughed, an indication that they weren't in any real danger.

"Coffee?" The Spanish-speaking drummer turned to Jacinto.

"Please." Jacinto took the warm metal mug in his hands. The coffee tasted strong and bitter, but was delicious after the cold night. One of the standing gringos pointed and exclaimed a word of English. Everyone turned their eyes back to the sea.

Impossibly, Tomás jumped to his feet upon that big board, and descended the watery ramp of an incoming wave. He managed to steer himself up towards the top of the unbroken face, and took a couple of steps forward before the whole thing exploded into foam.

Jacinto couldn't believe his eyes. He watched for another minute and saw Josue perform the same feat. It must've taken these gringos years to learn how to do such a thing. What a life they lived: playing music by night and walking on water during the day.

The drummer turned out to be quite a chef. After the coffee was served, he placed a skillet onto his little gas stove and filled it full of oil, eggs, and cheese.

Eventually, Jacinto and Tomás came in from the water, teeth chattering and lips blue. They stripped out of their rubber suits right there on the sand.

Jacinto stood up and walked to the water's edge. He put a hand in the ocean, wondering if this might be an opportunity to bathe. His fingers went numb upon touching it. This was the coldest water he'd ever felt, colder than the highest of mountain streams he'd touched in Honduras. He didn't know water could reach such a temperature without becoming ice.

"What cold!" he shouted to Tomás, who still shivered inside his dry clothes.

"You see," Tomás shouted back. "That's why we want to go to La Libertad: warm water."

The drummer scooped portions of the cooked eggs onto an assortment of bowls and plates. After the meal they were once again packing and moving. Jacinto, Josue, and Tomás said goodbye to the other carload in the parking lot, and the van headed north.

This time, their route followed the coast. Josue and Tomás pointed and craned their necks at certain beaches, scanning for potential spots to ride more waves. Not long into their trip, a dense fog overtook the road, and made it hard to see anything for minutes at a time. They continued on, hugging curves, crossing high bridges. Jacinto closed his eyes a couple of times, as the vertigo tingled in his fingers and the abyss appeared to shift below him.

In less than an hour, the landscape—hills, sea, fog, and a road—abruptly gave way to a city. The coast still lie on one side, but on the other nearly every hill was now covered with thick clusters of houses and apartments.

The van came to a stop on the shoulder.

"We want to look at the waves," Tomás said.

All three of them climbed out, crossed the street, and stood on the sand dunes staring into the wine-dark Pacific Ocean. A cold wind threw fine grains of sand at their faces.

"Look." Tomás pointed to the north. "That bridge is famous."

Through the fog, Jacinto could barely make out the red iron structure spanning out into the distant headland. Even from this odd angle, he did recognize it from television and magazines. The gringos continued to chatter about the swarming sea.

"*Vamos.*" Tomás put a hand on Jacinto's shoulder. "Too much wind."

Back in the van, Tomás turned down the volume knob and spoke to Jacinto over his shoulder. "We'll take you to the Mission," he said. "It's most likely where your brother-in-law lives. Everyone speaks Spanish there."

Jacinto nodded and said thanks. Soon, he would part ways with these friends, and bring an end to the most enjoyable part of his journey so far.

The city grew taller and denser as they drove on. The fog abated some. Great skyscrapers appeared in the distance. Josue struggled to park the van in a small space, but finally worked it in. The two gringos led the way to a busy street full of foot traffic. *Norteño* music blared from storefronts. Many of the signs were in Spanish. Jacinto was confused for a moment, feeling as if he'd come so far that he'd returned to his native country. If not for the cool weather, he might have thought his trip had been one giant circle.

He followed his friends inside a place that promoted itself as a Salvadoran restaurant. For the first time in months, he recognized items on the menu: *pupusas, sopa de gallina,* even *atole* and *riguas*—things that couldn't possibly be in season right now.

As usual, Tomás ordered a round of drinks. This time it was Regia, the Salvadoran beer that came in a big liter bottle—something Jacinto had almost never indulged in back home. They poured it out into small glasses, and clanged them together with a *"salud."*

For lunch, both gringos ordered *pupusas*—which seemed to be the one Salvadoran food they were familiar with. However, when the waitress—who looked to be from Chalatenango—asked Jacinto for his order, he couldn't resist the *sopa de gallina*: the dish that Mina made whenever they had a hen to spare.

The tortillas arrived first, and Jacinto was glad to see that they were thick and handmade. He could tell by the taste that they were Maseca or some other dry corn flour, but still a great improvement over the thin Mexican version. The soup was full of potatoes and rice, but did have a few fine chunks of meat and vegetables. Egg-shaped bubbles of oil floated atop its surface.

"Gracias." Tomás drew the word out and stared big-eyed at their waitress as he said it.

The young girl blushed and smiled back at him.

Once the waitress left, the meal was silent and somber. Josue rose and paid the bill, without consulting anyone, an act which Jacinto had come to expect but was still grateful for.

"You can keep that jacket." Tomás finished his meal and sat nursing a glass of beer. "It gets cold up here."

"Thanks." Jacinto managed a smile and tugged on the lapel of his new gift.

"Will you be alright?" Tomás asked.

"Oh yes," Jacinto said, understanding how helpless he'd seemed whilst in their care. "Trust me, I've been in far worse situations. Soon, I'll find my brother-in-law." There was a pause in which they each took a sip of their beer. Josue returned to the table. "But I'm sad to say goodbye to you two."

Tomás let out a broad grin. He always seemed afraid of being judged by Jacinto, as though the plight of undocumented workers were some fault of his own.

"Give me that paper with your brother-in-law's number."

Jacinto did as he was told. Tomás wrote another phone number down upon it, and insisted that Jacinto call in the case of any emergency. Jacinto thanked him, but had a hard time believing he would see these two gringos again.

"Well." Tomás looked down at his watch. "We have a long drive back to Santa Barbara," he said.

"Yes." Jacinto nodded. "You should get on your way. I can't thank you enough for everything. When you come to El Salvador to ride waves, you must stay in my house."

Both gringos exploded in laughter.

"My wife will make you some real *pupusas*, much better than this Maseca garbage." He checked to see that none of the restaurant staff listened.

They exchanged a round of hugs and goodbyes. The bell on the door clanged as the two gringos left. Jacinto watched them disappear down the street, then sat back down. A couple inches of beer inside the big bottle was all that was left on their table.

Jacinto poured the rest of the Regia into his glass and pushed the soup bowl—now full of only bones and a spoon—to the other side of the table. He had to think of his next move. There was a little over forty dollars in his pocket. It was enough to try Chano's possible numbers, but if anything went wrong, he'd be flat broke. He could tell from his last couple of restaurant meals that his savings wouldn't feed him for long in this city. First and foremost, he needed to get more income.

The waitress came and cleared away a handful of dishes. Jacinto saw the red, white, and blue logo of his nation's ARENA party hanging from a pendant around her neck.

"Excuse me." He emphasized his Salvadoran accent, something he'd tried to hide until now. "Do you know where one of your fellow countrymen might be able to find work?"

"Psshh." She rolled her eyes. "Everybody looking for work here is one of my countrymen."

Jacinto smiled. "I suppose so. But I thought it might be worth asking."

She stood up straight, a stack of plates in one hand, the empty beer bottle in the other. "Did you just arrive?" she asked in earnest.

"To this city, just now. I crossed the border a couple of weeks ago."

"Those gringos are friends of yours?" That brief flirtation with Tomás must've left an impression.

"Yes, close friends. They are great men, those two." Already, Jacinto felt nostalgia for his days with the surfer-musicians.

"Hold on a second." She carried the dishes to a back counter and shouted "Rigo!"

Jacinto sipped his beer. He couldn't see who she was talking to for a curtain by the kitchen, but he could hear her words: "There's a man here, just arrived, a Salvadoran; he needs work, anything."

She appeared to be listening, and nodded her head a couple of times. A big round man with curly white hair came out from the kitchen wearing an apron. Jacinto was the only customer left in the restaurant.

"You need work?" the big man bellowed.

"Yes, sir," Jacinto said.

"You mind dirt or garbage?"

"No sir."

"You mind working at night?"

"No sir, not at all."

"Can you be back here at sunset?"

"Yes sir, I can. That's no problem."

"See you then."

"Thank you, sir."

The man walked back to the kitchen. Jacinto lifted his glass and drained the rest of his beer. The waitress took a rag and wiped down the oilcloth of the table.

"Thank you," Jacinto said to her as well.

"Don't thank me yet," she said. "You haven't seen the work or the pay."

He smiled, and stood to leave. She put out her hand, and he placed the empty glass in it.

Outside, Jacinto felt good about himself. If he worked through the night, not only would he get paid, but he wouldn't have to find anyplace to sleep. And if it was dirty work, he need not buy new clothes just yet. With about three or four hours to kill, he decided to get the lay of the land.

As Tomás had said, the place was populated almost exclusively by Latinos. Pawn shops, taco stands, and bodegas all bore their signs in Spanish and catered to Mexican and Central American clienteles. He felt a little sleepy from the beer and the big meal, but worried it would be impossible to find anyplace to nap before the start of his job. Finally, he found a bench in a small plaza, and sat down to rest his feet.

*

Wilmer's mother came home late. He carried out her supper, and a smaller plate of reheated tortillas. From the evangelical church, a slow and repetitive hymn drifted in. Renegado curled up upon the dirt floor underneath the table.

Wilmer watched his mother eat. She was tired, her back stiff, the tips of her fingers pricked by the needles she'd handled all day. Neither of them spoke as she wolfed down her dinner. As the minutes went on, Wilmer could make out the lyrics of the hymn they overheard, something about the Holy Spirit, and the singer's trials soon coming to an end.

Suddenly, the distant choir was interrupted by the bouncy accordion riffs and oom-pah rhythms blasting through car speakers. Renegado rose and made a grumbling sound.

"Don Noe," Wilmer's mother said.

Wilmer stood up and knocked his plastic chair backward.

"Niña Mina." The *coyote* walked in, louder and more shameless than usual. "We can do this the easy way, or the hard way."

Wilmer could tell that he was drunk simply by smell, but the slurred speech and stumbling swagger offered further proof.

"What are you doing inside my house? At this hour!" Mina rose and waved her hands. Over the years, she'd used this technique to shoe away intruding *bolos*, as though they were confused livestock. But Wilmer could tell that the *coyote* wasn't that far gone.

By the wrist, Don Noe grabbed one of the hands Mina waved in his face. He twisted it hard so that Mina gasped. "I'm here to collect my interest is all."

"Get your fucking hands off my mother!" Wilmer grabbed the *coyote*'s forearm, a thick and hairy trunk of flesh bigger around than Wilmer's thigh. He pulled downward with all his weight. His eyes pinched shut with the effort. Renegado barked. The ground disappeared underneath Wilmer's feet. The cool dirt of the floor rose to meet his back. Next, a stinging pain on one side of his face, and a warm salty wetness inside his mouth.

When he looked up, Don Noe stood over him. That same stiff scorpion jiggled at his belt buckle; that same small revolver pointed at Wilmer's face.

"Listen to me, boy." The *coyote*'s eyes were bloodshot; a few greasy strands of hair hung before them. "I've told you before not to trifle in grown-up affairs, but you don't listen."

By now, Wilmer wasn't looking into the fat face. His gaze focused squarely on the revolver. From this angle, he could see bullets in each of the chambers. He could see that overstuffed sausage of an index finger, which needed only to budge a few fractions of an inch in order to end his life.

"Here, here! Get out of my house! Take it and go, you without shame!" Wilmer's mother waved a wad of bills in front of the *coyote*'s face. He moved the gun to his side and stood up straight. Though the scent of liquor still drifted from his pores, he didn't seem as impaired as when he first walked in.

Wilmer leaned up on one elbow and licked the wound on his lip.

"Get out already!" Mina screamed.

Don Noe shoved the money in his back pocket without counting it. "I've told you before, Niña Mina: there is an easy way to settle this debt." He turned to leave, muttering as he went: "Loyalty to a husband she won't ever see again, *que jodido.*"

An engine gunned hard and was followed by loud *norteño.* Wilmer rose and went out to the road. Behind him, Renegado followed, looking confused. Uphill, the taillights of the *coyote's* truck still showed, illuminating the *EXODUS* script through a cloud of dust. The evangelicals walked back to their homes, white shirts and headscarves shining under the moon.

"Fucking hypocrites!" Wilmer said. To seal the curse, he spat a mix of saliva and blood onto the dirt.

*

Jacinto arrived at dusk and stood outside the restaurant. He hoped for some free food or perhaps a cup of coffee, but didn't count on it.

The big man from before—Rigo—came outside along with one other young man. He lit a cigarette and said. "He should be here soon."

Jacinto had no idea who "he" was, but got the impression that this new young man was also waiting for work.

A rattling old pickup truck stopped on the street in front of them but didn't kill the motor. A dark-skinned man got out of the driver's side and went straight to Rigo. The two of them shook hands, spoke in soft voices, then the driver gave Rigo a handful of bills.

"Did you just arrive?" The other waiting worker asked Jacinto.

"To this city, yes," Jacinto said. "Earlier today." He kept his eyes on the exchange between the two bosses, not liking the looks of things.

"I'm Hernán," the new co-worker said. "From Guatemala."

Jacinto turned and shook the man's hand. He was young and short, with straight shining black hair and a wide grin that reminded Jacinto of Israel's.

"Jacinto, from El Salvador."

"*Vamos!*" the driver of the pickup said. He had an odd accent, perhaps from Cuba or Panama. All three of them crammed into the cab of the pickup truck. Thankfully, Hernán rode in the middle. Jacinto hoisted his feet up over piles of food wrappers and tools scattered about the floor.

"Okay." Their new boss spoke mostly to himself in a sort of droning chant. "We're going to work now. These men want to work." He struggled to shove the stick shift into gear.

What the job turned out to be was a cleaning service for several local restaurants and stores. In most cases, they spent hours scrubbing grime and hairballs out of the honeycombed rubber mats that covered the kitchen floors of this city. They started with a couple of butcher shops and a fish market. Then as the hour grew later they moved on to an upscale grocery store and delicatessen.

The work was dirty, as promised, but also wet. The front sides of Jacinto's pants and jacket got soaked in filthy water. His eyes and sinuses stung from the harsh cleaning agents. His fingertips grew raw and withered. Their boss never introduced himself but his clients all referred to him only as "El Negro." He seemed to have a firm command of English, as well as an encyclopedic knowledge of where they were going and at what time.

Before midnight, they took a break at the same street where they'd all met up. At a stand on one corner, a woman sold coffee and bacon-wrapped hot dogs. Jacinto ordered one of each, hoping for a second wind.

The exhaustion caught up with him during their short break. Now, they were on to restaurants and bars. In one place, they were asked to clean out the grease traps, a chore which left Jacinto's new jacket covered in an oily black film. Though he prided himself as a hard worker, this night was a trial for Jacinto. He wasn't used to being cooped up inside for long hours with all those chemicals and kitchen steam. Hernán proved to be a good kid with a decent work ethic, and wasn't squeamish about the filth, but the night hours broke his endurance.

Jacinto felt that he'd nearly worn his mop out as he finished up a floor they'd been promised was "la ultima." His eyes closed as he pushed it across the tiles of this small and nasty bar, stopping to bend over and pick up a few bits of broken glass.

"That's it; we're done already!" called El Negro in his raspy voice.

Outside the bar, the soon-to-rise sun turned one edge of the sky orange. They loaded their mops, brooms, and brushes into the back of the truck. Their boss passed them each a handful of bills. Jacinto counted them quickly and flew into a rage.

"Thirty dollars!" he shouted. "I made more than this in two hours!" This was true, considering what the hippies had paid him for the move.

"Tomorrow you'll make fifty." El Negro was unperturbed. "I had to pay Don Rigo his share." He took the lit cigarette from out of his mouth and shrugged. "Finder's fee."

Hernán looked at Jacinto, as if awaiting instructions. Jacinto turned back to the bills in his hand. There was nothing to be gained by fighting over this.

"See you tonight," Jacinto said to El Negro, then turned and walked off down the street.

From the sounds of the footsteps on the sidewalk, he gathered that Hernán was following him. Jacinto didn't mean to be rude, but he wasn't feeling social. More importantly, he had no friends or resources in this town, and could be of no help. They'd each be better off, Jacinto reasoned, if they went their separate ways and regrouped tonight.

Looking for a place to rest, Jacinto turned off the main drag onto a quieter street. His shoes sloshed with mop-water. After a couple of blocks he found a great green park, full of trees and ball courts, even a public bathroom. It was nearly empty at this hour of the morning. Jacinto wasted no time finding an inconspicuous spot to lie down. He took of his shoes and placed them in the sunshine by his head, then drifted off into an exhausted sleep.

16

IT WAS LATE MORNING, NEARLY MIDDAY, WHEN JACINTO WOKE up. A strong section of sun shone through the clouds. He propped himself up on one elbow. The park was now full of people. Most of them lay on blankets or bits of cloth chatting to one another. Some played odd games—throwing balls or slinging a round disc. In a circle, three thin gringos bounced around an imaginary football—off their knees and toes, sometimes their shoulders or heads. Jacinto blinked his eyes a couple of times and saw that they were, in fact, kicking around a tiny beanbag.

"Ice cream!" a voice shouted in Spanish. A Latino man stood above Jacinto, a Styrofoam cooler hanging from his shoulder. "Ice cream, *amigo?*"

"Yes," Jacinto said. Some quick calories might help him take on this day.

The vendor took his money and served him a pre-packaged vanilla cone coated in a shell of hard chocolate. Jacinto thanked him. The vendor smiled and moved on.

To the touch, Jacinto's shoes had dried. He rubbed his bare toes through the warm grass and watched the gringos play their games. The ice cream was sweet and cold across his tongue.

Once the cone was finished, he checked his feet for funguses or blisters and put his shoes on. He walked to that same familiar main drag—Mission Street—and went into the first bodega he came to. Armed with another pre-paid calling card, he found a pay-phone on the corner.

Once again, Jacinto went through the same humiliating ritual: dialing the different possible numbers while those that answered either hung up, spoke only English, or told him in his own language that there was no Chano there.

The card was soon spent and Jacinto wasn't yet halfway through the possible combinations. He walked back to the bodega, bought an egg sandwich and a coffee, and counted out the rest of his money. There was just enough to buy another card, but that would leave him without much cushion. With all he'd spent calling numbers, he could've sent a sizeable chunk back to Carasucia already.

Several hours still stood between Jacinto and his appointment with El Negro's cleaning service. For lack of a better idea, he walked back toward the park, hoping for a bit more rest. On his way, he overheard an argument in his own language. He stopped to listen and realized that he was in front of the supermarket that he'd cleaned last night.

"Go on!" one voice yelled. "Give me back that apron and get out of here!"

The speaker stepped from out a garage door beside the storefront. The man that he'd been yelling at stepped out as well. He chucked a wadded-up white cloth in his boss's chest. Jacinto saw that the fired man's eyes were squinted and bloodshot.

"*Pinche marijuanero!*" the boss muttered. He was tall, with wavy hair stuck fast to his head.

"Excuse me." A surge of opportunism rose in Jacinto's chest. "If you need a worker, I can help."

The man was taken aback. He gave Jacinto a once-over, from his toes up to his head. "Do I know you from somewhere?"

"I cleaned this place last night. El Negro brought me by. We did your floors and the rubber mats."

"Right, El Negro." The boss nodded. "If you can put up with that *pendejo*, I suppose you can put up with me."

"I'm a good worker," Jacinto said.

The man held the balled-up apron out to him. "Wash your hands."

This new boss was called Eduardo and came from Mexico City. He let Jacinto loose on several deliveries that had backed up in the small storage bay behind the garage doors. Jacinto carried a load of cow and pig parts into a walk-in freezer. His apron grew bloody and damp, but he was glad that the work was dirty; it justified his filthy clothes. Eduardo showed him where to stack a load of canned beverages. The concrete hallways that made up the store's innards were all lined with ceiling-high stacks of non-perishables.

Later, a small load of produce came in, and for the first time Jacinto was asked to enter the actual store. It was a simple matter of stocking garlic and onions, but it made him self-conscious. He worried that the customers might ask questions in English, or that his dirty clothes and mop-water scent might offend the real employees. The space itself was overwhelming. The noise of cash registers, the rip of butcher paper, and the chatter of customers all made for a loud din. The products closed in around him. Jacinto finished the garlic and onions then went back to the garage for a new assignment.

"Well done," Eduardo admitted. "You work twice as fast as that kid I sent home today." He took fifty dollars from his pocket and handed it to Jacinto.

"Can I come back tomorrow?"

Eduardo sighed. "Can you get some decent clothes?"

"Of course." Jacinto nodded vigorously. "Right away."

"What about a social security card?" Eduardo looked from side to side, as if concerned that somebody might overhear them.

"I don't know what that is."

"It's like identification, a little cardboard thing with your name and a number."

"Oh." Jacinto shook his head. "I thought you understood. I'm..." He swallowed. "I'm not here legally."

Eduardo let out a short, sharp laugh. "You think I don't know that, *cabrón?* I'm not as dumb as I look." He smacked Jacinto playfully on the shoulder then re-lowered his voice. "But you need a fake one if we're going to take you on full-time. They're not hard to get. But keep it between us."

Jacinto nodded.

"Look," Eduardo said. "There's a place up on Mission. That way." He pointed. "Their sign says 'Soledad Hotel.' You go there. Tell them you need a shower. If you want, they can give you a room for the night. Once you're inside, ask about a social security card. As long as you have it by the end of the week, you should be fine."

*

The rumors were true: the Mara Salvatrucha had taken over Rosario's school grounds. The police must've cut their losses and let them have it.

Wilmer walked up in his stiffest pair of blue jeans. He'd drunk several strong cups of coffee before leaving home; his bowels felt loose and jittery. This is the only way, he told himself again at the chain-link gate. Thirteen seconds. It's not so long. He'd gone without air for longer than that.

At the gate, a boy even younger than him—with "MS-13" tattooed across his bird chest—said: "What the fuck do you want?"

"I need to talk to him." Wilmer pointed to Teardrop, who stood against the wall at the far end of the courtyard.

Teardrop nodded and motioned for the young doorman to let Wilmer in.

No wall was left without graffiti. One long "Mara Salvatrucha" spread across the main classroom building. The numerals "13" were everywhere, done with every manner of ornate script. Cartoon hands—with long demonic fingernails—flashed gang signs along the buildings.

Most of the young *mareros* were inside one old classroom. They'd pushed all the desks out of the way and played cards on what had once been a teacher's table.

"What are you doing here?" Teardrop appeared to remember Wilmer.

"I have a problem," Wilmer said. "And there's nowhere else I can go."

"You know how this works, don't you?" Teardrop had his back and the sole of his foot against the cinderblock wall. A t-shirt was draped over one shoulder. His eyes wouldn't look straight at Wilmer, and instead scanned the grounds—this kingdom of his.

"I know about the most basic," Wilmer admitted.

"You can't fight back. You can't beg for mercy. You can't defend yourself. You endure, and nothing more."

Wilmer nodded. Put that way, their initiation ritual didn't sound so unfamiliar.

"You sure this is what you want?"

Wilmer nodded again.

"What kind of problem do you have anyway?"

From behind them, the card game erupted into a roar of hoots and giggles.

"There's a man who threatens my mother." Wilmer neglected to say who the man was. "He has a gun; I don't."

"And your father?"

"My father is no longer with us."

Teardrop looked at Wilmer for the first time during the entire exchange. "Look, go home tonight. Sleep in your bed. If you're still sure in the morning, come back this same time tomorrow."

Wilmer looked down at his feet and didn't hide his disappointment.

"This here is permanent," Teardrop said. "Better to doubt now than later."

＊

If Jacinto expected some kind of a humanitarian effort aimed at helping immigrants, he was promptly disillusioned. The Soledad Hotel was a seedy small-crime operation geared to profit from undocumented workers. The poorly lit interior smelt of mildew. A nasty carpet held together the floor of what might be called the lobby.

"What can I do for you?" A woman in heavy eye makeup sat behind a scratched desk and lit a cigarette.

Jacinto took a seat in the chair across from her. The clothes he'd purchased on the way over rested inside a plastic bag upon his lap. "I need a card, the identification. Social security?" the term sounded funny as it came out of his mouth.

She took a yellow legal pad out from a desk drawer and told him to write his name down clearly.

"Just the social security? No driver's license?"

"I don't know how to drive." Jacinto was puzzled. "But I would like to take a shower."

The woman smiled and exhaled smoke. "One hundred dollars."

The figure was like a punch to the stomach for Jacinto. "I don't have that much."

"It takes a few days." She wasn't surprised. "Give us twenty-five now and we'll get started. I'll throw in the shower for free."

By now, Jacinto was doubly suspicious of down payments, but saw no alternative. He trusted Eduardo, and didn't want to lose the store job. With the shirt and pants he'd just purchased, there would be only a few dollars left. If he continued to make fifty per day, he'd have to save almost everything to pay off this silly fake card. It would be a while before he could try Chano's number again, let alone send anything to El Salvador.

"Alright," Jacinto said. He had the exact change and handed it over to her.

She wrote down "twenty-five paid" next to his name on the yellow pad. "You can use the one down the hall. The water is nice and hot."

Inside the bathroom, Jacinto locked the door. He stripped off his soiled and stinking pants and Mexican football jersey and shoved them into the wastebasket. With a bar of soap, he made some sudsy water in the sink and let his old underwear—the phone number at the waistband well frayed—soak.

Jacinto took the first hot shower of his life. It stuck him as a cross between a great feat of engineering and a colossal waste of resources. Perhaps this entire nation could be described that way. At any rate, the hot water did rid him of the cold damp feeling he'd carried around since the night before. He found a kind of scrub brush on the rim of the tub, and used it to grind the layers of black filth from off his skin. He soaped up head-to-toe several times, and still the lines of water that went down the drain looked grey and grainy.

The towel that hung on a hook by the door felt as though it had been used by others, but Jacinto managed to get dry. In the cabinet behind the mirror, he found a pair of small, dull scissors. He checked the lock on the door again, wiped condensation off the mirror, and gave himself a crude and hasty haircut. Into that same wastebasket he chucked handfuls of his matted hair. Hiding underneath his old clothes Jacinto spotted a flattened tube of toothpaste. He retrieved it, picked the hair off of it, rolled it up, and managed to squeeze out a single short bead. With his forefinger, he gave his teeth a long overdue cleaning.

Finally, he put on the fake designer jeans and the second-hand button-down shirt that he'd bought on the way over. It was as clean as he'd been in months. He rinsed his underwear, and rang out all the water that he could. He'd keep the warm jacket that the hippies had given him, of course. He placed the still damp underwear inside the plastic bag where his new clothes had come, and tucked the bundle into one pocket of his baggy jacket.

Somewhere in the back of his head, Jacinto must have known that the shower was a sort of last luxury before this night. He wouldn't go back to El Negro. It wasn't worth soiling his clothes. He couldn't show up at the store that dirty and tired again. Now, as clean as he'd been in months, Jacinto would have to spend the night on the street.

He thanked the woman as he left the hotel, said that he would see her in a couple of days. His only plan was to return to the park and hope not to be hassled by the police.

But this too unraveled as Jacinto opened the hotel door. A heavy rain fell all over the city. The hustlers and homeless that normally populated this street were all gone or running for cover. Sleeping in the park was not an option.

Jacinto paused under the awning of the hotel. Even if he had the money on him, it would be hard to justify paying for a room, what with all his other expenses. A few blocks up the street, he saw an elevated section of freeway. Cars and trucks cornered up above, sending out fans of rainwater. Jacinto pulled up the collar on his coat, shoved his hands deep into the pockets, and ran.

Only one other homeless man was set up under the wedge of dry space below the overpass. Inside a kind of lean-to made from a tarp, he didn't rise or look out. Surely, others would join them as the night went on.

Jacinto walked up the angled pavement of the overpass a little. He used his once-clean hand to brush away some of the dirt and pebbles. Gingerly, he sat down, not wanting to grind dirt into his pants. From his pocket he pulled out the wet bundle of underwear and plastic. He lay down and placed it under the back of his head. Before falling in to an exhausted, dreamless sleep, Jacinto's last thought was this: At least if I get robbed tonight, I have nothing on me worth taking.

17

JACINTO WOKE IN THE MORNING WITHOUT INCIDENT. A FEW
other homeless bodies were strewn about under the overpass—all of them
with some manner of mat or blanket. Jacinto stuck out as a rough-sleeping
amateur.

He rose to his feet and brushed the dirt from his pants. With no idea of the
actual time, he could tell the sun would break the horizon soon. It looked to be
a clear day.

For such a big city, San Francisco took its time waking up. Jacinto struggled to find a cup of coffee, and finally succeeded in one of the bodegas along
Mission Street. He checked the clock on the wall and saw that he had half an
hour to kill before Eduardo expected him. After the coffee, Jacinto was left
with only a few dollars and decided against breakfast.

"You're early," Eduardo said.

Jacinto shrugged.

"Come on in. Hungry?"

Inside, Jacinto was shown where to hang his coat. An overloaded box
of sweetbread sat on a small table in the storage bay. Jacinto gathered that
they were from yesterday and hadn't sold. The smell roused his hunger and he
wasn't bashful. He wolfed down two of the filled pastries in quick succession,
not bothering to notice how they tasted, and then licked the sugar from his
fingers.

"Okay," Eduardo said. "First thing: produce."

With boxes of fruit, Jacinto headed out to the shop floor straight away. He
didn't feel as self-conscious this time around, now that he was clean and the
store was less crowded.

He stocked several loads of citrus—oranges, lemons, grapefruits. Jacinto wondered if he'd picked any of these fruits, and which were still in season. Over the course of the morning, he noticed that the prices in this store were higher—much higher—than he expected. The gringo customers browsed the aisles aimlessly, as though unsure what to buy. As he put away fruit, he did the math. With what it would cost to buy eggs and bread from this store, he could buy several prepared egg-and-cheese sandwiches from one of the bodegas along Mission. What sense did that make?

After several hours of produce, Eduardo asked if he was ready for lunch.

With some hesitation, Jacinto nodded out a yes. Eduardo disappeared into the store for a moment. To Jacinto's relief, he came back with two sandwiches and said nothing about their cost.

"You'll need to eat early here," Eduardo said, "before the kitchen gets busy with the noon rush."

"That's no trouble," Jacinto said.

They sat on a couple of upside-down buckets in the storage bay and tucked into the meal.

"Did you go see the Soledad?" Eduardo asked.

"I did." Jacinto made an effort not to eat too fast. "I should be sorted out by the end of the week."

Eduardo nodded and held a fist in front of his full mouth. "Do you know any English?"

"No," Jacinto admitted. "I haven't done much work around actual gringos."

"It wouldn't hurt, if you could learn a little."

"Can I ask you something?" Jacinto said. "Isn't this store quite expensive?"

Eduardo laughed out loud. "Don't say that to the boss."

"Seriously though: I don't know about wine, or the fancy meats, but things like bread and eggs, fruits and vegetables—it must be twice the price."

"You're from El Salvador, right?"

"That's right," Jacinto said.

"In your county, do the rich people eat beans three times a day, the way that the poor people do?"

"I suppose not."

"It's the same here, the same everywhere. People want the best; they pay for it. We might think they're wasting money. But this is food, *cabrón*. You put it in your body. Makes more sense than cars or jewelry, don't you think?"

Jacinto took another bite of his sandwich, worried that he'd insulted Eduardo's profession.

"Shit," Eduardo said. "If rich gringos were to stop throwing their money at overpriced things, a lot of us guys would be out of work."

"You're right, of course," Jacinto said. "Also, they say that hunger is the sweetest sauce, and because the poor never lack that they always eat heartily. Maybe wealthy folks need richer food, to make up for it."

Eduardo laughed. "Who told you that?"

"A friend," Jacinto said. He finished his sandwich and got back to work.

*

As Wilmer walked once again up the road to the former high school, he didn't feel as though he were making a decision. Bad or good, right or wrong—such things weren't part of the equation. Choice was one of those luxuries—like airplane travel—that might be available to gringos or San Salvadorans, but not to people like him.

This time, Teardrop met him at the gate. "Once you cross this, there's no turning back; get it? Go home now if you're not up for it." The gangster turned and looked over his shoulder, to check that none of his colleagues heard.

"I have no alternative," Wilmer said. "Let's get this part over with already."

Teardrop stepped aside and swung open the chain-link gate.

A gaggle of tattooed teenagers emerged from out one of the classrooms and assembled in the schoolyard. M and S and the number thirteen were written on all of their bodies, mostly their foreheads and chests. Lazy, full of vice, without shame—that's how Wilmer's mother might describe them. But all Wilmer could think was: at least they can protect each other. At least they're not helpless.

"*Oye chicos!*" Teardrop spoke to a rapt audience. "*Pobre* Wilmer wants to become one of us."

The boys all smiled and nudged each other.

"And as you all know, there's only one way in."

What followed was a half second of silence, and then: "One!"

Wilmer's world went sideways. His ear rang and he felt the cool pavement of the courtyard against his cheek.

"Two!"

The calls came in unison. The beating was a blizzard of sneakers and steel-toed boots, elbows and knees.

"Three!"

Wilmer's own head suddenly seemed enormous, too big to cover with his tiny arms.

"Four!"

Almost halfway through, he felt his lungs constrict. Every second was like a year, and his air passages needed no time to close completely.

"Five!"

It made the blows seem secondary, a minor irritation compared to the impossibility of drawing oxygen. His vision became an out-of-focus blur.

"Six!"

Wilmer ignored the kicks coming at him from all sides. Unable to see, he went to his knees and hands, hoping for some position that might allow a breath.

"Seven!"

One arm was kicked out from under him; he was back to a fetal position. The wheezes were audible even over the ringing in his ears.

"Eight!"

A swift kick went straight to his diaphragm. That's it, Wilmer thought. Winded and with no way in for even the smallest breath. This is how he'd die.

"*Ya basta!*" A lone voice came in place of the collective countdown. "Jesus, we don't want to kill him."

Wilmer felt himself be lifted by his shoulders until he was standing. His lungs were buried underground. Slower than ever, he felt a couple of those imaginary ants excavate his chest.

Once he drew a real breath, his vision returned like an old TV catching a signal. He found himself seated on a bench at one end of the schoolyard, Teardrop standing over him.

"Fucking hell! What happened to you?"

"I have a problem." With his finger, Wilmer drew a line in the air, up and down between his mouth and chest. "With my lungs."

"I'll say you do."

The other gangsters made their signs and patted each other on the back, congratulating themselves on the rigor of their initiation.

"Did I make it?" Wilmer asked.

"No," Teardrop said. "Not even ten seconds. Go home now before I lose any more face."

As Wilmer left the schoolyard, he felt the network of bruises and cuts running all up and down his body for the first time. How would he explain them to his mother? He had failed even in the task of becoming a confirmed fuck-up.

*

After lunch, the produce tapered off. Some canned goods arrived and needed to be stacked along the hallways. Another load of beef to the walk-in. A truck dropped off a cooler full of whole fish. Eduardo instructed Jacinto to take an armful of them into to the kitchen for somebody named Alberto.

This was Jacinto's initial trip to the kitchen, the rear-most part of the store. He was surprised, first of all, by how many people were crammed into it and working away within such a small space. Second, he was shocked to see gringos and Latinos working side-by-side, speaking a chaotic mix of English and Spanglish.

"Alberto?" Jacinto asked.

Everyone in the kitchen suddenly went quiet. The other employees all turned to stare at Jacinto.

"Over here." A voice answered in Spanish. "You can put those down right here." Alberto was a big man holding a knife. He motioned to the stainless-steel table in front of him, a surface covered in blood and rags.

Jacinto did as he was told, and dropped the fish. He felt as if he were on stage, all those workers watching.

Alberto thanked him and Jacinto turned and left. As he passed through the door to exit the kitchen, their giggles and chatter started up again.

Back at the storage bay, the day's deliveries appeared to be over. Jacinto swept the concrete floor.

"Those guys in the kitchen," he said to Eduardo. "Do they have something against me, against Salvadorans maybe?"

"Don't mind them," Eduardo said. "Everybody gets a little odd around newcomers. People start to think they own things, you know. There are only so many jobs. It makes people nervous to see more workers coming all the time, workers willing to do more for less. You stay here long enough, you'll start acting the same way."

"I don't plan to stay that long," Jacinto said it to the handle of his broom as much as anybody.

Once they finished, Eduardo again handed Jacinto fifty dollars cash.

"We'll do it like this until the end of the week," Eduardo explained. "Once you get that card, we'll fill out some paperwork and then it's once a week, understand?"

"Thank you," Jacinto said.

As he left the store, Jacinto's mission was to find some bedding and a cheap dinner. He checked in a couple of dumpsters on his way back towards the main drag, but found nothing promising. As it grew dark, he broke down and went into the secondhand store where he'd purchased his shirt the day before. There he bought a wool military blanket for two dollars. Inside of a plastic bag, he carried his bed toward the overpass. He stopped at a Mexican restaurant on the way and ordered a burrito to go. While he waited, he filled his pockets with napkins and his belly with ice water from a pitcher that sat on the counter beside a stack of plastic cups.

Once again, he was among the first occupants at the overpass and staked out a good spot higher up the ramp. He sat eating his burrito and offering stink-eye to any passersby who stared too long. Dinner over, he salvaged a bit of cardboard from the dumpster across the street.

He made a mattress from the flattened boxes, a pillow from his shoes plus a pile of napkins and plastic bags, and covered himself up with the scratchy wool blanket. Jacinto wondered how many nights he'd spend like this, and how many blocks away his brother-in-law lived.

*

Mina didn't return home until late, for which Wilmer was thankful.

After the workday, she seemed too tired to scream. Instead, his mother looked over Wilmer's face—the blackened eye, the split lip, the bruises that streaked his neck—then collapsed into the plastic chair and wept, her face down in her elbow.

"Moises?" she asked after a few seconds.

Wilmer nodded. He hadn't planned this lie, but now realized how harmless and fitting it was. And to seal his mother's sympathy, he added: "He spread lies about my father again."

Mina sobbed a bit more, but didn't show anger.

Wilmer went to the kitchen and brought out the supper he'd saved for her: beans, hard cheese, re-toasted tortillas. She thanked him, rubbed her eyes, and dug in. Between mouthfuls, Mina kicked off the shoes and wiggled her toes.

"Who would imagine..." She paused, half a tortilla still in her hand, her eyes puffing but tearless. "Your father goes off to suffer in the north—for your health." She pointed at Wilmer with her lips. "And you find other ways to destroy yourself."

"What has my father done for my health?" Wilmer's emotions got the better of him. His whole ruse had been based on defending his father's name. "He left months ago. I still have no medicine. We have more debt than ever. We'll be the last house in Carasucia without water. How does that help anyone?"

Mina sighed and broke up the dry cheese with the back of her fork. "He tried," she said. "One controls little more than one's intentions. He set off to help you. What happens along the way..." She shrugged. "What could he do about that?"

Wilmer didn't agree, but felt bad for forcing the issue after her hard day of work. He didn't want to clean his teeth, what with the split lip, and so lay down in the hammock while his mother finished eating. The bruises rang with a pain much worse than he'd let on. He winced as he lay back and waited for the hammock to settle into position.

*

The rest of the week went on like this. Jacinto arrived early at the store, did as he was told, and kept a low profile. He drew some realizations about this sort of work. While not as backbreaking as fruit picking or construction, it caused a separate sort of exhaustion. One had to maintain a state of smiling alertness. The kind of sighing or bellowing or spitting or farting that was all but expected in the fields was not tolerated here. And the cleanliness presented a constant challenge.

But it was a good job, all in all. He was lucky to have it. The fringe benefit of free food had already saved him many hours of wages. Eduardo's help with the process of false legality was invaluable. Perhaps, Jacinto thought, he would succeed in this country after all.

18

AFTER HIS FOURTH DAY OF WORK AT THE MARKET, JACINTO had enough to pay off the social security card. Eduardo sent him home with a box of expired fried chicken. A hard rain fell on each side of the overpass. The same old man lay beneath his lean-to. Jacinto thought of this man as the Mayor of the overpass. In the past several days, he and Jacinto had established an unspoken peace based on little more than not bothering each other. During the workday, Jacinto hid his blanket and cardboard bedding amongst the iron beams of the overpass, and the old man didn't touch them. In fact, he may have looked after them. The old man offered a non-confrontational nod each evening as Jacinto retrieved his bedroll, and that was the limit of their communication. Tonight, Jacinto considered offering some of his chicken, but feared this might cross some invisible line.

The other homeless were mostly docile or mentally ill. They didn't seem to suffer from a lack of food, and pushed carts full of picked garbage. Many were timid, harmless to Jacinto. The ones he worried about were the young people, those without carts. They came and went, not staying the night, writing graffiti upon the concrete or gathering in anxious circles to share drugs.

As he sucked the last dry meat off his chicken bones, Jacinto kept a close eye on one such group, laughing loudly and pretending to fight each other. They were three—two white and one black. They all wore long military-style coats and torn jeans. Their hair was close cropped, ears full of metal studs. Jacinto guessed they'd taken a drug that made them restless and twitchy. He was thankful once they finally moved along.

That night, Jacinto lie awake in his makeshift bed for awhile. His immediate financial goal—paying off the fake social security card—would be fulfilled in the morning. Now he had some decisions to make. From here on, he'd be paid only once a week. Should he buy another phone card and try to contact Chano? Should he find a room to rent? Should he go ahead and send money back to Mina and Wilmer? Faced with these options, Jacinto realized how much of the household decision-making his wife had always handled. He'd never bothered to ask the price of anything other than the crops they took to market.

After all these worries had gone in circles through his mind, the drumming of the rain lulled Jacinto into an exhausted sleep.

The second that the ruckus woke him, Jacinto's hand went straight for the wad of bills at his crotch. He braced himself for a blow and used his elbow to cover the exposed half of his ribcage. And though he heard the sound of a boot to his side—the noise of his painful gasp even—he didn't feel any impact. It took a span of several seconds before Jacinto understood what was happening. As he lay unmolested in his blanket, the old man—the Mayor of the overpass—was being beaten by two of the youngsters that had been hanging around earlier.

Jacinto didn't know what to do. He didn't want trouble. Suddenly, he wished only to pay for his card and rent a room on credit if he could. This was, for once, a problem among gringos. If they allowed their youth to beat their elders without reason, then who was Jacinto to stop it?

But after another boot strike, he knew he couldn't abide this. What good was the unspoken peace he'd forged with the Mayor, if they wouldn't even protect each other from punks like this?

Jacinto took his hands away from his money and raised himself up. The two gringo kids laughed and grunted, trading kicks to the old man on the ground. Jacinto sized them up. They were both small, but one—with a tattoo of a spider web creeping up his neck toward his ear—was much fiercer than the other. He had to find a way to take the mean one out whilst scaring the meek one.

The Mayor let out a series of raspy moans as the boots hit his belly and sides. Spider Web held his arms outward, and took a half step before each kick. The other boy stood at attention alongside, laughing and cheering on his friend. That boy had a safety pin through his earlobe; Jacinto imagined ripping it straight out.

His first move was critical. With all the swiftness he could muster, Jacinto kicked Safety Pin's leg—from the side and right at knee level—then grabbed Spider Web. He hooked both his arms round the boy's shoulders, and linked his hands together behind the head. Pushing downward against the boy's neck, Jacinto finally glimpsed the blurry spider below his collar. All four limbs flailed about like loose snakes, but Jacinto had him under control. He turned and saw that Safety Pin was on the ground, holding his knee.

Now, Jacinto was at a loss. If Safety Pin got up and came at him, he'd have to let go of Spider Web. He could get Spider Web to the ground from here—he thought—but that would leave himself vulnerable. Jacinto grew so scared that he wished there was a wall nearby to bash this boy's face into.

Both gringos shouted incomprehensibly. Jacinto back-peddled, yanking Spider Web off balance every other second so that he couldn't get off any real kicks. Safety Pin rose, still favoring his leg. He looked down at the old bum on the ground and then up at the multi-legged monster formed by Jacinto and his friend. He then turned and ran away in a lopsided hobble.

Jacinto was relieved. He loosened his interlaced fingers and did his best to grab a handful of short hair on Spider Web's head. With his other hand, he made a fist and delivered a punch to the boy's floating rib. It worked. Spider Web doubled over and gasped for breath—arms hugging his own torso.

Jacinto went to the Mayor and helped him to his feet. The old man's lip was bleeding. The two of them stood and stared down at the boy on his knees. Suddenly outnumbered, the boy held up one hand as if to say, "stay," and made his awkward retreat, still struggling to catch his breath.

Now it was only Jacinto and the Mayor, standing side by side and lacking a common language. The Mayor said, "gracias," then spit out a bit of bloody saliva.

Jacinto smiled. He wondered if the Mayor needed a doctor, but realized that there was no way to ask. Both of them went back to their respective beds. Jacinto stayed up the rest of the night, holding onto the wad of bills and feeling thankful that he got out of this altercation without facial wounds or torn clothing that would compromise his job at the store.

*

Wilmer skipped school the rest of the week, while the bruises on his face healed. He did not however, neglect his ripening beans. Renegado followed him out of the house, toward the field. They passed the water-project workers on their way to their morning meeting. Men turned and stared at Wilmer's black eye and busted lip, but said nothing.

Wilmer's parents had fought with the guerilla, while nearly all their neighbors were with the army. His family had always been pariahs here. But now, after Wilmer's brawl with a son of the main village family, and their exclusion from the water project, they were more outcast than ever. The rumor mill would waste no time determining a source for his wounds. Perhaps Moises would get the credit as well as the blame.

"Wilmer? What happened to you?" Finally, somebody had the nerve to say what was on his mind.

Wilmer turned and saw Don Jefe, the village gringo. In baseball cap and sneakers, he was on his way to meet the workers and lead them to their aqueduct.

"Are you okay?" With a finger, the gringo pointed at his own eye.

"I fell," Wilmer snapped back, and kept walking toward the family parcel.

*

The woman with the heavy eye makeup sat at the same desk and spoke on the phone. She motioned for Jacinto to have a seat. Just before walking in, he'd moved his wad of bills from his crotch to his front pocket.

She muttered a string of uh-huhs and English yeses into the receiver. From the desk drawer, she retrieved the same yellow legal pad as last time, with Jacinto's name and the amount he'd already paid. The phone still pinched between her ear and shoulder, she then took out a small blue piece of paper, the size of a playing card, and handed it to Jacinto.

He read his name on the little card, and a long string of digits. The rest of the words were written in English. This was it? This was worth two day's wages? He took out his money.

"There you go sir." She slammed the receiver down; the phone's bell gave a dull ring.

"Thank you." He handed her the cash.

She counted it up then collected her legal pad.

"If I rent a room from you," Jacinto asked. "Could I pay the bill later, after payday?"

"Can you put down a deposit?" With her pen, she scratched out the amount he owed on the card, then wrote something else beside his name.

"A small one." Jacinto shrugged. What good was it to save if his money would be stolen by punks under the overpass?

*

In the field, Wilmer's beans had climbed up the dry cornstalks. Their red-speckled pods begged for harvest. Wilmer studied the sky and decided that it wouldn't be raining again this year. He would pick all the beans that he and his mother could eat fresh, then let the others dry on the vine and store them for the rest of the year.

The bruises along his ribcage and hips ached with each bending and picking motion. Renegado lay down under the *palapa*, looking bored. The work was hot and dusty in the dry field, but Wilmer was glad to have it. He took the harvest seriously. As far as he could tell, the fat *coyote* would steal whatever cash they had. If not for corn and beans, what would they eat? Also, there was an element of resentful pride: if his father was now of no use to them—alive or dead—then Wilmer would prove he could feed the household.

Once the bag was full of new beans, he joined Renegado under the shade of the *palapa*. In the distance, he could see the *maquílas* where his mother spent her days. Between here and there, a plane lifted off from the airport. There was a time when Wilmer loved to watch aircraft take off and land. Now, he found that the sight of them made him angry and he turned his head away.

*

Jacinto was disappointed to learn he could only work at the store five days per week. Over the weekends, he took on hours with El Negro's cleaning crew to make extra money. El Negro's morning cash kept Jacinto afloat while he waited for his first weekly payment from Eduardo.

Though the bedding stank of tobacco, and cockroaches ruled the bathroom, his own quarters made Jacinto's life much easier. He slept well and was able to work harder during the waking hours. Night shifts with El Negro required a second set of clothes, which wasn't expensive. Jacinto washed laundry in the bathtub and always had one set drying over the shower curtain. For the first time, he was bathing and brushing his teeth with regularity.

His hope was that, at the end of the pay period, he'd have enough to pay rent here, try Chano's number again, and finally send something back to Carasucia.

"Don Jacinto!"

"What is it?" Jacinto was in the middle of unloading a pallet of canned pumpkin.

"Something for you." Eduardo handed him an envelope, his first name written on the front. "Open it."

Jacinto did as he was told. Inside, he found a piece of paper with his name and a large number typed out. "What is this?" he asked.

"It's your paycheck, *cabrón!*"

"You don't have cash?"

"We don't do payroll with cash." Eduardo stifled a laugh. "This way is easier, and more secure."

"What can I do with this thing?" Jacinto kept staring at the foreign object in his hands.

"I assume you don't have a bank account?"

Jacinto shook his head no.

"There are plenty of check-cashing places on Mission Street. They'll charge you a fee, but pay you right away. Go to the one inside the pawn shop."

Jacinto knew the place. He hoped this would be as easy as Eduardo described. He took another look down at the paper. It was a great deal of money, more than he'd ever made before. The first thing he would do: send some back to his wife and child.

After work, Jacinto went straight to the check-cashing counter inside the pawn shop. There, amongst the electric guitars, circular saws, and tarnished jewelry, the clerk counted him out a big stack of American dollars. Jacinto added numbers in his head. Even after paying off his back rent, he'd have a couple hundred left over.

Jacinto put the money in his pocket. He was preparing to leave the store when he made out an old familiar sound, something he'd not heard in a while. Unconsciously, it stirred him to a state of frightened alert and he looked to see the source. There, by the door to the pawn shop was a small boy—about Wilmer's age—with his mother. From the boy's throat came a wheezing sound, almost identical to the one Wilmer made during those awful episodes.

"Here," the mother said in Spanish. From the boy's coat pocket, she pulled out a little yellow plastic device and put it into his mouth.

"*Tranquilo*," the mother whispered. "Breathe deep."

With a couple of draws from this yellow thing, the boy's breathing returned to normal. She put the device away and the two of them left the store, having entered only to deal with the asthma attack.

Jacinto stood staring, dumbfounded, after they left. He'd never seen one of those miraculous devices before, only heard about their effects from his wife and son. Several seconds passed before he came to his senses and ran out of the store—weaving his way between a drum set and a stack of televisions—in search of the mother and child.

He caught up with them several blocks up Mission Street, as they started down the stairs to the underground train.

"Excuse me!" Jacinto was winded from the chase; his words came out in huffs. "I'm very sorry to bother you."

The woman averted her eyes. She put her hands on the boy's shoulder and ushered him down the stairs.

"Please, just one moment." Jacinto struggled to come up with an idea. "Would you sell me that asthma device?" The plan had always been to send money to El Salvador, so that the medicine might be bought there. They were only given out with a doctor's prescription; Jacinto knew that much. But to see one such gadget the moment he was paid, and in the hands of a Spanish-speaking mother and child—it had to be a sign.

"Leave us alone." The woman continued down the stairs, refusing to look up at Jacinto's eyes.

"It's for my son." Jacinto followed them through the crowd of people moving in either direction up the stairs. He remembered the cold shoulder he'd been given in the kitchen by the senior migrants, Eduardo's words about their resentment. It took all his restraint not to grab this woman by her shoulders, so that she would at least hear him out. "He's back in El Salvador. He has asthma but we have no money for the medicine. That's why I'm here."

Once down the stairs, the woman took brisk paces toward the turnstile. In her hand was a magnetic card that allowed entrance—a card that Jacinto didn't have. Once she entered, he would have no chance. She dragged her son by one arm.

"Please!" Jacinto insisted. "Name your price."

Finally, the boy shouted, "Mama!" and resisted her pull. "His son is like me. We should help him." The boy took the inhaler from his coat pocket and held it towards her.

She looked into her son's eyes, and accepted the device. They stared at each other for several seconds. Jacinto wasn't sure whether or not he should speak further.

"One hundred dollars," the woman said at last.

Jacinto was taken aback. He'd not anticipated this high a cost, but was happy to pay it. It was a good thing he found her whilst carrying so much cash. He fished the money from his pocket, and they made the handoff.

"Thank you," he said. He clutched the device to his chest, terrified that somebody might try to pluck it from him.

Still suspicious, the woman nodded and walked away. As the boy followed her through the turnstile, he offered Jacinto a final wave.

*

Once he was nearly home, Wilmer saw one of the shining sport-utility vehicles that had brought Don Jefe to the party months ago. It was parked in front of the gringo's house. A logo-and-collar-clad man carried out a piece of luggage.

A small crowd of gawkers gathered across the street, by Don Valentín's store. Wilmer joined them. A second later, Don Jefe himself came out—his face red and rubbery, streaked with tears.

"What happened?" Wilmer asked Don Chus, who stood at the fringe of the crowd, his cow going after the weeds on the shoulder of the road.

"They say his brother died," Don Chus said. "Jumped off a building, apparently."

"Why?" Wilmer asked.

Don Chus only shrugged. "Who knows? Maybe he was crazy, or on drugs. They're sending Don Jefe home for the funeral."

Wilmer thought of the planes he'd just watched in Comalapa, how this gringo could be in that country tomorrow. "More fuss is made over a dead gringo than a live Salvadoran, no?"

Don Chus—always quick to a laugh—instead turned to Wilmer with a scowl, angry at the lack of sympathy for Don Jefe's plight. He tugged on the cow's rope, a small reminder of his authority.

Wilmer took the hint and kept his thoughts to himself. He stood watching as the big car carried Don Jefe off towards a place that Wilmer would never understand.

*

A Gigante Express counter was open two doors down.

The clerk smiled and welcomed Jacinto. "Courier or Flash Money?" he asked.

Flash money was their popular money-transfer service. It was cheap and fast, but couldn't deliver letters or goods.

"Courier," Jacinto said at first, hugging the inhaler higher up along his chest, still afraid to let go. But as he thought of the days it would take for it to get there, and the fact that his wife and child had still heard nothing, he said: "And flash money too. One of each."

"How much flash money?" The clerk began filling out a form.

"One hundred dollars. Let me pay the charges separately." Jacinto pictured the man on the motorcycle arriving whilst Mina washed corn. A nice, round, three-digit number was more poetic.

"Of course. And what would like to send via courier?"

"This." Jacinto placed the plastic device on the counter. "And a note."

The clerk offered a pen and a pad of paper. Jacinto did his best to keep it simple, not wanting to make mistakes and waste this man's paper. "Dear Mina and Wilmer," he wrote. "Here is one inhaler. I hope it helps. I had a difficult journey but I am here now. I hope to find Chano soon so that we may speak by telephone. All my love, Jacinto."

He knew that it was fraught with misspellings and errors, but hoped they would understand the sentiment.

"Are these both going to the same address?" the clerk asked.

"Yes." Jacinto spoke his wife's full name, the name of the village, the municipality, the department, and El Salvador itself.

The clerk smiled, gave a receipt, and thanked him for his business.

Out on Mission Street, Jacinto felt—for the first time in a long while— that he'd done exactly the right thing. He bought a phone card at one of the bodegas. Again, the same awkward ritual. Again, no Chano. It was nearly twilight now. His heart finally slowed from the excitement associated with this one paycheck. He watched the other undocumented workers, all set to enjoy their Friday night. He still had money in his pocket, on top of what he owed the hotel. Should he celebrate somehow? Buy a beer or a cigarette or a big dinner? None of these things held much luster for Jacinto. And now that he wasn't sleeping under an overpass, or worrying about his next meal, Jacinto could better imagine his family back home: suffering without him, having gone many months without a word or a dollar.

No, he'd not waste a minute patting himself on the back. Instead, he pulled the collar up on his coat, and walked toward the Salvadoran restaurant, hoping to beg work on El Negro's cleaning crew.

19

AFTER ANOTHER LONG NIGHT OF SWAMPING OUT BARS AND kitchens, Jacinto listened to the dull rings through the payphone receiver. His clothes smelt of grease traps and mop water. The sun was barely visible through thick grey fog. These calls had become a sort of thankless piety to him, like a child's prayers before bedtime. Jacinto wished only to get them over with so he could return to his room and sleep off the rest of the day.

"Chano? Is that you?"

"Who the fuck wants to know?" The voice on the phone sounded as though he'd just woken up, but the cursing was unquestionably Salvadoran.

"It's your *cuñado*, asshole."

"Jacinto? You're alive?"

"What did you expect? That I was dead in some desert?"

"Where are you?"

"Here in San Francisco, at the Soledad Hotel."

"Get your things. Check out. I'll be there in half an hour."

They hung up. Jacinto turned the phone card over in his fingers a few times, then threw it in the trash.

Outside the hotel, Jacinto held a plastic bag with his change of clothes and his toothbrush. He and Chano had never been close. Though they'd fought together during the war, Chano always struck him as lazy, undisciplined, and full of vice. In Chano's eyes, Jacinto was probably a sort of humorless country bumpkin—not good enough for his sister. Chano was no farmer; that was for sure. After the peace accords, he moved to an apartment in the capital straight away, and worked a series of odd jobs. He knew how to fix cars, and often made good money as a mechanic. Years ago—back when it was easier—he made the trip north with a couple of friends.

"Cuñado!" The call came from up the street. Chano grinned wide. Jacinto watched him approach. He'd gained a big belly and a well-kept mustache. In the region around the eyes and upper part of the nose, Jacinto could still see the resemblance to his own wife.

"Look at you!" Chano embraced him. "You're pure bones. Haven't you been eating?"

Words failed Jacinto. His brother-in-law's warm reception was more than he'd expected. "It's good to see you, Chano. I've been trying to contact you for months. Any news from Mina?"

That question appeared to take Chano aback. "She calls me, yes. She's very worried. What the fuck happened to you?"

"It's a long story."

"Come on." Chano took the bag from him. "You'll stay with me. Tell me on the way."

*

Wilmer watched as the men headed off to the water project, only minutes after his mother had left for the sweatshops. Rumor was that the project went well, even with the gringo gone. They'd finished a big concrete tank by the side of the road, and the main aqueduct line was meant to reach it in a matter of weeks. A couple of overzealous households had already dug a ditch for the distribution line that would eventually come right to their cistern.

In the rosy-fingered dawn, the working men of Carasucia looked happy and whole. They'd barely finished their harvest when this project came along. Now, they made good money and didn't have to travel far. By all appearances, this endeavor gave them a sense of satisfaction they wouldn't get from wage work in the capital or the coffee *fincas*. For years to come, this generation will tell younger Carasucians the story of this labor—each time they turned on the water, perhaps. Since Wilmer's fight in the schoolyard, none of the ADESCO members had visited to speak of the project.

"Guillermina Paredes?"

A stranger spoke his mother's full name. Renegado barked. Wilmer turned to see a man in long sleeves and a baseball cap standing beside him, carrying a satchel over one shoulder.

"Guillermina Paredes?" the man repeated.

"She's my mother," Wilmer said. "But she's at work."

The stranger shrugged. "Give this to her when she returns."

Wilmer accepted an envelope placed into his hand. Only then did he read the logo on the man's cap and shirt breast: Gigante Express.

Wilmer turned from side to side to see if anyone watched. The crowd of workers was gone now and nobody else had emerged from their houses. The Gigante man had parked his motorcycle at another home, and walked over. The cycle's engine turned over then left the village.

Wilmer went inside the house and put the envelope down upon the table. In the kitchen he found a sharp small knife. Renegado made a yawning sound as Wilmer sat. With a calm and careful motion, he cut open the short end of the envelope. Inside, along with a receipt that read 'Flash Money' at the top, was a single hundred-dollar bill. Wilmer took it out and examined its every side.

What did this mean, exactly? That his father was alive? That he'd made it to the north and was now working?

He must have failed to contact Tío Chano, or opted not to. Otherwise, his mother would have heard something at her last visit to ANTEL. Perhaps he'd been working all this time. How many months had gone by now? He might have started another family, for all Wilmer knew. Perhaps this was only a guilt-ridden way of saying goodbye.

Wilmer considered what would happen if he passed this money along to his mother, as was expected of him. She'd take it as proof that Jacinto was still alive, and her faith in his aid would be redoubled. And, one way or another, this bill would end up in the hands of that filthy *coyote*.

No, Wilmer decided. He couldn't go that route. As for his father, this was too little, too late. His mother couldn't be trusted with this money or this information. Wilmer would take this hundred-dollar bill and put an end to that fat fucker's harassment of this family for good.

*

Chano worked as a mechanic at a shop here in the city. He lived in a big house broken up into apartments. But where most of the men rented a bedroom and shared bathrooms and kitchens, Chano had a spacious unit to himself— with separate living room, refrigerator, a sofa, and telephone.

After the story of his near-fatal desert experience and trip through Mexico, Jacinto told about the job in the store and Chano advised him to keep it. This was a bad time of year to look for work. From the moment they walked into the house, Jacinto's eyes kept returning to that phone mounted to the wall.

"You can have the sofa," Chano said. "I often work late into the evenings, so we should be able to share without much trouble. I've got a key for you, but it can be a little tricky. Hey!"

Jacinto turned to face him. He'd not paid attention.

"She usually calls on Sundays." Chano must have noticed him staring. "Don't worry, you'll get a hold of her."

"It's been so long." Jacinto detected an emotional quiver in his voice. "What must she think happened to me? Does she believe I'm dead?"

"She doesn't think you're dead." That was the most definitive statement Chano had made on the matter thus far.

"What does she say to you, *cabrón?*" Under other circumstances, Jacinto might've grabbed his brother-in-law by the collar and shaken him. He couldn't help feeling that a secret was being kept.

But it was Chano who raised his voice: "When she calls me, she's hoping that I've heard from you, understand? When we speak—once a month, perhaps—I'm the one who must tell her that I've heard nothing. What do you think she says? She gets panicked. She gets emotional. You know how women are."

Jacinto realized that he didn't know how women were. Mina was the only woman that he understood even a little. And he never thought of her as prone to panic or emotional distress. She kept cooler than he did.

"Relax, Jacinto." Chano sat down on the sofa. "You're alive and you're here. That's what she wants. Now there's nothing to do but wait for her call and earn her some dollars."

20

LIVING WITH CHANO, JACINTO'S MONEY WENT FURTHER. WITH his next paycheck, Jacinto planned to send a sizeable sum to Mina and Wilmer—much more than last time, several hundred dollars, perhaps. He slept well on Chano's couch, and enjoyed his work.

Whatever food he was given—stale bread, expired cheese, apples with brown spots, or gummed-up egg cartons—he took back to Chano's and turned into simple meals.

For several hours each afternoon, Jacinto had the place to himself. During this time he would bathe, take his supper, do his best to straighten up the apartment, but mostly hope for a call from Mina. He worried that she might ring while both men were at work, or while Jacinto was in the shower. As he did the math once again in his head—how much his next paycheck would be—he wondered about the price of the mobile phones that had become popular in El Salvador just before he left. Perhaps he could buy Chano one of those machines that recorded messages. Mina's voice would be captured on it, no matter what time of day.

Once Chano arrived home, he went straight for the stash of canned beer in the refrigerator. He always offered Jacinto one, and Jacinto always declined. After that, the two of them sat on the sofa and watched the grainy television. A Spanish-speaking station played game shows and *telenovelas*. Jacinto did his best to act entertained. He'd have preferred to go to sleep early, but thought it polite to keep Chano company. Also, they sat on his bed.

*

Wilmer walked all the way to Rosario with the hundred-dollar bill in his shoe. He'd hoped to see Teardrop at the bus stop. Instead, a couple of the younger *mareros* manned that post.

With a hollow sensation in his abdomen, Wilmer turned towards the hijacked schoolhouse where he'd been beaten up not so many days ago.

"You shouldn't be here," was the first thing Teardrop said to him. "I've lost a lot of face for saving your silly life."

"I'm sorry," Wilmer said. "It's very simple. I want to know if I could...buy something from you."

Teardrop raised his eyebrows and came closer to the chain link of the gate. "*Mota?*" he asked. "*Coca?* With that, I can help you. What do you need?"

"No," Wilmer said. "Not drugs."

*

At the end of the first workweek they spent together, Chano came home early. "Put your shoes on." He unloaded a fresh box of beer cans into the fridge. "I want you to come with me, meet some friends of mine."

Jacinto had showered, but not yet eaten. He gave a glance to the telephone on the wall, worried that the call would come while they were out. He hoped it would ring right now and get him out of this social obligation. No such luck.

The evening in the city was oddly beautiful. At its edges, the sky had an orange glow and was not obscured by fog. For the past several days, Jacinto had gone from the apartment to the store and back, only veering off course to buy a few items at a bodega—some instant coffee or a bit of sugar.

"You don't want to be a hermit here," Chano explained as they walked. "All of us—especially the Central Americans—we're a community. If anything happens to your job, you need to know who to ask about more work. These things are important, understand?"

"Of course." Jacinto feared that they were embarking on a money-wasting evening. Truth be told, he did want to be a hermit here. He wanted to silently suffer through it, however long it took to get the family on firmer financial ground, then go back home.

They walked down a street foreign to Jacinto. Two well-dressed gringos stood in the doorway of a building, oddly close, as if whispering. Jacinto stopped short of gasping as one of them leaned in and kissed the other on the mouth.

"Chano!" Jacinto said. "Did you see that? Those two men, they're *mariones.*"

"So what?" Chano suppressed a laugh. "They bothering you?"

"It's not me they have to worry about. What if somebody sees them? In El Centro, men have been killed for doing such a thing in public."

"We're not in El Centro, *cabrón.* Nobody cares here."

Jacinto went silent.

Chano slapped him on the shoulder, entertained by his naiveté. "What a country, huh? Homosexuals can kiss in public, but you can't walk down the street with an open beer bottle! And you need a license to catch fish in the river!" He laughed out loud.

*

Teardrop led him to a small house not far from the school. The bottom floor was a paper store, full of pencils and notebooks for the students that once passed by. The upstairs appeared to be taken over by the MS Only a few of the gangsters were there, and they were all older—senior leadership, perhaps. Wilmer felt more at ease around them than the small and jumpy ones his own age.

Teardrop mentioned "doing business" and they were both given entrance to a private room upstairs. Posters of naked or nearly naked *gringas* lined the walls, gang tags written on the white rounds of their breasts and butt-cheeks. All across the floor were wooden crates and cardboard boxes.

"There are many options." Teardrop opened a box and picked out a device that looked like two interlocking pieces of metal pipe, handle on each. "This one is cheap, but it works." He aimed the business end at the floor. "You put your bullet in there, then push this as hard as you can." Teardrop demonstrated the move.

"No," Wilmer said. "I need something that looks like a gun."

Teardrop let the improvised weapon hang down at waist level. "Have you got money?"

Wilmer nodded.

"Why didn't you say so?" He pulled a wooden crate from along the wall and opened it up. From inside, Teardrop pulled out a tarnished but terrifying military pistol. It was much bigger and more impressive than the *coyote's* little revolver.

"This." Teardrop pointed it upward and held it at eye level, like he was posing on the poster for an action movie, "Is the *mero mero*."

He pulled a lever, slipped the ammunition out, and handed it to Wilmer.

At first, Wilmer held it flat on his two opened hands, appreciating only the weight and geometry of the thing.

"That's a Beretta, nine-millimeter," Teardrop went on. "That'll scare whoever's been fucking with you."

Wilmer wrapped both hands around the grip and pointed the unloaded pistol at an empty corner of the room. It felt reassuring; it felt like a solution.

"Who is fucking with you anyway?" Teardrop pushed the crate back into place.

"Some asshole that comes around and steals from my mother." Wilmer noticed how calm and measured his breathing had become.

*

Chano led them inside a dark restaurant. The place was full of Latinos, but with tacky Hawaiian décor. A jukebox boomed with the low notes of *norteño* music. They joined three men at a table full of beer and snacks: toasted corn, pickled carrots, peanuts, and radishes.

All three of Chano's friends were Salvadoran. What with the noise, Jacinto could only carry on a conversation with the one sitting closest to him: a thick-limbed man with a mustache who introduced himself as "Juan" but whom everybody else called "Cuca."

Chano brought Jacinto a Mexican beer with a lime stuck in the top. He took one sip and helped himself to the salty snacks on the table.

Juan Cuca told his story over the noise. He had a successful construction business here in the city. Apparently, Salvadoran laborers were highly regarded for their skill in laying *azulejos*—the small tiles favored by gringos for kitchens and bathrooms. Juan specialized in this and made good money.

"Do you ever get homesick?" Jacinto grew less inhibited as he worked his way through the beer. "Do you ever want to go back?"

"*Puta*, I go back!" Juan laughed. "I'm building my house there. I take vacations in El Salvador once a year."

Jacinto was dumbfounded. "You cross once a year? Both ways? How?"

"I have this now." Juan reached into his pocket and pulled out a black booklet. He handed it over to Jacinto.

It appeared to be a Mexican passport, but with Juan's name and photograph.

"Is this real?" Jacinto asked.

"Fuck no." Juan held a fist up over his mouth and crunched his way through a radish. "It would never work to get into this country, but it's good enough to get on the plane. Once I'm in Comalapa, I tuck a twenty-dollar bill into it, and make one of those teenagers working at Immigration very happy."

Jacinto grinned at the cleverness of it.

At the other end of the table, Chano and his two friends laughed like hyenas at some stupid joke.

"And to come back in?"

Juan sighed and shook his head. "Coming back is the hard part; make no mistake. I know a good *coyote*, a friend since childhood. But even he's become expensive. I've half a mind to stop returning so often. We're better off staying here and making all the money we can for a while, going back for good once we have enough."

Jacinto handed the false passport back. "When is it enough? When can one say it's time to go back for good?"

"Only God knows for sure." Juan shrugged and went for another sip of his beer. "If I finish my house, then buy a couple of buses perhaps, it could be a comfortable, secure life."

Jacinto nodded. Ideas took hold inside his head. So far, he and Mina had only thought about the short term: getting Wilmer his medicine. What about an investment in something that could pay off down the road? The bus business was foreign to him, and Don Valentín had the *tienda* covered. Maybe a mill would work? Now, the women of Carasucia had to walk all the way to Los Anhelos with buckets of corn atop their heads. Surely, they'd rather stay closer to home. No matter how bad the situation got in El Salvador, the village would always need tortillas.

His train of thought was interrupted by a waitress carrying plates of food. She dropped one in front of each of them. Nobody had asked Jacinto for an order or anything else, but he was hungry. All of them had the same thing: grilled steak, rice and beans, a bit of chopped tomato and onions. No one at the table spoke as they all tucked into their food. Jacinto did his best not to think of the two eggs back at Chano's that he'd planned to eat for dinner, along with a length of French bread that would be too hard to eat tomorrow. While he worried about the final bill, Jacinto had to admit that the food was tasty. The beef was the most tender he'd ever had. It went easily under the fork and knife, unlike the tough and leathery cuts he was used to in his home country.

The waitress brought out more beer. Once their plates were cleared, a tiny glass of tequila was placed in front of each man. Jacinto hesitated at first, but managed to slug it down along with the rest of them. He felt the familiar euphoria of being alive, having a job and some money in his pocket, not unlike what he'd felt back in Arizona when the rolling party car set up. Finally, there seemed cause to celebrate. His journey was complete at last. If anything were to happen to his store job, perhaps this Juan could offer him construction work. Soon, if not already, Wilmer would have his medicine. With Jacinto's next check, Mina could buy more and begin to put a little away. Perhaps Jacinto could return in a few short years. And most importantly: he no longer spent his nights shivering under a bridge and would never need to again. All that was missing from his life was Mina's call, and the chance to tell her that everything will be all right.

Beer bottles rose in the center of their table and a slurred *salud* sounded from the lips of one of the new friends. The jukebox exploded with the opening accordion riff to "Tres Veces Mojado," and a raucous sing-along ensued.

*

Wilmer walked all the way home with the gun tucked into his waistband. Teardrop had offered to take him into the woods for target practice, but Wilmer knew he'd never actually fire the thing.

At the house, he locked the door to his mother's bedroom. Wilmer pointed the barrel of his new purchase at his own reflection and rehearsed under his breath what he might say to that fat *coyote*.

"*You* ought to be careful with *your* little toys, *cabrón*. Now get out! Leave me and my mother alone. Don't come back to this house ever, understand?"

He practiced tucking the pistol in and taking it back out of his pants. This rehearsal went on for half an hour. Through the window, Wilmer saw that the sun had gone down. His mother could return at any moment. Renegado whimpered from outside the door, lonely.

Wilmer left the bedroom and set about hiding the gun. He wrapped it in plastic bags, then took it out to the latrine. Among the tree-branch rafters that his father had fashioned, Wilmer found a spot where the corrugated metal roof was intact and wouldn't let any water come through.

As he hid it, Wilmer didn't feel that he was doing anything sinister. Instead, he felt as if this were a gift for his mother. Once this was all over, she would thank him.

*

Jacinto woke up on Chano's couch the next morning with a splitting headache. He jumped to his feet, checked the clock on the stove, and searched for his shoes—terrified he'd be late for work. After half a minute of bleary-eyed searching, he remembered it was the weekend, and that he had no job to go to today.

Back on the couch, he tried to force another hour of sleep. He felt the pockets of his jeans and found no money there. A cloud of shame came over him, and rained down discreet and disconnected memories from the rest of the night. A bill was brought out and each man reached into his pocket. All that remained of Jacinto's cash went towards his share—most likely didn't even cover his share.

He recalled the five of them out on the streets, howling like jackals, passing around a lit cigarette. They were about to enter someplace more dubious, either to have sex with prostitutes or perhaps only to look at naked ladies— Jacinto never did understand. But he was broke, drunk, and so tired he could barely stand. Did Chano bring him home or did he come here under his own power?

In his head, Jacinto added up the money that he'd have earned and saved had he gone and worked for El Negro last night. It would have been a wad worth sending home. He told himself to calm down. This was a small indiscretion, not a major setback. His host had invited him; it would've been rude to say no. Consider it a roundabout form of rent.

The doorknob rattled, and a second later the door itself swung open. Chano stumbled in, his eyes half-shut and a boozy smell coming from his pores.

"Good morning." Jacinto had assumed his brother-in-law was asleep in the next room.

"*Cuñado!*" Chano kicked off his shoes. "You were smart to come home when you did."

For this perhaps, Jacinto could congratulate himself. "Chano, I want to thank you for inviting me out last night. I enjoyed meeting your friends—Juan Cuca in particular. But from now on I think I'll work on weekend nights. I need to raise money as soon as possible."

"Psshh!" Chano rolled his eyes and stumbled into the kitchen. He took a beer can from the refrigerator and popped it open. "Lighten up a little. This isn't Salvador. One meal in a restaurant and a few drinks won't cost you a month's wages. You need to take advantage of this place. Otherwise, you'll be miserable." Chano collapsed into one of the two kitchen chairs.

"That's fine by me." Jacinto turned his head away as the starchy beer smell drifted towards him. "I came here expecting misery. The whole idea is to sow short-term misery so that my family might reap long-term security. I'm not here for a party!"

"Alright, alright." In spite of his drunken state, Chano did sound sincere. "You know what? You looked like you were enjoying yourself last night. After everything you've been through, I thought you deserved that. I have a feeling things are about to get tougher for you."

"What do you mean?" Jacinto forgot all about last night.

"I didn't want to say anything." Chano took a dram of his beer. "But there's been a problem, with the *coyote*."

Jacinto was ready to rise from the sofa and throttle Chano's throat until he knew exactly the whole story. It took every ounce of self-control he could muster to calmly say: "go on."

The telephone rang and startled both men.

Without speaking, Chano rose from his chair and lifted the receiver. "Hello. One second." He held the phone out toward Jacinto. "It's for you."

Jacinto felt his eyes widen. He took the receiver and held it to his ear. "Mina?"

"Jacinto? Is that you? Is that really you?" It sounded as if she were in the next room.

"It's me, my life. I made it. You won't believe what I've been through. The *coyote* abandoned us in the desert. The rest of the group died. I was put in jail and then bussed all the way to Guatemala. Along with a *chapín* named Israel, we rode trains and busses all the way to the border. Israel was killed before we crossed. By the time I reached this country, the phone number that you stitched into my underwear frayed apart. I tried every possible combination until I finally got in touch with Chano. But now everything is okay. I'm sorry it took so long to send any money. Did you get what I sent last week? But the good news is this: I made the trip without any help from Don Noe. There's no need to pay the *coyote*'s fee! Now I know you're thinking that we should get the down payment back as well, but I say we forget about it and focus on the future. How is my son? Did he have a good harvest? Is he there? Can I speak with him?" Jacinto was breathless once his story was over.

Through the earpiece, he heard the rings and clangs from the other ANTEL phones in the background. But the sound which cut through that cacophony was the soft whimper of his strong wife weeping.

"Jacinto," she said between sobs. "Chano hasn't told you?"

"No," Jacinto admitted.

"Don Noe wants his money. He's come several times to take whatever we have. He says that you turned your party over to the *Migra*."

"That's a lie!" Jacinto shouted now. "The only ones left alive in that 'party' were me and the *pollero*. And we'd both be dead if the *Migra* hadn't found us! Don Noe is responsible for half a dozen deaths. Don't believe him!"

"I know he's a liar!" Mina raised her voice to match his. "He tried to tell me that you killed yourself in prison. But it doesn't matter. He's got his story and a chance to make some money. What do I have? The truth and nothing more."

"What does he want?"

"The full amount. He comes by now to steal whatever change we've scraped together and calls that the interest."

Speechless, Jacinto did the math in his head. He'd have to work for a year at least to pay that off, without even factoring in his expenses or Wilmer's medicine money. He wouldn't do it. He'd not be pushed around this way.

"I'll come back," Jacinto said. "I'll come back and tell Don Noe to his face what happened. If he doesn't settle this so-called debt, I'll be sure to ruin his reputation so that no man within one hundred miles ever asks for his services again."

"No!" Mina shouted. "Don't come back! Wilmer's condition is bad. I've been working at the *maquílas* to make ends meet. Jacinto, we need the money."

The *maquílas*? This was the sort of situation he came here to avoid.

"I'll handle Don Noe." A suspenseful pause, with a sigh like resignation, came through the earpiece. "I'll plead poverty. I'll tell him that you're dead. Send me a few hundred dollars—that should shut him up. I'll say it's the most I could get from my brother and ask for mercy. He'll understand. He can't expect blood from a stone. Even a without-shame like him wouldn't harm a widow and a young boy. It's bad for business."

Jacinto hated this idea. "Don't be ridiculous. That man isn't to be trusted. We can't reason with him." He could barely stomach the thought of his wife and son left alone to deal with this problem. He wanted to be with them, if only to share in their suffering.

"Don't leave that country, Jacinto. I'll handle the *coyote*, understand. I have some ideas. I love you. Goodbye."

Once the dial tone sounded and the receiver hung upon the wall, Jacinto would barely look at his brother-in-law.

"You should have told me, Chano." He stared at the ground.

"I'm sorry. I thought it best that you hear from her. I worried that you might do something rash, something a little crazy."

Jacinto finally turned his gaze up to Chano's eyes. "Like go home and be with my family?"

"Exactly."

"Let me ask you: what kind of *jodido*, upside-down world are we living in where such a thing—protecting my wife and son, doing whatever possible to keep damage from their doors—is considered rash and crazy?" Jacinto found his shoes and put them on. "This isn't fair, Chano. We had a deal with that smuggler."

Chano sat down on the kitchen chair and drained the last of his beer can. "All that you've been through in your life, *cuñado*—that war, the land reform, your son's illness, the awful trip you endured to come here, all that senseless killing and worthless suffering—I don't know how it is you manage to hold onto this idea that there's such a thing as fairness or justice to be had out there in this world."

Jacinto slammed the door and left the apartment.

He found himself in the lobby of the Soledad Hotel. Once back in that familiar seat before Eye Makeup, he realized why he was here: "I need another document, one of the fake Mexican passports that make it easier to go home. I need it as soon as possible."

"We must take your picture," she said. "Follow me."

In a back room, they had a makeshift photography studio set up. She showed him where to stand and worked the camera.

"For this one," she said. "Don't smile."

Jacinto had no trouble complying.

Back on the street, Jacinto saw that the sun was now low and the sky pink and grey. He knew that sleep would not be an option for him tonight, and so made his way to the Salvadoran restaurant, where he hoped to get a place on El Negro's crew.

IV

21

JACINTO'S HANDS SHOOK AS HE TORE OPEN THE ENVELOPE
around his paycheck.

"Easy there," Eduardo said. "You'll rip that thing in half."

Jacinto smiled awkwardly and did his best to calm down. It was more
than he'd expected: several hundred dollars. He'd pay off his fake passport
with a fraction of it.

"See you tomorrow." Eduardo lifted off his apron.

Jacinto looked down at the check. "Until tomorrow." He lacked the heart
to reveal his plans. Like everyone else, Eduardo would try to stop him. Jacinto
felt bad for not at least giving warning, letting him know he'd have to find
someone else. But this wasn't such a big deal. There was no shortage of Central Americans here to fill a decent job like this one.

Jacinto left the store and walked straight to the check-cashing pawn shop
on Mission Street. Once again, in between tubas and power tools, a clerk
counted out his money. At his next stop, the Soledad Hotel, it was he who
counted out the stack of bills, in exchange for a cryptic and official-looking
document.

Once Eye Makeup handed over the passport, Jacinto spent a while staring
at the photo.

"I look so old," he said out loud.

Eye Makeup laughed and put away his money. "It happens to the best of
us."

Jacinto decided that it was convincing enough, as real as the one that Juan
had shown him. "How do I get to the airport from here?" He saw no need to
go back to Chano's. All he had there was a change of clothes and a tube of
toothpaste.

"Which airport?" she asked.

Jacinto shrugged. "Whichever one has the flights to my country."

*

"I've spoken to your father!" Mina said, as though that were great news.

Wilmer dumped a load of beans onto the table. "Is that right?" So far as he could tell, it changed nothing at all. He fetched a *guacal* and set to peeling. "He finally got around to stopping by Tío Chano's house, did he?"

"Wilmer." Mina was hurt by his reaction. "Don't you understand what this means? Your father is alive!"

Wilmer knew this, of course. He'd received the news in the form of the hundred-dollar bill. But he'd kept that from his mother along with the bigger secret—the one wrapped in a plastic bag and hidden among the rafters of the latrine.

"So he's alive." Wilmer plucked furiously at the stubborn sheaths, green with speckles of red. "He left in August. Where's he been? Where's the money?"

"He was in a Mexican jail, Wilmer, abandoned by the *pollero*. Many people died." Mina's voice took on a tone of authority that had been missing for the past several weeks. "Careful how you speak about your father."

"Some father," Wilmer said. "Where is he when that fat smuggler comes by to shake us down? Where is he while you're off in the *maquílas*? When I'm being beaten up at school behind his reputation? When water is finally coming to the homes all around us in exchange for a few *pinche* days of hard work?" He threw a fibrous pod of beans against the table and looked up. "It takes more than one phone call"—he stopped himself short of saying, *and a hundred dollars*—"to be a father."

The slap caught him by surprise. She'd managed to connect to the flesh of his cheek with a sharp, stinging whip of her palm.

Wilmer turned and saw his mother's face—trembling, on the verge of tears. He knocked over the bowl of fresh beans he'd been working on so that they spilled across the table and rolled to the floor. No longer willing to play the child in need of discipline, Wilmer turned and left the house.

*

Inside a puzzling piece of architecture like a warehouse crossed with a maze, Jacinto was passed from one Spanish-speaking attendant to another, until at last a young female agent from TACA airlines took up his cause. She was sweet and patient, probably from a Salvadoran family herself, and had apparently seen this sort of thing before.

"I only need to go one way," Jacinto explained, worried about the cost.

"In many cases, it's less expensive to buy a roundtrip ticket." Her nametag read *Marta*. She lowered her voice. "Also, it's less conspicuous when you pass through Immigration."

Jacinto nodded, glad to have an ally but still curious as to why he could never fool anyone in such matters.

"If you wish to leave soon…"

"As soon as possible."

"You chose a good time. We have a flight leaving in two hours which has extra seats."

"Look." He took all the money he had out of his pocket. "This is what I can pay. I need to get to El Salvador."

Marta turned from side to side, then gathered the bills together. She made them into a neat stack and counted them once, twice, three times.

"Alright then." She handed Jacinto back one of his ten-dollar bills, then typed furiously at the keyboard in front of her. Seconds later, a slip of sturdy paper jumped out of a machine on the desk. She handed it to him. It reminded him of his paycheck: a string of incomprehensible letters and numbers which were supposedly of great value.

"That's your gate there," she pointed. "Come and see me if you have any problems."

*

Wilmer would accept no excuses. No stories of prison or corrupt *polleros* or anything else. All he needed to know was that his father disappeared during a time of great need. His anger left no room for explanation. His face still stinging from the slap, Wilmer walked aimlessly down the village's main street.

For the first time in many days, Don Jefe's doors and windows were opened. Had the gringo returned from his homeland already? With nothing better to do, Wilmer went to investigate.

"Don Jefe?" Wilmer banged on the door and shouted.

"Yes?" The gringo rose from his hammock, but then sat back down when he saw it was Wilmer. "Come on in," he said. "Have a seat."

Wilmer sat on the bed. The gringo had a lit cigarette and let the ashes drop onto his floor. Wilmer wasn't aware that he smoked.

"You returned," Wilmer said.

"That's right. This morning."

"Most people around here thought that you'd stay in your country."

The gringo smiled, appreciative of Wilmer's honesty. "Not until we're done with this aqueduct."

"I'm sorry about your brother," Wilmer said.

"Thank you."

"Was he crazy, or on drugs or something?" Wilmer still couldn't fully get his mind around the death.

"Not exactly." Don Jefe stared at the cigarette in his hand, burning dangerously close to his fingers. "He was...sad, I think."

"Sad." Wilmer repeated the explanation, but was no less puzzled. He remembered his father's words about rich people and poor people doing things differently. Perhaps they suffered differently as well.

"What's the situation with your father now?" Don Jefe asked.

Wilmer shrugged. "He's in your country. My mother spoke to him on the phone this morning."

"That's wonderful." The gringo forced a smile. "So he's alive."

"Yes. I had a feeling he was." Wilmer couldn't quite bring himself to tell Don Jefe about the money he'd received, or what he'd bought with it. "But I'm not sure it matters. He's been gone a long time, and we've heard nothing from him. Meanwhile, his smuggler harasses us constantly. In my opinion, it's too little, too late."

"That man in the pickup?" The gringo threw the cigarette onto the ground and stomped it out with his flip-flop. "He's the smuggler?"

"That's right. He comes to steal whatever spare change we have, claiming it as interest on the amount we owe for my father's voyage."

Don Jefe's face contorted into a state of confused sympathy. "Is there anything I can do to help?"

"No." Wilmer looked the gringo straight in the eye. "He won't be a problem for much longer. I have a plan."

*

Never—not even in his wildest moments of hope or fear—did Jacinto imagine he might one day fly. The first steps inside the airplane were tentative, frightened. It took every ounce of will he could summon not to run screaming out of the thing. He was shocked by how casually the other passengers treated the experience. They sipped soda bottles and flipped through the pages of magazines, everyone in normal clothes. What had Jacinto expected? Were they to wear helmets? Flight suits, perhaps?

The seats were set up with a system of letters and numbers. Jacinto found his with little trouble: against a window, near the back. He sat down and looked out the oval of thick glass. Several men—some of them possibly Salvadorans—wore orange vests and drove small tractors full of luggage and other supplies. Jacinto could see the whole wing—the jet engine hanging underneath it like a machine from the future.

A large white man with a crew cut and a knobby round nose sat down beside Jacinto. Something about him suggested American military. At the front of the fuselage, a tall and beautiful flight attendant gave a demonstration. She held up a model of the seatbelt, which she locked and unlocked. Jacinto felt underneath his ass—careful not to disturb the crew-cut man—and found the strap. He fumbled with each end, flipping the metal pieces and twisting the belt, until he finally heard a click.

When he turned his eyes back up to the beautiful woman in uniform, she had an inflatable device around her neck and a yellow cup over her mouth and nose. He'd missed that part. Did they need to wear those things during the flight? What was she saying? He looked around at his fellow passengers. None of them paid attention. Crew Cut flipped through a catalog. Jacinto tried to relax. The plane began to move.

Somehow, Jacinto had underestimated his fear of heights when he'd formulated this plan. It came to him as the worst sort of shock—that which is immediately and retroactively obvious—when the airplane came unglued from the ground. He'd imagined the experience would be akin to looking at footage of clouds and sky on a television screen. But with the noise and the inertia, and the up and down motion of the wings visible from his seat, it was all too clear that he was being shot through the sky inside of an aluminum tube.

The worst of it occurred once they'd climbed to a great altitude and the plane went into a turn. Outside his window, downtown San Francisco shrank below, became some tiny three-dimensional memory of a city. With the motion of the plane, it felt as though he were about to be staring up at it. He wondered if he might fall from his seat and hit the plane's ceiling. A film of sweat lined his palms. The tingling in the soles of his feet grew into a painful, piercing throb. His breathing turned shallow. He clutched the armrests on each side of him, as though he might be able to hold the plane together by those two bits of upholstery. How would he possibly survive more than six hours in this machine?

*

After dinner, the sound of hymns from the evangelical church was broken by the *norteño* music again. Wilmer and Mina dropped their spoons and tortillas onto their plates.

"Stay here," Mina insisted.

Wilmer nodded. She walked out to the road.

As soon as his mother left the house, Wilmer rose from the table and ran to the latrine. His hands shook as he brought his gun down from the rafters and removed it from the plastic bag. Renegado waited outside. Wilmer wished the dog wouldn't follow at a time like this, its white form visible even in the dark. He made a hushing sound—finger before his lips—as if Renegado might understand.

Wilmer ran around the far side of the house and hid behind the kitchen. Thankfully, the truck's headlights were off. As if in an action movie, he trained the weapon on the teenage driver in the cab. "Pow," Wilmer whispered, drawing the sound out on the ends of his lips. He turned it closer to the house, where his mother and the fat *coyote* stood talking. She didn't curse him this time. Their conversation appeared oddly civil.

"This is all you had to say, Niña Mina. Your troubles with me will soon be over." Don Noe spoke in a tone that was sickeningly kind. Wilmer aimed at his back—where he imagined the lungs were—and made the gunshot sound to himself again.

"Come back tomorrow," he heard his mother say. "While my son is at school. And come alone."

"Of course." The *coyote* nodded.

For a half second, Wilmer wondered why his mother would invite their enemy back the following day. But that notion was quickly eclipsed by this knowledge: the *coyote* would be here, alone, and expecting Wilmer to be absent. It was a perfect setup.

From behind, Wilmer heard footsteps and the repeated address: "Brother." The evangelical service must have ended, the parishioners now returning to their homes. He tucked the pistol under his shirt and went back around the house. By the time he stepped inside the latrine, the truck engine fired up outside with an accordion blast on the stereo. Once he'd stowed the gun, the truck was gone.

Mina sat at the table again, hugging her own arms. Wilmer went by the cistern and washed his hands, as if he'd just made a routine visit to the latrine. They both sat down and resumed their meals.

"Soon," his mother said, "that awful man will be gone from our lives."

With calm and even breathing, Wilmer replied: "I know he will, mom. I know he will."

*

After dark, the plane made its first landing. Jacinto thought he heard the word "Texas," but wasn't sure where they were. Mostly gringos disembarked, while more Latinos boarded. Many of them appeared to be the spoiled children of San Salvador's upper class, but some were older folks—perhaps granted visas to visit their stateside families, now that the US consulate considered them too old to work. Crew Cut stayed put. Jacinto was confused by the time zones and hour changes, but gathered that he'd be travelling through the night.

The second takeoff felt less terrifying. This time, the city below was reduced to nothing more than a series of colored lights, like stars. After they reached their cruising altitude, the flight attendant rolled a cart down the aisle. The smell of warm food filled the fuselage. Jacinto hadn't eaten all day. How much were they charging for the meals? He craned his neck over the seats in front of him to see if any cash was exchanged.

By the time the cart finally came to his row of seats, Jacinto was ravenous. He watched how Crew Cut lowered the seatback tray, and then did the same. Jacinto found himself smiling at this bit of clever design. The gringo exchanged a few words with the flight attendant. Then she turned to Jacinto.

"Chicken or pasta?" she asked in Spanish.

"How much does the chicken cost?" he said.

She smiled wide and stifled a half laugh. "It's *gratis*, señor."

Jacinto felt a mix of relief and embarrassment, then said, "chicken, please," not knowing what she'd meant by pasta.

She handed him a tray and turned to serve the gringo his supper.

This food had an odd texture, but Jacinto had no trouble finishing it in a few minutes, going so far as to wipe up the dregs with the sphere of soft bread that he'd been given—inside its own transparent wrapper. Soon, what he found before him was a pile of disposable plastic and cardboard. The airline, it seemed, was well versed in the gringo manner of mixing ingenuity with wastefulness.

Once the food and its paraphernalia had been cleared, many of the passengers slept in their reclined seats. The physical symptoms of Jacinto's fear— the sweaty palms, the rapid heartbeat, the needle-like sensation in the soles of his feet—abated and allowed him to relax. His eyes finally closed and he let his head fall against the wall of the fuselage.

The first bump shocked him straight awake. Had they crashed? Were they under attack? Another great bump shook the entire aircraft. Jacinto looked around in a panic. A few people adjusted their pillows, but as a whole the passengers were nonplussed. What was wrong with everybody?

The bumps continued, as though this section of sky were full of potholes. Jacinto clutched the armrests again and swallowed the fact that this must be acceptable for such a trip. He closed his eyes and told himself to calm down. "You're in no danger," he said under his breath. "You lived through much worse on the journey north."

As the aluminum tube bounced and jostled, Jacinto looked up and around. Where was the escape route from this thing? Were he atop the train again, he would jump off and try his luck later. What could one do to get free of this contraption?

"*Amigo*, hey, *amigo?*" Crew Cut spoke to him now, aware that something was wrong but also that the two of them shared no common language.

Jacinto stared back with big eyes and short breath. "I want to get off this thing." Jacinto whispered in Spanish. A metallic sensation lined his throat and started down into his stomach. He braced himself.

The gringo shoved the open end of a waxy white paper sac over Jacinto's mouth. With a laborious and painful wrenching, the barely digested supper spewed forth into the bag. Jacinto coughed and hacked up the last bits. His face grew hot and broke out in beads of sweat. The gringo offered a clean napkin and pressed a button on the ceiling.

The vomiting forced Jacinto's breathing to calm, as though some of the anxiety was expelled along with the contents of his stomach.

The attendant came and carried away the paper bag, then offered Jacinto a moist towel made of real cloth and an open can of fizzy soda. Crew Cut patted Jacinto on the shoulder.

Jacinto spent some hours with the moistened towel draped over his face like a boxer. At some point, a sharp needle of sunlight pricked its way through both the towel and his eyelids, and he rose to have a look. Too exhausted for fear now, Jacinto gazed out the window and saw a landscape below. Upon first glance, he knew that he stared down at El Salvador: the narrow valleys, the volcanic hills, clusters of light still on in what must have been the outskirts of the capital.

He scooted forward and pinned his face to the glass—the surface cool against the skin of his nose. He saw a road, which he thought to be the La Libertad highway. One valley over, he found another road. Was this the one that ran through Carasucia? The very road he lived on? It was hard to tell from this angle, but he saw no reason to believe otherwise. In a matter of hours, Jacinto estimated, he'd be telling Mina and Wilmer about his experience of flying, of looking down upon this, his native land.

But the plane cut too tight an angle and Jacinto lost track of his road. El Salvador's surface grew closer as they lost altitude. He saw what had to be the Highway Litoral below. A cane-field fire sent up a cloud of black smoke. Semi trucks moved like square beads along a string. He saw the coastline, the white caps of waves crashing into rock and sand. Now, Jacinto didn't find it odd or funny that his gringo musician friends had wanted so badly to come here and walk upon warm water. It was a beautiful country. It had everything one might ask for, except work.

To Jacinto's surprise, the plane's trajectory took them far out over the sea, not straight to Comalapa as he'd assumed. With only water below, they banked hard to the left. Thankfully, Jacinto sat on the upside of this turn. Once they straightened out again, he saw that the ground was much closer. Ahead, he caught a glimpse of the airport's concrete tower, lit up orange by the rosy-fingered dawn.

And then, just a moment later, with a bump and a soft rattle, a squeak of rubber upon asphalt, Jacinto was home.

22

IN THE IMMIGRATION LINE, JACINTO AGAIN FELT A RUSH OF vomit-inducing anxiety. He took the very last bit of American currency he had, a mangled ten-dollar bill, and discreetly tucked it between the pages of his fake Mexican passport—the corners of which were already coming apart. The line puttered forward like a funeral march, only two officers working the counter. Had Jacinto his *cedula*, he could go through the national line and be done with all of this. But that document was with his wife, some few fifty miles from here. If he were caught now, and thrown into prison, would there be any way to prove that he was a citizen of this country? Would his countrymen recognize him as a fellow national, the way that every single Mexican seemed able to do at a glance?

Jacinto finally reached the counter. The agent in whose hands he placed both his travel document and his fate couldn't have been more than nineteen. The fuzzy beginnings of an ill-conceived mustache clung to his otherwise smooth face like residue from a dark beverage.

The bill fell awkwardly out onto the young man's counter. He looked over his shoulder to check for attention from his supervisors. With his index finger, he rubbed at one eye. Jacinto realized that this young man must've worked through the night. He fingered the split corner of the fake passport, chuckled at little, and looked up at Jacinto. One of his hands stuffed the ten into his front pocket, while with his lips he pointed toward the exit and motioned for Jacinto to go on.

*

Wilmer and his mother passed an awkward morning together, each with their own secret plan for the *coyote*. The collected women of Carasucia gathered across from their house, with baskets of dirty clothes and water receptacles, to wait for the bus which would take them closer to the river. Wilmer watched them from near the front door. This was proof positive that the rainy season had ended. Now, Mina would have to factor such trips into her schedule. The months of hoarding and hustling for water—which Don Felix and his gringo sought to end forever with their aqueduct—had begun again. Wilmer caught his mother stealing a glance at the level in their cistern.

Wilmer prepared for school. He gathered his notebooks and backpack, put on the starched white dress shirt and dark blue trousers. They ate a lunch of soup made from new beans, a bit of chopped onion on the top. In a memory as fleeting and elusive as a ghost, Wilmer recalled how his father used to crack an egg onto this steaming soup and let it cook there inside the serving bowl.

Wilmer cleaned his teeth after the meal, careful not to waste water. His mother hauled their dishes to the *lavadero* at the side of the cistern.

"Goodbye, Mama," Wilmer said as his mother stood washing, then walked toward the school.

*

Once free of the airport's kiosks, crowds, and uniformed officers, Jacinto felt that he was in familiar territory for the first time in months: the sunrise from over the *cerros*, the salt air mixed with the pungent smell of burning cane, the sound of insects that he could name, even the dust itself was familiar here.

It must've been a good rainy season, Jacinto decided as he crossed the parking lot. The shoulders of the road were verdant and lush with weeds and vegetation. An empty cane truck rattled its way around the bend and came toward Jacinto. He stuck his thumb out, noticing several other men in the back.

The driver was kind enough to pull over. Thankful to be in a country without silly laws against such a thing, Jacinto climbed into the back.

Along with two other men, he stood clinging to the wooden walls—still sticky with cane juice—as the truck bounced its way down the road. Jacinto widened his stance and bent his knees, thinking again of his gringo friends and the way they'd held their balance whilst riding waves. Between the boards, Jacinto watched a miniature film of his native country. Men swung machetes out at their sides on their way to their fields. With *guacales* of corn balanced atop their heads, women walked toward their local mills to make *masa*, always reaching up to sample a course kernel or two as they went.

Skinny children with coins in their hands sprinted toward *tiendas*, sent by parents or neighbors to buy a bit of cheese or cream for breakfast. Jacinto smiled broadly at the sight of it. This was what he knew, the way he wanted to live. And while he still wasn't sure how he'd handle his son's illness, or his family's harassment by that corrupt *coyote*, he was never more certain that he had to handle it himself, and here. The landscape, the air, the dirt—they all cried out in a chorus of affirmation for this, his homecoming.

The truck slowed at the *desvio* and turned inland. To Jacinto's surprise, they were about to head toward the capital. This was odd, as most of the sugar cane fields lie further west, along the coastal planes. Perhaps the truck needed maintenance. He shuffled forward along the flatbed and tapped upon the back of the cab—the national hitch-hiking vernacular for: "stop and let me off here." The driver obliged.

*

Wilmer walked slowly across the village, past the gringo's house, past the spot by the soccer field where they'd sold tamales and *elotes* for naught. He paused and watched the children file in and out of the schoolhouse, the teachers rising out of the crowd and shepherding it like a flock of livestock.

As he stood at the outer fringe of this herd of pupils, Wilmer questioned his plan. Would he find a way out of class once inside? The *coyote* might arrive at any second. How would he know when to leave? It occurred to him now that once he crossed these gates, there might not be a chance to turn back.

At his rear, Wilmer felt the push of fellow students. He side-stepped his way out of the crowd and turned toward home.

"Wilmer, Wilmer!"

He heard the shrill call of a schoolteacher and turned to see Señora Miriam staring at him.

"Where are you going?" she hollered.

"I have to return home," he yelled back. Their gazes were locked and Wilmer could see that she remained unconvinced. "I don't feel well," he heard himself say over the crowd of disinterested kids. Then, for the first time in his life, Wilmer faked shallow breathe and an asthmatic wheeze. He put a hand to his chest and bent at the waist a bit.

Once free the teacher's sight, Wilmer stood straight up and walked normally. He came again to the main road. This time, the fat man's pickup was parked in front of his home, the *EXODUS* across its tailgate shining like a cruel joke.

Wilmer looked from side to side. Few neighbors were about; nobody paid him any mind. The village women were still at the river, not here to fuss and gossip over the problems of the Paredes household. With a light and stealthy step, Wilmer crossed the street and walked right up to the truck. For once, nobody waited inside. He tried the handle. It was locked, of course. Through the window, he had a look around the inside. There was no sign of the *coyote's* little revolver.

Down the side street along the far end of his house, where the evangelical church sat, Wilmer walked with his backpack held up over his face. If his mother caught sight of him through the fence and the trees, she'd assume from the uniform that he was another pupil heading home from morning classes. Once past his house, Wilmer cut into the wooded yard out back, through his mother's banana and papaya trees, around the piles of rinds and food scraps that Mina threw out here to rot.

With careful steps, Wilmer ducked inside the latrine. As he unwrapped the gun from the plastic bags for the second time in as many days, he noticed that not only were his hands trembling, but that his breathes had grown fast and shallow, for real.

*

As the heat of the day set in, Jacinto walked along the Litoral. A public bus trolled past, baskets strapped to its roof rack. The *cobrador* hung off the side and shouted destinations. The bus pulled off onto the shoulder a couple blocks ahead, and two ladies disembarked. Jacinto touched the front pockets of his jeans, feeling for coins, but found nothing. Many hot miles stood between him and the road that cut inland towards Carasucia, and he might have to walk it all. A cane truck went by, and Jacinto diligently held out his thumb, but the truck was travelling too fast to stop. All the driver offered was a blast of exhaust-laden wind. Jacinto kept walking.

Soon, he came to the *"zona franca"*—a clever euphemism for a giant cluster of sweatshops. Buses of young men and women came in and out, some of them obviously having worked all night. Flirtatious giggles were passed amongst the younger ones. Work here mainly held a social function. Despite the Salvadoran president's repeated proclamations that single mothers could support their families in such jobs, it was well known—at least in Jacinto's village—that one could scarcely afford lunch and bus fare after a ten-hour shift in the *maquílas*.

Even in the few months he'd been gone, the *zona franca* had doubled in size. Jacinto feared that it would soon creep its way dangerously close to his home, that this whole country might soon become similar to the city of Chihuahua—a wasteland of factories, construction sites for new factories, and squatter camps for the poor folks who worked on both.

He knew that nobody would stop to pick up a hitchhiker here; too many others would try and climb aboard to save their bus fare.

Once free of the sweatshop zone, Jacinto's highway followed a great expanse of cane fields. A large square of green stood out amongst the others—which were black and bare, recently burned. Jacinto stopped walking for a second and stretched his legs. A semi passed and broke the heat. He checked to see if anyone approached, then ducked in amongst the stalks of cane. Wishing he had a machete with him, Jacinto selected a slender piece and broke it off by hand. After a short and vigorous series of twists and pulls, he managed to free it from the plant.

The next mile or so was a bit more bearable, with a fresh length of sugarcane to suck on. Jacinto peeled back the skin, bit off chunks of the flesh, and chewed them until the sugar was all gone. Along the road, he spit out mouthfuls of dry fiber in between fresh bites.

The distance was greater than Jacinto remembered. His stomach ached with emptiness and dry skin rose in clumps upon his lips. He eyed a few tall coconut palms and wondered if he could overcome his fear and climb them. But how would he even open a coconut without so much as a machete? No matter, he told himself. Soon he'd be drinking coffee in his own house, eating tortillas made by his wife's hand, from corn harvested by his son. One long walk was nothing, in the big picture.

It was well into the afternoon by the time he reached the *desvio*, where the little village of Santa Cruz clung to one side of the Litoral. Though he had no money for the fare, he sat down upon the log that served as a makeshift bus stop. His feet ached and he hoped to rest them a bit before the harder uphill hike. He closed his eyes and forced himself to imagine the village, his home. For some reason, the only image he got was that of a raging fire. He tried this several times with the exact same result, then gave it up and opened his eyes.

A number seventeen bus, Carasucia's local, passed in the opposite direction, coming from the village. Jacinto stared up. Through the dust and the glare, he spotted several familiar faces—women he knew. On the roof of this bus, nets of twine held down *cantaros*, buckets, and baskets of laundry. Already, Jacinto thought, the women travel down here to wash clothes. An idea took hold: might Mina be among them? They often went as a group, to avoid harassment from the ladies who lived here. The bridge under which they washed was only a mile or so out of his way.

Jacinto rose and walked fast in the bus's wake, hoping that Mina might have a few spare coins for his own bus fare. Again, with his tired legs and dehydrated head, the distance grew longer than he'd remembered. He passed a bicycle repair shop, in which a shirtless young man banged a hammer upon a metal bar. A group of school children, younger than Wilmer, stopped at the iron cage of a *tienda* on one corner. They bought plastic bags full of colored drinks. One by one, they bit off a corner and squeezed red syrup into their mouths.

By the time Jacinto reached the river, the women had all unloaded and were engrossed in the laundry process. Each set up upon a separate stone, and spread their articles of clothing out along with soap and a stiff brush. Jacinto took a visual inventory—once, twice, three times—until he was sure that Mina wasn't among them.

He was not the only onlooker upon the bluff. Two young men sat atop bicycles much too short for them. With their jaws hung slack, they stared down at the women of Carasucia, hoping for a peek of nipple through a soaked blouse. Immediately, Jacinto felt shame for appearing to seek the same cheap thrill. He considered walking down to the riverbed, reminding them of who he was and telling his story. Perhaps someone would lend him a few coins for the bus. But he didn't wish to explain. In his mind's ear he could already overhear the village rumor mill: Mina's husband paid a *coyote*, only to return penniless.

This ill-conceived idea had already cost him too much time. Jacinto turned and walked back the way he'd come, towards the *desvio* and then uphill.

*

When Wilmer emerged from the latrine, Renegado waited at the door with a wagging tail. The dog cocked his head. The gun felt heavy in Wilmer's hand. The whole arm trembled like it was broken and needed help from his other limbs. His breathing passages constricted. Whatever he was about to do, Wilmer realized, he'd have to do it fast.

He leaned against the cistern with one hand as he made his way into the house proper. Where were they? He saw no sign of his mother or the fat *coyote*. Wilmer had half a mind to check the road and see if the truck still sat there. For a moment, his diaphragm relaxed and his breathing calmed.

It was Renegado who noticed it first. The dog went right up to Mina's bedroom door, nose first, then let out a series of confused barks. Wilmer followed with the lightest steps he could manage.

The door was made from two rectangles of tin mounted to a wooden frame—his father's design, no doubt. Above the barks from the dog, and barely muted through the metal door, Wilmer heard another set of animal noises: a squeal of base male pleasure, a groan of endurance from a woman.

Wilmer's breath left him in an instant, as if he'd been kicked in the belly by a horse. He fell against the vertical beam that held up the roof of the house. His mother was in there, in the bedroom, with that most loathsome man. Wilmer's vision grew grainy and his world spun.

He hugged the stripped-branch beam with both his arms. Wheezes whistled through his sinuses. Renegado's relentless barks masked the sound of Wilmer's asthma. The boy pulled himself together. His hatred for Don Noe filled his chest and felt a decent substitute for air. He breathed it deep.

*

The hill was steep and long. Jacinto had rarely walked its entire length. The shoulder allowed some nice views of the sea and coastal plains. He passed by the unofficial dump: a ravine with easy access, where people threw anything too big or chemical-laden to burn or bury in their yard. He had a look down: car batteries, old cans of paint. What looked to be the carcass of a small dog poked out from a plastic bag, teemed with flies, and would soon attract buzzards. The wind shifted and brought the ripe smell of decomposition. He turned his head and kept on walking.

Jacinto had abandoned hope for a ride and resigned himself to walking all the way when the banana truck rose on the horizon. He dutifully put out his thumb, but was surprised to see the silver pickup pull off the side and stop. Jacinto climbed into the back, careful not to crush the yellow fruit.

Even the engine struggled with this hill. It revved up and down in starts and stops, trying to find the right gear. The road leveled off, approaching the plateau on which Carasucia sat. The truck's speed increased. Jacinto looked ahead. For a moment, he thought he was hallucinating. Not a half-mile away, the road became a tunnel of fire—almost like the vision he'd had a few moments ago. He ducked down behind the cab and covered the sides of his face with his forearms. All around, he saw nothing but orange and yellow flames. Had he hitched a ride into some circle of hell, rather than to his home? Had he somehow caused this to happen, simply by imagining it? As a sweat broke out all over his skin like a rash, the fire abated. He studied it from behind and understood that somebody had set fire to the fields on either side of the road. The flames leapt nearly all the way across. Burning the scrub in a spent corn-field was a common practice. It increased yield in the short term, but damaged the soil after a few years. His heart still beating hard, he told himself to calm down.

Carasucia crept up on him. His puzzlement over the fire had distracted Jacinto from their progress. The truck came to a stop and Jacinto noticed that he was parked in front of Don Valentín's *tienda*. The driver came around to fetch a crate of bananas. Don Valentín walked over as well. Jacinto's eyes caught his.

"Don Jacinto?" the store owner said.

"Don Valentín." Jacinto nodded, as though it were a polite greeting and not a confused inquiry. "Good afternoon." He rose from the bed of the pickup and turned to his home.

*

Wilmer backpedaled until he stood by the cistern. He picked up his moth-er's cake of laundry soap and hurled it at the bedroom door. The metal rang like a gong. One hand still wrapped around the gun, Wilmer's other hand found the scrub brush and chucked that as well, then a near-ripe mango his mother had set along the cistern's rim. The door sounded with a chorus of rings and clangs. Confused voices came from inside.

Finally, the *coyote* pulled the door open, spouting a storm of grunts and curses. "*Hijo de la gran puta!*" He wore a blood-red button-down shirt. With one hand, he still pulled dark jeans up over the white of his underwear. The scorpion belt buckle hung slack at one side.

"You little fucker." The fat man came toward Wilmer. "So many times I tell you but you don't listen." He lifted an arm across his chest, as if preparing to deliver a backhand strike.

Wilmer raised the gun.

The *coyote* noticed it for the first time and froze. He set his teeth into his lip and held both hands up.

Wilmer was underwater now. The airway to his lungs tightened to the size of a pinprick.

"Now you be careful with that thing, son." The *coyote* attempted a calm and peaceful tone. "Why don't you give me that before anyone gets hurt?"

"I'm not your son, you fat fuck!" Even to Wilmer, his own belabored voice sounded like it belonged to a cartoon frog.

"Wilmer? Is that you?" His mother came to the door, the bed sheets wrapped about her otherwise naked body. "My God!" she shouted upon seeing the pistol. "Put that thing down!" Tears formed in her eyes.

"Listen to your mother," the fat man continued. "Me and her, we've sorted out our problems. I won't be bothering you anymore." He took a step toward Wilmer and held out an upturned palm. "Give me that thing, son."

"For the last goddamn time, I'm not your son!" The small amount of air still in Wilmer's lungs all left along with that curse.

*

Jacinto had only gone a few steps before he noticed the familiar truck parked alongside his house, the airbrushed *EXODUS* upon its tailgate. His clip sped and then slowed a little. He looked around for something—a machete to borrow, a stone that would fit inside his fist, a big stick, a broken bottle, even a baby-food jar to use as a weapon the way that Israel had atop the train. Jacinto wouldn't need to wait to settle his score with this cheating scoundrel of a *coyote*. It would be his first act as prodigal father.

He would be smart, Jacinto decided. He wouldn't run in full of rage. No one else appeared to be inside the pickup. The *coyote* had come alone. Two skinny girls in dirty Sunday dresses dashed by on their way to the store. He looked around for his neighbors, these people he'd never made a sincere-enough effort to befriend. Who in this village might give him a sharpened machete? Did anybody have a gun to lend?

The second that the word "gun" went through his imagination, Jacinto heard the first shot. He wondered briefly if he'd developed some sort of telepathic superpower. And if he had, why not imagine something good happening at a time like this?

Another shot sounded. Then another. Renegado ran out the door, past his long-absent master, frightened by the noise. Jacinto forgot all about finding a weapon or a strategy and ran the remaining half block to his home.

*

The first shot nearly knocked Wilmer over. For the next two, he used both arms. The pistol was like a bucking horse he had to wrestle control of, a fire hose. But surely, at least some of the bullets found their fat target.

Wilmer's vision blurred, but not before he saw a bit of blood cough up from the *coyote*'s mouth and mingle with his mustache. After that, Wilmer lost the ability to see.

His mission complete, he felt the asthma attack he'd kept at bay for so many minutes finally wash up through him like a wave.

*

Upon entering his home, Jacinto's first sight was of two bodies strewn across the floor. The smell of spent powder and a sulfurous smoke hung about the room. Jacinto remembered such odors from his days in the conflict. A woman screamed. His wife, wrapped in a sheet like she was a toga-clad character from some Greek tragedy, fell to her knees at the threshold of their bedroom.

He looked down at the bodies. Don Noe lay still on his back. His pants were undone and his shirttails hung out. The scorpion belt buckle lay to one side. Several bullet holes were in his chest, Jacinto now realized. The blood that seeped out soaked into a button-down shirt the exact same shade of red.

He turned to the other body and at last recognized it as his son. Lying by his side—as casually as the belt buckle—was a class of handgun which Jacinto also recognized from the conflict. His son's chest rose and fell—a motion more akin to coughing than breathe. Jacinto composed himself and ran over, fell to the ground. "Mina!" he shouted, "Did you get the inhaler that I sent? Did you buy one with the money that I wired?"

"What inhaler?" she cried. "What money? I've received nothing!"

"Coffee then!" Jacinto screamed.

She rose with a nod and ran to the kitchen. Jacinto lifted his son's head off the ground.

"Wilmer," he said, "Wilmer," incapable of speaking any other word. Jacinto suspended judgment on this bizarre scene. His journey had taught him that searching for reason can be as worthwhile as a dog chasing its tail. As if on cue, Renegado walked back in and cocked his head at the pair of them. Wilmer wheezed in his father's arms. Jacinto wished he could reach down the boy's throat and pull something out.

"Wilmer, Wilmer, Wilmer." He chanted the boy's name. Eyes closed, Jacinto put his forehead against his son's. He recalled how thinking of a gun resulted in the shots a minute ago. How thinking of a dog caused Renegado to appear. Within the last hour, a vision of fire had resulted in a real one. If he thought of something miraculous right now, was there any chance it might actually come to pass?

Mina came back with a cup of dark liquid and a spoon. She frantically mixed instant coffee into water. Jacinto lifted his son by the armpits so that he sat a little straighter, held up his forehead with one hand.

"Here we are," Mina whispered like a lullaby. "Here you go, m'ijo." She poured the coffee into the boy's mouth. Wilmer made a best effort at drinking. The unbearable wheezing sounds stopped for a second, and Jacinto allowed himself to believe that there was a less-than-tragic end to things.

He looked around the room. Had his son shot the *coyote*? Such a thing seemed unthinkable, and was a distant second to his primary concern.

*

Wilmer felt as if he were swimming upward—trying to reach the surface only to rediscover the infinity of the sea. Finally, he let a bit of ocean into his mouth, held it there, swallowed. In what must've been an unconscious cross between dream and memory, he thought he heard the voice of his far-away father calling his name.

The boy didn't understand exactly what was happening, but he knew this attack was different. It wouldn't end the way the others had. Wilmer was okay with this. After so many minutes—so many years, really—of struggling for breath within an indifferent world, he was well prepared for something new. Wilmer ceased fighting against the change.

Wilmer had been taught to fear this situation from an early age. He'd suffered many close calls during his short life. Still, once it finally came for him, death gave his heart no notice.

*

Wilmer's mouth exploded in a cough. Dark liquid spiked with solid crystals of instant mix flew everywhere. Jacinto felt his son's spine contort like a snake. The wheezing gave way to the sort of worthless gasps a fish makes upon the ground. His chest still pressed against the boy's back, Jacinto felt something else. The fight drained out of Wilmer's body. He'd given up; his father could feel it as sure as a candle blowing out. Renegado let go a sad bark as if he noticed it too. Seconds ticked off with no sign of struggle from the boy. He ceased to move altogether.

"The water has to be hot; otherwise it won't dissolve," Jacinto shouted at his wife.

"You think he can wait for it to boil?" she snapped back.

Mina embraced her son's body. Jacinto let her take the weight of the torso. They formed a sort of pieta there—the mother and son—this one more awful than any Jacinto had seen on a church wall or stained glass window.

Jacinto shook his head. He rubbed his fists into his eyes. With his palms, he slapped his own face. He kept waiting to wake up—on Chano's couch, in the Chiapas jungle, under a California overpass, atop a train even—anywhere that wasn't still inside this awful nightmare in which his son wouldn't live. Every decision Jacinto had made, every bit of toil and trouble, it was all aimed at preventing this, Wilmer's death by asthma, Jacinto's greatest fear. What was it that Israel had told him about fear and hope? Had Jacinto somehow caused this tragedy, by trying so hard to resist it?

As the sulfur smell abated, he caught a whiff of something else. It was the same odor that caused him so much shame back in that orange grove. His wife smelt of sex. He looked back to the slain body of the corrupt smuggler and finally did the crude arithmetic of debt and survival. He didn't blame his wife for fucking that awful man, any more than he blamed his son for shooting him. He blamed himself for having left them both to such a fate.

23

WHEN JACINTO SAW THE GRINGO IN THE DOORWAY, HE thought for a second that he had indeed awoken from a dream. Perhaps he'd fallen asleep while inside the store in San Francisco, and now was seeing one of their regular customers—dressed like a slob but with pockets full of money.

A wheezing sound came from his son, and Jacinto immediately remembered where he was.

"Wilmer? Niña Mina?" The gringo looked inside and couldn't make sense of the sight. Soon, his eyes settled on Wilmer there on the floor. The color drained from his face. The object in his hands—was it a box?—fell with a thud against the dirt floor. He made a breathless statement in his own language. Jacinto thought he heard the English word for God.

Only once the gringo had forgotten it entirely did Jacinto recognize the small box on the floor. It was a Gigante Express package. It was his package.

As he went to pick it up, Jacinto cursed his cut-short nails and the strength of gringo tape. By the time it was in his hands, he was prepared to chew through the cardboard if necessary. He made a dull point from his thumb and forefinger and pressed it like a drill into the top of the box until the clear tape gave with a pop.

Mina must've thought her husband was taking his anger out on this box for no reason. But when she saw the small plastic device that he produced from it, she immediately understood what he was doing. She held the boy up. Unsure how the inhaler worked, Jacinto gingerly placed it to Wilmer's lips and waited for something to happen. The strange gringo was the one who finally pressed down on the tin canister and released the mist.

The first burst barely made it into Wilmer's mouth, but by the second one, Jacinto had the hang of it. All too slowly, in unbearably small increments of coughs, wheezes, and breaths, Jacinto's son came back to life. The three adults set him in a plastic chair, the inhaler by his side, and watched as he began to breathe normally.

If his descent into death had been a slow and gentle fading, Wilmer's return to life was abrupt, violent, and without grace. The organs inside his chest clamored for blood and air. They knocked greedily against his ribcage and spine. A fit of dry coughing sanded away at his throat. Slowly, with a series of floating lines and bright blurs, vision returned to his eyes. The first sight of his second life materialized in an image of his father, holding a vaguely familiar plastic device. His mother stood behind him, along with a gringo whose name escaped Wilmer.

Their three mouths moved with what must've been speech. Hearing seemed to be the one sense that still stubbornly refused to return. Both Wilmer's ears were filled with a dull ringing noise. For the first minute or so, his memory was worthless. But when he had a look around the house and saw the fat man on the floor, the events of the past days and months came back to him in spades.

*

Once sure that his son was alive, Jacinto considered the dead man inside his house. He picked up the pistol and locked the safety, as though scared it might do more harm. Mina stroked Wilmer's hair. The gringo stood watching. Jacinto walked out to the street.

The northbound bus arrived and the women of Carasucia disembarked. Husbands and sons ran out to meet them and help. The entire village surrounded the bus, ferrying laundry and jugs of brownish river water—the first time this year that they performed the dry season's weekly ritual. Jacinto studied their faces, remembering who they were, wanting more than anything to be part of such a family chore.

It only took a second or two before a few of the women stared at Jacinto and whispered. They pointed to the pickup parked along his house. Jacinto looked down at the end of his arm and was shocked to see the gun still there. He nearly threw it to the ground, as if it were a stinging insect landed in his hand. No wonder they pointed and whispered. He tucked the pistol into the waist of his trousers, at the small of his back. People kept staring. They seemed ready to watch him and what remained of his family for the rest of the day and on into the night. This wasn't over.

Back inside, Mina continued to stroke Wilmer's hair. The boy breathed normally, but had not spoken. He put a hand on each of their shoulders.

"Mina, Wilmer," he said. I think we might be in some trouble. How have you been getting along with the neighbors?"

"Horribly," she said.

Jacinto nodded, then turned his head toward the body on the floor. "This man was murdered. Nobody's likely to believe that it was done by a thirteen year old."

"You don't think the police will believe it?"

"The police are one thing. Don Noe's people are another. His circle of friends and associates are not known for their forgiving nature."

"So what do we do?"

Jacinto exhaled, looked at his wife, then his son, then back to his wife again. "I think we have to run."—the one thing which he wanted most not to do anymore.

Mina nodded.

"Do you have the keys to the truck?" the gringo asked in passable Spanish. "I could drive you to the border."

Jacinto turned to face him. "Who are you?"

"They call me Don Jefe." He extended his hand and they shook.

"He's my friend, Papa. He's a good man." Those were the first words Jacinto had heard his son speak since leaving.

He turned to face Wilmer. What was he meant to do in this situation? Wasn't this an occasion for discipline or perhaps some fatherly wisdom? But Jacinto could muster no such thing.

Instead, he rifled through the fat man's pockets and found his wallet, which contained a good deal of both Salvadoran and American cash. Jacinto decided he didn't want to look at the smuggler's ugly face anymore. He took a blanket off his wife's bed and covered the body up. Next, he took the pistol out and had a look at it. The clip held two more bullets. Jacinto returned it to his waistband and let his shirt hang over it.

The gringo spoke to Mina, who still wore only the sheet. "Where will you go now?"

Mina turned to Jacinto.

"If we're going to be criminals anyway." Jacinto decided there was no harm in confiding in this stranger. "We might as well go north. There we'll at least have food in our illegal bellies."

Don Jefe didn't look surprised. "I have some things that might help you, along the way. I'll come right back."

Jacinto nodded then turned to his wife. "Mina," he said. "Pack a bag: whatever food we can carry, any cash we have around, some kind of warm coat. Put on work clothes and your sturdiest shoes."

*

Wilmer's heart was well tried with trouble, but this was too much for him to handle. They were leaving home? Now? What about the corn? What about Renegado?

A body and a gun lie on the floor. It was Wilmer's fault. Weren't his parents going to yell at him? Shouldn't he be apologizing, admitting his errors? He didn't want to cover up this crime, so much as to erase it, undo it somehow.

Once Wilmer turned and saw the three men standing at the entrance to his house, he understood that his family was altered for good. There would be no time for atoning, only for survival.

*

"Welcome home, Don Jacinto." The words came from the entrance to the house. Like a confirmation of Jacinto's fears, three men entered. "With permission?"

"Enter." Jacinto nodded. "It's been a while, Don Felix."

"I hope you have a very sound explanation for this." Don Felix gestured to the fat body on the floor behind him. "I don't take deaths in my village lightly."

"My son shot this man." Jacinto didn't mean to expose Wilmer, but he was so sick of lying.

Don Felix rolled his eyes. "You're going to blame this on your boy?"

"No." Jacinto placed a hand on his waistband. He felt the pistol's presence poke against his lower back. "My son pulled the trigger, just as I said. But I blame myself."

"I'm going to have to ask you to stay here, while we send for the police."

One of Don Felix's sons took a half step closer to Jacinto and Mina.

"I'm afraid that's quite impossible." Jacinto's free hand tingled. How many years had it been since he'd last held a gun at another person?

The tension was abruptly broken by the returning gringo. Don Jefe walked in with an armload of gear and gadgets. He greeted the new visitors.

He dropped the goods on the table then turned to Don Felix. "What are we going to do?"

"*Pues...*" Don Felix was taken aback. "Perhaps we should call for the police."

"The police? Are you joking? We need to get rid of this body, as well as that truck. Quickly."

The gringo spoke to Wilmer who still sat in the plastic chair. "Some of these things might help, on the trip."

Wilmer nodded and went to pick one up. Jacinto's eyes lingered on the sight: his son no longer the killer, once again a boy excited about some new toys for a moment.

The gringo turned back to Don Felix. "Is there anyone here who knows how to make a car disappear?"

Mina and Jacinto also turned to Don Felix, watching what went on behind his eyes. After a long and pregnant pause, he said: "One of my sons-in-law has experience with such things. I'll speak to him."

The gringo nodded then looked to the body on the floor under the sheet. "What do we do about this?"

"Him? We'll throw him in the fucking dump down the road, with the dead dogs and the car batteries." Jacinto no longer cared who the gringo was, only that he seemed to wield influence over Don Felix.

The gringo, Jacinto, and each of Don Felix's sons took a limb and carried the body out to the truck.

Don Felix's son-in-law Tito did offer to help. From San Salvador, he'd married one of Don Felix's daughters and moved to the village, but still commuted into the city for work. The risks were explained, but Tito assured everyone that he would sell the truck for parts once their mission was complete. He knew the right people, or so he claimed.

Jacinto wolfed down a simple supper of beans, tortillas, and the hard-cooked eggs which had split while Mina cooked the rest of them for their trip. He changed into a fresh set of his own clothes. The gringo had brought over a couple of canteen-type water bottles, a plastic rain jacket similar to those the army used during the war, and what looked to be an expensive collapsible pocketknife.

Before leaving, Jacinto took Don Felix aside. "Look after my little house, please, and my parcel of farmland as well. If somebody from the community needs a place to farm, or a place to live even, they are welcome here. We don't know when or if we'll be back. But don't offer my things to the highest bidder; offer them to those with the most necessity."

Don Felix nodded. "You have my word."

"The same goes for the corn and beans in the granaries. Better they be eaten than left to rot."

"I'll see to it," Don Felix said.

The two men shared a handshake.

The gringo climbed into the driver's seat of the pickup and started the engine. Mina and Wilmer loaded into the small space that passed for a back seat. Tito sat in the middle, his legs against the gearshift. Jacinto climbed in last, and immediately turned off the stereo.

The gringo popped the clutch and drove off. He hesitated once the ring of fire came into view, but Jacinto insisted that he drive fast down the center of the road and they'd be fine. Minutes later, they pulled off at the makeshift dump.

Jacinto felt no guilt as he tugged the *coyote*'s body down the length of the pickup bed. All the tragedies associated with the border and the trip north, so that men like this one could profit. Jacinto didn't despise the governments involved; they were designed to act in their own self-interest. But human beings should be different.

Jacinto put his arms under the fat man's shoulders and sent him tumbling off the truck and into the ravine. Good riddance, he thought, as the body thudded against the rest of the trash. He wiped his hands on his pants and climbed back inside the cab.

They took the Litoral west towards the border, a seldom-travelled route along cliffs above the wine-dark sea. In the gringo's hands, the truck bore them over broad ridges of land. It was a beautiful country, Jacinto decided. He wished there were some way he might stay.

"The United States," Tito said dramatically. "I hope to get there someday."

He was a kind young man, Jacinto thought, but naïve.

"I'd like to make some real money, you know. Build a house for my family. Maybe have my own business someday—fix motorcycles, perhaps."

"It's not that simple," Don Jefe said it before Jacinto had a chance to.

Tito had a romantic vision of that country to the north, based mainly on television and movies. Like so many Salvadorans of his generation, he dreamed of another America, one that existed in a sense, but that wasn't available to them. Their dream didn't include the America of smugglers, of crooked employers, of counterfeiters, of laborers sleeping on the street. Perhaps Jacinto had dreamed of a similar place when he started his travels so many months ago. But now, he had no illusions about which America he was heading to. Their destination was the lesser of evils, a place that might grant you a paycheck, but could take everything else in return. Now, he went without romantic notions, but with a heavy heart and no better ideas.

In the end, Jacinto decided not to disabuse Tito of his American dreams. Perhaps they did him more good than harm.

24

THE GUATEMALAN BORDER WAS OFFICIALLY CLOSED WHEN they arrived. Tito and Don Jefe said goodbye and drove off towards San Salvador, to get rid of the truck. Jacinto offered half the dead *coyote's* Salvadoran cash to the immigration agent on his side, the rest to the Guatemalan agent on the other. They walked through without trouble.

From there, they took a bus to El Carmen and then a raft across the river into Mexico. Again, the most treacherous stretch came atop trains in Chiapas. Jacinto showed the gun to three different would-be stick-up artists, but never fired either of the two remaining bullets.

Once in Oaxaca, they rode buses the rest of the way, courtesy of the fat man's fat billfold. Outside Laredo, they were ferried across the Río Bravo in inner tubes, along with many others. The *polleros* led them to a greyhound bus station. From there, it was easy. The three of them spent many hours on cramped buses, and slept inside the stations a couple of nights, but didn't miss meals and felt little danger. For more cash, Jacinto sold the pistol in Phoenix.

They made their way from Carasucia to San Francisco in less than two weeks. Part of their success was certainly due to the knowledge Jacinto had gained from his prior attempts. Much more was owed to the cash and the gun—two things that produced results in every nation of this continent. Still, Jacinto couldn't help but believe that there was another force at work.

This voyage had already taken so much from them. It had turned each of them into something they never wanted to be: an unfaithful wife, a bad father, a killer. They wore this indifference like armor as they travelled, and were made invincible by it. Perhaps that was the great irony of the migrant's trail north: those that go for the right reasons will have the hardest time. Those that go for the wrong reasons—with the wrong dreams—will find it no more difficult than walking through an open door.

Chano welcomed them warmly. He never again questioned Jacinto's return to El Salvador. Straight away, Mina found employment in the grocery store, with Eduardo. She worked hard and showed an uncanny capacity for the English language. The independence associated with her own job and her own paycheck suited her well; Jacinto was glad she got to experience it.

Though hesitant at first, after enough positive testimony from other Salvadoran families, they eventually sent Wilmer to the nearby public school. The boy was initially scared by the idea of a classroom full of gringos, but he soon learned that he was hardly a minority in his new neighborhood. He studied with more enthusiasm than ever before. His parents considered this a result of his near-death experience—the appreciation of his second chance. But in Wilmer's eyes—after watching how hard his parents worked and had struggled to get here—it was simply the least he could do.

Jacinto was advised to hold out for a more lucrative position on Juan Cuca's construction crew. This materialized within days, and paid even better than packing gear for gringo musicians. Within a month, they moved into their own apartment in the same building as Chano's. Chano joined them for meals several times a week. Mina made tortillas and *pupusas* from the dried corn flour sold in the shops along Mission Street.

Finding care for Wilmer's condition turned out to be far more complicated than anyone guessed. Conventional doctors and drug stores demanded prices outside of their means, even with the two American salaries. Finally, a kind employee from Wilmer's school accompanied him home one day. She directed them to a local clinic, where they waited in line for a while and filled out some incomprehensible paperwork, but were eventually given inhalers at a significant discount. Oddly, the climate in San Francisco seemed not to aggravate the boy's asthma as much as that of home.

By all accounts, it was a good life. If measured by the standards of rural El Salvador, theirs was the story of great success. But months went by, and Jacinto never could overcome the hollowed-out feeling he'd had since that single day in Carasucia. Though his son was thriving here, Jacinto hated the thought of Wilmer's life spent in a land where he wasn't welcome, where his very presence was considered an infraction of law. The boy's innocence, his childhood, was shot down that day, killed along with the fat *coyote*. Both he and his wife went through their lives worn and spiritless—Wilmer being their sole bright spot—each of their thoughts still dwelling on the Salvadoran home they'd failed to make.

Juan Cuca had Jacinto installing *azulejos* in a gringo family's bathrooms. The big house was in a hilltop neighborhood called Twin Peaks, which looked down on the Mission district and the rest of the city. On clear days, Jacinto could see the downtown skyscrapers. They called to mind the Mayan pyramids that once stood upon his homeland. He wondered about the poor working people who had built those stone structures for their noble and priestly castes: what sort of injustices did they suffer along the way? What would the archeologists of the future make of this city? Would they measure its significance by any standard other than the height of its buildings, the ambition of its architects?

In the second week of the job, a squadron of military airplanes performed acrobatic flight patterns over the city. Juan explained that they were part of an elite division called: "The Blue Angels." Other workers were endlessly amused by their flips and twists, the flamboyant cursive of their vapor trails. Jacinto could hardly imagine a greater waste of time or money. He remembered being bombed at Guazapa, and fought the urge to lay flat and cover his head whenever they passed over.

Winter weather in San Francisco was a daily coin toss. Mornings were either overcast and rainy or sunny and warm. The second Friday at the Twin Peaks house proved to be the clearest day he'd ever seen in the city. Charged with hauling out bucket-loads of old tile-work from yet another bathroom, Jacinto paused at Juan's truck and took in the view. He was able to see not only the famous Golden Gate Bridge and downtown's tall towers, but also the ports and smaller cities on the other side of the bay. The beach he'd stood upon with his two favorite gringos sparkled with sunlight and sea foam. He saw the broad golden hills of Marin County to the north, and—for the first time— two small islands far out in the Pacific.

As he gazed upon all those structures built by immigrant hands, all that land cared for and farmed by immigrants, Jacinto indulged in his own dream of another America. He dreamt of one that didn't cut itself up with razor wire, or stare at its own flag until its eyes were crossed. In his dream, America admitted one obvious truth: for any hard worker with a starving family, the laws of another nation are as meaningless as the foreign tongue they were written in.

But as the Blue Angels buzzed overhead with a great whoosh of spent fuel, Jacinto knew this was an unlikely dream. He thought of Wilmer again, as the planes made a wide turn above the bay. This America could allow its sons to fly as if it were the easiest thing in the world—something so dull and commonplace it needed to be spiced up with summersaults and spirals. Whereas Jacinto could hardly allow his son a single unobstructed breath of air—not without a long trail of injury, deceit, and broken laws. The familiar sting of shame burned the pit of his stomach.

What was it Israel had told him about hopes and fears? That they were not so different? Perhaps the same was true of dreams and shames. Both showed the disparity between the lives we lived and lives that might be.

The angels in their airplanes flew straight toward the sun, now much higher above the horizon. As his eyes followed them, a bright smudge burned orange and red upon Jacinto's field of vision. He held his stare. The blinding blur overwhelmed the jets and the buildings, made the city look small and insignificant. With nothing in the sky to stop it, the strong morning sun cast all its light and heat down upon this, the America that was and the America that might be.

Acknowledgments

THIS NOVEL OWES A MASSIVE DEBT TO MANY AMAZING WRIT-ers and journalists. The following books provided both inspiration and infor-mation. I can't recommend them strongly enough. *The Devil's Highway* by Luis Alberto Urrea is perhaps the most important book ever written about im-migration; it provides an incredible account of the tragedies that occur along the southern border. *Coyotes* by Ted Conover is a compelling look into the challenges faced by recent arrivals. *Crossing Over* by Rubén Martínez is a beautiful depiction of how immigration is changing both Mexico and the US *Enrique's Journey* by Sonia Nazario chronicles the harrowing route that Cen-tral Americans endure in search of a better future. *Lives on the Line* by Miriam Davidson offers a unique insight into those who make their homes along the border. *The Massacre at El Mozote* by Mark Danner is required reading on the war in El Salvador.

I'm so grateful to J. Reuben Appelman, who gave an early and insightful reading of the manuscript. His advice and encouragement were invaluable.

But above all, I owe the greatest debt to the Ayala family of Cantón Palo Grande in El Salvador. I cannot thank them enough for sharing their table, their warmth, and their stories with me.

About the Author

Tyler McMahon is the author of the novels *How the Mistakes Were Made* and *Kilometer 99*. He teaches writing at Hawai`i Pacific University, edits the *Hawai`i Pacific Review*, and organizes the Ko`oalu Writers Workshop.

More from Gival Press

The Spanish Teacher by Barbara de la Cuesta
That Demon Life by Lowell Mick White
Tina Springs into Summer / Tina se lanza al verano by Teresa Bevin
The Tomb on the Periphery by John Domini
Twelve Rivers of the Body by Elizabeth Oness

For a complete list of Gival Press titles,
visit: *www.givalpress.com*.

Books are available from Ingram, Follett, Brodart,
your favorite bookstore, the Internet,
or from Gival Press.
Gival Press, LLC
PO Box 3812
Arlington, VA 22203
givalpress@yahoo.com
703.351.0079

www.ingramcontent.com/pod-product-compliance
Lightning Source LLC
Chambersburg PA
CBHW031940010726
47493CB00007B/2006